P9-DWH-235

D0037568

With

By the Author

The Cherry Pit (1965)

Lightning Bug (1970)

Some Other Place. The Right Place. (1972)

The Architecture of the Arkansas Ozarks (1975)

Let Us Build Us a City (1986)

The Cockroaches of Stay More (1989)

The Choiring of the Trees (1991)

Ekaterina (1993)

Butterfly Weed (1996)

When Angels Rest (1998)

Thirteen Albatrosses (or, Falling off the Mountain) (2002)

With (2004)

Donald Harington

The Toby Press

Toby Press (Second edition) 2004

The Toby Press LLC
POB 8531, New Milford, CT. 06676-8531, USA
& POB 2455, London W1A 5WY, England
www.tobypress.com

Copyright © Donald Harington 2003

The right of Donald Harington to be identified as the author of this
work has been asserted by him in accordance with the Copyright,
Designs & Patents Act 1988

All rights reserved. No part of this publication may be reproduced,
stored in a retrieval system or transmitted in any form or by any
means, electronic, mechanical, photocopying or otherwise, without
the prior permission of the publisher, except in the case of brief
quotations embedded in critical articles or reviews.

This is a work of fiction. The characters, incidents, and dialogues are
products of the author's imagination and are not to be construed as
real. Any resemblance to actual events or persons, living or dead is
entirely coincidental.

ISBN 1 59264 050 8 *hardcover*

A CIP catalogue record for this title
is available from the British Library

Typeset in Garamond by Jerusalem Typesetting

Printed and bound in the United States by
Thomson-Shore Inc., Michigan

For Brian Walter
and Lynnea Brumbaugh-Walter
who believed

Part One:
Parted with

Chapter one

She tried to run away. You're not supposed to do that, it's a
blow to the whole idea of devotion, and she ran away not because
she lost even a smidgin of the true blue faith that bound her to him
forever but simply because she began to believe that he might do her
greater harm than he already had, might even do away with her.

She had been bad. He had told her to watch the truck, to
stay with the truck, to guard the damn truck, and she had done her
best, patient as only she knew how to be patient, as he had gone
away with his arms full with a box and then had come back by and
by and had taken another box and disappeared once again and then
kept on doing that, box after box, and she had yearned to go with
him, the late afternoon had been coming on, and he had been gone
such a long, long time, and she had convinced herself that there was
nobody else around, nobody was going to bother the stuff left in the
truck, she couldn't catch the faintest wind of any person anywhere
for miles, and therefore what harm could it be if she just explored
a little bit, not going far from the truck, keeping it always within
range, and keeping a closer guard for the first sign of his return? But
a deer with two fawns had come into view and she had been thrilled

to pieces, especially by the fawns, so cute and innocent and curious, and before she had realized what she was doing, she had followed them off into the woods for a considerable distance before she had realized that she had completely lost touch with the truck.

And when she had returned, he had been there, and he had been furious. The very tone of his voice had hacked and slashed her, and then he had taken a stick and had beaten her with it. She had protested and whined but he had kept on beating her until she could hardly stand up. Then he had told her to get back onto the truck and stay there and not even think about leaving it again. He had taken another box and gone away once more, and she had lain in the truckbed among the few remaining boxes and had inspected some places on her ribs and her legs where he had actually drawn blood. She had been very sad. She had understood why he had beaten her, and she was terribly ashamed for having disobeyed him and abandoned the truck, and she had been miserable in her guilt and in her unhappiness.

The next day he had done the same thing, going into a town to a store and loading up the truck and driving it back and up, up the mountain road so rough and bouncy she was nearly thrown out of the truckbed, more than once, and then making her stay with the truck all afternoon while he unloaded it, box by box, sack by sack. And the next day, the same. And the next.

Now she thought and thought about the whole situation, and felt a nagging wonder about the possibility that somebody else might be a lot nicer to her than he was. Mostly he was good to her, but ever since he had taken her away from her mother he had not shown her much affection or even much attention, except when he had needed her for something. He had provided a good home for her, and had fed her well, and she had liked the place a lot, but now it appeared that he was getting ready to move, and she didn't think she wanted to move. Why else would he be toting all those boxes and sacks up here to the different place? Once or twice (or was it three times?) in the beginning he had allowed her to walk with him to the different place and look it over. The truck could not get to it, or even near it, and she managed to understand why. The road ended at a deep gully where rains had washed the road away. And even if the road had not been washed away *there*, the road later fell to pieces all over the place, and they had to go down into deep ravines, so steep she sometimes slipped if she didn't watch her footing, and very hard to climb out of, and once they climbed out of it they were on a very narrow bluff ledge that scared her with its height and danger. She tried to picture him alone with his arms full of those boxes and bags trying to climb down into those ravines and then back up out of them and across that awful bluff ledge, and she could almost understand why he would be in such a bad mood that he would beat her unmercifully. Then after trekking up and down through all that rough rocky land and across that bluff ledge and into the deep dark forest again, the road, or path, what barely remained visible of it, climbed sharply and trickled out for good, rising to an old homestead in a bramble-clogged meadow on the very top of the mountain. She had been stunned by her first view of the old house, and of the house's view of distant miles of mountains. She could tell that nobody had been up there for a long, long time. It was in her nature to search, upon first seeing any strange house, for signs that might betray any information about the inhabitants. But there was no information whatsoever there. After he had taken her inside the house and she got a whiff of the interior, she began to sort through a cluster of old stale smells, not one of which was familiar to her, except that of rodents. Clearly whoever had lived here had departed ages ago.

Behind the house, near an orchard that was swallowed up in brush and briars, were the remains of an old barn, and there she could detect the fact, barely, that it had once been inhabited by a cow and a pair of mules. There was the rodent smell again. Another building, smaller than the barn, but unlike it not in danger of collapse, was just an open shed with benches along its walls and an assortment of round wooden drums or casks unlike any in her acquaintance. There was one other tiny little building by itself between the barn and the house, its door ajar, and inside she saw a bench-like seat that had two large holes cut in it. There was a distinct odor of fresh poop overlying an assortment of ancient poop-smells, and she assumed that he had been using this little building to do his business.

A few of the small things which he had already moved into this place had come from his house, and thus she managed to understand that he was indeed planning to transfer the contents of that house, her home, to this place. She didn't like it. Or did she? Strangeness, unfamiliarity in any form disturbed her at the same time that it piqued her curiosity. She was adaptable and could easily learn to enjoy life here, if that was what he wanted. But why did he want it?

Why was he going to take her away from her home and move her into this strange, stranded dwelling-place? So many times already he had taken the truck, empty, to huge stores in big towns, where he had loaded it up and brought it up here and slowly unloaded it, a box or a bag at a time, and carried it to the remote house. Maybe he just liked all the exercise. But why did she have to stay with the truck? In the beginning it had been fun to watch but now it was old and dull and she was tired of it. And she had no idea how much longer it would go on. He had been mean to beat her so cruelly. She began to think seriously about the startling idea of running away. First she had to think seriously about where she would go if she did run away, and to consider what her chances would be of an alternative existence elsewhere. Then she had to make a mental list of all the things she didn't like about him.

What he called her, for instance. *Bitch.* On the surface, there was nothing wrong with that, because that's what she was, but it was such a neutral name, no affection in it, and the way he said it sometimes made it sound like he was cursing her. She had a perfectly nice name, Hreapha, and it was a great pity that he would not call her that. Probably he just couldn't pronounce it properly. It was a name that she liked to declaim to the entire world, enthusiastically or warningly, depending on the occasion. "Hreapha! Hreapha!" she often declared. It was what she told him whenever he returned to her after one of his foot-trips to carry boxes to the old house, but when she'd said "Hreapha" after his return the time she'd gone to watch the deer and fawns she had meant for the sound of it to carry abject apology, and yet he had beaten her viciously anyway.

The name had been given to her by her mother, whose name was Whuphvoff. Her mother had taught her everything she knew about the world, especially how to fight and take care of herself. She had never known her father, whose name was Ralph-Alf, but her mother had often described Ralph-Alf as beautiful and irresistible, albeit not half her size. Her mother had spent most of her life in dwellings; her father was strictly the outdoor type. Hreapha had sextuplet brothers and sisters, but while still young one by one the others had been removed from the family until only Hreapha remained to enjoy her mother's company and instruction, and this she had for a long time, until her mother had taught her everything she knew about the world.

Then one day he had taken her away from her mother and quite possibly Hreapha had never forgiven him for that, and she made note of it now as one more reason for running away. He had never even bothered to tell her what his name was. She had grieved for her mother unceasingly, but he had said, "Bitch, you aint never gon lay eyes on your maw again, so you might as well snap out of it." And oh, if only he had done anything to help, like taking her out for a run or a walk or even playing fetch with her in the yard, but he just left her all alone to endure her loss. Her mother had explained to her the enormous benefits of being loyal and devoted to one's master, but Hreapha had rarely taken pleasure in any such benefits with this man.

He had two vehicles, and when he took the truck he always made her ride in the back, even in the coldest part of winter. Riding in back was not without its satisfactions: she had a full exposure to all the fascinating smells and sights that ordinarily she could only get by sticking her head out the window, which she couldn't do when he kept the window rolled up because of the cold. When he took her, as he sometimes did, in the other vehicle, she was permitted to sit on the seat beside him and sometimes, if it wasn't too cold, to stick her head out the window on that side. The other vehicle had no back end like a truck, just a back seat, with a wire fence separating it from the front seat. That vehicle also had lights on the roof that sometimes flashed. When the lights flashed there sometimes came from deep within the vehicle a hideous screaming sound as if the vehicle was going through angry death throes. Then the vehicle would stop behind another vehicle alongside the highway and he would get out and go over and talk not nicely to the other person and give that person a slip of paper.

He usually did not take her with him on these trips in the flashing, screaming vehicle, in which he departed nearly every morning, leaving Hreapha to entertain herself in the front or back yard. But one time she happened to be riding with him when the person he stopped and spoke not nicely to took a metal thing that he pointed and it made a loud explosive noise and caused the windshield over Hreapha's head to be punctured in three different places, and then her master had taken another metal thing and pointed it at the man and made the loud explosive noise and the man had fallen down. He had searched through the other vehicle for a long time, and from its trunk had taken a large canvas bag and put it into the trunk of his own vehicle. Returning to her, he had remarked, "Well, now, Poochie-wooch, me and you are in the goddamn clover!" She had no idea what he meant but she was delighted that he had called her something other than Bitch.

That had been the last time that the flashing, screaming vehicle had ever been used. From then on, he didn't go off to whatever his dealings were each day but stayed home, day after day. As the weather warmed he even went fishing, and took Hreapha with him, and she greatly enjoyed that although she could not begin to imagine why anyone would want to eat a fish. But then he gave up fishing and started taking the truck to those huge stores in several different towns and loading it up with all those boxes and bags. In the beginning, at least, she had loved all that travel.

Hreapha understood how important the boxes and bags must have been to him. So he could almost be forgiven for his anger at her for her failure that one time to guard the truck constantly. She told herself she could let that go, his beating her. But there were so many other things she couldn't let go. One of them had happened not too long ago on a night so cold she had dreaded the thought of trying to sleep in the backyard in the crude little house he had made for her, lined only with a stinky old blanket. He had surprised her by, instead of putting her out at the usual time, suddenly saying to her, "Hey,

Bitch, how'd you like to sleep in the house tonight?" His breath had reeked of the beverage that made him stumble when he walked.

Hreapha had never slept in a house, and she knew that only masters and mistresses and their children were allowed to do that. She could not for the life of her understand why he was making such an invitation, and she could only sit and stare quizzically at him as he repeated himself. She got up and walked in a circle twice as if searching for a proper place to lie down and spend the night. It didn't matter. The hard kitchen floor was good enough, and warm enough. He pointed to a place there. She licked his hand, and then lay on the floor. He poured some more of his brownish liquid into his glass and then poured some into a saucer, which he set before her, saying, "Here, old gal, try a snort." Dutifully she dipped her tongue into the liquid but it was penetrating and burning, and she left it alone. "Hey, come on!" he said, "Let's us me and you tie one on!" She whimpered, as if to tell him thanks just the same but she really didn't care for any of that beverage.

After a while during which he repeated his invitations to drink, he became unhappy with her. "Goddamn," he said. "Thankless mutt. I got a mind to leave you here when I move away." Then he kicked her. He opened the kitchen door and kicked her again, and as she scampered out of the house he kicked her several more times. "I hope you freeze to death!" he yelled, before slamming the door on her.

The memory of that night remained with her now as she pondered the decision to run away. She was tired of living in dread and expectation that he might hurt her again, as he had then, and recently when he'd beaten her with the stick for failing to guard the truck. She knew that he had increased his use of the beverage that made him stumble when he walked. She had been in the back of the truck when he had stopped at the places where he obtained the beverages. They were in two different towns and he had to drive a long way to get to them. But she knew they were the beverage-places because as soon as he had loaded the truck he opened one of the boxes and took one of the bottles to the truck's cab and began drinking from it. He had loaded many, many boxes of the bottles into the truck, and later had carried them, laboriously, carefully, into and out of all the ravines, over the rough trail that led up to the new place. Hreapha bore no illusions about her intelligence but she knew she was smart enough to realize that if several sips from the bottle made him get loopy and rocky, then he had taken possession of enough entire boxes full of bottles to cause him to fly over the moon or kill himself, whichever came first.

Part of her felt an obligation to stay and protect him, if she could. Her protective instincts were all-consuming and she was even proud of them. But a stronger part of her, perhaps not a natural part of her, was self-protective and therefore selfish.

There was only one box left in the truck, and he would soon be coming back to get it. She jumped down from the truck. She had thought about which way to go; her compass or simply her sense of the whereabouts of her *in-habit* told her that the tiny town that had become her home lay south but that south was also the direction of the different place, albeit uphill. So she had better head north, and go downhill. She decided to wait until he came back into view, so he could watch her taking leave of him.

Her mother had once explained to her the meaning of a most common imprecation of people: *bad dog.* Her mother had told her that she could expect to be called a bad dog if she ever, ever did anything contrary to the best interests of people. Her mother told her that the imprecation was meant as a corrective but it usually just had the effect of causing undue guilt and remorse and anxiety. Her mother had advised her to always remember that regardless of how good she was, she would always be somebody's bad dog.

Now he came back into view. She watched him as he approached the truck, and she said "Hreapha!" to him in a way that clearly meant "goodbye." And then she said, *Bad man.* And turned and ran.

Chapter two

Let her go. In his whole life he'd known only a few dogs as good as she was, but damned if she was worth the bother of chasing after her or trying to find her. Driving the truck back down the mountain, bouncing over the twisting, unbearable trail or what was left of it, he thought he caught a glimpse of her in his headlights, and he stopped and turned off the engine and called to her. "Bitch!" he hollered and only then for the first time regretted that he'd never bothered to give her a real name. It sounded like he was cursing her and challenging her to defy him and show her head. He tried sounding gentler. "Bitchie old girl," he called. "Come on back." He took his flashlight from the glove compartment and shined it around through the deep, dark woods. "Poochie-wooch," he called, pleadingly, but already he was debating with himself whether to get another dog or try to do without. It would really be stupid not to have a dog, just as a watchdog in case anybody ever found the old Madewell place, which wasn't likely, since nobody but himself had ever found the place in many a year. In fact the first time he'd gone up there with Bitch to reconnoiter the place, he was surprised to discover in the dust on the floor his own footprints and nobody else's, and yet it had to be nearly twenty years since he'd last set foot there, that time he'd been out searching for that kidnapper Montross that he'd finally found and killed, not anywhere near that place but far down below it, in a glen by a waterfall.

That had been his first accomplishment as a state trooper, and now, twenty years later, still only a sergeant in highway patrol although he'd tried for years to get into the criminal investigation division, he had completed his last act as a state trooper, which had made possible this fulfillment of his dream, as well as his retirement. He wasn't even concerned about the possibility that somebody still held a title to the old Madewell place, or leastways to the hundreds of acres of forest that it was on. He doubted that old Gabe Madewell had actually sold it to anybody when he pulled up stakes after the war and headed for California. Gabe had been a barrel-maker all his life—he tried to remember what the trade was called, something like somebody's family name, Carver or Turner or Cutter or somebody—but the market had dried up on Madewell and he took his wife and kid and just left everything there like it was, resting on top of one of the highest mountains in Newton County and practically impossible to get to nowadays.

"Well, just you stay out there, Bitch, and see if I care!" he hollered, starting the engine again. "I hope you starve to death!" He went on down the mountain, jouncing over the ledges in the road as if he were driving down steep steps. The poor truck was probably not going to hold up for more than a couple more trips, and he began to think about what he'd bring with him on those last trips. He was putting off bringing the crates of chickens, and he still wasn't certain about trying to bring the davenport, but knew the time was coming when he'd have to make up his mind whether or not to try to bring it. How in hell was he going to get the davenport down into those ravines and back up and especially across that goddamn ledge? He could carry it over his back much of the way, and maybe use ropes to raise and lower it in the roughest places. Any way you sliced it there was going to be hell to pay, but by God he'd sat or laid on that davenport since he was just a kid, and his mother had loved it, and he sure wasn't going to put it in the yard sale he was planning on having next Saturday "before going to California." He laughed. That was a good one. And everybody believed it. Or anybody who gave a rat's fart what he did or where he went. He had told so many people he was pushing off for California that he halfway believed it himself.

He knew Bitch wouldn't starve to death in the woods. She was a smart dog and could probably catch something to eat, coons or possums or squirrels. He thought of the three fifty-pound bags of Purina Dog Chow that he had taken the trouble to tote up to the Madewell place, one hundred and fifty pounds of doggie nuggets just to feed Bitch with. Hell, if she was so damn smart she'd probably get it into her head to go on back up to the Madewell place and get in there somehow and chew open one of those bags of Purina. He wouldn't be a bit surprised to find her there with a big grin on her face the next time he came back.

But more'n likely she'd just keep on a-walking until she came to somebody's house who would feed her. The nearest house in this direction was a mile or more, down toward Parthenon, and he didn't even know for sure who lived there. It was an old farmhouse some ways beyond where this trail met up with the dirt road from Wayton to Parthenon. He rarely saw the folks who lived there; he'd waved at the woman once or twice as he went by. If the woman had happened to notice him driving the truck up the road so many times loaded up with stuff, she might have wondered. But once he got that davenport and those chickens up there, assuming the poor truck could make that next-to-last trip, she'd never see him go by again, because the last trip would be made in the dark of the wee hours, with his passenger.

He'd be "gone to California." Which is where near about everybody from this part of the country had gone anyhow. His mom and dad had gone out there, and died out there. His sister Betty June wrote him once or twice a year from some place called Santa Monica, where she was doing real well. He figured he'd probably have to answer her latest letter, which he hardly ever did, just to let her know that he didn't live in Stay More any more and not to write him there any more. He wouldn't tell her he was "gone to California" or she'd expect him to come visit her.

But now he could go spend a couple more nights at home

and get ready for that yard sale and heft that davenport up onto his back experimentally just to see if it would fit and how heavy it was. He knew he didn't need to have the yard sale, not for the money anyhow. The only reason he was having it was to make it look a little more convincing that he was really leaving for good. He'd had a realtor's FOR SALE sign in his yard for weeks now, and might not ever find a buyer for such a rundown old place, but he didn't need that money either. He didn't need any money. He'd bought himself a steel fireproof Sentry® security chest and put all the money in it, except for what he thought he'd need to buy whatever he needed to stock his new home, and he'd buried it under the front porch up there at the Madewell place, and he didn't expect he'd have to dig it up for a good long while. It was dirty money anyhow, probably collected from all kinds of poor folks addicted to the dope that they'd had to buy with it.

His CID buddies—not friends because he didn't have a one but good old acquaintances from way back, Lieutenant Morrow's men in Company E of the Criminal Investigation Division at Harrison—had been puzzled about what had become of the money, but they hadn't suspected him, or even questioned him about it. His twenty years of service were spotless, and made him eligible for the retirement he'd taken, and nobody thought to make any connection between his retirement and his shooting of that drug runner, except that, as he'd put it, he was damned tired of being shot at, and it was time to hang it up.

They assumed that if the DOA perp had made a delivery in Tulsa and was on his way back to Memphis, he must have had a huge amount of cash on him, which maybe he could have dropped off somewhere or laundered or something. Why had the guy been so far off course, not taking I-40 but US 65? Maybe he'd taken the money to Branson and delivered it to one of the mob who hung out there. The case was closed, although some shady-looking characters had been reported sniffing around Harrison to see if they couldn't find the money.

The buried security chest had about four hundred thousand still left in it; he hadn't counted, but he'd spent only about forty or fifty. He'd bought everything he could possibly want, including a real fine set of the best firearms, with enough ammo to last forever, but he had the sense not to do any conspicuous spending, like getting a new truck, which is why he hoped this old crate would hold out for just a few more trips, a couple more shopping trips and then a trip to take the davenport and chickens and a final trip to take the girl.

And of course during those last shopping trips he'd also be shopping for the girl herself. Tomorrow he planned to park the truck alongside one or more of the elementary schools and maybe visit some of the playgrounds and parks. He registered what he had just thought, and realized the ambiguity: no, he wasn't fixing to shop for the girl, meaning do some shopping on her behalf, which he had already finished. He was fixing to shop the available display of eligible girls and pick out one: *shopping for a girl.*

He'd already got her whatever she'd be a-needing at the Harrison Wal-Mart, where he'd bought her a whole bunch of some clothes and shoes and stuff, telling the saleslady they were for his daughter and not knowing her exact sizes but only able to say what you'd expect a girl of seven or eight to wear, summer, fall, winter, spring. The saleslady had helped him load up three carts and just said, "Your girl is sure going to be thrilled with all this." And he'd said, "I hope she will." Then he'd gone to the toy department and filled three more carts with enough dolls and toys and games and stuffed animals to serve as birthday and Christmas presents for years to come.

Sog Alan went on home to spend the night, had all the good bourbon he could handle, went to put Bitch out and realized she wasn't in anymore, then went to sleep. Next day fairly late he took his truck and headed to Harrison for one more shopping trip, reflecting that one more ought to do it, and he'd better avoid visiting any of the places he'd already shopped, although he'd tried to spread his shopping out among as many different stores as possible. He'd already used almost all the various supermarkets in Harrison, Berryville, Huntsville, and driven down to Russellville for others, gone all the way to Eureka Springs for his huge hoard of good liquor, and picked up odds and ends at small stores all over creation, buying several cartons of cigarettes at each of maybe a dozen different places. He had enough smokes to last at least a couple of years, and then he'd just have to plant some tobacco and grow his own. He had seeds enough to grow anything in creation.

Now this time he pulled into a discount supermarket up over on the east side of Harrison where he hadn't been before, and, as usual, loaded up a couple of carts with all kinds of stuff he was buying by the case load or carton or gross.

The check-out clerk, a real pretty but saucy gal, rang up his stuff and said, "Twenty-four quart jars of pickled pigs' feet? You must really hanker after this stuff."

"I'm partial to it," he admitted, and truly it was one of his concerns, that he might some day run out of them. He liked them on occasion, not every week or even every month but he liked them.

"Are you going into hibernation in the early spring?" she asked. "Or do you have a family of thirty-seven to feed?"

He smiled. "Something like that," he said.

She studied him. "Say," she said. "Aren't you Sergeant Alan? I know who you are. You stopped me in Valley Springs and gave me a ticket that wiped out all my savings!"

"What was that name?" he asked.

"Karen Kerr," she said.

"Yeah, I do believe I remember you, on account of that name that sounds phony. I reckoned as how it might just be a alias, but it's sure-enough your real name, aint it?"

"It's not my maiden name," she said.

"I seem to recollect you was doing fifty or so in a thirty-five mile zone."

"I was late for work, and I nearly got fired."

"Well, I reckon you told the judge that, but the law is the law. Aint my fault you broke it."

"I'll get a boy to help you bag and load all this stuff."

"I can do it."

After driving away he reached for a cigarette and found the slip of paper with a list of a whole bunch of other stuff he'd meant to buy at that market, and he looked it over and swore at the items he'd have to go back for, or get somewheres else: Vienna sausages, canned orange juice, Pet milk, and *coffee*, for godsakes: he already had several cases of big-can coffee but it was something he couldn't grow and he drank his share of it and was bound to run out by and by.

He stopped, turned around, and drove back to the big parking lot of the supermarket, where he parked inconspicuously and turned off the motor and just sat and waited patiently for a long, long time to see when Karen Kerr might leave work. Whenever she took off, he could go back in that store for the rest of the stuff on his list, including beef jerky: somebody had told him that beef jerky would keep forever. He wouldn't take the chance of her seeing him load up a lot of other stuff.

For a while as he waited he entertained himself by watching an occasional youngster go by. School had let out and kids were either going grocery-shopping with their moms or in some cases by themselves or with their friends, and every now and again he'd see a pretty cute one, and imagine in his mind what it would be like if she was the one. But not one of those he saw really grabbed him. He knew that when he found the girl of his dreams he would know it on the instant.

He went around to the back of the truck to fish in one of the sacks for the new issue of *Police Gazette* he'd just bought. He reached to give Bitch a little pat on the head and found her missing and realized she wasn't his dog anymore. Then he sat and read through *Police Gazette,* a lively tabloid which was his favorite reading-matter, shoot, practically his *only* reading matter, and he knew that he was going to miss it in the months and years ahead. It was always a real pleasure to come across the articles on the disappearance of kids, that had lots of photographs. He knew backward and forward what made up the profile of a so-called child molester, which he wasn't, because he hadn't never in his life *molested* nobody. Sure, he'd done a couple of naughty things with a couple of little bitty old gals, but not against their will, and he was hoping that the companion of his coming months and years would never once have any occasion to feel that what he was doing was against her will. He had for several years assisted his buddy Jack Samples in the CID's pedo squad, helping Jack make collars and interrogations, and in their time they had nabbed dozens of fellers who were genuine pure-dee pervert *molesters*, old boys who raped and killed tykes and even tots. Jack had once said to him, "Sog, I be damned if you aint got a nose on you that can smell out pedos where I'd never of found 'em." He hadn't told Jack the reason he could find pedos so easy was because he really felt a kind of…not brotherhood or nothing but a real understanding of the way their minds worked and their hearts felt and their dicks stood. Your typical straight-up-and-down pedo generally had in his house a huge assortment of dirty pictures of kids, and unprintable printed matter that showed photos of 'em naked and even doing things to each other, and over the years him and Jack had confiscated such a heap of this stuff that Jack hadn't even noticed that Sog had "borrowed" a good little bit of it. His favorite, which he'd looked at so often it was falling apart, was a book called *Nudist Moppets*, and he was planning on keeping that up there at the Madewell place, although he hoped he wouldn't really need it because his truelove would want to romp and play without a stitch.

He decided that the next little gal who came along would get herself undressed by him in his mind, right then and there. And then here she came. Walking right in front of his truck, as he quickly stripped off her dress, was not just a girl but the girl of his dreams. He knew it so surely he put her dress right back on her, to be nice. The cutest thing you ever did see. Blonde and blue-eyed and full-lipped—oh, those lips were something else! And she turned her head and saw him and *smiled* at him with all kinds of eagerness and readiness. He couldn't remember the last time he'd seen any child with a smile like that. And her skin! Her skin was so soft and fresh and touchable that Sog had to restrain himself from getting out right then and there and giving her a big squeeze. His heart swole within his shirt and his dick swole within his pants; it was the first spontaneous hard-on he'd had in God knows when. But he could only sit and watch as she went on walking by and strolled over to the part of the parking lot where the employees kept their cars, and she went up to this blue Camaro and tried the door and then just stood there beside it, for a long little while, as Sog wracked his brain for a sure-fire way to grab her and take her away right there in broad daylight. Eventually it dawned on him, maybe because he recognized that Camaro, that this lovely little lady, his intended, might be waiting on that selfsame Karen Kerr that he was waiting to see come out of the store.

A bright idea hit him. He could just start up the truck and drive right up beside her and say, "Your mother's in the hospital, and I've been sent to take you there!" It wasn't an original ruse, he'd heard variations of it used by other abductors that he and Jack Samples had caught, but it might just work. The problem was, he hadn't finished all his shopping, and he didn't intend to get the girl until everything was ready for her. While he was pondering this quandary, Karen Kerr came out of the supermarket and sure enough walked right over to that Camaro. He nearly perished with envy when the girl gave her mom a big hug, both of those soft arms reaching around her mother's waist. And then the girl commenced a-talking, and never stopped. She got in the car with her mother and they drove off, and Sog waited just a bit and followed them, keeping at a distance but close enough that he could tell the girl just went on talking and a-talking.

They didn't drive too awful far. He found out where they lived, on the east side of Harrison not far from the Fairgrounds, on just a old country road with no neighbors in view. It wasn't much of a house.

And then he drove on back to that supermarket to finish his shopping. By the time he got the load up the mountain it would be too dark to tote any of it to the house but he might just sleep there in the truck and get a early start the next day transporting it on foot along the terrible mile of ravines and the rocky ledge along the bluff and a godforsaken forest trail. Who knows? Tonight or any time tomorrow he might even get a visit from old Bitch with her tail betwixt her legs and a shit-eating grin on her face.

Chapter three

She had made it clear to Robin that she should never come to the store except in an emergency. But Robin just couldn't wait, she was so excited with the news that Kelly Brewer had invited her to a sleep-over birthday party. At least Robin hadn't come inside the store, where Mr. Purvis would have seen her, but waited at the car, which wasn't an awfully smart thing to do. In a sense that violated Karen's rule that Robin should never be alone in public. Karen was going to have to have a talk with her about the fact that she seemed to be forgetting a lot of her rules, or else was deliberately flaunting them. Robin seemed to be growing more willful and reckless, along with acquiring a reputation in school for being something of a bully. Possibly Robin was upset by the absence of her father. She seemed to have changed since the divorce last Thanksgiving. Robin's second grade teacher, Miss Moore, had called Karen in for a conference, with the principal sitting in, to discuss Robin's behavior problems, specifically, as Miss Moore put it, "her need to bombard others with her presence." Their solution, surprisingly, was to promote Robin. They felt that Robin was too precocious and too intelligent, already reading at fourth-grade level, and promoting her would not only put her where she belonged but also would remove her from those classmates she had been bullying. "She's just too smart for her friends," Miss Moore had said. Of course Robin didn't want to be promoted, and Karen had said she would have to think about it.

Karen's mother, who fortunately didn't live in Harrison but down the road twenty miles at Pindall, tried to tell Karen that there were two reasons Robin was becoming so headstrong; one was because Karen was needlessly over-protective and the other because Robin never saw her father any more. Or saw him rarely. Billy had returned to town only once since the divorce, and had tried to take Robin to the roller rink, but Karen had been afraid he might try to abduct her (such things often happened) and she had refused to let Robin leave the house with him. If that made Robin tough and rude, and caused her to pick on other kids, then it was more Billy's fault than it was Karen's. It had been Billy who had taught Robin some kind of rough sport called taekwondo, which probably had helped Billy over his frustration at not having the son he'd so desperately wanted, but it didn't do anything for poor Robin other than leave her prancing around the house kicking out her feet and chopping the air with her hands in an extremely unfeminine manner.

Driving home, listening to Robin run on and on about that birthday party, not able to get a word of caution in edgewise, Karen was happy that Robin seemed so lively and animated in contrast to her usual self these days. It reminded Karen of what an incredibly sweet child Robin had once been. She had been, as they say, bright-eyed and bushy-tailed, full of love and wonder and joy, singing her childish songs all the time. Robin had had a speech impediment that made her unable to sound her *r*'s and *l*'s properly, so that she said even her own name as "Wobbin," a charming pronunciation, really. But the kids in the first grade had called her Wobbinhood and teased her with songs about The Wed Wed Wobbin Comes Bob Bob Bobbin Along…until Robin discovered that she could smack them a good one and get them to shut up. Although Karen couldn't afford it, and Billy wouldn't help, Karen had spent some money on a speech pathologist for Robin, and now at least she could say her own name correctly, except when she got too excited, as she was now:

"And Gwetchen Scott will be there! And Webecca McGraw! And so will Bevewwy Nichols!"

When Robin paused to catch her breath, Karen asked, "Have all their folks given them permission to spend the night?"

"You better believe it," Robin said.

"How do you know? What if I called their mothers and asked them?"

Robin stopped bubbling and scowled. "Why would you have to do *that?*"

"Have any of those girls ever been to a slumber party before?"

"Sure. Gwetchen had one last month but she didn't invite me."

"That's pretty young for sleeping over, don't you think?"

"How would *I* know? I've never been invited."

"You don't have to get surly with me, Miss. I wasn't invited to my first slumber party until I was eleven or twelve."

"I'm not you," Robin said, which was her second-most favorite expression, the first being the two words, "But, Mommy..."

"Let's just talk about it later while we fix supper."

Karen decided to stuff Robin with her favorite food, spaghetti (which she had early pronounced as "basketti" and still said that way for the fun of it) and then perhaps Robin would be less moody when Karen rejected her request to attend Kelly's birthday slumber party.

Robin helped in the kitchen, as she'd been taught to do. Robin wasn't allowed to use the stove, but she could time the boiling of the spaghetti noodles and tell Karen when they were done so Karen could strain them. It was also Robin's job to stir the Kool-Aid and put the ice cubes into the glasses, as well as to set the table. While they worked, Robin broached the subject again. "It just surprised me so that Kelly would ask me. I didn't think she liked me at all."

"Because you usually make fun of her?"

"I don't make fun of her. But everybody in Miss Moore's class loves her to pieces, and they don't know what a crybaby she is."

Karen smiled wryly, trying to remember the last time that Robin had cried. "Maybe if she's still a crybaby, she's not old enough to be having a slumber party."

"Becky said she'd give Kelly fifty cents if she could get through the whole party and sleep-over without ever crying," Robin declared, "and I think Kelly has made up her mind to try and see if she can. Being eight is too old to cry."

"If it's Saturday night, probably all you girls will stay up past midnight talking and goofing off and you'll be too sleepy to go to Sunday school and church the next day."

"*Mommy*," Robin said. "Why do you really not want me to go?"

Karen needed a moment to ponder the question. "We've never spent a night apart except when you stay at Grandma's house," Karen said. "I'll be lonesome without you."

"Do you want to come?" Robin invited, and laughed at the image. "You'd have to take Kelly a present."

"Speaking of which, where do you plan to get the money to buy Kelly something? You know we just don't have any." Before Karen had been hit with that hideous ticket for speeding, she'd used up a good chunk of her savings account getting Robin the bicycle, which had been a big mistake, because she couldn't let Robin ride off on it without supervision, and Robin simply wasn't the outdoor sort anyhow, preferring to stay in the house most of the time.

"But *Mommy*, it might only be a couple of dollars. If you don't have it, Grandma would give it to me."

"She would, and she'd also hop all over me if I wouldn't let you go, isn't that a fact?"

Robin smiled. "She could sure make trouble if you wouldn't."

It was hard enough to raise a child without help from a spouse. But it was harder to raise a child with too much help from a parent. Karen's mother had her own ideas about childrearing…which hadn't been so bad, as far as Karen herself had developed. Louisa Spurlock believed that only God should supervise the comings and goings and growing of a kid, that leaving well enough alone and in God's hands was all the watching-out that a parent needed to do. But Louisa still enjoyed the help and companionship of a husband, although Grandpa Spurlock wasn't Karen's father and therefore not the real forebear of the golden-haired beauty whom he doted on so much. Leo Spurlock was so infatuated with Robin that it made Karen uneasy. She had stopped just short of telling Robin not to sit on her grandfather's lap.

Men, Karen was convinced, were mostly creeps. The world was full of old goats who couldn't think of anything else but sex, unless it was simply ways to make the opposite sex feel miserable. Her boss, Mr. Purvis, had tried so many times to get into her pants that she'd finally had to report him to the police, and this lecherous cop had sneered and drooled as he explained to her that she wouldn't have a case without witnesses and it was pretty hard to prove anyhow and his advice was, if she couldn't stand the thought of giving old Purvis a little enjoyment, to just try not to get into a situation she couldn't get out of.

Cops were just as bad, or worse, than the bad guys. Take that jerk she'd seen again this afternoon, buying out the store, that Sergeant Alan of the state police. He had given her the ticket for going a little too fast on a stretch of Highway 65 where everybody else was going the same speed she was. That guy was a typical tough, unfeeling, uncouth law officer: getting into middle age, paunchy, thick, the image of a redneck, and probably the owner of an extensive private collection of pornography.

"Do you know how fast you were going?" he'd asked her when he stopped her.

"No, I don't," she'd said honestly.

He'd laughed and said, "Then I can write anything I want on this ticket, can't I?"

"Why are you picking on *me*?" she'd asked him. "All those other people are going the same speed I was."

"What other people?" he'd said.

"Look!" she'd said, and pointed. "Look at that guy! He's going faster than I was."

"I'll catch him," he'd said, and had finished writing out the ticket for her.

Robin was eating her salad quickly, to get it out of the way before touching the spaghetti. Robin hated salad, or anything green, but Karen had demanded that she eat what was good for her, so Robin had developed a habit of quickly finishing anything she didn't like before starting on what she did like.

Karen reflected that if she'd flirted with that cop, maybe he would have let her off. Or maybe not. Maybe he had a quota to fill, so many tickets to write each day, in order to earn his bonuses and feed that family of thirty-seven that he was buying all that food for. Karen shook her head, and laughed.

"What's funny?" Robin asked.

"I was just thinking about a man at the store today who bought a whole case—that's twenty-four quart jars—of pickled pigs' feet."

"What's *that*?" Robin wanted to know.

"When they butcher hogs and take off all the bacon and hams and good parts, they've got leftovers like feet, which they preserve by pickling, and sell cheaply."

"Ew," Robin said. "That's gross."

"You've never had any, and I hope you never have to."

"What did he look like?" Robin asked.

"Why do you ask?"

"Anybody who eats lots of pickled pigs' feet must look weird. Maybe like a monster."

"He's a state trooper," Karen said, "although he wasn't in uniform." She attempted to describe him: mid-forties, strong build but potbellied, plain grizzled brown hair, bushy eyebrows. "He might not look weird but he certainly wasn't good-looking. Just an old country boy without a brain in his head. He was buying case loads of everything. Maybe the state police are going to have a big picnic."

Robin laughed, and said, "A zillion pigs chomping on pigs' feet!" Then she said, "Let's not get off the subject, okay?"

"What subject?"

"I want to go to Kelly's slumber party."

Karen sighed. This was going to be difficult. She tried to tell herself that Kelly's parents, whom she'd never met, were thoroughly responsible people and would do a proper job of riding herd on the party. They would make sure nobody got hurt and that all of them behaved themselves, as much as girls of seven and eight possibly could. Maybe the parents would even make sure the kids put out the lights and went to sleep before dawn came. Still, Karen would worry herself sick the whole time Robin was away.

The whole idea just wouldn't work. Robin had a daily schedule that she was required to observe, from the time she woke up until the time she went to bed, that included her chores around the house and her homework, as well as her "fun" things like watching television and reading comic books and talking on the telephone and playing with her paper dolls, most of which she'd made herself. She was particularly responsible for strict observance of the rules while Karen was at work and Robin was home alone. She was not allowed to invite her friends over unless Karen was home. Robin had memorized the numbers for the fire department, the family doctor, the police, and Karen's place of employment. Robin was allowed to use the vacuum cleaner but not the toaster, the electric can opener, the mixer or the stove.

Robin was permitted to check the mailbox quickly when the school bus dropped her off, but then she had to go directly to the front door and unlock it with her key that was kept in a special pocket under the lid of her lunchbox. Karen had timed her: it took only twenty seconds for her to step down from the bus, glance into the mailbox and then walk to the front door and, before unlocking it, check the house for any sign of a broken window or anything that didn't look right. Karen had requested that the bus driver wait those twenty seconds until Robin was inside before driving off. If Robin noticed *anything* about the house that didn't look right, she was supposed to get back onto the bus and ride back to the school and phone for Karen from there. After actually entering the house and locking it from the inside, including the deadbolt, Robin was supposed to give the house its inspection, looking for anything amiss: back door ajar or unlocked, windows not closed, any smell of smoke or gas or anything suspicious.

If anyone phoned for Karen while she was gone, unless it was Grandma, Robin was required to tell the caller that Karen couldn't come to the phone and to take a message, and never to tell the caller that she was home alone. Robin was not to unlock the door for anyone except Grandma and Grandpa, and they had a special code knock which Grandpa called shave-and-a-haircut-six-bits; a rhythm of knocks that was easily recognizable, so if Robin heard a voice on the other side of the door saying, "Open up, it's your Grandma," even if it *sounded* just like Grandma, she was not to open the door unless she'd heard that code knock.

Despite all these rules and procedures, Karen still worried constantly about leaving Robin home alone. And today Robin had violated her routine by coming to the store to meet Karen instead of taking the school bus home. That was not excusable, and Karen considered punishing Robin for it by forbidding her from attending the birthday sleep-over. If nothing else could persuade Robin to back down, Karen might have to resort to that.

"Did you just walk from school to the store?" Karen asked her daughter. Robin nodded. It was only a few blocks from Woodland Heights Elementary to the store, but still, Robin knew she was not allowed to walk alone. "That's not permitted, you know. You must never forget 'stranger danger.'"

"I never forget," Robin said.

"What if a man had driven up beside you and told you that I was in the hospital and he'd been sent to pick you up?"

"I would've told him that I know where the hospital is and I could walk there by myself, thank you very much."

Karen smiled. "That's good, but what if he had tried to get out and grab you?"

"I would have given him a *chagi* in the nuts."

"A *what* in the *what?*"

Robin stood up from the table and said, "*Chagi* means kick in taekwondo. Watch." And she delivered a swift kick into the groin of an imaginary man who somehow took the form of mean old Sergeant Alan in Karen's mind.

"I didn't know you knew those words," Karen said.

"And if that doesn't crumple him up," Robin declared, "I'll give him a *chireugi* right in his windpipe." And she demonstrated, making a spear of her fingers and thrusting them toward his neck.

Karen flinched. "Wow. That hurt, I bet."

Robin dusted her hands together, and sat back down. "Next question."

"I wish you wouldn't drum your fingers on the table," Karen said. It was a bad habit that had gotten worse in recent months. On one hand, it was clear proof that a career as a concert pianist was waiting for Robin, if only they could afford piano lessons. On the other hand, it was annoying and showed a complete lack of patience. "Tell you what," Karen offered, "if you'll clean your room, and I mean *clean* it, I'll give you two dollars to buy Kelly a birthday present."

Robin thought about that. "You mean that I could *take* to the party?"

"How else would you get it there? Mail it?"

Chapter four

Few things frightened her. She was scared of thunder but not of the lightning that went with it. Thinking about this, and about the explanation that her mother had tried to give her about the connection between lightning and thunder, how the latter is the sound of the former (even though this was hard to grasp because she often saw the lightning long before she heard the thunder), she decided that what most frightened her about thunder was the noise. Not just because it was so crashing and booming but because it was inexplicable. What was *happening*? Was the whole world blowing up and coming to an end? She had lived through many thunderstorms and always found that the next day the world was just as it had always been, but every time she heard a sudden loud noise (gunshots too and, at least once in her short life, the fireworks that accompany July 4th) the sound seemed to be suggesting mass destruction.

And because she was not afraid of the lightning, or of any sudden light, or of light in any of its forms (not even the moon, although it sometimes seemed to be an intruder), she was not afraid of the absence of light either. The dark did not bother her at all. This seemed to her an unreasonable lack of fear, when she ought to be rightly apprehensive about all the unseen things out there in the dark which could cause her harm. Often she could hear them, and smell them without being able to see them, but she reflected that their odor and their sound were fearsome but not their invisibility. She hated the high-pitched echo-shrieking of bats; she knew they had to do it to find their way around in the dark, but she couldn't stand the sound of it.

She didn't need to make any sounds to find her way around in the dark, and so now she trotted easily and effortlessly down the remains of the old logging trail that meandered up the north face of Madewell Mountain. But her tongue, hanging out of her mouth to catch all the night's fragrances, was becoming dry. She was very thirsty, and hoped she'd soon catch a sniff of a spring bubbling out of the earth, or a rivulet in a ravine, and she realized too it was well past her suppertime, with no prospect of anything to eat in the offing. Sure, she could catch a squirrel or a rabbit, or even one of the night birds whose plaintive advertisements for a mate filled the air sweetly with pleasant sounds, but the simple fact was that she had never in her life killed a thing. Not a thing. Well, of course she'd caused the demise of various fleas who had burrowed into her coat and fallen victim to her chomping. But that was self-protective murder.

She encountered along the trail many creatures, edible and inedible, none of whom could understand her attempts to communicate with them: a porcupine, a green turtle, an armadillo, a family of raccoons, and a possum. In the dark she could see clearly enough to tell what an ugly creature the possum was, but she knew from experience that possums were good folk, and friendly, and she was sorry she didn't know their language. Overhead were flying squirrels whose sounds were too mild to frighten her but noisy enough to be distracting. There was also an occasional owl, whose hoot stopped her in her tracks and reversed her ears.

After a long time the logging trail met up with a larger trail, a dirt road, and she came to a habitation. She and the other dog caught wind of each other at the same instant. The other loudly announced her name: "Arphrowf!"

"Hreapha!" she answered.

Soon they met, and took turns sniffing each other's identities. Arphrowf wanted to know where in tarnation she thought she was a-heading, this time of night. Hreapha explained that she'd been up on the mountain with her master, but had decided to revolt against him and to disaffiliate herself from his activities. Good gracious to Betsy, said Arphrowf, you don't mean to tell me. I never in all my born days heard tell of nobody a-quittin out like that. Hreapha explained, He wasn't a very nice man. I had all I could take.

Say, said Arphrowf, does he by any chance drive a old beat-up Chevy pick-up? I reckon I've seen that feller go past here a hundrit times lately. And wasn't that you a-settin in the back end? Amidst all kinds of passels and totes and plunder? Where's he a-haulin all that freight?

Hreapha sat for a spell (she needed the rest) and told her new friend all about how her former master had taken possession of an old farmstead up on the mountaintop and was apparently stocking it up with enough food and supplies to last forever, including enough hard liquor to enable a flight over the moon or an early death, whichever came first. She asked Arphrowf if she'd ever been up there to that old abandoned house. Her new friend said, I caint say as how I have. I think I know where it is, though. It's just too fur and snaky for me to want to mess with. Hreapha observed that she hadn't seen any snakes yet. Then she asked, You wouldn't happen to have any surplus food lying around loose, would you? Arphrowf apologized: I done et in the forepart of the evening and they won't be a-layin out my breffust till the sun comes up. But you're shore welcome to stay and share it with me.

I guess I'd better be getting on, Hreapha declared.

Don't be rushing off. Stay more and we'll visit till they lay out the chow.

I thank you, Hreapha said. I reckon I'll see you again some-time. "Hreapha!"

"Arphrowf!" her friend bade her goodbye.

Hreapha possessed an unerring sense that told her which way to go to meet up with her *in-habit* in what remained of the tiny village where she'd lived recently and where she still had a friend or two. While this sense depended upon a collaboration between her ineffable internal compass and her memory of the complex of odors she had sniffed the many, many times she had been in the pickup on this road, it was primarily a knowledge of that part of herself she had left behind at home, which her mother had told her was called her *in-habit:* an invisible, unsmellable presence, a second self beyond the senses. So now she headed down the dirt road that would lead there sooner or later. Hreapha was a little sad to be leaving Arphrowf, who was a good old friendly country girl, and she had ever-so-briefly considered the possibility of hanging around and seeing if Arphrowf's people might want to have her, or at least feed her. But she believed her chances for a meal or a new master might be better in or near the village. Home is home, after all, where your *in-habit* remains and never wants to leave. There was even the possibility that after her former master had completely moved out of his house, she could move back into it, and continue to enjoy living there, in her old familiar home, the only real home she'd ever known, and if she didn't have a master, if nobody took possession of the house after he had left it, she could just count on a friend or two to help her forage for food. Possibly, even if somebody did take possession of that house, they might adopt her! She really did have a bright future, and her steps quickened as she trotted along the road. Almost as if in celebration, she came to a spring trickling out of the roadside bank, with a small pool where it fell, and she quenched her thirst at length before trotting onward.

It was a long way to the village, and she passed very few houses along the road, most of them vacant, and the few inhabited ones domains of her kindred, who continued sleeping or perfunctorily called their names to her as she trotted past. She knew none of them, and only occasionally called her name back to them.

The only difficulty she had on the long road was an abrupt encounter with a striped skunk. She recognized it instantly and knew that if she antagonized it she'd carry its foul squirtings on her face for days and days. In her own language she tried to assure the skunk that she meant no harm and simply wanted to go her own way, but the skunk spoke a complex foreign language and began circling her with its tail raised and then, at the instant she sensed the animal was about to fire its fetid spray, Hreapha took off, running as hard as her legs would carry her. Thus she escaped the full brunt of the foul vapors, but not entirely their all-encompassing effect. Further along the road she had to stop and burrow her nose into the dirt and hold it there for a long time until the worst of the hideous smell had gone.

She still carried the awful stink when she finally arrived on the outskirts of the village sometime after daybreak, at one of the very few houses still occupied, where lived a very good friend of hers, a big shaggy fellow named Yowrfrowr. He was always thrilled to see her, especially because his only companions other than his mistress were the countless cats who filled the front yard. Yowrfrowr was a jovial and gentle fellow, but he had little affection for or tolerance of his yard mates, who were now eyeing Hreapha with mean and unwelcoming looks.

"Yowrfrowr!" he greeted her, but then he backed away from her and said, Ew pee-you, that kitty must've had a pole down its back!

Sorry, she said. I guess I didn't jump out of its way fast enough.

They're a botheration and a pestilence this time of spring, Yowrfrowr observed. A body can't take a little constitutional without the danger of being squirted by one of their fulsome atomizers.

Hreapha didn't always understand Yowrfrowr's language, which she assumed could be the result of the fact that he was purebred, not of mixed ancestry as she was. He was well-behaved and kind, as well as extremely good-looking, and she thought she liked him more than any other dog of her acquaintance, although he did constantly hint at his sexual attraction toward her.

You wouldn't happen to have any of your breakfast left over, would you? She asked.

Didn't that bastard give you enough to eat? Yowrfrowr demanded.

He doesn't know I'm in town, she said. But even if he did, I wouldn't want him to feed me. I've forsaken him.

Yowrfrowr's big soulful eyes grew enormous. You *what*?

I just decided I don't want to live with him anymore. So I ran away.

35

High time! Yowrfrowr exclaimed. Though I must say I've never heard of such apostasy before. Good riddance to bad rubbish.

But I haven't had anything to eat since yesterday breakfast, Hreapha said, and I've been walking for miles and miles.

Yowrfrowr tilted his head and looked at her sideways. Miles and miles? It's less than a mile from here to his house.

He has another house. He's moving. Way off to some godforsaken run-down homestead on the mountaintop far north of here.

No wonder you left him. He has no right to take you away from this town…and from me. Yowrfrowr winked at her.

So? She reminded him of her request. I'd really appreciate a bite or two.

Sweetheart, I'd give you *all* my breakfast if I still had any. Truth is, I've cleaned the dish, at least those morsels which I could beat the blasted felines to. But tell you what: I could go over there and scratch on the door and whine piteously and maybe she'd come out and give me some more.

Which, bless his heart, he proceeded to do. You hide behind that bush, he told her, and then he scratched at the door and whined for a while. As the door opened, he said "Yowrfrowr!" eagerly. The old woman stood there looking down at him. Yowrfrowr had once explained to Hreapha that his mistress was the oldest woman in town, was the grandmother of some of the others who still lived nearby, and was also, despite her age, the most beautiful creature on earth. Her only grave flaw, her *hamartia*, was her fondness for worthless felines.

The woman said to him, "What's bothering you, Xenophon?" The woman never called him Yowrfrowr. Usually she just called him "Fun" for short, or sometimes "Funny."

He rose up on his hind legs, holding his forepaws in a begging gesture, smiling broadly all the while. Hreapha thought he was indeed funny, perhaps ludicrous. The cats averted their faces in disgust.

When that failed to convey his message he went to his empty food bowl and nudged it with his nose toward the old woman's feet. "You want more food?" she said. "Good heavens, boy, I gave you as much as you always get. You don't want to get fat." She scratched him behind the ears and closed the door.

Well, you tried, Hreapha told him. Thank you.

I know where there's a dead pigeon, he declared. If one of those mewly pussies hasn't found it first.

Thanks, but I'll be running along, she said.

His soulful eyes looked heartbroken. Aw, dearest, don't depart, he whined with theatrical emphasis. Stay more and let's frolic.

I know what 'frolic' means to you, you old goat. "Hreapha!" She turned tail.

"Yowrfrowr!" he called after her mournfully.

As she went on, she reflected that there might come a time when she'd gladly eat that dead pigeon. But if worst came to worst, she could catch and kill one of the chickens at home, although that would surely outrage him if he knew it was her, not to mention violating her principles about not killing anything but fleas. She trotted down into the main street of the village, which was deserted. She had explored it many times and never found any sign of recent activity or life in it. There wasn't much left to it: a few empty houses, one of them big; a couple of stores, a big one and a little one, both long abandoned. She had explored the pile of hewn stones that Yowrfrowr told her had once been a bank where people kept their money, and a huge cellar which had been the foundation of a gristmill.

The derelict village wasn't her destination. That was another half mile or so beyond it, up the main road that led out of it. She passed one other occupied house, and spoke only briefly with Ouruff, who wasn't very sociable because she was preoccupied with the rearing of a litter of puppies and didn't have time for Hreapha. They were practically next-door neighbors, although the house where Hreapha had lived was another quarter-mile beyond Ouruff's house. She didn't want to ask Ouruff for food, because she knew that Ouruff was still nursing and needed to eat everything she could lay her paws on. How's the pups? Hreapha asked politely as she moseyed on past. Jist a-feelin hunkydory, Ouruff said. Stay more and take a look-see.

Got to be getting on, Hreapha declared. "Hreapha!"

37

She arrived at home. Or what used to be home. Although her *in-habit* was clearly there, and glad to see her, the pickup wasn't there. She hadn't expected it to be, didn't want it to be. She went at once to her food dish, just an old green plastic bowl that he hadn't washed in ages. It was empty, of course. What had she expected? Well, she knew how absent-minded he was, and half-hoped that he might have put food out for her, just from force of habit. She looked around for the chickens, who were ordinarily free-ranging and had the run of the place and even left their droppings in Hreapha's favorite spots. But they were all gone! Hreapha visited their coop but they weren't there either. Had he also taken the chickens to the other place?

She sighed, and suddenly remembered that the back yard was a cemetery for a great number of bones that she had interred in the course of time, and she had but to remember the best and biggest one, and she could dig it up and gnaw happily on it. She had dug up the back yard not just to bury bones but also to make herself a den, to keep warm in cold weather and keep cool in hot weather, and a number of pits she had dug simply out of boredom. But most of the holes had been for the burial of bones, which he had generously thrown to her after gnawing most of the meat off himself.

The disinterred bone might not provide much substance for her stomach but the very act of chewing on it kept her from feeling hungry, and it also controlled tartar and prevented build-up and gum disease.

Hreapha spent the rest of the morning digging up and gnawing bones. There was still some water, rather stale, in her water bowl. Everything around her had her stamp on it; these were her things and smelled like her and therefore belonged to her, and she was happy among her possessions. Eschewing her doghouse with its stinky blanket, she climbed down into one of her holes and curled up and took a long nap.

As usual, her sleep was full of dreams. She knew that the purpose of dreams, sometimes disturbing and sometimes blissful but always mysterious and puzzling, was to help her make some sense out of her life, and to know what to do day by day. Sometimes she dreamed of being chased by people, other dogs, and monsters.

Sometimes she dreamed of chasing people, other dogs, or monsters. Sometimes she had dreams of being able to fly like a bird. Sometimes she had weird dreams: once she was required to put on a dress and a hat to cover her nakedness. Most often though, she dreamed of houses: big houses, little houses, henhouses, doghouses. Doors. Attics. Porches. Windows. Kitchens. Roofs. Bedrooms. None of the houses were actually places she had ever seen or lived in. Always the houses in her dreams were dilapidated, even the doghouses, and had been abandoned, were not being used, although each of them was inhabited by at least one *in-habit*. And they were not necessarily empty. They were cluttered, and it was somehow her responsibility to move the clutter.

Whatever she dreamed during her long nap this afternoon, she woke up from it having come to a most disturbing decision. She looked over the rim of the hole in which she had slept and noticed that there was no sign of him or the pickup. Much as she liked *this* house, which was her home, she was going to abandon it. She was going to reverse her direction and hike all the way back up to that mountaintop, to that other house where her master was moving. For the life of her, she could not understand why she decided to do this. But she knew she must do it. Something in her dreams had persuaded her.

She gnawed on one more bone and did not bother to bury the remains of it. She took a long drink of the unfresh water. She considered stopping to tell Yowrfrowr where she was going, but she did not. She summoned up her *in-habit* and said to it, I'm sorry but you've outgrown this place. Let's go.

Chapter five

He decided to take the chickens first, as a warm-up for the much harder task of carrying the davenport. He'd already had plenty of exercise chasing them down and catching them and putting them into the two crates. The crates were the real McCoy, the same kind that Tyson used to coop and ship all their birds in, made of wood that could rail in twelve to fifteen four-pound hens, and he'd helped himself to a couple of them several weeks before when he was still driving the cruiser and a Tyson truck had stopped along the highway. But the crates were big and he had to use both hands to lift and carry each one of them, and it was real tricky. In fact it was a son of a bitch. He'd toted so many boxes and sacks on this same path so many times that he knew almost every step by heart and could do it in the dark, although part of it amounted practically to no-hands mountain-climbing, getting his boot up into this crack and then raising the other boot above it to that crack. Christ almighty. For the pure hell of it, he'd tried to calculate just how far he'd gone already, moving everything into the Madewell place. It was just under a mile from where he had to leave the pickup to the front door of the old house. That meant that it was practically a two-mile round trip. Multiply that by the number of sacks and boxes and bags he'd carried, and it came to the equivalent of walking all the way to Little Rock and back. But any fool walking to Little Rock would stick to the nice smooth road, and his route had been steep down and steep up, reminding him of the old joke that if you was to iron Newton County out flat it would cover the whole state of Texas.

And he'd never had to carry anything as big as a chicken crate. That was one hell of a hefty job, and it lathered him with sweat not from the heat but the nervousness of it. And then there was the damn birds a-cackling the whole time and even pecking his goddamn fingers. He sure did relish fried chicken and he had to have his scrambled eggs two or three mornings a week, but he just didn't know if it was worth all the trouble.

On the trickiest part of the trail, that goddamn ledge against the bluff that was just barely wide enough to stand on, he had to turn sideways and hold the crate sideways and move sideways a step at a time, bit by slow bit. That ledge was such tough going that even Bitch had shied away from it. He hated to remember Bitch now. He truly wished he'd been nicer to her.

His thoughts lost on the damned dog, he took a misstep, lost his balance, lost his hold on the crate, tripped, and the whole fucking crate went flying off the bluff and it was kind of a miracle he didn't go flying after it. It landed in a treetop down below, the tree boughs breaking the fall so the crate and birds weren't smashed into the ground. But the impact tore open the crate's door and the birds flew out. Some of them landed on branches of the tree, others fell to the ground, a couple of them lay motionless as if dead, but all the damn chickens were out there loose. He wasn't going to try to climb down there and recover them, and he knew he couldn't get that crate out of the tree. The hell with it. Their wings was clipped, and they might come home to roost, ha ha. He figured they'd find their way on up to the house, those that didn't get eaten by foxes or bobcats or whatever was waiting for them out there in the woods.

He went back to the truck and got the other crate and was even more careful transporting it, sweating and winded both, and especially careful along that ledge where he'd lost the first crate. The second crate contained a rooster, at least, and he could start in to breeding the flock right away, and as soon as the eggs hatched he'd have nearly as many as he'd lost.

He reflected that all of this labor of hauling and carrying all the supplies for his new home had been a peck of trouble but it had slimmed him down a good bit. His beer gut didn't hang out over his belt buckle anymore. His biceps were thicker than he'd ever known them to be. He was in good shape for doing the repairs that needed to be done on the house, which was the first big job as soon as he got the girl moved in and settled.

He got the second crate of chickens to the house successfully and turned them loose beside the henhouse, then opened a bag of chicken mash and broadcast it liberally around the yard, near the henhouse. He didn't intend to feed the chickens regularly, and had only one thirty-pound bag of mash. When that ran out, they'd have to learn to feed themselves on bugs and worms and whatever they could catch. But the mash would tell them that this was their new home and they'd better stay here and maybe they'd better cackle loud enough for those other chickens down below to come up and join 'em.

Sog dusted his hands and made himself a little drink of Jack Daniels before going back for the davenport. He'd prefer to have his drink on the rocks, but the only rocks he was ever going to have up here was the real rock kind of rock. No ice. He sipped his drink and watched the chickens out in the tall grass a-scratching around for the mash he'd scattered. He hoped the girl would be partial to fried chicken as much as he was, and maybe even learn how to cook it. Serafina, his first wife, had been the best chicken-fryer in the country; must've been something she put in the batter. Fina had been just too good to last, and he'd had her for just a few years after he'd come home from Korea and found out her man Gene had been killed there, and had taken her and her sweet little daughter Brigit into his house. Brigit had been just five at the time, and he'd waited patiently for two years before he'd ever tried anything with her, and then he made sure that she really wanted to do it and that she understood it was just between him and her and never to be told to a soul, and he rewarded her as much as he could, and sweet Brigit had just loved him to pieces and was completely heartbroke when her mother decided to move on. Fina never found out about them. She just didn't like living in a dying town like Stay More, and she didn't think Sog had much future. At least that's what she tried to say in the note that he found when he come home from work one day. He was so pissed he went out and wrote tickets all over the place, stopping everybody for everything, especially for driving one mile over the speed limit.

He could still enjoy Brigit in his fantasies, although it had been fifteen years since last he'd enjoyed her in the flesh. The funny thing was, and this was something he'd been asking himself about, this girl of his dreams that he had found and was going to be moving into this house any day now didn't look anything at all like Brigit. She was far lovelier, for one thing. Brigit had been real cute, black hair in bangs and a cute little mouth with just the right size lips, but this Harrison girl that was his truelove was just something else, completely.

He finished his drink and went back for the davenport. It was clouding up and looked like it might come on to rain, which they sure needed. It hadn't rained a drop so far this April. He told himself that if he could just somehow get that big couch into his new home, the very worst would be all over. He wouldn't have been surprised if the davenport wound up in a treetop like the chicken crate, but he was bound and determined to get his dear mother's favorite possession into his final home. The experience with the first crate of chickens was good in the sense that it had taught him there was no way he could get the davenport along that same narrow ledge. He had plenty of rope and was going to have to figure out a way to rig the rope over a tree limb on top of the bluff and tie it around the davenport and either swing the davenport over and across the ledge or else hoist it all the way up the bluff. But first he had to get the davenport through those ravines. He'd already carried the davenport upside down on his back to get it into the pickup, and he knew it weighed just about a hundred and fifty pounds. That wouldn't break his back, stout as he was, but the footing was sure going to be tough going.

It took Sog all of an hour to lug that davenport on his back down into and up out of the three ravines that had to be traversed before he could reach that precarious ledge. He was just climbing out of the last ravine, huffing and puffing and sweating like a studhorse, when sure enough it come onto a rain, just a light sprinkle at first. He told himself not to hurry because getting the davenport across that ledge had to be done carefully, but by the time he'd rigged his ropes and tied them proper and was ready to swing the davenport across, it had commenced to rain pretty steady and he sure hated his mother's davenport getting drenched like that. In his impatience he climbed aboard the davenport and rode it as it swung across the ledge, and he grabbed aholt of a tree trunk on the other side, telling himself what a smart boy he was to have devised that system of ropes for getting the davenport beyond that ledge…although if it hadn't worked he and the davenport both would have crashed a hundred feet down to the earth below.

Getting the davenport the rest of the way through the forest was fairly easy and he cleared the front door of the Madewell house just as thunder crashed and a real toad-strangling downpour hit. He righted the davenport into its place in the living room, and admired it there for a long moment before he went to shut the front door and just as he did a flash of lightning illuminated a creature dashing into Madewell's shop out across the way. The open-ended shed was the place where Madewell had rived his staves and assembled his barrels and buckets and piggins and churns, and it had a little forge in it for the metal bands. That creature wasn't no wild beast of the woods. Damned if it wasn't old Bitch, sure looked like. He wasn't going out in this downpour to investigate. If she took a notion to come on to the house, he'd be nice to her. He wondered if maybe she'd never really left but had just been hanging around here waiting for him.

Sog made himself another Jack D and sat on the davenport and enjoyed it. The davenport was wet but not too wet, and it would dry off. It was going to be real comfy a-sitting here with his truelove, and he could hardly wait to do it. After all this work, there were just two things left: holding the yard sale Saturday, and finding some way to take possession of his truelove. He wished he knew her name, so he could think of her by name instead of just "truelove." He knew her last name, which was on their mailbox: Kerr. He hoped she would have a real nice first name. He sure didn't have a very good one hisself, although his grandpap had explained to him that Sugrue, which was his grandpap's family name, was a distinguished Irish name that went all the way back to the Irish Siocfhraidh, meaning victory and peace. Kids in school had started calling him Sog in the first grade, although the teacher called him Sugrue all the way through the eighth. He didn't mind, except Sog sounded a little like soggy, which everything was getting in this downpour. He had told his second wife, Arlene, to call him Sugrue instead of Sog, but she had preferred to call him Daddy, though of course they never had any children, and she was just a overgrown child herself, which was probably what had drawn him to her in the first place. Every bit of thirty-five when she'd married him, she was just a little bitty old slip of a girl, flat-chested and baby-faced. She could have passed for ten or less. Most people thought she was his daughter, or even his granddaughter, for heavensakes. But she sure wasn't innocent. Nor sweet. Nor fresh. She'd had a fairly wild past that he never learned all the particulars of, but he suspected she might even have been a whore at one time. He'd rescued her from a guy who beat her and was now serving time at Cummins. Worst of all about Arlene, compared with a genuine girlchild, was that she wouldn't mind him; he never could tell her what to do, and she was headstrong and did as she pleased. Arlene hadn't lasted as long as Fina before she commenced complaining that he simply couldn't hold out long enough for her. She had a fancy name for it that she taunted him with: *premature ejaculator.* She said his fuse was too short. One day she said, "You go off too fast so I'm going off, period." And she left him. Just like that. Fuck her.

As the rain kept beating down, Sog figured this would be a good time to check the place for leaks. Gabe Madewell and his daddy Braxton who'd built this place had been real craftsmen, and the same tight workmanship they'd put into all those barrels and buckets and piggins and churns had gone into the house. The roof was covered with cedar shingles that Brax Madewell had rived with even more care than he'd rived his white oak staves, and those shingles was still tight and solid, although the ones on the north side was all covered with moss. Except for a couple of window lights that Sog was going to have to replace (and he had lugged in a box full of glass pre-cut to the exact size of the window lights), the house was tight, a miracle in view of how long it had been abandoned. Why hadn't anybody ever wanted to take it over after Gabe Madewell left? Probably because they couldn't find it! No, honestly, the only reason anybody would want the place, assuming they knew it was there, would be because of one of two things: either they wanted to become a barrel maker like Madewell or, like Sog, they wanted it as a hideaway, a hermitage.

There was, Sog discovered, one leak in the roof, which was coming down into the smaller bedroom which Sog was using entirely as a storage room, with boxes stacked to the ceiling, a ceiling which was steadily dripping water upon the boxes. Hastily Sog took a bucket and climbed his stepladder and positioned the bucket to catch the drip of the leak. He watched the bucket for a while to assure himself that it wouldn't fill up and overflow for a good long time. Then he resumed his inspection of the house and took satisfaction in seeing that it was practically all ready for the arrival of his truelove. It was a good old house. They had everything they needed for years. And it was reasonably clean. When he'd first entered it, it had been inhabited by a pair of buzzards who'd laid their eggs right on the floor and hatched 'em and there was a bunch of godawful ugly baby birds a-screaming and also a-puking. One of them baby birds could hit you with puke from twenty feet away. Once he'd shot 'em or shooed 'em off, he had to clean up the terrible mess they'd left behind. Buzzards was the unsightliest, grossest bird on earth, and they'd probably flown in through one of those missing windows. Sog wasn't superstitious, not compared with most of these here so-called Ozark hillbillies, and he didn't believe the superstition that buzzards will puke upon any man who commits incest. It didn't matter to Sog because he would never think of committing incest anyhow if he had a real daughter. But he did believe, or knew for a fact, that buzzards are a sure sign winter is over, that there will not be another freeze after buzzards are seen. It hardly ever froze in April anyhow, but Sog knew when he saw the buzzards that good times as well as good weather lay ahead. He also believed what was simply a matter of fact: buzzards will fly and soar and hover over anything dead.

Late in the afternoon the rain stopped. Sog went out to the

workshop, where he thought he'd seen Bitch disappear. She wasn't there. Sog even peered into the two big barrels that for some reason Madewell had left behind and not sold with his other barrels. Sog intended to use one of them as an old-fashioned rain barrel, to collect water, although there was a good deep well behind the house, still with its operating pulley, to which Sog had attached a new chain and a new galvanized tin bucket. He didn't think they'd ever run out of water, but wanted the rain barrel for insurance, and maybe just as a kind of tribute to old Madewell, who had made all of this possible.

"Bitchie babe?" he called. But she wasn't around. Maybe he'd just imagined her. Or maybe it was her ghost. Yeah, probably she'd been eaten by a coyote or a bear off in the woods and her ghost was here to keep him company. But just in case it was her, he opened one of the bags of Purina Dog Chow, filled a new plastic dish he'd bought in the pet aisle of a supermarket, and set it out for her.

Then he hiked back to the pickup, and drove to Harrison. He checked the gas gauge and noted it was getting low. He didn't need a full tank. He needed just enough to make this trip to Harrison, then one more trip to Stay More for the yard sale and one last trip to Harrison to pick up his truelove.

Chapter six

Ifyou stare and stare at a mirror, and not because you're getting dressed or fixing your hair, does it mean that you're vain? She liked to just look at herself and try to imagine what she'd look like when she was eighteen or twenty. If she wasn't badly mistaken, she would be a dish, which is what her grandfather often called her. Grandpa Spurlock liked to say to her, "Honey, you're going to break hearts all over the place." She'd had explained to her what he meant when he called her a bombshell, and she knew what he meant when he called her "cutie pie" and "turtledove" and "chickabiddy" but she had trouble understanding what he meant when he called her "jailbait" and especially when he called her a "killer," because she couldn't be blamed if somebody's heart broke over her and they died. She would never deliberately kill anybody, although actually she might kill Jimmy Chaney if he didn't back off. Today at school during that horrible thunderstorm he got very flirty with her and even talked nasty. Thunder petrified her, and Miss Moore had stopped teaching the class and allowed them to take cover in the cloakroom, and Jimmy had snuggled up beside her. He said he was going to crash the birthday party and sleep with her. Jimmy was really the only boy she liked, usually, but he was ill-behaved and unpleasant, the same as all boys are. And possibly he had a wicked mind. She would never forget the time last fall when he'd come over to her house after school, breaking the strict rule that she was never allowed any visitors—girl or boy—when her mother wasn't there, and the fact that he wasn't supposed to be there made her dizzy and so titillated she didn't know what she was doing, and she probably encouraged him. He suggested that they ought to uncover their genitals and show them to each other. "Parts," he had said, and maybe if he had used some other word she might have been willing, but the fact of the matter was that she didn't have any parts. There was nothing there. This in itself didn't bother her too much—she had taken shower-baths with her mother at a very early age and one time she and Becky McGraw had not only shown each other theirs but had drawn pictures of each other's, so she knew this was a fact of the way all females were made, without parts.

But she hadn't wanted to compare what she didn't have with whatever he did have. She'd never seen a part. She had heard several things it was called besides "part"—the thought of that word made her giggle at the idea that it could be replaced, like automobile parts. Becky said it was just called "thing." Beverly knew it was properly called "doodad." Gretchen had heard it referred to as "pecker." Only Kelly had ever actually seen one, belonging to her father, and she said it was called "weenie" and attempted to describe it, and the two little pouches drooping from it, called, everybody knew, "nuts," although sometimes simply "balls." Robin had never seen a weenie and doubted that it looked anything at all like a hot-dog-type weenie, or frankfurter. Although blessed with a fabulous imagination, she had difficulty imagining what it looked like, and just out of curiosity she nearly allowed Jimmy to take down his pants. But instead she had told him that she was very sorry to have to tell him that they would both have to wait until they were much older before they could exchange peeks as he suggested. "You're so smart you won't ever have any fun," he said.

Once a couple of years ago while she was sitting on Grandpa Spurlock's lap and he was telling her one of his stories—he told such great stories about the old-time folks who had lived in these Ozark mountains—she had noticed some kind of bump or lump beneath her bottom and reached down to squeeze it and ask, "Grampa, what is *that?*" And he had squirmed and got real red in the face and said, "Aw, Cupcake, that's jist my mousy. Don't you be a-foolin with it." And she hadn't tried to squeeze it again. But later when her friends were talking about what a part could be called, she contributed "mousy," although she didn't say she'd learned it from her step-grandfather.

She just loved Grandpa Spurlock. He was the only male she knew (including Jimmy and Mr. Palmer, her Sunday school teacher, and Dr. Vanderpool, her pediatrician) toward whom she really felt respect and affection. She knew he wasn't really her grandfather but just married to her grandmother. Still, she felt closer to him than to her mother, who was so strict and distracted, or even her dear grandmother, who was so religious she had once told Robin she didn't care what she did so long as she got into Heaven, by and by.

The reason she was thinking of Grandpa this afternoon was not because of his mousy but because she was playing with her paper dolls, and every time she did that she thought of him, because one of her paper dolls was Grandpa Spurlock. It had been he who had given her a book of punch-out paper-dolls when she was four, and who, upon discovering that she liked to create her own paper dolls, had provided her with reams of paper and pasteboard with which to cut them out and clothe them. He had even given her a very good pair of scissors so that she didn't have to use her mother's, although her mother was very upset at the idea of Robin owning something so sharp and pointed. Although Grandpa Spurlock had also given her Paddington, her beloved teddy bear without whom she could not sleep at night, it was the paper dolls that really made her think of him, and even name one after him as a citizen, in fact the mayor, of her little town. Robin had created a whole village of paper dolls: men, women and children, families named White, and Brown, and Green, and Black, and Gray, and she had her hands full managing their wardrobes, not to mention inventing a life story for each one of them, and creating enough struggles and entanglements among them to give drama to her private world. Paddington sat in the chair opposite and watched her solemnly while she snipped and snipped and snipped. Her village, which was called Robinsville, even contained a paper bear named Paddington.

In fact she was running out of paper, but Grandpa had promised to bring some more the next time he came, and she hoped he might even come today.

Now it often happened in Robin's life that whenever she thought about something, or was hoping for something, that that something actually came to pass, it really occurred, it appeared as if by magic, the magic that was in Robin's head. It made her feel powerful and it made her wonder if she had the ability to perceive things that other people could not.

Anyway, there came a knock at the door. There were hardly ever any knocks at the door. Once in a great while there might be a couple of women selling a religious magazine and she had to tell them that she was not allowed to open the door. Robin ran to the door and called, "Who is it?"

And the voice said, "It's your grandpa. Open up."

And she turned the deadbolt and was about to open the door, ready to jump into his arms and be lifted up, when suddenly she realized that he had not knocked with the code, shave-and-a-haircut-six-bits.

"You didn't knock wight," she called to him, sorry that the return of her speech impediment robbed her voice of authority.

"I didn't? Well, drat my hide." He sure sounded like Grandpa. "How's this?" And he knocked a sort of knock knockedy-knock knock that sounded like the code. But it wasn't quite it. Robin fled to the living room window and peered out. Grandpa's car was not out there. It was just an old pickup truck.

She returned to the door. "What's your name?" she called.

"Grandpa."

"What do people call you?"

There was a silence, too long, on the other side, and she was convinced that this man, whoever he was, was a stranger, and therefore a danger. "Please open the door," he said.

"Go away," she said. "You're not my grandpa and if you don't go away I'll call the police."

"I'll huff and I'll puff and I'll blow your house down," he said.

She couldn't help giggling. "Not by the hair of my chinny chin chin!" she said.

She could hear him making some exaggerated breathing and blowing on the other side of the door, huffing and puffing. Then he said, "Piggy-wiggy, that didn't work. Your house won't blow down. I don't rightly recollect how the rest of it goes. Does the big bad wolf climb down your chimney next?"

He sure sounded like Grandpa, and she wondered if Grandpa was just playing with her. "No," she corrected him, "you're supposed to say you'll take me at six o'clock in the morning to Farmer Smith's turnip patch."

"Okay. Will you meet me at six o'clock in the morning?"

"I'll be there at five o'clock but with a bunch of police."

"Piggy-wiggy, I aint the big bad wolf, no foolin. I'm your lover boy. Me and you are fated to spend the rest of our lifes together, so we might as well get started right here and now."

She thought, *Something may be wrong with me, but I will never be in love. I will never have a lover boy. I love Paddington so much, but he's not really a boy.* She said, "I'm going to count to ten and if you're not gone I'm calling the police."

"Don't you even want to see my face? For all you know, I could be your Prince Charming. Open the door and have a look."

"You sure don't sound like anybody's Prince Charming," she said. "Now *get!* One... two... three...."

"Awright, I'm a-going, but you'll be sorry you turned me away. I'm fated to have ye, and I'll have ye one way or t'other, wait and see."

She waited, not commenting on that, and she waited, and finally she heard the truck start up. She ran to the window and looked out and got just a glimpse of him in profile driving away. He was just some old guy. Not a Prince Charming at all. More like the frog before he turned into the prince.

She returned to Robinsville and tried to resume her supervision of the lives of its citizens or at least of their wardrobes, but she was breathing hard and could feel her insides were all out of whack. She thought of calling the police anyway. Or calling her mother. Yes, she had better call her mother at the store. She went to the phone and started dialing but was stopped by the realization that if she reported this visitor to her mother there was no way on God's earth that she would be allowed to attend Kelly's birthday slumber party. It was bad enough already that Robin had refrained from telling her mother that Kelly's parents planned to take all the girls to the roller rink for the earlier part of the birthday party. Robin loved the roller rink more than any other place in Harrison, but her mother would never, ever let her go there, and if she knew that Kelly's parents were planning to include it as part of the party she wouldn't let Robin go. Robin sighed, and put the phone down.

There came another knock at the door! She actually jumped. But wasn't it the code knock? She went to the door and called, "Who is it?"

And the voice said, "It's your grandpa. Open up."

He was back! Whatever bluster and courage she had had during his first visit was now lost. She thought she would faint. "What's your name?" she asked.

She recognized his laughter. "Why, Leo Spurlock, I reckon," he said. "Last time I looked, anyhow."

She ran to the window again and looked out and sure enough it was Grandpa's car out there. She opened the door and leaped into his arms.

"Cupcake, you're trembling," he said. "Did I give you a scare?"

"No, but there was a man here. He was pretending to be you. Where's Grandma?"

"Aw, she wanted me to drop her off at the shoe store. Which means I don't have to go get her for another hour. So I thought I'd just run out and bring you some more cutting paper. I've got two reams in the car, one white and one colored." He returned to his car and brought her the big packages of paper, which would provide a summer and fall wardrobe for everybody in Robinsville. Then he sat in his favorite chair and patted his lap for her to sit in it, but she was getting too old for that. "What's this about somebody pretending to be me?" he asked.

She sat on the sofa and started telling him the whole story of the stranger's visit, but she got only as far as the huffing and puffing part when Grandpa laughed and said, "That's a great story, sugar bun, but you sure it aint jist a story?"

"He was *here*, just a little while ago, just before you came."

"Hmmm," said Grandpa. "I seen a feller in a pickup driving down the road as I was coming in."

"That was him. He was in an old pickup."

"Didn't git a good look at him but he shore didn't look like me."

"I told him I was gonna call the police, and he went away."

"Well, you know, there's lots of fellers like that in this world. Your beauty just swept him off his feet and he didn't know what he was doing."

"But he never saw me!" she protested.

"Might've seen you get off the school bus." Grandpa nodded his head and kept on nodding it, as if that was the answer to the whole matter. Some stranger had seen her get off the school bus, had greatly admired her and even—what was the word? yes: *lust*—the stranger had lusted after her and wanted her body. Miss Moore had given the class information about why it was so necessary for both girls and boys to avoid strangers and not allow themselves to be lured, and afterward Becky had said to Robin, "I still don't get it. Why would a stranger go to all that trouble? What does he want?" and Gretchen had said, "Silly, he wants to *fuck* you!" Robin had heard that word several times and had a fairly good idea of what it meant. It was something very wicked that some people did for fun and nastiness. Gretchen had tried to tell them that mommies and daddies did it too, and Robin had become so angry at Gretchen she hadn't spoken to her since then. "Why don't you sit on my lap," Grandpa said, "and I'll tell you a story or two, like old times."

She realized she had never been alone with Grandpa before, without Grandma or her mother present. She wasn't comfortable, and that bothered her, especially because she adored her grandfather. "I

55

was hoping," she said, "that I could ride my bike with you here to look after me." She had a perfectly wonderful bicycle, the most expensive thing that was her very own, but she hardly ever got to ride it. Her mother wouldn't let her go out and ride it off by herself, and the only times she could ride it was when her mother would supervise her, and there were hardly any times like that. She really needed the exercise. Since the weather had started warming up, at school recess the girls (and boys too) had taken to removing their shoes and socks to play their games, but Robin hated to go barefoot. She could understand why other kids liked it and liked the feel of the cool earth or grass under their feet, but Robin couldn't stand it. So she had been avoiding the recess games, and wasn't getting enough exercise. When it got too bad, she could always skip her rope by herself, which she often did, alone in the house, in relief against all that sitting-down to manage Robinsville, but skipping rope or even practicing her taekwondo moves wasn't as much fun as riding the bicycle. Her father one time had taken her to a martial arts class where the taekwondo teacher had told her she would be a black belt within six months if she came to class regularly. But of course her mother wouldn't let her go, and her father just didn't come around any more.

"Okey-doke, I reckon," Grandpa said. "If you're a-hankerin to ride your bike, I 'spect I could oblige ye."

So she put on her jacket and got her key and locked the house and Grandpa got in his car and drove it slowly behind her while she rode her bicycle down the road. It felt so good. She liked to pump with her legs and feel the wind in her face. It really wasn't very cold. She liked to swing the bike frame back and forth as she pumped harder. Soon she had left Grandpa a good ways behind. If only she had her dog running along beside her. But she'd never had a dog, or a cat, because her mother said it was out of the question. She would simply adore having a good dog, and have it now running with its tongue hanging out beside her bicycle. Bicycle riding was really the only time she liked to be outdoors. Not that she was a stay-at-home, and she certainly wasn't allergic to fresh air, but she just had no appreciation for the world of nature, and woods bothered her. She disliked the few times that the teacher had taken the class on a "nature walk," and she had no interest whatever in being able to identify trees or plants or flowers or anything. Even the Sunday school teacher had once tried to take the class out into the woods to discover how God was out there in those woods, but she never found Him. If she were God she wouldn't want to be in the woods. "I have never seen God," she told her mother later, and from then onward refused to say her prayers at night or anytime.

Now she stopped peddling and squeezed the brakes on the handlebar. Right there up ahead beside the road was that man parked in his pickup truck. She looked behind her to see how far Grandpa's car was. She couldn't see it. She shouldn't look over her shoulder like that while the bike was still moving. She lost her balance and before she could stop the bike or get her balance she had crashed into the earth.

Chapter seven

My goodness alive but wasn't she the pertiest little thing that ever walked God's earth—or rode a bike on it? He didn't much believe in God; he'd seen or heard about too damn many plum loco things in this world to believe that nobody as smart as God was supposed to be could possibly have saw fit to allow it, let alone have planned it in the first place, but whenever he laid his eyes upon Robin he was struck all of a heap with the certainty that nobody but God Hisself could have had the cleverness to have created somebody so splendid. Oftentimes he wondered if Louisa had looked like that when she was just a young 'un. He'd seen photos of Louisa looking tiny and cute, but nothing at all like her granddaughter, why, there was scarce even a family resemblance. Of course it was hard to think of Louisa without resentment. Even besides the fact she hadn't wanted him to touch her for years and years, she was so all-fired churchy and had to go three times a week and drag him along with her, she had also made it hard for him to give Robin all the loving she needed. When that worthless asswipe Billy Kerr had taken to fooling around and then split for good, Leo had wanted to step in and take his place as a kind of daddy for Robin, but Louisa had suspicioned that he had the hots for Karen and wanted to take Billy's place in bed, which wasn't true at all, not at all. Karen was a sightly-enough woman, and Leo couldn't understand why she hadn't found herself another man, but he didn't have any sort of attraction to her whatsoever. He just wanted to be a daddy for Robin. He wanted to take her to her martial arts classes that Billy had been taking her to but that Karen couldn't find the time for. He wanted especially to take her out to the roller rink now and again, because she was already real good at what was called "artistic" skating, and if she got a chance to keep it up, why, there was just no telling how far she could go, maybe even switch to ice skates by and by and become another Sonja Henie or one of those such as Leo liked to watch on the TV. But damn her hide, Louisa had not allowed him to follow his intention to do all those things for Robin. The best he could do was buy her toys and things and make sure she had all she needed to follow her interest in paper dolls and paper things. He'd been allowed to help her in that line all he liked. In fact, not only had he started it all when he gave her a book full of paper dolls a few years before, but he had also demonstrated to her something that she ought to have learned from Karen or somebody but nobody had ever bothered to learn her: you can make yourself a whole string of paper dolls holding hands if you just fold up a sheet of paper proper and then cut just the profile of the doll, so that when you unfold your paper you've got a whole line of identical ones. As soon as she learned how to do that, Robin had to give a different name to each and every one of the identical dolls in the string, and that was how she got started a-populating her whole town full of little paper people, which she called Robinsville, and wasn't that clever of her? Robin was not only the pertiest thing he'd ever seen, and the smartest to boot, but she had an imagination that would make you shake your head in wonder and keep on a-shaking it.

Leo had a thing for paper himself. He had also shown her how to take a sheet and fold it just right so that it became an airplane that would really fly. You had to do it just right. It was a trick Leo had learned in the Navy. He wanted to take Robin up one of the hills in Harrison and show her how to launch them paper planes out across the air and watch 'em fly and fly and just fly away. But he had to make do with being allowed to just take her out in the back yard and let her fly her planes back there, and they didn't go very far without a drift of wind to catch 'em.

Today was the first time he'd ever been truly alone with Robin, and here he was with just a back view of her a-riding along ahead of him, with that golden hair a-streaming out behind her. Personally he liked the hair better in braids, which Karen was real good at fixing when she wasn't too busy, but now Robin had taken the braids out so she could have her hair blowing in the wind while she rode the bike. And all he could do was foller and watch.

Leo took his foot off the gas, and coasted, and let his thoughts coast too. When he returned his attention to the road, he noticed that Robin had done pedaled right out of sight! He mashed the gas again and cleared the little curve in the road, and Christ all Jesus! If she hadn't done had a wreck! Her and the bike were all crumpled up flat on the earth.

Leo braked to jump out just at the same time that another feller was rushing up to her. Blamed if it wasn't that feller he'd seen a little bit before, the one that Robin thought maybe had been knocking on her door. He and the feller got to her at the same moment. Him and the other feller each bent down and took one of her arms.

She wasn't hurt bad, maybe a scrape or two, and she wasn't even crying. Leo had never in her life known her to cry, over anything. But she was in great pain, he could tell.

The other feller was trying to lift her up too, and he was a pretty big and stout feller, half again as big as Leo, and sure enough he just lifted her up easy as a loaf of bread and made as if to carry her to his pick-up.

"Grampa," she says through her big lips that was all twisted in pain.

"Yeah, it's Grampa," says the other feller. What the heck? And started a-carrying her toward his truck.

"Hold on!" says Leo and grabbed aholt of one of her arms. "I'm her grampa!"

"The hell you say," says the feller, tough and mean. "I'm her grampa."

Leo had never met Billy Kerr's dad, who lived over in Oklahoma somewheres and had never been to Harrison as far as Leo knew about, and he wondered, could this maybe be Billy Kerr's daddy? If that was so, then he'd really be her grandfather because Leo wasn't actually her blood grandfather.

"Well, I got to her first," Leo says, somewhat lamely, and wraps his arms around her possessively.

"But I picked her up first," the other feller says, in all truth. "How do I know you're her grandfather?"

"Ask her?" Leo says.

The feller looked down at Robin and says, "Is this man really your grandfather?"

"Well, no, not really," Robin says. "But his wife is my grandmother. Oh, I *hurt!*" And she walked to Leo's car and opened the door and sat down. She made some painful faces and then she bit her lip and says, "Besides, you're that creep that tried to break into my house!"

"Is that a fact?" Leo wanted to know, and says these words to that man.

"Goshdarn, I wasn't trying to break into her house. I just wanted to talk to her, and see if she'd maybe seen my lost dog. My damn dog is lost and I can't find her."

"Is that a fact?" Leo says. "Then how come you're a-claimin to be her grandfather?"

"I didn't know who ye was," the other feller says to Leo. "For all I knew, ye might've been one of them there child molesters, and I was just a-claiming to be her grandfather to get rid of you."

Leo knew that if the other feller really wanted to, he could whop Leo upside his head and lay him out cold, and make off with Robin as easy as pie. The fact that he wasn't whopping Leo meant that maybe he really was looking for that pore lost doggie. "Well," Leo says, "I sure hope you find that there lost dog, and we'll keep a eye out for it."

"What's the dog's name?" Robin says.

"Bitch," the feller says, and for a second Leo felt his hackles a-rising, thinking the feller is cussing at Robin. But Leo thought about it for a while and decided the feller wasn't cussing. Then Leo put Robin's bike into the trunk of his car, half a-hanging out with a bent wheel and fender that would need some work. He got in the car and drove off with Robin.

He took her back to her house. "I reckon we ort to of ast him what the dog looks like," Leo says

"He's not looking for a dog," Robin says. "That's just an old trick that bad men use to lure children with. That's what Miss Moore told us, anyhow."

"What if a dog was to show up?" Leo wondered.

Back at the house, after unloading the bike, he got into the medicine cabinet and found some antiseptic ointment and some Band-Aids and tended to Robin's elbow and her knee. "Say, listen, Cupcake," he said to her, "if your maw wonders what happened to your knee and elbow, I reckon ye better just tell her you had a accident at school or something. It wouldn't do for her to know that I allowed you to go out on your bike."

"Okay," Robin agreed. "And I'm not going to say anything at all about that man. Mommy said that I can go tomorrow night to a friend's sleep-over birthday party. She wouldn't let me go if she knew I'd been bothered by a strange man."

"I guess not," Leo said. "I know your momma." Fact was, Karen Kerr was the awfullest worrywart he'd ever known, and it was a wonder she ever allowed the poor child to do nothing.

"Also," Robin confided in him, "Kelly's parents—it's Kelly's birthday party—they're going to take us six girls to the roller rink for a special birthday party there before the slumber party, and I didn't even tell Mommy about that. She really wouldn't let me go if she knew about that."

"I hope ye have a good time," Leo said, and wondered if there was some excuse he could give Louisa tomorrow evening so's he could come all the way back into Harrison and go to that roller rink himself. Not to skate, because he'd never been on skates in his life, but just to watch. Thinking of Louisa, he said, "Now I'd best run and get your grandma, and we'll see you in a bit, maybe before your maw gets home.

He drove to downtown Harrison and Louisa was standing outside the shoe store waiting for him. She had just one box of shoes under her arm, which at least was an accomplishment. Sometimes she spent the whole afternoon in there and never got nothing.

"Where've you been?" she wanted to know.

"Aw, I just dropped in at the pool hall to see some buddies," he said.

"You don't have any buddies," she said.

Leo didn't like that. Matter of fact, he did have fellers all over the place that he could pass the time of day with. Maybe not ary a one of them that he'd lay down his life for, or vicey versa, but Louisa made him out to sound like some kind of hermit.

"Where was it ye aimed to go next?" he asked.

"We might as well get on out to Karen's," she said.

He drove on back to Karen and Robin's place, the second time today. Third, come to think of it, counting the trip down the road behind her bike.

As they were getting out of the car, Louisa said, "Where's those reams of paper you got for Robin?"

Leo realized he'd already given them to her. "Uh, I reckon I must've went off and forgot 'em," he said.

"What?" Louisa was upset. "We just stopped at the Wal-Mart for them a little while ago." Louisa peered into the back seat in search of the Wal-Mart sack, which, Leo realized, was probably in plain view on the table at which Robin had spread out Robinsville.

Leo hung his head. It sure took a heap of sneakiness to get anything past Louisa. He had never been able to learn all the tricks and ruses that most fellers use in order just to have a little fun in this sorry life. "Louisa," he announced solemnly, "in my old age I seem to be getting more and more absent-minded. I'll be durned if I didn't already drop off them reams of paper."

She squinted her eyes at him. "Leo Spurlock!" she exclaimed. "You don't mean to tell me you've already been out here by yourself? And that little girl all alone?"

He nodded, feebly.

She hauled off and slapped him. Hoo boy it stung like the

dickens and knocked his glasses off. It wasn't the first time she'd hit him, and he knew it wasn't going to be the last. "I never did nothing," he protested, truthfully.

"You get back in the car, and you just sit there," she commanded him. "You just sit there and I'll visit with Robin and come out when I'm good and ready."

She went up to the door and knocked. After a while, she hollered, "It's your grandma. Open up."

Leo rolled down the window and hollered, "You forgot you're supposed to knock the shave-and-a-haircut-six-bits."

Louisa knocked proper, and Robin let her in.

Leo just sat there, for a long time. By and by Karen come home. She parked and come over to him. "Leo, what are you sitting out here for?" she asked.

Leo coughed. He coughed because he didn't know what to say, but the act of coughing provided him with a excuse, "I been feelin porely. I jist might have something I don't want Robin to catch."

"Sorry to hear that," Karen said. "Mother won't be long. I've got to take Robin downtown to shop for a birthday present for a party she's going to tomorrow night."

"Yeah, Robin told me all about that party," he said.

"So you have seen her?" she said and looked at him peculiar. "I thought you meant you didn't want to see her so she wouldn't catch anything from you."

Leo come mighty close to smiting hisself on the brow on account of his stupidity in not knowing how to pass even the time of day without sticking his foot in his mouth. Was there ever a feller on earth who had more sawdust where his brains ort to be?

Chapter eight

O kay, okay. Let's us just clamp on the blinders and hold our horses. He was not just going too fast and reckless but he was doing it assbackwards, all on the edge and itchy to get the girl. He knew damn well that he'd have to hold that fucking yard sale *before* he took possession of her, and it wasn't advertised until tomorrow morning. Probably nobody would show up for it, but he had to have it anyhow just for the look of things.

He'd meant this visit to Harrison, his next to last, to be only a sort of reconnaissance, to see whichaway the wind was blowing and get the lay of the land. He just wanted a good idea of the girl's comings and goings, and if there was maybe any chance she ever went anyplace by herself. But coming into town he realized he was driving too fast at the same moment he heard the siren and saw in the rearview mirror the blue lights flashing atop the trooper's cruiser.

It was old Hedge Larrabee, who he'd trained years before. "License and registration," old Hedge said from behind his dark sunglasses, without even bothering to take a good look at him.

"Hedge, you dipshit," Sog said. "It's *me.*"

"Sarge?" old Hedge said, and for a second looked like he was about to salute. "Goshdawg, Sarge, I thought you'd gone to Californy. You were doing sixty-five in a forty mile zone, did you know?"

"Yeah, Hedge, I'm heading for Californy the day after tomorrow."

"Well, good luck and God bless and all that crap," Hedge said. "You take it easy now, you hear?" Hedge turned to go but then he turned back. "Sarge, if you're going to Californy, you'd better have this heap looked at. You've got hardly any tread on the tires, and the whole damn muffler is about to come loose."

"I'll probably junk it and take the bus," Sog declared, and drove on. He'd gone hardly half a mile before he discovered how heavy his foot on the gas was, and had to force himself to let up. Then he drove on out the road to the Kerr place and parked near it so he could sit there and watch for the school bus to let the girl out. He wished he knew her first name so he could think of her as something besides "the girl" or his truelove or whatever. After a while the school bus pulled up, and she got off and his heart swole mightily, once again amazed at how beautiful she was. He waited for the school bus to drive off, but the driver just sat there watching until she had checked the mailbox and then gone to the front door and let herself in. She had her key inside her lunchbox.

He hadn't meant to try anything today, but the very thought of her being alone in that house was just too much for him. He and Jack Samples had known of several cases where the kid was so trusting or just plain gullible that they would open the door for anybody. He thought he might as well give it a try. He drove on a little and parked out front, and went up and knocked on the door.

But it wouldn't work. He pretended to be her grandpa, but she wasn't fooled. In the first of what he knew would be thousands of conversations in the years to come, he discovered right off the bat how smart and clever she was. He couldn't get her to open the door, and finally he gave up, and drove down the road a ways and parked and sat there for a good bit thinking about the ways that he might possibly take her into his custody. He could just bust out a window in the house. There wasn't no other neighbors within view, and even if she hollered probably nobody would hear her. But he didn't want to scare her too bad, and he put on his thinking cap to see if he couldn't come up with the words to keep her gentled down. He already told her that him and her was fated to spend the rest of their lifes together and that he was her lover-boy, but he doubted she'd believed him. Shit, when you got right down to it, he was old enough to be her grandpa, and she would probably prefer a much younger guy to spend the rest of her life with.

"Lord, lord," Sog said aloud, "help me to find a way to get her to go with me to our new home." Sog wasn't hardly religious at all, and when he said this prayer he wasn't even picturing the Lord Above, but he was sure earnest in his request.

And be damn if, at the very moment he said those words, she didn't appear! Riding her bike! "Thank you, Lord!" he said. But when she caught sight of him she threw on her brakes or something and the bike crashed.

And then here came that feller who turned out to be her real granddaddy, or her step-granddaddy leastways, a guy some years older than Sog and kind of puny and Sog was prepared to fight him for the girl, but then he figured it was already bad enough that he was letting the man get a good look at him so that later on when Robin disappeared the man would be able to describe him and maybe even help 'em draw a picture of him. Up at CID they had a real sketch artist who could talk to you and get you to give him enough info about a suspect to get his likeness down exact on a piece of paper.

So Sog he figured he'd better get on out of there, and he drove off, hoping the feller hadn't bothered to take down his license number or nothing. But come to think on it, the feller didn't seem to be loaded with brains.

He went to the drive-in for a couple of cheeseburgers and a milkshake. He was going to miss cheeseburgers and milkshakes and maybe these was his last ones, because tomorrow evening, his last evening here in town before heading off home with his beloved, he intended to have his "last meal," that is to say, his last restaurant meal, and he'd already decided on Western Sizzlin', where he could get himself a nice big cut of steak, something he'd never be having again up there on the mountain. He'd considered but rejected the idea of keeping some beef cattle up there; it would be just too hard to get them up there unless he carried them when they were still calfs, and he might not be able to do that. Probably a calf weighed more than a davenport and was harder to manage and carry unless it was tranquilized.

Thinking of tranquilizers, he remembered that he'd already given some thought to the possibility of using some chloroform on the girl. But buying some of the stuff was out of the question. You can't get it at the drugstore. He'd thought of trying to get some from a vet with the excuse of using it to put his old sick dog to sleep (his dog, if he still had her, was young and fit), but there again, when the news of the girl's kidnapping was announced, the vet might remember him and put two and two together.

No, his best bet was just to make his own. A few years back he'd arrested this guy in Yellville who ran a meth lab and made a lot of other chemical stuff besides, and the feller had told him how to make chloroform real easy: you just take you some Chlorox bleach and mix in a little acetone with it and stir it up. Hell, he could get the fixings for that right over at Wal-Mart. What would have acetone in it? Why, any old nail polish remover would do.

So he went to Wal-Mart once again. He knew he probably wouldn't run into that saleslady who had sold him all the clothes and toys and stuff for his girl, because that was a different department. First he went to the laundry soap aisle and picked up a jug of Chlorox bleach. He reflected that he was sure going to miss being able to take his dirty clothes to the coin-op laundry in Jasper. But they were going to live in the manner of the old-timers and wouldn't need such as that. There was a big old black iron kettle or wash pot that the Madewells had left behind, and such had been good enough for his grandmother to boil up enough water for a wash of clothes, and it would be good enough for him, and maybe the girl too if she really wanted to help could learn how to do laundry.

Then he headed for the cosmetics aisle to get the nail polish remover. He was checking the back of the bottle to make sure it said acetone on it when he looked up, and here come that woman Karen Kerr with her daughter his darling! Sog ducked behind the aisle just in time and they didn't see him. He spied on 'em from a distance, ready to duck if they looked his way, and saw that the girl was picking out a bright pink bottle of what looked like bubble bath mix. His head was filled with visions of her in a bubble bath. They wouldn't have a bathtub as such up on the mountain but there was a big galvanized tub with handles that they could carry around and set up on the kitchen floor to fill with hot water from the stove and maybe even both of 'em get in it at the same time.

From a distance Sog followed when they went on to the greeting card aisle and the girl got a package of bright wrapping paper and then spent a while picking out a card from the rack that said "Birthdays." Sog didn't have to be a genius to figure it out: the girl was planning to give a friend a birthday present of bubble bath stuff and maybe even go to a birthday party. Maybe a party where they'd be playing in the yard or something and Sog could watch for a chance to grab her and chloroform her. But probably the party would be tomorrow, Saturday, when Sog had to be out at Stay More running the goddamn yard sale.

Sog kept himself hidden until they'd left the store, and then he went back to the cosmetic aisle and got a whole case of that bubble bath mix and put it in the cart with his Chlorox bleach and nail polish remover. Then just a couple more things: he needed some sponges, one good one for the chloroform, plus a little plastic bucket to mix the stuff in, and a wooden spoon to stir it. Then he was all set.

If he'd had the sense God gave to people to pound sand in a rat hole, he would have gone on home to Stay More and done a few things to get that yard sale ready and then got a good night's sleep in preparation for the biggest day of his life tomorrow. But, idiot that he was, he had to drive once more down the road to the Kerr place, or near enough to it to park down the road and spy on it, just to see if anything was going on. There was always a chance the birthday party was being held there, and always a chance it was this evening instead of tomorrow. His burning eagerness to get it all over with had already cost him a bad moment or two and now here he was a-scheming to try something else. As he sat there, he even thought about the idea of asking Karen Kerr for a date sometime, and taking her out, and step by step making friends and then watching for a chance to make his move on the girl. But no, the girl would recognize him if he tried that. And besides it was just too damned slow. He had to act now, and get his business all settled so him and the girl could live happy ever after up on the blessed mountaintop. There was only two ways to abduct a kid, Jack Samples had once told him, one, by ruse, the other, by blitz. It was time to blitz.

The house was still, but the car was in the driveway, so they were home. By and by the lights went on as it come on to dark. As he sat there pondering, Sog finally made up his mind what he had to do: he had to get Karen to open the door and then he was going to chloroform her first, and then, after she was down, he would chloroform the girl.

He got out his stuff, and set the bucket on the seat beside him, and commenced to do his chemistry. He poured a pint or so of the Chlorox bleach into the bucket, then tossed in several dollops of the nail polish remover, then took the wooden spoon and began to stir 'em together. Whew, did those fumes stink. He figured he'd better protect himself against it, and was fishing in his pocket for his handkerchief to wrap around his nose when it suddenly got too black to be just plain dark.

When he came to, the black was being replaced by a sliver of light in the east. He looked at his watch, and although his watch said five-thirty, his mind was only thinking about his determination to get rid of the watch as soon as he was settled on the mountaintop. Next his mind became aware of how his whole damn head felt—like it was being pounded into a rat hole. Next it was not his head screaming for his awareness of its pain, but his stomach. He had just enough mind left to think to get the fucking door open, and then he puked out into the road. He went on puking until there wasn't nothing left. Then he had sense enough to pour out what he'd already mixed in the bucket. He started up the truck and turned it around and headed for the highway, and at the first culvert he passed he slowed down just enough to toss the Chlorox and the acetone out into the ditch. He had to stop once more to puke, and then he headed for Stay More.

And goddamn it all to hell if he wasn't stopped by the fucking state police once again! And wouldn't you know it was ole Hedge again.

"I wasn't doing sixty-five," Sog protested.

"Naw, Sarge, you was only doing forty. But you was driving erratic. Better let me sniff your breath." Hedge got his face up close and drew a big breath and said, "Wowee, have you been drinking varnish?"

"I aint been drinking," Sog said.

"What are you out this time o' night for?" Hedge wanted to know. "Or early morning, I ort to say."

Sog thought fast. "Some friends of mine were giving me a goodbye party."

"'Scuse me, Sarge," Hedge said, "but you aint got no friends." Sog wouldn't challenge the accuracy of that shitty observation, so Hedge went on, "And if you was at a party, you would of been drinking, wouldn't you of?"

"Hedge, I wouldn't take a drop because I knew you'd catch me," Sog said. "Now if you'll just let me go on, I'll drive more careful."

"You better do that, Boss," Hedge said. "Oops, you aint my boss or nobody's any more, are you?"

"Then you ort to be glad of that," Sog said and drove off fast. Tomorrow—or, more exactly, *today*—when he came back to Harrison, coming and going he'd have to take back-roads to stay out of Hedge Larrabee's territory.

It's forty twisting miles from Harrison to Stay More. As soon as he got home, he popped a fistful of aspirin, which helped just a little, took half a glass of bourbon, which helped more, and then dragged what possessions he had left out into the yard. Just as he figured, almost nobody showed up for his yard sale. Stay More was practically a ghost town anyhow, and only a few people from hereabouts took a notion to come. George Dinsmore came and offered to buy his chickens, and he had to explain he'd already sold 'em. Latha Bourne, who used to be postmistress of Stay More before it lost the PO to Parthenon, offered to buy his davenport, and he had to explain he'd already sold it.

Mid-afternoon he stuck the unsold stuff back into the house

and shut it up and locked it, which he never had done before. He taped a sheet of paper on the door: GONE TO CALIFORNIA. He took one quick drive around what little was left of the town, including the old empty schoolhouse across the creek, taking a kind of farewell look. If it hadn't been for his headache he might have allowed himself to get nostalgic over the scenes of his boyhood but he wanted to just tell them all to go to hell.

Back in Harrison for the last time, he skipped the last supper at Western Sizzlin' because his stomach still wasn't settled.

He took up his spy post near the Kerr place and waited and followed when Karen Kerr drove the girl away and across town to somebody else's house, and left her there, probably for that birthday party. The girl was carrying the gift-wrapped bubble bath. He parked down the street for a stake-out on that house, and hadn't been waiting very long before two of the cars took a whole bunch of the girls, six or seven of them, back across town to a roller skating rink.

There is kind of a little balcony at one end of the roller rink, where the skaters stop and step out to take a breath of air or to goof off or whatever. Sog drove his truck around behind the roller rink so that he could watch that little balcony.

It began to get dark. Usually two or more of the girls would appear on that balcony together. Sog got out and stood so he could reach up to the balcony, which wasn't very far above the ground. His eyes was level with the rink floor and he could see inside the rink, where a whole bunch of skaters was a-gliding all over the place, and there in the midst of them was his truelove, doing all kinds of fancy turns and spins and even leaps. She took his breath away. And he loved her more than ever.

He waited patiently, and just like they say, everything comes to him who waits. By and by, she come out onto the balcony by herself, breathing hard after all those stunts. She was too winded to put up any struggle. He grabbed her and gagged her and took her away.

Chapter nine

She didn't mean for him to see her. She intended to take possession of the yards and fields and to let her *in-habit* know that this was her new home, and live in peaceful co-existence with the mean bastard without being *his* dog. She kept herself hidden in the grass, spying on him while he brought in a crate filled with chickens from the old home and turned them loose in the yard near the dilapidated henhouse, then broadcast chicken feed around the yard. The chickens discovered her while scratching around for their feed, but they knew her and did not even bother to cackle in recognition, and of course she wasn't making a sound. Later she watched with great interest as he appeared, coming up the trail from the forest with some enormous thing on his back. It took her a while to recognize it, possibly because it was upside down and didn't seem to belong on a man's back out in the woods, but she caught a distant whiff of its scent and realized it was the big soft feel-good piece of furniture that had been in the old house, that she herself had once tried to sleep upon because it was so comfortable. He had kicked her off of it, and had said, "Bitch, don't never let me catch you on there again." Well, she reflected, whatever doubts she might have had that he intended to forsake the old place entirely and move into this mountaintop homestead were now laid to rest. He loved that piece of furniture more than he loved anything else in this world. That piece of furniture was his wife, and now the new home was complete.

When she had heard the first distant thunderclaps she had cringed and burrowed her belly into the earth, lowering her ear flaps down over her ears. But then the thunder came nearer and louder and the hard blankets of water fell from the sky and she started losing her mind, and decided to make a mad dash for safety and shelter in the building that had been a workshop. She didn't care if he saw her or not. Inside the workshop she was protected from the waterfall but not from the terrible noise, and she took a leap and landed inside of one of those tall round wooden things, where she cowered and trembled. The walls of the wood around her offered only a little protection against the crash of the thunder, and once again she was convinced that the world was coming to an end. Eventually the hideous noise stopped, and she had to make three or four jumps before she could extricate herself from that deep drum. She sniffed the air and detected that he was approaching just in time for her to hide herself in a dark corner of the shop.

It was while she was hiding that she became unmistakably aware of an *in-habit* that was so present and clinging that for an instant she thought another person had been there recently. But like all *in-habits,* it had no scent. And yet this *in-habit* was so powerful she knew it had been around for a long, long time, and she had to choke herself to keep from calling "Hreapha!" to it, which would have given away her hiding place to him, who was now peering into the wooden drum as if searching for her, and then was calling "Bitchie babe?" in such a gentle voice she was tempted to answer him. She could almost *see* the *in-habit* shying away from him. No, she couldn't *see,* but she could perceive, and this *in-habit* was a tousle-haired boy in overalls. She wanted to lick his hand, which he held out to her, but she didn't want the man to see her. She waited until the man was gone, and then she attempted to lick the *in-habit's* hand, but the hand, darn it, simply was not there.

One night she and Yowrfrowr had taken a stroll together to

the Stay More cemetery, an interesting place to play, and Hreapha had detected her very first ghost, if that is what it was. Yowrfrowr had nudged her and cautioned her not to call her name to it, because ghosts hate barking. So they had both pretended the ghost wasn't there, and it had gone away.

What's the difference, she had asked Yowrfrowr, between a ghost and an *in-habit*?

A whole world of difference, my dear, he had said. The primary difference is that ghosts are the spirits of creatures who no longer live. *In-habits* are the spirits of creatures who are still alive.

Do you mean that when an *in-habit* dies it becomes a ghost?

Yowrfrowr had chuckled and grinned. Not exactly, he had said. Many ghosts have never been *in-habits*. And many *in-habits* never become ghosts. An *in-habit* is part of someone who loves a particular place so very much that regardless of where they go they always leave their *in-habit* behind. If I should ever have to leave Stay More, perish the thought of that unlikelihood, my *in-habit* will fiercely take possession of this whole damn town.

She had only been able to look at him with wonder, trying to understand just what an *in-habit* was.

Yowrfrowr had gone on grinning. Now if you'll hold still, he had said, my *in-habit* would like to climb up on the back of your *in-habit*.

You're as silly as you look, she'd said, and had run away from him.

Now she perceived that the man had gone, perhaps back to the truck for another piece of furniture, and she came out of hiding. Her hunger pangs were getting the better of her, and she was nearly tempted to turn one of those chickens into a ghost. But she knew all the chickens personally, although they had never exchanged names or made any attempt to communicate beyond Hreapha occasionally beseeching them to stop defecating all over her favorite lying-places.

She went up to the house and discovered to her delight that he had left out a bowl of her favorite kind of commercial chow on the porch. So he knew she was there! He was going to feed her! This would be ideal, to share the premises with him without any servitude to him, or any ill-treatment from him, and yet retain the right to be regularly provided for. She decided that when he came back again she would say "Hreapha!" at least once, just in gratitude. She licked the bowl clean.

But he did not come back. She waited a long time and then took a hike the harsh mile down the mountain to the place where he customarily left his pickup, but it was not there. She supposed he had gone back to Stay More for yet another load. Returning up the mountain trail, stepping gingerly along the ledge where not even goats could step and telling herself not to look down, she couldn't help looking down at the sound of some familiar cackling, and she noticed, far down below, a whole flock of her feathered friends from the old place. Looking closer, she saw the smashed crate that had been their container in the treetop. Brainy as she was, it didn't take her long to surmise that he must have accidentally dropped a crate of the chickens while negotiating the treacherous trail.

It took her a while, more than a while, to find a way to get down there. But she did, and announced to the chickens that she intended to shepherd them to their new home. Of course they couldn't understand her language, but she went on communicating, reassuringly, telling them that her great-grandfather on her mother's side, whose name was Yiprarrk, had been a sheep dog, and knew how to herd the animals and get them to move in the desired direction. She thus had inherited at least a semblance of the ability to herd creatures. She went up behind a big fat hen and snapped "Hreapha!" and sure enough the hen moved in the desired direction, although casting Hreapha a malevolent and supercilious look. There was a rooster who responded to Hreapha's commands by attempting to rise up and stab her with his spurs, screaming all the while in a way that damaged her ears, and she practically had to get into a cockfight in order to convince him to accompany his harem.

It was slow work. All the rest of the afternoon was consumed in trying to get the birds moving in the same direction, up through the dark woods to the place where the remains of the trail could be picked up and they could march more smoothly toward their new home. A few stubborn hens ran the wrong way and she had to chase them down and pretend to bite them in order to get them turned around. She had shouted "Hreapha!" so many times that she was perishing of thirst. Surely Grandpa Yiprarrk had not had to work so very hard.

But she was permitted the elation of job satisfaction when finally, as evening came on, she managed to get all fifteen of the hens (and even that rooster) to the yard of the henhouse, where the sight of their former companions cheered them up so much they would have apologized to Hreapha if they could have. Although the henhouse looked as if a strong wind might blow it down, it was still usable, and inside it the former owner had attached wicker baskets lined with straw to the walls, which served as nests for the laying hens. Hreapha could see into one of the lower ones and was pleased to notice that it already contained an egg, which, after all, was what hens were supposed to do.

Hreapha did not understand any of the varied clucks, chirps, squawks, cackles, chuckles or chirrs with which the chickens communicated, but she managed to deduce that the newly arrived hens were inquiring of the already-settled hens about the possibility of drinking-water, a possibility that Hreapha herself needed to settle at once. One of the established hens peeped or piped an answer, and led her sisters a short distance up the hillside to a tiny building, just a shed of two sloping roofs and nothing else, which covered a spring emerging from the earth. The overflow of the spring collected in a small pool large enough for Hreapha and the chickens to jointly slake their thirst.

She was glad to know of the existence of that tiny spring-house. Going inside, she discovered how cool it was in there. The low temperature helped to freshen her body after its exertions, and she was so comfortable she lay down beside the spring and went to sleep. Not one of the chickens had made any attempt to thank her for helping them find their way home, but she would discover, in the days and months ahead, that they were all extremely polite and friendly to her, and they made an effort to refrain from defecating on her favorite napping spots.

In fact, the very next day, when the man had still not returned, and Hreapha could not devise a method for breaking into the house to get at the bags of commercial dog chow (there was a missing windowpane but it was too high for her to leap through), a chicken appeared at the patch of grass where Hreapha was lying, sat down, stared Hreapha in the eye, clucked, and then stood up and walked away, leaving an egg behind. Hreapha studied the egg. She was almost certain that the hen intended it as a gift. She was touched. Hreapha had never eaten an egg. Yowrfrowr had once explained to her the meaning of "egg-sucking dog," which was often considered an insult, he said, but it was quite possible, he assured her, to puncture an egg with your teeth and then suck the contents out of it. He himself had not tried it, but he knew from other dogs that it was delicious, although a dog who developed a taste for eggs was considered worthless at guarding the henhouse and therefore was customarily shot. Yowrfrowr had said, Still, I would much rather be an egg-sucking dog than a shit-eating dog. And he had also told her about coprophagy, which was commonplace among certain malnourished dogs and probably, she realized, accounted for their bad breath.

"Hreapha!" she called after the generous hen in a way meant to express her thanks, and then she punctured and sucked the egg, which constituted her only victuals for the day, since she could not bring herself, as the chickens did, to scavenge for worms and bugs and, Hreapha noticed, the early lettuce that was beginning to appear in the soil of the vegetable garden the man was attempting to start.

Night came again, and still the man had not returned. To amuse herself, for she had absolutely nothing else to do, she tried to imagine what was keeping him. She even imagined the worst: his truck had fallen off the mountain. Such things happened. Maybe, she conjectured, he had consumed too much of the beverage that made him stagger and had actually flown over the moon, or even suffered an early demise. Yowrfrowr had told her that just a few years previously men had actually landed on the moon, but not because they had been loaded up on spirituous beverages. You can't do it, he assured her. But you can certainly drink enough to bring about your death. She imagined what life would be like for her here if he was truly dead and she was alone but for the chickens. Possibly, given time, she would find a way to get inside the house and into those bags of commercial chow. Or possibly she would just have to become a wild dog, a feral dog, howling at the moon. It was not a happy thought but it was not outside the realm of possibility. But no, she could not imagine life without human company, and she knew she'd probably have to go back to Stay More and hope to find somebody who needed her. The trouble was, there were so very few people still living in Stay More.

Thus, despite whatever revulsion and bitterness she had sometimes felt for him, her heart leapt up and her tail began oscillating crazily when she detected, shortly after dawn of the following day, his imminent arrival. Despite her resolve to keep herself hidden from him, she could not help shouting "Hreapha! Hreapha!" joyfully, and dancing in circles.

He was coming up the trail with yet another piece of furniture on his back. What was it? No, it was not furniture. And it was not exactly on his back, but draped over his shoulder. As he came nearer, and she continued calling her name in exuberant greeting, she perceived that the furniture was a person, a small person with long light hair, a little female person.

At the moment of this perception, he took the person down off his shoulder and stood her on her feet and said to her, "Look, here comes our doggie!"

And she ran to join them.

She danced around them, jumping up and down continually, her tail going a mile a minute, her voice announcing her name over and over. But almost at once she saw that the little female person, the charming girlchild, was extremely unhappy. Hreapha could smell the girl's unhappiness, and her fear and her panic.

"Down, Bitch," he said, and she stopped dancing. Then he addressed the child, "She shore aint much to look at, is she? But she's the smartest dog ever there was. Now I aim to let ye walk on the rest o' the way to our house yonder. I don't reckon you'll try to run away, now will ye? Just wait till ye see what-all I've got for you."

And then, with him leading the way and the girl following

slowly behind, her back bent and her head down, and Hreapha trotting last, they made their way up to the house.

"Why, lookee here," he said, "I do believe all our chickens has done come home to roost. We'll shore have all the eggs we can eat and plenty of fried chicken besides. And that rooster will get us out of bed in the morning." He opened the door, and they all went inside the house. Hreapha could see the opened bag of commercial chow through the door to another room, and she couldn't wait for him to dole her out some of it. "Now you jist sit here on the davenport and get comfy," he said to the girl, "and I'll make a little fire in the stove to keep ye warm. Are you chilly? And then I'll scare us up some breakfast. How bout some pancakes and syrup?"

The girl did not answer.

"Jam or jelly or molasses instead of syrup?" he wanted to know. But she would not answer. "I reckon I could run out and see if our hens has laid any eggs yet, and fry you up a bunch of eggs, if you'd druther have 'em." The girl made no response. "Listen, sugar, you got to eat you some breakfast and keep up your strength," he said. "I'm starving myself."

The girl did not answer, so he disappeared into the kitchen and Hreapha listened to him banging around some pots and pans in there. Hreapha studied the girl, who looked as if she wanted to jump up and run out the door. Hreapha tried to understand who she was and what she was doing here. Could she possibly be his daughter perhaps, long lost and now home? Granddaughter, even? Was she conceivably a stray he had found somewhere, or who had followed him home? Part of Hreapha felt a certain jealousy, if not resentment. She knew she was going to have to share the place with this girl. But part of her felt a powerful sense of attraction and protection. The child was lovely, and innocent and uncorrupt, and potentially loads of fun. Hreapha wagged her tail and moved closer to the girl and nuzzled her ankle.

The girl spoke her first words. "Get away from me!" And she kicked Hreapha, who whimpered and backed off.

Chapter ten

And he wapped a wag awound her eyes so she could not see. And he knotted it too tight. And the twuck started up and she could not tell where they were going. And she could not bweathe. And then he. And the twuck went on and on. O why is this happening why why why? And then he finally started to talk. "I don't aim to hurt ye," he said. And he said. He said. She could not see him in the dark. And she knew it was him. It was him who. But why? The twuck went on and on. Bouncy bouncing bouncy. And she tried to cwy but could not. Why not? She wanted to cwy but the gag in her mouth kept her from cwying, yeah, she would cwy except for the gag. But she could not cwy with her eyes either. And why? And she was just too scared to cwy. And no, and no, she had not cwied since she was three years old. A long time ago. Why? And she heard him talk again. "Are you cold?" And she would not nod or shake her head. She had stopped sweating. All that skating had made her sweat, was why she'd skated out onto the balcony to catch the breeze. And she heard him talk again. "Here, let me put this blanket on ye." And she felt the blanket on her, which she did not need because she was still all wet with sweat and the twuck's heater was running and it was hot.

And she was too scared to cry. And in the dark she reached with her hand to feel for where the door was, and she reached for the door handle. And she heard him talk again, heard him yell, "Hey now! Don't do that! Take your hand off there!" And felt him reach across and grab her hand. "You don't want to be trying to open the door, honey. If you was to open the door and you was to try to jump out, it would kill you!"

And the twuck went on and on. The woad was wough, the wough woad went up and down, the woad started to climb, and it climbed and climbed and she wondered if maybe they were on their way to Heaven, and maybe she had already died and he was some kind of angel who was taking her to Heaven, and there really was a God and God lived at the end of this climbing woad. Yes. But then she thought no, no, he was not an angel but the Devil and he was not taking her to Heaven but to Hell because she had committed the terrible sin of vanity, too gosh proud of herself because her skating made all the other girls look like clumsy yo-yos, which they were. None of them could skate backward as she could, no. Nor do heel-to-heel spins. She put them all to utter shame and now she was paying the price for her dazzle. That was why. And the twuck stopped. And she heard him talk again. "Now, sugar, I'm a-taking off the gag, though I cain't take off the blindfold just yet." And he took the gag out of her mouth. "You can scream if you take a notion, but won't nobody hear ye. We're way off away from everybody." And she did not scream. She could not cry and she could not scream. And the twuck started to move again and it climbed and climbed and bounced and bounced and she could not imagine that there was a woad anywhere in the world that climbed and turned and twisted and bounced like this woad. And she heard him speak again, talking very loud over the sounds the twuck was making. "You can talk now, sweetheart. You can tell me your name." And she could not talk. No talk. She would not talk. "My name's Sugrue Alan. You can call me Sugrue. Can you say 'Sugrue'?" And she would not say anything. "I reckon I've gave ye a bad fright, but there aint nothing you need to fear from me. Like I told ye the other day, me and you are fated to spend the rest of our lifes together, and I mean to love ye more'n you've ever been loved. So I sure do hope that you can get over your scare and learn to be mine and—" His voice was lost behind a horrible sound, a scraping grinding wrenching banging. She jumped. "Well, there went the goldarn muffler!" he said, and drove on, the twuck motor so noisy that surely God could hear it if He was anywhere, but He was not.

And the woad went up and up and up and then the twuck stopped, the noisy motor went off, and then she heard him speak again. "This here's as far as the trail can reach. Good thing too on account of they's just a drop or two of gas left. I reckon I'll just take off your blindfold now, but you won't be able to see nothing, out there in the dark. We're nearly home but there's still the worst mile to go and we caint do it in the dark, so we might as well just get cozy here in the truck and wait until daylight, when we can see to find our way along the rest of the trail. I promise ye you'll be tickled to pieces with your new home as soon as you can lay eyes on it, come dayspring." And she would not speak, nor move, nor see, nor feel, nor be. "You might as well go to sleep, honey," he said to her. "You could stretch out here on the seat, or even put your head in my lap or whatever you want to do to get comfy." And it was late at night, and then it was later at night, and she was very sleepy, very sleepy, but she could not sleep without Paddington. She really really needed to sleep but she could not sleep without Paddington. Of course she wanted her mommy but she wanted her bear even more. She could sleep without her mommy but she could not sleep without her bear. And she began to think that she might never see him again.

"Here, no wonder you caint sleep with them there skates still on your feet. Let's take 'em off." And he got out of the truck and came around to her side and opened the door and lifted her feet and untied the skates and removed them and tossed them into the back of the truck. "Don't reckon you'd ever have no use for 'em no more, which is a shame, the way you was flying around that roller rink looked like you'd been born on skates."

So then yes maybe he was the Devil punishing her for her vanity at the skating rink. "I'm sorry," she whispered.

"*What's that?*" he said. "You said something, didn't ye? I was afraid you'd turned deaf and dumb on me. Did you say your name is Sarah?"

But she could not say anything else. He got back into his seat and talked a while more and told her she had better try to sleep and he said sleep so many times that the sound of the word put him to sleep. He even snored. She waited a while and then she gently opened her door and got out. Behind the twuck must have been the woad they had come up on. If she could follow that woad and get down there before he woke up, she would be free. But it was so dark, and nothing scared her more than the dark did, and the gravel hurt her feet in her sockies and worst of all she hated the woods. She walked just a few steps beyond the truck before she realized she was already lost, and there were monsters out there in the woods waiting for her who were much worse monsters than he was.

She returned to the truck, glad to be back, but could not sleep. It was very cold now. She wrapped the blanket tightly around herself. She imagined her mother somewhere crying. She imagined Kelly and Rebecca and Gretchen and Beverly still wide awake at the slumber party, maybe crying too, and Kelly's party was ruined and maybe the parents came and got the other girls and took them home. And Grandma and Grandpa were at Mommy's house with the lights on and staying up all night waiting for her to come home. And if all those people could be staying awake there was no reason for her to sleep.

But she must have drifted off out of sheer exhaustion because the next thing she knew he was shaking her shoulder and there was some light out and she could see all the trees surrounding them in the deep, deep forest. "Time to get on up home," he said. "Watch your step getting out, because there's lots of wood up under the truck." She got out and he got out and she saw that while she had slept he had crammed many sticks and logs up underneath the truck. "Now you'd better stand back on over here," he said, and led her a good ways off from the truck to the edge of a steep ravine and then he went back and knelt down and started a fire in the sticks and logs which blazed up and roared and then there was a whooshing boom as whatever gasoline left in the tank caught fire and exploded. And the truck burned. And in the back of it her skates, that weren't her skates but just rented from the roller rink and which she'd have to pay for if she lost them, her skates must've burned too. When he came back to her he was smoking a cigarette. She really hated people who smoked.

He watched the truck burn for a while, and then he said, "I reckon I ought to put the blindfold back on ye for the last awful mile, but it wouldn't make no difference nohow even if you could see where we're a-going, because you'd never be able to hike it by yourself. Now you'd better get on my back." And he picked her up and put her up on his back, and then he climbed down into that ravine, so steep she yelped in fright, and he said, "Don't worry, honeybunch, I've done this a many and a many a time." And he reached the bottom of the gorge and climbed up out the other side, and went on. And then there was another ravine, with water in the bottom of it that he had to step across on rocks. And then another ravine with a tree-trunk fallen over the water at the bottom of it that he walked across carefully like a tightrope walker, and then climbed way up out of it like a mountain climber. If she had not been so frightened she would have enjoyed the ride. It was thrilling. "Here comes the tricky part," he said, and it was really the worst part: on a narrow ledge across a bluff high above the forest below he had to turn sideways and walk sideways, holding her to his chest, saying, "Dropped a whole crate of chickens here yesterday morning, but don't ye worry, girl, I don't aim to drop *you*. Close your eyes if it skeers ye too much." And she had to close her eyes.

When she opened her eyes there were no more ravines or ledges but just a little path that climbed up through the deep dark forest, and he carried her a little ways on his shoulder up that path until it escaped from the forest and they were in a wide field rolling up to the top of the mountain, and there stood a house! "Yonder's our home," he said as if she hadn't already noticed it. And as they climbed to it, she could see for miles and miles out across the valleys and mountains all around. Everything blue and green and it was almost like Paradise, so maybe this was some kind of Heaven. He took her off his shoulder and stood her on her feet and said, "You can walk from here." And coming to meet them was a dog. He pointed, "Look, here comes our doggie!"

It was the ugliest dog she had ever seen, some kind of mongrel cur, mostly white, not very big, and it was barking and prancing around and swishing its little tail back and forth, and for a moment she thought the dog was going to jump her. "Down, Bitch!" he said and the dog stopped dancing. And they went on to the house and they went in it. It was a very old house and it was all dusty and faded and there were cobwebs all over the place. There was a fairly clean sofa and he had her sit on it while he built a fire in the room's heater-stove to warm it up, and then he went to fix her some breakfast.

The hideous dog was trying to lick her ankle. "Get away from me!" she said to it, kicking, and it backed off whimpering.

The man came running from the kitchen. "Hey, you talked! Is Bitch bothering you?" He opened the front door and gave the revolting dog a hard kick that knocked it outside, and he shut the door after it. "If she ever bothers you, just let her know who's boss."

She was, come to think of it, hungry, and he had her sit at a small table in the kitchen near the kitchen stove, one of those old-fashioned iron wood-burning stoves, not a great big one but a sort of squat one that was cute, and it was very warm and nice. He gave her scrambled eggs with some kind of oval-shaped meat stuff. "That's Spam," he said. "I reckon we won't have fresh meat unless I can shoot a razorback one of these days. Now what do you like to drink with your breakfast? You don't drink coffee, I bet."

And she spoke. "Milk," she said.

"Well, I hope you don't mind powdered milk too awful much," he apologized and fixed her a glass of something that just sort of tasted a little bit like milk. "'Course they's Pet Milk too, but it's even worse."

He talked all the time they had their breakfast but she did not say another word. He apologized a lot. He apologized for the cobwebs, saying he'd been too busy trying to get the place stocked up and ready for her and starting a little spring vegetable garden and all, and he intended to give the place a thorough dusting and cleaning today or tomorrow. He apologized for the darkness of the kitchen, saying the windows needed to be washed and of course there wasn't no lectric lights. He apologized for not having no orange juice, just something called Tang which was the same color and wasn't very cold because there wasn't no ice. He apologized for not having no ice cubes. He apologized for the awful dog. She waited to hear him apologize for having kidnapped her, but he did not. "Just tell me anything you need whenever," he said.

"I need to go to the bathroom," she said.

He hit himself on the forehead. "Now why didn't that cross my mind? 'Course, we aint got any indoor facilities, ha ha. No runnin water. But I'll show you to our outdoor accommodation, ha hawr." He started to lead her out of the house, but stopped. "I reckon you need something to put on your feet." And he ran into the other room, leaving her. She was really desperate to pee. It had been such a long time and she had tried to hold it but now she couldn't hold it any longer. Her panties started to get wet. He came back with a whole bunch of shoes. "Just take your pick," he said, and she was amazed to see so many nice shoes, nearly all of them in her size, and she picked out the prettiest pair of sneakers she'd ever had. And put them on, real quick, hoping she wouldn't pee any more until he showed her where the bathroom was. He had to help her tie them because she still had not completely mastered the tying of shoes.

The bathroom, if that is what it was, was outside about a hundred feet from the house, off where the woods started. It was just a shack, and there was a bench sort of thing with two holes cut in it. "I'll just wait outside here, this time," he said, and closed the door after her leaving her alone in it. His voice called, "Have you got enough paper in there?" And she looked and there was a roll of toilet paper on a stob on the wall. She pulled down her blue jeans and her already wet panties and tried to sit on the hole. She had never been in one of these outhouses before although she had heard about them. She hadn't been told they were so smelly. The hole was too big for her and she had to be careful not to fall into it.

After a long time he called, "Are you okay in there?" But it was so hard and awful and stinky and sad and she could not say anything. But she finished and got out of there.

"Now," he said, "do you want to take a look at all the rest of the place, and see where the well's at, and the henhouse yonder, and what's left of the barn and all? Or would you rather see the real surprise I've got for ye?"

"It's cold out here," she said. So they went back in the house, and first he let her take her pick of several jackets which he had bought for her. They were all very neat jackets and warm and comfy and beautiful, especially the one she picked and tried on, which was a perfect fit.

Then he said, "And here comes your first surprise!" And he went into the other room and came back with the biggest doll she'd ever seen. It was nearly as big as she was, and was dressed better than she'd ever dressed, with a yellow/orange kimono type of dress, and fancy shoes. She had long dark hair and long eyelashes and such a sweet look on her face. If Robin had been a couple of years younger she would have adored the doll, but she had outgrown dolls of this nature, and much preferred her paper dolls.

"You don't like it?" he said, and demonstrated how it had a string with a ring on it that you pull to make her change her great big eyes from orange to green to blue to pink. "I got one with dark hair so's I could tell you'uns apart! Hawr hoo!" The man had an ugly laugh, nearly as ugly as his dog.

She sat on the sofa with the doll beside her and pretended to allow the doll to join in their conversation. She wanted the doll as a witness. She asked him the first of the many, many questions she would ask him.

"Are you going to take me home?"

His face got all wrinkled up. "Why, *hon*," he said, "I figured you knew that I never intended to do no such a thing as that. We're here forever, don't ye know? Just you and me. This is your home."

She asked him the second question. "Why did you pick *me?*"

"That's easy," he said. "I picked you on account of you're the pertiest gal I ever laid eyes on in my entire life. Lord if you aint. They just don't make 'em the least bit pertier than you are."

She asked him the third question. "Are you going to fuck me?"

Part Two:
Sleeping with

Chapter eleven

I t took all of whatever sawdust he had for brains to devise a way to get out of the house Saturday night. He knew that there was lots of fellers on this earth who just "went out with the boys," but nobody never bothered to tell him how they got away with it. She was right that he didn't have no buddies to speak of, so he couldn't have used that as a excuse anyhow. In all the years he'd been married to her, she had never let him leave the house on Saturday night, or any other night as far as that matter goes, and now that she was ticked off at him on account of his going out to see Robin by himself yesterday afternoon she was keeping a close watch on him and spending all her time thinking up ways to punish him.

He thought of the idea of putting something or another into her iced tea at suppertime that would knock her out for the evening. Of course she'd be madder than a wet hen whenever she woke up, but at least he would've been able to spend the whole evening at the roller rink watching his sweet Robin on her skates.

When he was mighty close to giving up on the whole idea, it suddenly hit him that he did have a good relative if not a buddy, Benny Samuels, a cousin, living down the road at Western Grove, and Benny owed him a couple of favors and now was a good time to call in one of them. So he watched for a chance when Louisa was busy and he phoned Benny and whispered into the phone what he wanted him to do, and sure enough a little while later the phone rang and Louisa answered it and Benny told her that his wife was in the hospital and he was all alone and could Leo please come over and keep him company for just a little while tonight? Louisa told him she'd think about it, and hung up. She was suspicious, and said maybe she'd better go with him to keep Benny company, but at the last minute she said all right but don't you stay too long, you hear me? And you take your pickup and leave me with the car. And he hopped in his pickup and tore off lickety-split out of there and got to the Harrison roller rink just as the girls was hitting the floor.

And didn't he have him one heck of a swell time! He got him an Orange Crush sody pop and a sack of pork skins and he sat in the bleachers sort of place with the other spectators, moms and dads and the folks who were handling the birthday party, part of which they had right there in the rink, with favors and hats and tooters handed out, and they let Leo participate, so he didn't need that sody pop and pork skins because they was handing out fresh pizza and then birthday cake. And wasn't Robin just thrilled to pieces to have her grandpappy there! And after the party part was over and they'd et all the cake and the girls went back out onto the floor to do their skating, she more than once hollered, "Grampa, watch me!" as if he needed to be told, because he couldn't take his eyes off of her. She was a sight to behold, and he was just a little afraid she was a-fixing to hurt herself with one of them jumps and spins and turns and even skating backward besides!

He wondered what happened. At the far end of the rink was this little balcony place where the skaters sometimes stepped out between numbers to grab a breath of fresh air, and he never took his eyes off her but she went out there, and it was dark, and the next thing he knew it looked like some feller just reached up and plucked her right off the balcony! Leo started to run out across the floor, but they hollered at him because you aint supposed to be on the floor if you aint wearing skates. So he had to turn around and run out the front door and around the side of the rink to reach that balcony. And she was plumb gone. Not a sign of her. He couldn't believe it, and wondered if his old eyes was a-playing some kind of crazy trick on him. He looked around all over for her. Not a trace. He went back into the rink and looked around in there, thinking maybe she'd not really gone on the balcony, or maybe gone to the Ladies' or something. But he couldn't find her nowhere. He started to ask. He asked the little girl that they was giving the party for, "Say, have you seen Robin?" But she hadn't. He got the same answer from the other girls. He went to the manager of the rink and said, "Excuse me but it seems like my little granddaughter has turned up missing." And the manager asks her name and he tells him and the manager gets on the P.A. and booms out, "WILL MISS ROBIN KERR PLEASE COME TO THE FRONT DESK?" and they wait and wait and then the manager says on the P.A., "HAS ANYBODY SEEN MISS ROBIN KERR?"

After a good long while, the manager says to Leo, "Maybe her momma came and got her."

"I doubt it," Leo says. "I think maybe you'd better get the cops to come over." So the manager makes a phone call.

By the time the police arrived, the skating had all come to a halt, and all the girls and their parents that brought 'em was just milling around talking to one another and looking as sick with worry as Leo felt himself.

One of the officers set in to asking him a bunch of questions. What was the victim's full name? What was the victim's age? What was the victim's physical description? What was the victim wearing? When and where had he last seen her? Leo led the officer over to the balcony and told him about the feller plucking her off of there. You're sure it was a man, then? the officer asks. "Couldn't no woman have just snatched her like that," Leo said. What was the man wearing? the officer asked. How old was he? "I'm sorry, I didn't get a good look at him." Leo said. "You see, he was out here in the dark and it happened so fast." And you say you're her grandfather? "Well, actually I'm just married to her grandmother."

Somebody was tearing at the back of his jacket and he turned

97

around and there was Karen. "LEO! WHAT HAPPENED?" she hollered. Leo explained to the officer that this lady was the girl's mother, and the officer helpfully explained the situation to her so Leo didn't have to do it. But Karen looked like she was fixing to murder the officer. "BUT WHAT WAS SHE DOING HERE AT THIS ROLLER RINK?!?!" Karen screeched, and the officer looked at Leo and waited for Leo to explain because the officer sure didn't know what she had been doing here at the roller rink. And because he didn't know, both of them were staring at Leo waiting for him to explain.

"Skating," Leo said, and that was all he could say for the moment.

"DID *YOU* BRING HER HERE?!" she yells into his face.

There was a crowd of people gathered around them, girls and parents and cops and sheriff's deputies and state troopers, and somebody in that crowd must've been a friend of Karen's or maybe a mother of one of the other girls, because the woman said, "Karen, we were having the party here. Didn't Robin tell you?"

"NO SHE DID NOT!" Karen screamed. "DO YOU THINK I WOULD HAVE LET HER GO TO THE GODDAMN PARTY IF I'D KNOWN YOU WERE TAKING HER TO *THIS* PLACE?" Karen broke down and commenced bawling. Leo tried to hold her and for a moment she looked as if she was going to let him hug her but then she backed off from him and cried, "I want my mother! Where's my mother?"

"She didn't come with me," Leo admitted, and, thinking of Louisa, said to himself, *Boy, am I going to be up ole Shit Creek without nothing to steer with.*

"She didn't come with you," Karen said. "She didn't come with you, huh? So she didn't come with you." And then she says, still calm but very loud, "LEO, WHAT HAVE YOU DONE WITH HER?"

"I reckon she's just a-settin at the TV up at the house," he says.

Karen bursts out laughing. "So you've just got her at your house? And Mother's with her?"

It got through Leo's sawdust that they were talking about different hers. "Aw, I thought you meant your mother. I haven't done nothing with Robin. She's been kidnapped."

A policeman spoke to Karen. "Ma'am, let me ask you: are you married?"

"What's that got to do with anything?" she wanted to know.

"Yes or no, ma'am, please."

"No, I'm divorced."

"Then maybe the girl's father came and got her. That often happens, you know, especially if there's any kind of custody dispute."

"Then Billy has got her!" Karen said. "That asshole! Oh, it's just like him!" And Karen commenced bawling again.

The cop said, "Let's get off the rink and go sit down and you can tell us how to find him."

Everybody got off the rink, and a table was set up with chairs around it, and other people sat in those bleachers, and each of the girls at the birthday had to answer a few questions before she was allowed to go, and one by one the parents took the kids away. Leo figured the best thing for him to do was just slip on out and get on home and maybe even pretend to Louisa that he didn't know nothing about nothing. But as he was stepping slowly and softly toward the door, a cop came and took his arm and said, "I hope you're not going anywhere."

"My wife," he said, "she's the girl's grandma, and I reckon I ought to go get her."

"We'll send a trooper to pick her up," the cop said. "We need you here. Have a seat."

The place was really filling up with all kinds of officers and the FBI besides. Somebody was even taking flash photos of that balcony and running a tape measure across it like you did when somebody has a wreck.

Leo was mighty glad to have all those law enforcement people surrounding him for protection when Louisa arrived, or else she might've killed him on the spot. It took a couple of 'em to hold her back from attacking him. Her behavior was really inexcusable and was probably the reason they decided to keep him for questioning. He didn't relish spending a night in jail but it was sure a lot better than spending the night at home with her. Either way he wouldn't have been able to sleep a wink. It wasn't the disgrace of being arrested that preyed on his mind as much as the fact of Robin's disappearance. She meant the world to him and now she was gone. They could suspect him all they wanted to and it wouldn't bring her back.

They fed him a good breakfast at the jail and there was a TV with the morning news having a big story on Robin, and her picture broadcast for all the world to see. It wasn't one of her best pictures and didn't do justice to her beauty. Right soon after breakfast a feller from the state police, name of Jack Samples, who was in charge of child molesters, and two of Lieutenant Samples' men, sat Leo down at a table and commenced asking him a bunch of questions. They had even checked him out and found his Navy rap sheet, which mentioned that he'd spent some time in the brig after being caught during shore leave with a eleven-year-old whore. That had been twenty years ago, goddammit, but they acted like he'd just been picked up last night.

They grilled him. What was his exact relationship to the victim? What was the nature and extent of that exact relationship? Had the victim ever said or done anything inappropriate or of a sexual character during that relationship? Had he ever said or done anything inappropriate or of a sexual character during that relationship? Had he ever fondled her? Where had he touched her? Had he sat her upon his lap? When and how often and with what conclusion? What sort of kisses had he given her and received from her? Was it true that he had given her a large stuffed bear, named Paddington, whom she regularly slept with?

Leo did a lot of sweating during this interview, but the worst had only just begun. Maybe he had given the wrong answers to the questions because by and by they started in to trying to get him to confess where he had taken her and where he was keeping her. In the trunk of his car maybe? Tied up in the woods somewhere? In an abandoned house somewhere? They promised him they would try to get him off lightly if only he would confess and lead them to the girl. Did he want to spend the rest of his life in prison? No? Then why didn't he come clean and help them find the girl?

Trying desperately to divert attention away from his own innocent self, Leo suddenly remembered the man from the other day, the man who Robin said had pretended to be him, the man they'd later encountered out on the road after Robin's bike wreck who at first claimed to be her grandfather because, as he'd said later, he had suspected that Leo was a child molester and wanted to protect her against him. The sawdust began to sift away as Leo realized that man was probably the number one suspect. Maybe that man was some kind of stalker who wanted Robin specifically and had taken the trouble to follow her to the roller rink and abduct her.

Leo told the officers all that he could remember about the man and what he had done and said. He concluded, "Maybe he was just looking for his lost dog, like he said, but that could've just been a excuse."

The officers looked at each other, and mumbled some stuff to one another, and then Jack Samples said, "Or maybe he was your partner in this deal. Maybe he was the one who actually grabbed her at the rink but you put him up to it. Huh?" All Leo could do was shake his head vigorously and keep on a-shaking it. They led him off to another room and hooked him up to a bunch of wires and stuff that was some kind of lie-detector machine. Then they asked him all kinds of questions, including all of the questions they'd already asked him, and he did his best to tell the honest-to-God truth. He told the truth when they point-blank asked him if he knew where she was. When they were all done, and he was plumb wore out, he said, "Well, did I pass?" but they didn't say yes or no.

Finally one of them asked him, "Do you think you can describe this man you were talking about?"

And later that morning they brought in a police sketch artist who wanted to do something called a "composite," and the feller started off with simple questions to Leo like age, height, weight, hair color, eye color, etc., and then got to more complicated ones like how close together the eyes was, and how long the nose was and how much the ears stuck out. Leo had a pretty hard time trying to remember just what the guy had looked like day before yesterday, and finally when the artist had come up with a sketch and showed it to him Leo had to offer his humble opinion that it didn't look too awful much like the feller. "His eyebrows was bushier than that, and his mouth was some wider," Leo criticized the artwork.

By mid-afternoon they had a sketch that was a fair likeness of the guy. Jack Samples studied it and laughed and said, "Aw shit, that sort of looks like old Sog!" But nobody took the trouble to tell him who this Old Sog was. They made copies of the picture and sent 'em out to the press, and it appeared on the evening news and Leo was even a little proud, as if he'd drawed the picture himself.

Jack Samples said to him, "Well, I guess you're free to go, for now. Probably the girl wasn't even abducted, she was just a run-away."

"On roller skates?" Leo said, and somehow they all thought that was funny, and laughed. But Leo wasn't laughing. One of the cops, not Samples, had told him that in most sexual kidnappings the child is never found alive, and Leo was starting to get powerfully haunted by the notion that poor Robin could be dead and raped somewhere at this very moment. His heart poured out for her, and for his loss of her. She had been the light of his life. Such as his shitty life had been. Now some real son of a bitch who had made careful plans and carried them out had removed Leo's darling little girl from this earth. Leo did not intend to take it laying down.

He drove on home, prepared to face the worst yet. It's twenty miles from Harrison to Pindall and that gave him plenty of time to think about what he would say to Louisa. But by the time he got there he realized there was only one thing he was going to say to her: "Screw you." Honest.

So he was even disappointed when he got there and discovered she wasn't there for him to say that to. The car was gone. He suddenly remembered that this was Sunday and if she wasn't at one of her constant church services or meetings or whatever, she was most likely keeping Karen company during this time of grief and anxiety and waiting.

Leo went up to the bedroom and got his revolver out of the closet and took hold of a fistful of bullets. Then he turned right around and drove those twenty miles back to Harrison. He didn't go to Karen's. He went to the roller rink.

It's funny how things come to you. Maybe because of not having any sleep the night before and being in a kind of daze still, or maybe because without even thinking it out loud he had already determined that if need be he would spend the rest of his life searching for the girl, he suddenly experienced a flash of a minor little detail that he hadn't even known he had noticed: that feller's pickup didn't hardly have no tread to speak of on the tires. They was bald.

Leo searched the parking lot behind the roller rink until he found some bald tracks in the mud, and they went out onto the highway turning south, but he lost the tracks on the asphalt. He started driving slow down that asphalt road, watching every little side road that he came to for any sign of the bald tracks again.

It was the slow but steady beginning of Leo Spurlock's long, long quest.

Chapter twelve

How in hell was he supposed to answer a question like that? He was struck all of a heap that she would use that word, which didn't belong on the sweet lips of such an innocent child. And yet. And yet, he couldn't help but be kind of excited by it, because the way she used it seemed to mean that she at least knew what it was and therefore he might not have to learn her as much as he thought he'd have to learn her.

Even so, he choked on his coffee and needed a minute to gentle down. And then he asked, "Where'd you pick up that word?"

"Everybody knows it," she said, staring him straight in the eye, feisty and brash as all get out.

"Sweet little girls don't know it," he said.

"You should hear all the words Gretchen Scott knows," she declared. "She knows all of them."

"Who's Gretchen Scott?"

"One of my best friends at school."

"Did Gretchen tell you what that word means? Did she explain what happens when you go to bed with somebody?"

"Sort of," she said. "But you're not answering my question. Is that what you're going to do to me?"

"Not today," he said, and that was all he could think to say, which was true. He didn't intend to rush things. He wasn't one of these here goddamn *rapists*. Aw, of course he knew what statutory rape was, but this wasn't the same thing. He really hoped that whatever they did would be consensual on her part. He wasn't never going to force her to do nothing. And besides for some strange reason he wasn't feeling an awful lot of lust, not at the moment, anyhow. He'd thought for a while that he wouldn't be able to hold himself back, once he got ahold of her, but now that he had her he didn't seem to have the itch in his britches that he'd expected.

"But tomorrow maybe?" she said. "Or sometime?"

"Not if you don't feel like it," he declared, and then, because the subject was something that ought not be discussed too much but just acted upon whenever the occasion called for it, he decided to change the subject. "It's warming up out there," he observed. "You want to take a look at the place?"

"I want to brush my teeth," she said.

"Fine and dandy. What color toothbrush do you want?"

"Blue."

He got her a nice blue toothbrush out of the box of new toothbrushes, and then, because she'd never brushed her teeth without running water, which they didn't have, he showed her the new system of using the wash basin and a gourd dipper filled with water from the water bucket. He had to hold the dipper for her at first, but she got the hang of it, and brushed her teeth and then he wanted to show her how to draw water herself. He took her out to the well, and showed her how to let the well bucket run down on its chain down and down deep into the well and then you let the bucket submerge itself and you pull it up on the pulley with the chain. She had a struggle, at first, pulling that chain with the bucket full on the other end of it, but she finally got it up and then he showed her how to pour the well bucket into the kitchen bucket and take it to the house and set it on the bucket shelf and put the gourd dipper in it.

"See?" he said. "Nothing to it."

She frowned. "It's not nearly as easy as just turning the faucet handle."

"If you think that aint easy, let's see if you can split some stove wood," and he took her out to the woodpile, where a chopping stump was surrounded by a good stack of logs he'd dragged in from the woods and cut up with his chain saw. The chain-saw was one of the few things he'd sold at the yard sale. He hated to let it go but knew they had to learn how to cut timber with just a axe and crosscut. He had some doubts about showing her how to use the axe, not that he was afraid she'd hurt herself but she might just get it into her head to take a whack at him while he was asleep or something. But that was just a risk he'd have to take, because he wanted her to do her share of helping with the stove wood. He started off with little pieces, propped steady on the chopping stump, and made sure she stood with the axe in such a way that it wouldn't slip and hurt her. Bitch was watching them, and the girl asked him to make the dog go away. Then she missed her first few licks but got the hang of it and actually managed to split a piece in two. "Hey, you did it!" he said and tried to give her a hug, but she backed off from him. Then he showed her where the stove wood was stacked in a big wooden box beside the kitchen door. Even if she wasn't very good at splitting wood with the axe, she could be handy at toting the wood to the wood box.

He showed her the little springhouse, and explained it was the nearest thing they had to a refrigerator. If they had any fresh cow's milk or butter, which they didn't and never would, they could keep it in the springhouse. He did have some powdered lemonade mix and directly he'd show her how to mix a jar of it and get it cooled in the springhouse. "We could keep our Kool-Aid here too," she offered, and it was the first thing she'd said that made it sound like she really wanted to participate in this life. That made him happy but he was real sorry to realize that it had never occurred to him to buy any Kool-Aid mix because he never used the stuff himself.

"Sweetheart, I really do hate to tell ye, but it complete slipped my mind to get us any Kool-Aid," he said.

She looked as if she was about to cry, and he wished she would, just to prove that she still knew how to cry. "You're not ever going to the store again?" she said and he wasn't sure whether it was just a statement of fact or maybe a question. Either way, it didn't need to be said.

He showed her the rest of the place—the barn, which they wouldn't have no use for since they didn't have any cows or mules or any need to store hay. And it looked like it might fall on their heads anyhow, and he told her she'd better not even play around in or near the barn. That wasn't true of the shop, which was still a pretty sturdy shed and still had all the tools and stuff that Gabe Madewell had just abandoned when he pulled up stakes. He explained to her that this had been the workshop of the barrel-maker who had lived here but hit the trail some twenty-odd years before. He showed her one of the two barrels that had been left behind and attempted to explain how the staves were cut from the white oak timber in the surrounding forests and shaped to go inside the steel bands to make a barrel that was probably used for whiskey. Madewell had also made wooden buckets and tubs and churns, and there was still one churn left behind, never used but slightly damaged. Sog showed it to her and explained how it would have been used to make butter. They wouldn't have no use for it, but it sure was a handsome piece of woodwork to look at. "There was some kind of name for the work he did, which was a family name or something—Turner or Carver or Cutter."

"Cooper," she said.

"Yeah, that's it! How'd you know it?"

"I read it in a book," she said. Then she asked, "Why did he build his house way off up here on this mountain?"

"Well, I believe it was probably his daddy, Braxton Madewell, who was also a cooper, who built the place way back around the turn of the century. I reckon he built it here because it was handy to all the timber."

"How far is the nearest neighbor?" she asked.

He started to answer but then realized it could be a trick question. "If you was a crow and could fly, and headed thataway," he pointed toward the south, "you might fly over a house where people still lived in about three mile or so, in a place called Stay More, just a ghost town, really. But there just aint no way to go from here to

there on foot." He decided to tell her about Adam Madewell. Gabe
had a boy named Adam who'd been several years behind Sog at the
Stay More school, and Adam had to walk it, getting up before daylight
every morning and hiking four miles over the roughest trail you could
imagine and him not but a first or second grader, just a kid, hiking
eight miles round-trip every day of the school year, carrying his dinner pail and his schoolbooks in places where he practically had to do
mountain-climbing, until finally he'd had some kind of accident at
home, helping his daddy make barrels and gashing his leg so badly he
couldn't walk on it, and they never saw him again at the schoolhouse.
Ad Madewell had been a real smart and proud and hardworking kid
at school, and the teacher, Miss Jerram, had loved him and was sorry
to see him go, or rather stay, because he must've stayed home from
school for a couple of years before they left for California and the
school itself didn't last much longer than that. But folks on the store
porch—Latha Bourne's General Store—used to kid Ad because his
paw and maw never did come to town for anything. "Hey, Ad," they'd
say, "why don't ye show 'em that trail you come in on?" Adam's trail,
which went through a lost holler with a big waterfall in it, had been
washed away after he quit using it, and now there wasn't a sign of it,
although Sog had been in that lost holler one time and in fact had
shot a bad man there when he was with the state police.

"You were a policeman?" the girl asked.

"Yeah, that's what I did most all of my life," he said.

The girl was staring at him in a way that bothered him, as if
she was trying to picture him in his uniform or just trying to figure
out why a law-abiding officer of the law would do something illegal
like stealing a little girl. "What did you shoot the bad man for?" she
asked.

"He had kidnapped a little girl," Sog said, and felt he might even
be blushing. "Yeah, I know, it sounds ironic, don't it? As it turned
out, this feller, Dan Montross was his name, just an old hermit, he
was the girl's grandfather. But I didn't know that."

She fixed him with that look again and said, "Somebody is
going to shoot you." She sounded like she meant it. He hated to hear
her talk mean like that.

"They've got to find me first," he said.

It wasn't a good day. Both of them were tired from lack of sleep the night before, but he had a lot to do, and there was plenty he could find for her to do. He asked her what she'd like for lunch and she said a peanut butter and jelly sandwich. He had plenty of jars of peanut butter and plenty of jars of jelly, but no bread. He explained that bread gets stale, and it gets moldy, and you can't keep it in a jar, and he hadn't thought to buy even one loaf to hold them until they could make some. He had all the fixings for making bread and he intended to show her soon how to do it and how to bake it in the woodstove, and maybe bake some pies and cakes and biscuits while they were at it. But not today. They had all kinds of crackers, plain saltines as well as fancy ones, and he asked her if she could just make do with peanut butter and jelly on crackers. For himself he had a hankering for some pig's feet, and opened a jar and forked a couple of 'em out. He fixed himself a generous glass of Jack D to wash them down with.

"I'm going to throw up," the girl declared.

"You aint even et yet," he said.

"If you eat that stuff, I won't feel like eating," she said.

"Here, try a little taste. Won't kill you, and they're scrumptious when you get to know them."

She got up from the table and left the kitchen, taking her plate of peanut-buttered crackers with her.

"Don't eat on the davenport!" he called after her. "My momma wouldn't never let me eat a-settin there."

After lunch he had to go work a while on covering the trail to where the truck had been parked. He asked her if she didn't feel like taking a little nap. She claimed she didn't. What did she feel like doing then? What would she ordinarily be doing this time of day on a Sunday afternoon? She said she'd be working on Wobbinsville. What's Wobbinsville? he asked. Just a town she made up for her paper dolls to live in, she said. Did he have any paper she could use to cut some paper dolls and clothes for them? Well, of course they had enough toilet paper to last for a few years, but he had to apologize that there wasn't any other paper except the brown paper sacks that stuff had come in from the grocery. That would do, I guess, she said, if you could let me use the scissors.

Sog looked and he looked in the boxes of kitchen gadgets he'd brought from home, and there wasn't no pair of scissors to be found nowhere. Maybe it was just as well. He didn't want her fooling around with something sharp like a pair of scissors that she could stab him with. But he went out and searched the shop for scissors. There was a pair of what looked like sheep shears, but that wasn't the same thing. "Bitch," he said to the dog, "you haven't seen any scissors anywhere, have you?" Bitch was a real smart dog but she couldn't answer that one. He went back to the house and informed the girl, "I sure do hate to have to tell you but it appears they just aint no scissors nowhere."

She hung her head and for a moment there he was almost sure she was finally going to let herself cry. But she didn't. He went into the storeroom and rummaged through the toys he'd got for her, and brought out a little Fisher Price xylophone which had different colored bars and he showed her how it would play itself if you pulled it across the floor. But maybe she just wasn't musically inclined. There was a whole bunch of board games but they required two or more to play and he was going to be busy all afternoon. He went ahead and showed her the one called *What Shall I Be?* Career Game for Girls, which features a nurse, a teacher, a airline hostess, a model, a ballet dancer, and a actress. He promised to play the game with her later, but right now he had work to do. She could maybe learn it by herself. No? Well, he wasn't going to drag out any more of the stuff right now, because he had to save it so that he'd have something to give her at Christmastimes and on her birthdays.

"You'd better try to take a little nap," he urged. "Come on and I'll show you our bedroom." He took her in there, where he had rehabilitated the old iron bedstead and springs the Madewells had left behind along with a real mattress stuffed with feathers, so soft he figured it must've been goose down. "You never slept on a featherbed before?" he asked, and when she shook her head, he said, "Well, just climb up there and see if you don't fall right to sleep."

She laid down and closed her eyes and he tiptoed out and on

out of the house and told Bitch to keep an eye on the door. He told Bitch it was okay for the girl to go to the outhouse if she had to but not to go anywheres else. Then he took his axe and shovel and hiked the mile back to where the truck, or what was left of it, was still smoldering. The embers had died out enough that he could commence cutting a lot of saplings and brush and stacking them on top of the remains of the truck to cover it up. He didn't think anybody would ever come up the old trail this far, but if they did they wouldn't see nothing but a brush pile. Then he went over the trail to the house, walking backward and covering up any signs of the path and covering them with brush. All of this wasn't so much to keep anyone from finding the path as it was to keep her from finding it.

When he was done late in the afternoon it was time to give thought to supper, and he considered killing one of the chickens. But he was just too blamed tired and sleepy himself to bother with it. The girl, however, wasn't asleep. She was talking to that big doll he'd given her. He was pleased to see she'd found some use for the doll. "What would you like for supper?" he asked her.

"Basketti," she said.

"Say what?" he said and she repeated herself and it finally dawned on him that she was just baby-talking spaghetti. That too was something he didn't have in stock. "Wop food," he said.

"What?" she said. "It's my favorite of everything."

"It's what Eye-talians eat," he said. "I never could abide it, nor even tried it. Like pizza, it's for Wops."

"I love pizza," she said.

"Well, I'm sorry but we just don't have the makings of any of that Wop food."

And again she seemed right on the edge of hauling off and having herself a good cry. This has been a bad day, he reflected, but he was confident that given the passage of time she could learn to overcome all her likes and dislikes. For supper he opened a can of beef stew and for dessert they had canned peaches with cookies. At least there was plenty of cookies, enough bags to last them until they learned how to make them.

When he lit up after dessert she said, "Please don't smoke."

"You'll get used to it," he assured her.

After supper they played board games. He had a good one called *Dealer's Choice* that involves purchasing cars and maintaining a used car lot, with lots of vintage car cards. But she didn't like it much. It grew dark and he lit one of the kerosene lamps and he tried to show her how to do it but she said she was not allowed to play with matches. "You don't play with 'em," he said. "You just light the darn lamp with 'em." They tried a game called *Clue* but it seemed to be over her head and maybe his too. They briefly played a game called *Sorry,* and fooled around just a bit with a game called *Charge It: The Family Credit Card Game.* They played a board game called *Goldilocks and the Three Bears*, the object of which was to help Goldilocks escape. Then it was bedtime. Well, actually, he had thrown his wristwatch that they'd given him at retirement off the bluff and didn't know what time it was, and maybe it was early, but he was bushed. He didn't feel a smidgin of desire. He told her that tonight he'd sleep on the davenport and she could have the featherbed all to herself. She told him that she couldn't sleep without Paddington, and it took her a while to explain just who the hell this Paddington was. He went into the storeroom and came back with a stuffed rabbit, a big one, and told her to give it a hug and pretend it was Paddington. Then he tucked her in, in her nice new flannel jammies, and gave her a little kiss on the forehead.

"Mommy always leaves on the night light," she said. "I can't sleep in the dark."

"Well, tough titty," he snapped, growing short. "As you can see we don't have no lectricity up here." He could leave a kerosene lamp turned down real low but that was dangerous and he didn't want to try it. Ditto the idea of leaving a candle lit. He had an emergency flashlight with enough spare batteries to last until maybe she got old enough to grow out of her stupid little fear of the dark. So he set up that flashlight but she complained it was too bright. He covered it with a handkerchief and said goodnight, wiping his brow and thinking *this sure has been a shitty day.*

In the morning she was gone. And the feather mattress was soaked. She had really done wee-wee all over it. He dragged the mattress out of the house into the sunlight, and wondered how much air and sunlight would be required to dry it out and remove the smell.

Bitch was just sitting there and didn't even bother to wag her tail. "Which way did she go?" he asked. "Did you happen to notice?"

Chapter thirteen

She wished she had some friends handy to help her make sense of this whole situation. Her haunch really hurt where he had kicked her out the door, which seemed to be his way of saying that she was being replaced by the girl. She had examined the child closely and determined that the girl probably could not fetch or beg, nor guard the henhouse nor bite intruders. So the girl was intended for some other purpose which escaped Hreapha. If that purpose was companionship, the girl obviously was not going to be very companionable, agreeable, or even pleasant. Maybe the man was just giving her a trial. Maybe the girl had found him somewhere on his travels and had decided to follow him home and see if he wanted to keep her. Hreapha's own mother, Whuphvoff, had once upon a time when she was young secured her own position in a good family by that maneuver: she had just followed a boy home and the boy had said, "Mom, she followed me home. Can I keep her?" and Whuphvoff had thus been absorbed into a good family, where Hreapha had been eventually born. Hreapha's mother told her that she hoped she would never have to resort to that method of securing a family, but it was something to keep in the back of her mind, where Hreapha already had so many things stored that they were crowding into the front.

The very fact that the man was probably preparing breakfast for the new girl (Hreapha could smell the coffee and some kind of awful prepared meat frying) and had neglected to fill Hreapha's dish made her sure that her place in this world was being supplanted by the newcomer. After a while the man came out and ran to the henhouse where he gathered up two handfuls of eggs, and Hreapha whimpered her name softly to him in hopes he would notice her and remember to feed her, but he did not. She had not had anything to eat since that thoughtful egg that the charitable hen had laid for her yesterday, and she was getting very hungry.

Later the man brought the girl out of the house and showed her to the little building where people poop, and again Hreapha made mild whimperings to call attention to herself, and again she was ignored. And after that, they came out again so that the man could show the newcomer how to draw water from the well. During the operation, Hreapha positioned herself nearby and tried to look nice and eager and hopeful without outright begging, but again it did not dawn on the man that he had neglected to feed his faithful dog. Next the man attempted to show the newcomer how to chop wood, and after repeated attempts the girl was able to split a piece of it. *Well now, at least that's something I couldn't ever do,* Hreapha reflected. Nor could she draw water from the well. She did not need to, because, as she next discovered, the man was showing the girl to the springhouse, which was a perfectly good source of water. Hreapha followed, maintaining all the while her pleasant hopeful look and posture, but the man and the girl were caught up in a discussion about something called Kool-Aid and neither of them gave Hreapha a glance.

Later in their tour of the premises, the girl was shown the barn and warned to stay away from it and then shown the shop, which, Hreapha had long since discovered, the *in-habit* liked to inhabit and where he could usually be found. Or, since "found" doesn't apply to *in-habits*, perhaps "detected" was the word. The *in-habit* studied the girl with great attention and curiosity but did not reveal himself to her. Nor did the man discover the *in-habit*. The man did, however, begin to talk about the *in-habit,* or rather about the *in-habit* when the *in-habit* had actually inhabited the place, as a young schoolboy named Adam Madewell. Hreapha listened with great interest to what was said about Adam, and wished she could communicate with Adam *In-habit* and compare notes with him about his impressions of this newcomer. Did he think she was just a stray who had followed the man home? Should we keep her? *Could* we keep her? Even though the girl was not sociable, certainly not to Hreapha, whom she seemed to dislike intensely, the girl was, after all, lovely, even if she could not fetch and beg, and she might be loads of fun. Didn't Adam think so? But Hreapha did not know how to ask these questions of Adam, and wasn't sure he could answer. That would come later.

And then she heard the girl say to the man, "Somebody is going to shoot you." It did not sound very sociable at all.

And she heard the man answer, "They've got to find me first."

After they had gone inside to have their lunch and she was left with only the prospect of becoming an egg-sucking dog, she pondered these statements and reasoned that the man was perhaps hiding from someone who wanted to shoot him. That would help explain all the trouble the man had taken to relocate, to abandon the house in the village of Stay More and stock up this mountain hideaway with enough food to last forever and enough drink to fly over the moon. It also gave Hreapha notice that one of her duties in the foreseeable future might be to protect the man against somebody trying to shoot him.

Later, the man threw her some kind of small bones that had been pickled and were virtually inedible, so she did not try to eat them, but went on starving. Later still the man came out and rummaged through the shop and finally took notice of Hreapha and said to her, "Bitch, you haven't seen any scissors anywhere, have you?"

She stood on her hind legs in a begging posture, licking her chops and wagging her tail and sparkling her eyes in an attempt to communicate *If you'll give me some food I'll find some scissors for you.* But he could not hear her, and went back into the house.

And still later, after Hreapha had gone to the henhouse and

actually drooled upon an egg but resisted the overpowering urge to suck it, the man came out once again and said to her, "Bitch, keep an eye on this door. If she comes out to use the privy, that's okay, but don't let her wander off. You hear me?" Once again Hreapha rose up on her hind legs in the begging posture, licking her chops and smiling hopefully, but once again the man failed to get her message, and she began to conclude that he might actually be pretty dense. He took his shovel and his axe and disappeared down the trail in the direction of the truck's parking place.

Hreapha obediently guarded the door for a long time but the girl did not come out. Hreapha was bored. She'd much rather have followed the man to the truck, or accompanied the child to the privy, but there was nothing to do, and nothing to think about except her empty stomach. She was nodding off and ready for an afternoon nap when out of the corner of her eye she noticed a hawk circling overhead. She knew it was a red-tailed hawk. Even though she was colorblind like all her kindred, she had learned from Yowrfrowr that it was called a red-tailed hawk, even though it didn't have a tail, at least not like a dog's. Anyway, the big bird landed on a high tree limb and just sat there giving the evil eye to Hreapha and then to the various chickens who were pecking around in the yard. What intimidating eyes the hawk had! Hreapha tried to return the bird's malevolent stare, but couldn't maintain eye contact. It occurred to her that the hawk was sizing her up, trying to determine if there would be any resistance if the hawk made off with one of the hens. "HREAPHA!" Hreapha declared, letting the hawk know that Hreapha intended to protect the flock.

But Hreapha's warning went unheeded. Suddenly with a hideous bloodcurdling scream the hawk dived from its perch and headed straight for the selfsame hen who had benevolently provided Hreapha with the only sustenance she'd had in ages, a single egg.

Hreapha sprang into action. She reached the hen too late to spare it from being snatched in the hawk's talons but she was quick enough to leap and seize the hawk's head in her mouth, feeling its skull crunch beneath her teeth. The hawk screamed even louder, the sound deafening and petrifying Hreapha, who hung on for dear life as the three of them plummeted back to earth.

The hen's life was spared and she ran off squawking bloody murder. The hawk continued to thrash and shriek for a few interminable moments and then lay still. It was the first time that Hreapha had ever killed anything (if we do not count assorted sinister fleas). She was too stunned to move, for a long time. She could only stand and contemplate the dead hawk, a really huge bird with an enormous wingspan, now disheveled and askew. There was another hawk circling high overhead, possibly the wife or husband of this slain bird, but the other hawk did not come down to investigate.

Good dog! said a voice behind her, and she, having never been called that before, turned eagerly, only to see nothing, or rather only to perceive the presence of the *in-habit*, who, at least, had demonstrated that he could communicate.

After a while, first looking around to see if she was observed by anyone "real" and noticing that all the hens and the two roosters were watching her with awe, Hreapha ate the hawk.

It was not easy. It was in fact very messy. The feathers got in the way of the meat, and Hreapha had to constantly spit out mouthfuls of feathers. She eschewed the drumsticks and the wings but chewed the breast and thighs and made a welcome meal of it. The meat was somewhat gamy—although Hreapha had absolutely no other game to compare it with. Perhaps "wild" would be a better word, and Hreapha was somewhat concerned that eating this hawk might make her feral and even vicious. But her hunger pangs were temporarily eradicated.

When the man came home from whatever he'd been doing with the shovel and axe, obviously tired from his work, he saw the remains of the hawk and hollered, "Goddamn it, Bitch, have you been eating one of the chickens?" She cowered and whined, and he kicked the hawk's remains preparatory to kicking her. When he did so, the enormous wingspan and the beaked head became evident to him and he said, "Well, what do you know? It's a *hawk*!" He stood there looking at the hawk and counting the chickens and taxing his limited intelligence and finally said, "This hawk must've got in a fight with a fox or something. Shitfire, what kind of *watch*dog are you?"

He went on to the house and she did not see him again until he came out at bedtime to use the pooping-perch. It was dark and after the lamps were extinguished within the house it remained dark and quiet for the rest of the night. Hreapha brooded about what kind of watchdog she was. His mention of a fox reminded her that the chickens had more to fear from foxes than from hawks. More than once at the old place in Stay More she had had to chase foxes away from the henhouse, and had fought a couple of them, and knew that they were mean. She understood that foxes were dogs and therefore her cousins, but she intensely disliked them. And vice versa.

She napped fitfully through the night, perhaps dreaming a time or two. It seemed that in one of her dreams she was a hawk, soaring high above Madewell Mountain with a fine view of this homestead, which, however, was completely abandoned again, except for its *in-habits*. But now there were three *in-habits*, including that of a female dog.

She woke at dawn from this dream at the scent of the girl-child stepping out the front door. "Shhh!" the girl said to Hreapha with her finger over her lips, and then left the premises. In one hand she was carrying a flashlight, not lit; in the other hand a small paper sack which had the scent of edibles, possibly crackers.

Naturally Hreapha followed, but once they had left the yard the girl turned and stomped her foot and hissed at her, "Get home!" and swished her hands holding the flashlight and sack. Naturally Hreapha did not get home but waited just a while and resumed following the child, who seemed to be trying to find the path that led to the trail that led to the truck's parking place, but she could not find it. If the girl had asked Hreapha politely, the latter, who could easily smell the trail, would have shown her where it was. But the girl tried to find it by herself and got extremely off course. Hreapha said "Hreapha" in a gentle way that was meant to correct her bearings, but the girl picked up a rock and threw it at her. It missed. "Get home!" she said again, and threw some more rocks. None of the rocks succeeded in finding its mark. But Hreapha understood that the girl did not want her company. She waited, and allowed the girl to wander on out of sight, and waited some more, and then easily picked up the scent and followed unseen from a distance.

The child really had no idea where she was going, and began drifting southward instead of northeastward where the truck parking place was. Soon, Hreapha perceived, the child was hopelessly lost, but she kept plodding on, and circling back, while getting deeper into the tall white oak forest. Even from a distance Hreapha could smell the child's extreme fear and panic as well as her unreasonable determination. Nothing smells worse than unreasonable determination.

It had not been too awfully long ago when Hreapha herself had reached the momentous decision to run away, and thus she understood and empathized with the girl, and even wondered if possibly the man had beaten the girl with a stick as he had Hreapha. But the essential difference between this girl's running away and Hreapha's was that the latter at least had *some* idea of where she was going, and this girl had none whatsoever.

At least the act of running away made it pretty clear to Hreapha that the girl was not a stray who had followed him home.

After a while the girl came upon a marvelous but useless discovery: there was a pond of water where beavers had felled trees and made a beaver dam. From a distance Hreapha could smell the animals' scent, although she knew they were nocturnal and would not be visible now. She was delighted to discover that beaver were living here on the mountainside so near the farmstead, and she was keen to investigate their dam and lodge, but did not want to be seen by the girl. The girl herself had paused in her flight to study the pond and the beavers' log structures, which seemed to fascinate her, as if she knew what sort of creature had built this remarkable edifice.

Hreapha was fascinated too, but she realized the man would be waking soon and would be exceedingly angry at finding that Hreapha had abandoned her post. So Hreapha ran home quickly. And just in time. The door opened and the man struggled to drag an entire piece of bedding out of the house. Having seen him transporting a davenport on his back, Hreapha was not surprised to find him in this act, but she soon perceived that the bedding bore the strong scent of the girl's marking. Hreapha herself did a lot of marking, as was the nature of any canine, but the girl was not a canine and Hreapha did not understand why she had so thoroughly marked the bed, unless it was a kind of defiant farewell gesture to the man.

The man dragged the mattress on out into the yard, where he left it, and then he turned to Hreapha. "Which way did she go?" he asked. "Did you happen to notice?"

Of course this was one of those occasional situations when Hreapha wished that she could use the human language, but all she could do was turn a circle, reverse the circle, and then begin trotting in the exact direction from whence she had just trotted. Although the man's thinking faculties were somewhat slow, even retarded, he managed to understand that she intended to lead him in that direction, so he followed her. She led him out across the field and to the edge of the woods and into the woods and down into a dale and over a knoll and into the deeper woods and down the hillside to a little stream which flowed and flowed and culminated in a beaver pond. She was not unmindful that she was thus betraying the child, if indeed the child was trying to run away. But her first allegiances and responsibilities, after all, were to her master, bastard though he was.

The girl was not at the beaver pond. The man paused for only a moment to marvel at the beavers' engineering achievement, then he said to Hreapha, "Well, Bitch? So where is she?" For a moment Hreapha wondered if maybe the girl had gone underwater with the beavers into their lodge, a ridiculous conjecture. But she sniffed along the sluiceway of the dam for a while and picked up the girl's scent again, and followed it not very far to a glade in the sunlight where the child was sitting on a rock, nibbling on a cracker.

"Get home!" the girl snapped at Hreapha and began looking for a rock to throw at her. But at that moment the man came into view, and she stood up and tried to run away. The man quickly caught up with her and swept her up off her feet and held her in the air.

"*Honeybunch!*" he said. "You don't know what you're doing. You could get real bad lost out here and just *perish!*"

The girl's eyes were dampening and it looked as if she were trying very hard to cry. But she did not. He set her down, and put his hand on her shoulder and steered her in the direction of home. Hreapha followed happily along after, and the man stopped to reach down to pat his dog on the head. It was the first time she'd ever been patted. "Good ole Bitchie," he said, and he said to the girl, "she might not have the sense to keep the foxes or hawks away from the chickens, but she knew how to find you. If it weren't for her, you'd of got hopeless lost out here and you'd of been et by the bears or the wolves, I guarantee you."

The girl kicked at Hreapha and connected, right in the ribs. "I hate your dog and I hate you," she said. "I want to go home."

"We're going home, sweetheart," he said. They came again to the beaver pond. "How about me and you come over here sometime and do some fishing?" he suggested.

Chapter fourteen

In the days ahead she acquired a mission in life: to do away with that horrible dog. Watching her captor shave one morning, watching him open the blade and sharpen it on the leather strop and mix the soap in a dish and brush it on his cheeks and then lift his nose with his thumb while he drew the blade slowly down across his upper lip, she plotted the idea of getting that razor and sneaking up on the dog while the dog was asleep and slashing its throat. Then the next time she ran away there would be no dog to follow her and she could just keep on walking and walking and if she started early enough in the morning she might find that place called Stay More before the sun went down and there might be somebody still living there.

The awful dog slept a lot, and in the days ahead she watched for a chance when the man wasn't around or not watching and she could snatch his razor and slash the dog's throat. The man was spending a lot of time in his garden, so it would be easy to do it while he was out there if his back was turned or if she could find the dog sleeping somewhere where he couldn't see her from the garden.

Day after day, he tried to get her to help with the garden, but she would not. They had their first real fight about that. Usually the man tried to be nice to her, and he hadn't lost his temper yet, and he hadn't even been angry at her for wetting the bed, which had compelled her to apologize to him for the first and only time, saying she couldn't help it and she didn't mean to and she wouldn't do it again, although she did do it again, every night of the nights ahead, until finally he made her sleep on what he called a "pallet": just some quilts on some pillows on the floor. And she wet that pallet too, and he made her put it out each morning to dry and air in the sunshine.

But they had a fight about the garden, because she didn't want anything to do with it, and she came close to having to use her taekwondo on him.

"Darn your little hide, you want to eat, don't you?" he said. "And not just today but this summer and next fall and winter? It's hard work to raise a little truck garden but it pays off in the long run."

"I hate veggies," she said.

"How come?"

"Because they're *green!* If I wanted to eat something green, I would eat grass or leaves."

"Shoot, I'm planting lots out there that's not green. Maters aint green. Crookneck squash aint green. Taters aint green. Hell, corn aint green. Don't you like corn on the cob? Roastin ears?"

Come to think of it, she did, but it had never occurred to her that corn on the cob was something you could grow. It came from the store, like all the many other things that came from the store which they would never ever have again because they'd never go to the store again. Bananas, for example. She loved bananas, and liked them sliced on her Fruit Loops at breakfast. But she couldn't even have any Fruit Loops because he hadn't bought any, although he had Wheaties and Corn Chex, which didn't taste very good with that powdered milk on them instead of cream.

"If you could grow bananas in that garden, I'd help you plant them," she said.

"I'm sorry about the bananas," he said. "But late this summer there will be pawpaws aplenty hereabouts, and a pawpaw is just as good as a banana if you develop a taste for it."

She had never seen a pawpaw and didn't like the sound of it. She didn't tell him that the main reason she wouldn't work in the garden is that she had to watch for a chance to catch the dog sleeping and slash its throat. But there were other reasons. When he was out there working hard and sweating it made him smell bad, and she hated to get close to him. She had already told him his breath was bad but that wasn't because of the garden work, it was because of his bad teeth and his cigarettes and all that whiskey he drank. She couldn't imagine any woman wanting to be married to him, and she certainly wasn't going to even pretend to be his wife. It was bad enough she had to be near him at the kitchen table and when they played their board games; she didn't want to be near him in the garden. "You stink," she said to him, more than once, and all he could say was that any day now they'd both have to get out the old washtub and have a bath. Or take a swim in the beaver pond when the water warmed up one of these days. She did not know how to swim; her mother had never allowed her to go swimming, for fear she'd drown. But the beaver pond was the only thing she liked in this whole world where she was trapped. In the days ahead when she missed her daily routine of getting up and taking a shower with Mommy and getting dressed and going to school, and she wondered if her classmates were really missing her and if they were even sorry that they had ever criticized her and called her names like "snot" and "pest" and "meany," she thought of at least one advantage of being a prisoner in this wilderness: in school they had been studying mammals and rodents and beavers and she had even seen a film about the busy beaver, which fascinated her, and here she was actually in the presence of real live beavers! Wouldn't she have a lot to tell in school if she could get back and tell it? She had studied up on the beaver so much that she recognized the dam the moment she saw it, and she knew that beavers come out only at night and thus she hadn't seen any, but she hoped she could go back to the beaver pond sometime at night with the flashlight or a lantern to watch the beavers and maybe even make friends with them. Of course the man would have to go with her.

"The least you could do," the man whined, "since I've took the trouble to spade up all that there soil and plant the strawberries, is for you to help weed them and also pluck off the blossoms, because we can't eat them this year but just get them ready to eat next year."

But she would not work in the strawberry patch. She couldn't conceive of doing something *now* that wouldn't have any benefit until a year from now, when she was sure she would no longer be here. If she couldn't find her way out of this place, or if someone didn't come and rescue her, she would be dead a year from now, either from being eaten by bears or wolves while trying to escape, or else, if it came down to that, she would just decide to stop living and figure out some way to die.

"Help me mulch the sweet potaters?" he would whine. "Don't you just love sweet potaters baked with marshmallers on top?"

"I hate sweet potatoes," she would say. And then she would say, "I'll help you plant the marshmallows, though."

And he would look at her to see if she was kidding, and say, "We've got bags and bags of marshmallers."

In the days ahead he worked every day in that garden, and not once but twice she took his razor from the place where he kept it and unfolded it and went off looking for that dog. The first time the dog woke up and saw her coming with the razor and jumped up and ran off. The second time the dog stayed asleep and she was just about to slash its throat when the man came up behind her and snapped, "What are you doing with my razor?"

"We don't have any scissors. I need it to cut my paper dolls some clothes."

"You don't have any paper dolls," he said.

"I need to cut some out of something."

"And you'll slice your finger off. Give me that." And he took the razor and hid it in a place where she couldn't find it. So she had to think about other ways of getting rid of the dog.

In the days ahead there was not much else to do. She had already spent so much time brooding and moping about her predicament that she had nothing else to think on the subject. There were no books to read, not even comic books. She had been addicted to comic books and being weaned from them so suddenly gave her real heartbreak. There was a stack of some kind of magazine called *Police Gazette* full of stories about murder and crime and evildoing, but she read one issue and lost interest. She was bored. There was no music to listen to or any way to play it, and all she could do was sing to herself. Worst of all, there was no television. If Sugrue Alan thought that he was going to deprive her of television for the rest of her life, he had another think coming to him.

She reflected that the only other thing she liked about this place, besides the beaver pond, was the fact that she didn't have to worry about burglars. All her life, one of her biggest fears had been that somebody would break in and rob them. Her father, when he had still lived with them, had tucked her in at bedtime every night and reassured her about her fears that they would be poor or that he would leave her or that they would be robbed. He had left her, so she was right about that one fear. But way up here on this mountain they were so far away from everybody that no burglar would ever find them. For whatever comfort that was worth. Yet even though they were so far away, she knew that there were other people *somewhere* out there. At night when it was dark and still and she sat out on the porch and listened very carefully, above the sounds of the frogs ("peepers" the man called them), she could sometimes hear, far away, the sound of a truck shifting gears, or, sometimes, what seemed to be a gunshot. And sometimes the sound of airplanes far overhead. So there *were* people out there. Would she ever see them again?

As the days dragged by she tried to alleviate her boredom by making believe that she was in school and that Miss Moore was giving her a lesson which she had to learn. But such make-believe only got her to first recess, and there was nowhere to go, because the other girls and boys were out in the yard barefoot and she couldn't stand being barefoot.

She missed her jump rope. She wondered if, among all the things he had got for her, there might be a jump rope somewhere. Was he saving it for her birthday in September? She went into the storeroom where the boxes were stacked to the ceiling and the sacks and packages were stacked on top of them, and she wondered what-all was waiting for her in there. She couldn't open anything. Finally she came right out and asked him if he had a jump rope in there anywhere and he wasn't sure what she meant. "For skipping, you know?" she said. He had lots of rope, and showed it to her, but most of it would have made a good lariat or lasso or noose but not a jump rope.

In the days ahead, with nothing better to do, she practiced her taekwondo moves, getting her feet and hands into their best maneuvers. The dog watched, and she knew that if she wanted to she could kick the dog up under the throat with a *chagi* that would snap its neck and kill it.

"What in tarnation are you up to?" he wanted to know.

"It's martial arts," she said. "I'm practicing, and when I get good enough, I'm going to protect myself against you."

"I aint done nothing to ye," he protested. "For one thing I'm just too blame tard. I'm too tard to lift a finger against ye." And he went out to his blamed garden to get himself more tard. They ate out of cans at every meal because he was too blame tard to work in the kitchen. He kept promising that he'd kill a chicken and fry it and he kept promising to show her how to bake bread and cakes and everything, but he hadn't yet.

Eventually, because she had absolutely nothing better to do, she approached him in the garden and said, "Okay, what do you want me to do?"

"When?" he said.

"Now," she said. "Here." And she spread her hands to indicate the garden. If she didn't stand too close to him, and practiced holding her breath, she could stand him.

"It's time to plant the beans, I reckon," he said. "And if you don't like green snaps, we could plant a few yellow snaps."

She didn't know what a snap was, but she followed his directions and together they planted two rows of beans, yellow for her and green for him. It wasn't very hard. Then they planted shell beans and pinto beans and kidney beans.

And when they were all finished he said, "Let's run over to the pond for a dip." She didn't know what a dip was, but she followed him when he fetched towels and a bar of Palmolive soap from the house and they hiked to the beaver pond. The dog followed them, but she didn't mind too much. When they arrived at the pond, the man took off all his clothes and jumped in. She had to turn her head aside during the few seconds between his removing his underpants and his submersion in the water. She caught just a glimpse of this thing, the very first time she'd ever seen one.

"It's just a mite chilly," he said. "Come on in."

"I can't swim," she said.

"You don't have to swim. It's shaller enough to wade in, over yonder."

"No," she said. She was not going to take off her clothes even if the afternoon was almost hot.

"Suit yourself," he said. He gave himself a bath with the soap, which she was glad to see. No, not *see,* because she tried not to watch, but she was glad that he was getting himself clean for the first time since she'd known him. He looked funny, suntanned on his arms and face but still white on the other parts, including his fat belly. While he was exposing himself, she strolled down where the dam was and searched for any sign of the beavers, but she knew that they'd built what was called a "lodge," and they were sleeping all day in the lodge unless the man's jumping into the water had waked them up.

When he was finished and dried himself off and had his clothes back on, and didn't stink so much, he said to her, "If you'd like to go over there where it's shaller and give yourself a bath, I won't watch."

She really needed a bath. "Take your dog," she said, and she waited until they had wandered off out of sight, and then she removed her jeans and shirt and, taking a look around to see if even the beavers were watching, she pulled off her panties and she stepped into the shallow water with the bar of soap. But it was *cold*! She quickly stepped out of the water, shivering. She took a deep breath and stuck one foot back in and got it wet enough that she could rub some of the soap on it. She liked the clean smell of the Palmolive. She reached her hand down and got a handful of water and rubbed it on her upper body, and soaped a bit. Bit by bit she got accustomed to the cold water and managed to reach the point where she could splash enough of it on herself to get the soap off. If her mother had been here she would have made Robin wash her hair, or have washed it for her, and Robin would have had to say, "But, Mommy…" which was something she said nearly every day of her life but had not had to say for a long time now, and this made her smile. She missed her mother so much but did not miss having to say "But, Mommy…" all the time. Then she toweled herself dry and dressed again. He came out of the woods with the dog and they went home.

"Looks to be some rain coming up maybe," he observed. "We sure could use it."

He declared that it was time they had a real supper and he wanted to show her how. He led her out into the yard. He picked up the axe in one hand and with the other hand he grabbed a passing chicken by the neck. The dog yelped. "Bitch, hush, I aint about to harm *you*," he said, and swung the axe and chopped off the chicken's head but it didn't kill the chicken, who went on flopping headless around all over the yard, while Robin screamed and the dog whined and whimpered, and off in the distance it began to thunder. After a while the chicken stopped its headless dance and lay trembling, and the man said to her, "Quit your squealing and help me pluck it." He showed her how to pull the feathers off the chicken, and then he took a butcher knife and cut the chicken up into pieces and showed her how to dredge it with flour and fry it properly. She felt really sick to her stomach.

He had to eat most of it himself. Or several pieces, and said he'd keep the leftovers in the springhouse. Then he toasted her with Hawaiian Punch and said, "Since it's our first real honest-to-God supper together, don't you think it's time you told me your name?"

She didn't want to tell him her name but she knew he'd pester it out of her eventually. "Wobbin," she said.

"Robin, huh?" he said. "That's a right perty name. Glad to know you, Robin." And he offered his hand. She took it and gave it a little shake.

By bedtime the thunder was booming, and she could hear the rain falling on the roof and all around. It grew steadily harder. One of her teeth had been working itself loose for many days and she reached into her mouth and wobbled it and pulled it and finally got it out. She put it under her pillow on the pallet for the Tooth Fairy to find.

Then the lightning bolts started hitting all around, and the thunder sounded like it was coming in the front door, right into the house. It was terrible. She had never seen such lightning nor heard such thunder. Was this the end of the world? The whole house would disappear with her and him and everything. She was shaking uncontrollably. Between peals of thunder she could hear that damned dog whimpering horribly outside the front door, and finally she heard the man get up from his bed on the davenport and open the door for the dog. She didn't want the dog in the house but almost felt sorry for the poor thing, having to endure such a thunderstorm as this. She felt sorry for herself. She even felt sorry for Sugrue Alan and wondered if he too was just a little bit scared. Anybody in their right mind would be terrified in a storm like this. But maybe he didn't have a right mind.

The next horrendous flash of light and peal of thunder lifted her right up from the pallet as if it had hit her. It was unbearable. She ran from the bedroom into the living room, desperate to be comforted and hugged. He was there on the davenport waiting for her.

The next morning she knew only two things: one, that she had spent the rest of the night cuddled against him on the davenport, and two, that she had had a long uncomfortable dream about finding herself at school in her pajamas.

Chapter fifteen

Mr. Purvis was kind enough to set up an area in a corner of the warehouse room, screened behind the cereals and the condiments, where she could go for privacy when she felt an uncontrollable need to cry. Or she thought it was a kindness at first, until Liz, one of the other checkers, told her that Mr. Purvis simply didn't want her using the employee's lounge for her crying.

The attacks came on her suddenly, triggered by almost anything, such as a customer coming through the aisle with a little girl, and sometimes Karen couldn't make it to the warehouse corner before she broke down. Sometimes the tears started streaming down her face while she was ringing up the items on the counter, and this disturbed the customers, although many of them recognized her because they'd seen her on television several times, and if they recognized her they'd say something sympathetic while she signaled for Liz to come and take over so she could run to the warehouse room.

The first uncontrolled fit of crying had of course occurred at the roller rink itself, that terrible place, that goddamned place which, one of these nights, she was going to set on fire and burn to the ground (although every day various people left bouquets of fresh flowers on that little balcony). The second fit had hit her not long afterward when she'd been required to find a good recent photograph of Robin for the officers, and she didn't know whether she was crying simply at the sight of Robin's face in the photo or out of embarrassment at the realization that she had so very few pictures of her daughter; neither Billy nor she had ever owned a camera.

And the third time the fit had wracked her with helpless sobs was when, at the police station, they had made her take a polygraph test. *Her*! Did they think she would do something to her own daughter?! The cop had tried to explain that it was "just by the book," as he put it, part of routine procedure. They had to delay the test for a whole hour until she could get control of herself.

"If you ask me just one more question I'm going to start screaming," she had said, several times that night and the next day, to several people, not just the cops but the television people and the reporters. But they had not stopped asking her. And she had stifled her screams. She had broken into tears again when they had asked her to describe what Robin had been wearing, and she was almost ashamed that Robin's jacket was cheap and too small for her. She had really bawled when they had made her show them Robin's room. They had "secured" the room and wouldn't let her touch anything in it, although again she was embarrassed that her whole house was a mess and needed straightening at least. They had taken several items of Robin's dirty clothes to be used for the bloodhounds to sniff. They had practically moved into her house and for several days she was a stranger in her own home.

The time she had cried the hardest was the worst, in the sense that it screwed up her first carefully planned television appearance. They had given her several hours to prepare her "message" and to rehearse it, but those hours hadn't been sufficient to prepare her against the possibility that she would break down so completely in front of the television cameras.

"Whoever you are," she had said into the camera, clutching the stuffed bear that Robin had called Paddington, "wherever you are, I know that you are listening, and I want to say just a few things to you. Robin Lee Kerr was my daughter, my only child. She *is* my daughter, my only child, and I say '*is*' because I know that you are keeping her alive, that you have not done any harm to her. Not yet. I can imagine what you plan to do with her, and I can only believe with all of my heart that you are going to keep her alive. I know why you selected *her*, of all the girls her age in this world. Because she is so beautiful. Oh, she is also full of mischief and spunk and humor, as you are discovering every minute she's in your company, but most of all she is so very, very *beautiful*...." At that point Karen had lost it. The cameras had had to avert their eyes and go to the announcer, who had tried to finish the message for her, begging him, whoever he was, wherever he was, to let Robin go.

Her doctor had given her sedatives for the first week only. After that, he said, the Lord would take care of it. Her doctor was also an elder in her church, and when she told him how much and how helplessly she was crying, he told her that her tears were necessary for her to come to terms with her grief.

She had thought she had cried so much that she simply had no tears left, and after a week off from work, the week when she was drugged with the sedatives and assaulted every day by contacts with strangers, she had needed to go back to work to pay the bills. But she had cried again when her fellow employees presented her with a check in the amount of the wages she had lost during her week off. They had taken up a collection for her.

And she had cried when she realized that if Robin were here, Robin would call her a "crybaby." Karen couldn't remember the last time that Robin herself had cried, although she had a fairly good guess: when Robin was about three, and they (including Billy) were at the supermarket (not the one where she eventually went to work), and Robin was crying about something she wanted to get, in the typical fashion that three-year-olds learn to cry for whatever they crave, and Billy, who wasn't in good humor for having been dragged out to help with the grocery shopping, had snapped at Robin, "If you don't stop that crying, I'll give you something to really cry about!" Karen didn't believe that those simple words were enough to have turned the trick, but for whatever reason Robin had never cried again.

"Are you crying *now*, Baby?" Karen asked of her missing child, having acquired the habit of talking aloud to Robin. "Is he doing something to you, and making you cry?" Karen waited for an answer with a real hope that somehow the words of Robin's answer might come back to her, but they did not. And once again Karen would see Robin at a younger age, lying in bed asleep, or sucking her thumb, or both. "Have you started sucking your thumb again?" she asked. But there was no answer.

Robinsville still lay untouched on the table where she had left it. Karen took literally the instructions not to disturb anything, and Robinsville was still spread out with its crudely cut and labeled store and school and post office and its houses with the dozens of people young and old in their paper clothes that Robin had designed and cut out for them. Karen would pause to stare down at the village, and would think it was a ghost town now despite its paper citizens. The thought gave her something else to cry about.

But she also remembered that the whole idea of Robinsville had been prompted by a gift of reams of paper and pasteboard and even scissors from Leo, and Karen hated to think of Leo. She had not seen that bastard again since chewing him out at the roller rink. Her mother said that her husband had simply disappeared, which reawakened suspicion that Leo was either responsible for Robin's abduction or was in cahoots with whoever had done it. Karen hated the thought that her mother had been married for a number of years to such a man...although she had often told herself that Leo was precisely what her mother deserved. Her mother offered to move in with Karen temporarily until Leo returned or was captured, but Karen didn't want it, couldn't stand the thought. For one thing, she was very resentful of her mother, because her mother had always had such a let-well-enough-alone attitude toward Robin's upbringing, chiding Karen for being such a worrier. Just recently Karen had lost it with her mother and had yelled, "You told me not to worry and look where it got me!" It was very hard not to blame Louisa Spurlock for Robin's misfortune; if she was not directly to blame, she was married to a louse who was conceivably at this very moment holding Robin captive somewhere.

And that "sketch" which Leo had provided for the police artist, which indeed reminded Karen somewhat of that jerk state cop Sergeant Alan, was obviously just a clever ruse that Leo had devised to divert suspicion from himself. State Police Lieutenant Samples, the specialist in child mistreatment, didn't think that the sketch was valid, and therefore they didn't have anything to go on.

The FBI agent assigned to the case, Henry Knight, out of the Little Rock office, seemed to Karen to be the only one who knew, as the expression had it, the distinction between his ass and a hole in the ground. He was efficient and knowledgeable and industrious, and in addition to all that he was kind and good-looking. Mr. Knight—or Hal as he insisted she call him—was the nicest, or the least unpleasant, of all the men she had had to deal with since it happened. She felt close enough to him to make her complaints about the other men to him. There had been a lot of rudeness and thoughtlessness and downright stupidity on the part of so many of the officers she'd had to deal with and answer a thousand questions for. Hal Knight understood her problems and her feelings so well that she wondered if perhaps he himself had lost a child. Finally she came right out and asked him, but he said he'd never had any children of his own.

It was Agent Knight who suggested to her that she keep a journal, and he even provided her with a spiral notebook. He told her the journal would not only be a good outlet for her feelings but it might also accidentally provide a key word or passage that might give a clue to something she'd previously forgotten. She was so touched at his thoughtfulness that she broke into tears, and he held her while she cried; it was the very first time that anyone held her while she cried. But it was also the last time, because she never cried again after that. Whenever she felt like crying, she would just whip out her journal and write something in it.

She leaned on Agent Knight and couldn't have done without him. She couldn't lean on her mother, or her doctor, or her minister. Billy came back to Harrison briefly at the request of the police, and spent the night at a motel, and she saw him for only a few minutes. They spoke but didn't touch. She was surprised to see how grief-stricken he was, but she couldn't lean on him. Somehow she got the feeling that he blamed her for Robin's disappearance.

A couple of weeks after her first dismal performance on television, she was invited back to try again, and she *willed* herself not to cry, and took her precious journal with her just in case. Agent Knight went with her and helped her get ready for it. She confided to Agent Knight her fear of repeating the break-down she'd had the first time she'd gone before the TV cameras, and was surprised to learn that he had been watching that.

"Don't dwell on your loss," Hal advised her. "Don't think about what a swell kid Robin is. Think about what a scumbag her abductor is. Get angry. Let it all out."

It was good advice. Instead of trying a placating tone as she had in the first TV message, she delivered a tirade. She even imagined she was addressing Leo directly. "We're going to find you," she said into the camera. "We're going to catch you, and if you have harmed a hair on that girl's head we are going to make you pay for it. You had better be taking very good care of her, and doing all you can to make her happy, because she is going to tell us everything you did, and you are going to be severely punished for every little wrong thing you did to her. The only way you can possibly prevent the terrible reckoning that awaits you is to bring her back *now*! We have no pity for you, none whatsoever, but if you search your heart you might find just enough common decency to allow you to lessen your hideous crime by ensuring her safe return." She paused, glowering fiercely at the camera for a long moment, and then she went on. "Now if you have her there with you and she is watching this, I want to say something to her too. Robin? Can you see me, Robin? Can you imagine how much I miss you? Not a moment goes by that I don't ache to hear your laugh and see your bright eyes and smile. Paddington misses you too, and everybody in Robinsville is counting the seconds until you return. I know you are brave and clever and nothing can hurt you. If only you knew how many people are spending every minute hunting for you. We will find you. We will never stop trying to find you. I love you."

Later, she asked Hal Knight, "Do you think she heard me?"

He nodded his head. "She heard you," he said. "I know, as I've never known anything, that she is still alive."

"But what if that creep has her somewhere where there's no television?"

"That's possible," he admitted. "But still she heard you."

Even with all the help she had from dear Agent Knight, and even though she had stopped crying, Karen felt helpless, and there was nothing she could say to her journal which would make her feel there was anything more she could do. What she needed was a book on the subject. Unfortunately Harrison didn't have a good bookstore. She phoned the library and spoke to the librarian. "Would you happen to have any books with a title like *What to Do If Your Child Is Missing?*"

"Is this Karen Kerr?" the librarian asked, and said she would check the card catalog and phone her back. Sometime later she phoned back to say that she'd even contacted larger libraries in Fayetteville and Little Rock, but there simply wasn't any such book. There were books on child victims of sexual offenses, and books on pedophilia, and books on abduction, but there were no manuals advising heartbroken mothers of missing kids on how to deal with their problems and their heartbreak.

The librarian said she was sorry, and then she said, "Have you considered trying a psychic? Don't laugh. I know a woman over at Batavia who is truly incredible. It's worth a shot." And she gave Karen the name and phone number.

Karen asked Agent Knight what he thought of the idea of using a psychic. She expected him to laugh but he didn't. And she hoped he understood: she didn't need a psychic to deal with her psychological problems. She needed a psychic to help her locate Robin.

"It's been known to pay off," Hal said. "Let's be sure the person won't try to gouge you." And he offered to drive her over to Batavia to interview the woman. The woman gave her directions over the phone and told her to bring something that had been special to Robin. Karen took Paddington.

"I certainly know who you are," the woman said, when they arrived. "You're becoming famous, and my heart goes out to you. Now y'all have a seat and I'll tell you my terms." The woman would require a down payment of "only" fifty dollars, but if the child was found as a result of any information given, the total fee was five hundred dollars. Karen was ready to leave, but Agent Knight said he'd gladly fork up the down payment out of his own pocket, and he did.

The woman proceeded to do her "reading." She took Paddington and hugged the bear and sat with it on the sofa with her eyes closed, for a very long time. Karen and Hal waited and Karen resisted the urge to drum her fingers on the table, as Robin would have done. But she thought of Robin and kept Robin fixed in her thoughts while the woman was doing her "reading."

The woman's eyes suddenly snapped open and the woman smiled broadly. "She's alive," she said.

Karen's heart ought to have leapt up but she remained emotionless. She waited and heard the rest of it: a man was keeping Robin in captivity, not tied up or anything but free to move about as she wished, although she couldn't run away because the place where they were was so far off in the wilderness that the child could never find her way out of there.

"Which wilderness?" Hal wanted to know. "There's wilderness all over the Ozarks."

"I'm sorry," the woman said. "I can't pinpoint it. It's remote but it's bright. It's a very bright place surrounded by deep forests. There's an old farmhouse. There are chickens all about. There is a dog."

"Can you tell what the man looks like?" Karen asked, wishing she'd brought a picture of Leo to show to the woman.

"He's not a young man," the woman said. "He's coarse. He's misguided. He's not very bright."

And that was all she could do for them. But she was so sincere in her belief that Robin was still alive that Karen's own belief was reinforced. One of the thoughtless cops had told her that the chances of finding the girl alive this late were "practically nil;" he'd quoted to her some statistic that nine out of ten girls abducted for sexual purposes, if they are found at all, are usually dead.

So she had a glimmer of hope, and life returned to Karen. Her landlord appeared on the Saturday he usually collected the rent and told her that a certain FBI agent had persuaded him to let her live rent-free until Robin was found. The Harrison Rotary and Lion's

Clubs had taken up a donation to offer a reward for Robin's return. In celebration, Hal invited her to have dinner with him. It was only Western Sizzlin' but eating out is eating out, and it was her first date in nine years.

And then Leo returned. The cops spotted his pickup and pulled him over. On the seat beside him he had a large roll of U.S. Topographic Survey Maps in a scale of 1:24000 for all of Northwest Arkansas and Southwest Missouri. Questioning him, the police relayed his answers to Agent Knight, who told Karen. Leo was quoted as having said, "What if I was one of these here child molesters? Where would I take her? Why, sure as shootin I'd take her to an abandoned farmhouse at the end of a dead-end road."

So all this time, with the help of those detailed topographic maps, Leo had been trying to locate each and every abandoned farmhouse in the Ozarks that was at a dead-end road. But his search, so far, had been a dead-end. He still had hundreds of other roads to explore, if only they would let him go.

Chapter sixteen

The first thing he did when he woke up, before he woke her, was to feel the davenport beneath them to see if she had peed on it. But she hadn't. That was good news. It had been such a terrible storm he'd come mighty nigh to wetting the bed hisself.

The bad news was that he still hadn't been able to get any lead in his pencil. Even now, with her still sound asleep against him, her face against his chest sweeter than ever, he couldn't get it up. He was just as out of commission as he had been ever since he'd first taken her. He'd thought at first it could just be from the same kind of anxiousness that had made him into what Arlene had called a premature ejaculator. But this kind of anxiousness, if that's what it truly was, was caused by something else. Did he really feel guilty or evil? No, he sure didn't. Did he feel sorry for the poor girl? No, there wasn't no reason whatsoever that he should feel any such thing, because he was doing everything in his power to create a new home and a new kind of life for her to make her happy and keep her happy forevermore.

Maybe it wasn't any kind of anxiousness but just plain old overwork. It was true he had been working awfully hard lately, getting the garden ready and tidying up the place, and there was a good chance he just didn't have any energy left over for thoughts of getting it on. Yeah, maybe that was it. The least little thing he did lately left him plumb tuckered out. Maybe he needed a rest before he'd be able to stand up stiff and salute again.

He'd hoped that when she took off all her clothes at the beaver pond he'd be able to feel his old dinger getting stiff just at the sight of her. And sure enough she was a sight to behold, much better in the flesh than any of the pictures in his *Nudist Moppets* book, and although he'd spied on her the entire time she was trying to give herself a bath, practically drooling at the loveliness of her little body, he hadn't been able to feel even a twitch of stiffening down below.

The two roosters were doing not a duet but a duel of crowing, the Rhode Island Red trying to drown out the Barred Plymouth Rock. It woke her up. She smiled up at him! It was the first time he'd seen her smile since that first time he'd laid eyes on her in the parking lot of the Harrison supermarket. She had such a lovely smile. He couldn't resist wrapping his arms around her and giving her a big hug, but even that failed to arouse his dead dood. She climbed off the davenport and said "I gotta go" and for a awful moment he thought she was fixing to try and run off again but he sat up and watched as she went out the door in the direction of the outhouse. Bitch followed her out, and he realized the dog had been in the house all night and he hoped she hadn't gone wee-wee or worse anywhere.

He got up and put on his overalls and started breakfast. When Robin came back, he said, "Maybe things is gonna get better. You didn't wet the bed last night." She had to go see for herself, but came back from the bedroom with a big pout on her face.

"What's the matter?" he asked.

"The Tooth Fairy didn't come," she said, biting her lip as if once again she was just on the verge of having a good cry. "I left one of my teeth under my pillow last night."

"The pillow on your pallet?" he said. "Well heck, no wonder. That wasn't your pillow last night. *I* was your pillow last night. What does this here Fairy generally leave you?"

"Fifty cents."

"Well, if I was your pillow the Fairy must've left it under *me*." And he went to the davenport and pretended to fish around with one hand while with the other hand he found two quarters in his pocket. "Sure enough, what did I tell ye? That old Tooth Fairy thought I was your pillow, which as a matter of fact I was." And he gave her the two quarters. "I can't imagine what you could spend those on, though."

"I'd put them in my piggy bank," she said. "At home I have a razorback piggy bank, and I probably have a whole lot of money in it. Maybe ten dollars."

"You wouldn't need a piggy bank around here," he said. "One of these days I'll tell you where there's all the money you could ever dream of."

"Really?"

"Really. I've got it stashed away in a good place. Hundreds of *thousands* of dollars."

"You're kidding. Where'd you get it? Did you rob a bank?"

He wondered if he ought to tell her. There was never going to be any chance for her to tell on him. He wanted her to know that as far as money was concerned he was her sugar daddy, even though there would never be any need whatsoever for money. So he went ahead and told her the whole story about the drug runner he'd stopped on the highway who had taken a few shots at him and been killed in return. He wasn't bragging but he hoped it would increase the respect she had for him. He'd never told the story to anyone and it was good to be able to tell it to somebody.

When he was finished, all she said was, "If you spent so much money buying all that stuff you've got in there, why didn't you get some scissors and some paper and some crayons?"

"Crayons?" he said. "Well now, I do believe we've got some of them." And he went into the storeroom and fished around in the bags and sure enough there was a big yellow box of Crayolas. A real big box, with maybe over a hundred Crayolas in it, of every color you could imagine. She was real tickled to have it, but made that pout again and said, "If only I had some scissors."

"Tell you what," he said. "You help me out around the house this morning, and this afternoon I'll take my pocketknife and get it real sharp and see if I can't cut out for you anything you want to trace on a piece of brown paper."

So they had them a deal. Since the rain had left it too wet to work in the garden, and it looked like it was a-coming up another rain anyhow, he put her to work sweeping the house and washing windows, although she had trouble reaching some of the cobwebs. "I've never seen a cob," she said. "What do they look like?" While she worked in the house, he went out to the cooper's shed and started to saw some pickets for building a picket fence to surround the garden, to keep the chickens out of it. And maybe the rabbits and any other critters that Bitch wasn't smart enough to shoo away. He ought to have thought to bring along a good big roll of chicken-wire to make a garden fence, but that was one more thing he hadn't even thought about, and besides he was going to have to learn how to make do. A picket fence, even if he didn't have any paint to paint it nicely white, was a lot more sightly than chicken wire anyhow.

There was old tools in the cooper's shed that he wanted to learn how to use to shape the pickets for that fence—adzes and froes and augers—but every time he went into that workshop he felt a kind of strange feeling like as if there was somebody else there, although there sure wasn't. Once, in there, he had without even thinking about it said "Hello?" as if he expected somebody to answer.

He couldn't do it. Not because of whatever or whoever was haunting the place, but because the effort of sawing just wore him completely out. He didn't have the strength to take a spit. It was all he could manage just to drag hisself back to the house and plop down on the davenport, where he could only laze around and watch busy Robin redding up the house. For such a little thing she did a fair job, and then she even got some lunch for both of them, and after lunch, true to his word, he took his pocketknife and used one of the whetstones from the shop to get the point real sharp so he could cut into pieces of paper on which she traced the outlines of teeny-tiny clothes: dresses and hats and pants and coats and what-all. It wasn't easy, and he felt dizzy with fatigue. It sure would have been a lot easier with a pair of scissors, but he rolled his tongue out and bore down and managed to cut up enough clothes for one paper doll.

"I wish you had something stiff," she said, and his eyebrows lifted in search of her meaning. What she meant was that she needed pasteboard or something to make the actual paper doll with. He suggested they could empty a cardboard box in the storeroom and use the cardboard but she said cardboard was too thick. "I have an idea," she said, and went out to the privy and came back with the almost-used up roll of toilet paper. She unwrapped what little was left on it, and took the cylindrical tube or core and picked at it until she found the seam that kept it in its shape, and she unrolled it and flattened it out and showed him how it made a kind of diamond shape of thin pasteboard! Then she took her pencil and drew a paper doll within that diamond shape, head at one point, feet at the other, hands at the others. "Now, can you cut this out?" she asked, and he took his knife and bore down and managed to cut into the outlines of her drawing and liberate the paper doll from the toilet paper tube. How about that? Wasn't she some kind of genius? And then she took the pencil and the Crayolas and gave the doll features and skin color and a pair of panties. "This is me," she said. And she dressed it with some of the clothes that had already been cut out of a paper sack.

"Are you a-fixing to make me too?" he asked.

"You're too big to be made out of a toilet paper tube," she pointed out. "But I have another idea," she said, and she went and got the board game called *Dealer's Choice* and said, "I don't like this game," and she showed him how the bottom of the box was just the right size and shape and thickness for making the paper doll of him. He kind of liked *Dealer's Choice* himself but if she didn't he could learn to live without it. So he let her use the box the game had come in. She traced the outlines of a paper doll three times the size of the one she'd done of herself on the toilet paper tube.

"I reckon you're right that we sure could use a pair of real scissors," he remarked.

They were interrupted by some loud barking right outside the door, and Sog managed to get up and fetch his rifle, and decided to get his revolver too while he was at it. He told Robin to get behind the davenport and stay down. He looked out the window but didn't see nobody. So he slowly opened the door, and there was old Bitch looking up at him with one of her grins on her face. And she barked again, at him, that silly kind of bark that sounded like "roffa".

"What is it, Bitch?" he asked her, but she just said that roffa again. And then he noticed. At her feet, on the porch floor, was a pair of scissors! "Lord God Almighty!" he exclaimed. "Who brought them?" His first thought was that somebody had sneaked up onto the porch and left them there.

As if to demonstrate that she herself had put them there, Bitch gripped the scissors in her teeth, picking them up. She trotted past Sog into the house, and presented the scissors to Robin. *Roffa,* the dog said to Robin.

"Don't that just beat all," Sog exclaimed. "Didn't I tell ye she was the smartest dog on earth? But where did she find a pair of *scissors?* Bitchie babe, where'd you get them scissors?"

Robin was just overjoyed with the gift, and even gave the dog a hug. Imagine that. Here she'd been bent on killing the dog and now she was hugging it.

Well, the scissors needed some work. They was somewhat rusty, but Sog summoned the energy to scrape and clean and file them good as new, and he oiled them, and then Robin was really in business. She went right to work, cutting paper dolls and paper doll clothes all over the place and you never saw anybody happier.

A good thing she had all that paper doll stuff to keep her busy, because it commenced raining again, raining pitchforks with tines on both ends, and there were howling winds. Sog had meant to get up on the roof while it wasn't raining and try to patch that one leak, and now he couldn't do it because it was raining too hard and also because he just didn't feel like doing anything.

For days and days it rained off and on, more on than off, and sometimes so mighty *on* that he feared the whole place would wash away. Robin was happy with her paper dolls but he had nothing much to do except watch her and drink his Jack D and smoke too much and sometimes get up from the davenport and show Robin how to fix some supper. He tried to show her how to bake bread but it turned out wrong and they could only throw the bread to Bitch, who sort of liked it. Sometimes Robin went out in the rain with a slicker on (the Wal-Mart lady had recommended a yellow slicker) to do her chores: bringing in firewood and water and gathering eggs, either in the henhouse or sometimes just out in the grass somewheres. Sog taught her how to fix reasonable scrambled eggs for breakfast, although once she burned herself on the stove and he had to get out the first aid kit and put some ointment and a bandage on it

When she was just giving all her attention to her paper dolls and not paying him any mind where he sat drinking and smoking on the davenport, sometimes he'd take out his sorry prick and fool around with it and study it and try to get it to solidify just a little bit. But he might as well have been playing with a dead man's cock, and the thought of that—touching another man's cock, even if the man was dead—gave him a bad case of fantods.

In time he realized that probably he would have to see a dick doctor, one of those specialists who could give you something for it or do something that would correct the plumbing. But that was out of the question, of course. The very thought of it set him to brooding about what would happen if either one of them, him or her, was ever to really need a doctor for something. Or even a dentist. In time she lost a couple more of her teeth, and he dutifully played the Tooth Fairy, but what if she ever got cavities and needed some drilling? He felt selfish and mean for wanting a dick doctor when she might need something even worse.

Hell, if any kind of doctor was needed it wasn't a peter specialist anyhow but just a plain old ordinary sawbones who could look him over and find out what was generally bothering him, that he didn't have no strength to speak of lately, and had dizzy spells besides and just generally felt like shit. He couldn't even walk right any more; his left leg had started dragging behind him. He never in his life had such problems before. He'd never taken a single day of sick leave the whole twenty years he'd been with the state police. He'd always prided himself on being fit and hearty and he was contemptuous of people who allowed some silly little illness to hold them back.

Now he didn't know what could be causing him all this distress. His feet were numb, he had a backache troubling him, and sometimes he couldn't tell whether his arm was up or down and even when he looked to see if his arm was up or down he couldn't make it out clearly because there would be two of them, one up and the other down, and both of them the same arm, the left one.

Even Robin noticed his discomfort, and asked him, "Are you feeling okay?"

He hated to admit it. "It don't appear that I am," he said. "But how come you to ask?"

"Your hands are shaking a lot," she said.

It sure was a good thing that such a smart and brave little girl had the ability to take over the running of the household, which was the only hold that needed running, what with the constant rain.

The garden was begging something terrible for its weeds to be pulled but he couldn't send her out to do it even if he could explain to her all the ways of knowing the difference between a useless weed and a useful plant.

After that night of the terrible storm when she'd come to sleep against him on the davenport, she decided that she liked that arrangement, or maybe since she couldn't have that old Paddington bear to sleep with that she'd claimed she could never sleep without, she decided to sleep with him. But the davenport was too small for both of them, and they couldn't really stretch out proper, so one night after she'd fallen asleep he took her to the featherbed, and lay down beside her, and that's the arrangement they had for sleeping from then on, although he wasn't good for nothing but sleeping.

He lost track of time. He'd decided from the beginning not to own a calendar, but even if he had one he'd have no inclination to get up and go take a look at it. And if he hadn't thrown away his timepiece he wouldn't bother to glance at it. He had a notion, but just a notion, of when May turned to June and June turned to July, et cetera. There were even some mornings when he felt like getting up, at least long enough to do something useful like go out and chop the head off a chicken. Not being able to work in the garden and not being able to put a fence around it had one advantage: the critters of the woods came out to nibble the garden stuff, and he could get up and fetch his firearms and show Robin how to use them, even the shotgun, which knocked her down the first few times she pulled the trigger. But in the course of time she managed to shoot a couple of rabbits who was pestering the garden, and he had just enough strength left to show her how to skin the critters and put 'em in a stew pot and cook 'em. Robin didn't like beef jerky and she didn't care for Vienna sausages or a lot of the other stuff they had in cans or jars, and she didn't much like the idea of eating bunny rabbits, but it was that or starve. Robin was skinny and he wished she'd eat more but she just didn't have an awful lot of appetite, or maybe it was just too much trouble for her to do all the fixing of all the meals.

He felt totally worthless and having lost his manfulness didn't help, at all. Things got so bad that Sog Alan began to wonder if it was God's punishment on him. Under ordinary circumstances he would never have given a thought to such a thing.

Chapter seventeen

Even the dumbest of dogs possesses the basic talent for *minding*, which, Yowrfrowr had once explained to her, most decidedly does *not* mean the ability to obey, but rather the faculty of knowing what is in one's master's mind. Not exactly mind-reading, Yowrfrowr had said, nor so-called telepathy, no, nothing so magical as that, but purely a sense of being in tune with the workings of the master's thoughts, which is necessary, after all, as a substitute for verbal communication. So. Hreapha's *minding* of her master quickly alerted her to the fact that he was sick as a dog, so to speak.

Searching for a reason for feeling like hell, you start with something you ate. And Hreapha didn't have to look far to find that: he had killed and eaten that nice hen who had kept Hreapha from starvation by providing an egg, and who Hreapha had spared from the clutches of the hawk. For several days after that event, Hreapha had felt morose and angry. And out of sympathy for that hen she had lost her appetite so completely that she wondered if maybe she herself was coming down with something as a result of having eaten the hawk. But she got over that. It remained to be seen whether he would ever get over having eaten the nice chicken. She sort of hoped not. He deserved punishment for numerous wrongdoings, including, Hreapha was beginning to believe, the taking and keeping of a very young female person against her will. Hreapha was convinced that the person, whose name was Robin, had not been a stray at all, nor even a willing companion to the man, but had been *stolen!* Theft should always be punished, and possibly the man's grave illness was what he had coming for snatching the girl.

Despite the general mood of gloom and doom that had befallen the place along with the impossible rainfall, Hreapha was at least cheered by the fact that the girl was no longer attempting to murder her. In fact, the girl had become caring and even affectionate, and had taken over the chore of making sure that Hreapha always had her dish filled with doggy nuggets once a day. And the girl always gave her a pat on the head and some kind words at mealtimes. This radical change in attitude was obviously the result of Hreapha's having presented the girl with the pair of scissors.

It was a dirty deal that Hreapha had never received any credit for having rescued the chickens from the woods or for killing the hawk or her various other good deeds, but her first thanks had been for something she didn't deserve credit for. It had not been she who had found the scissors. She had only brought them to the house and given them to the girl. She might never have known the location of the scissors (although she had looked all over the place, including the dangerous barn) if it had not been for the *in-habit* who inhabited the cooper's shed.

Hreapha had been asleep and thought she was just having another of her vivid dreams when she distinctly heard the word *scissors,* and looking around but seeing nobody, heard further, *Come go with me, old girl, and I'll take ye to some scissors.* It was rather difficult to "come go" with him, the *in-habit,* because she couldn't see him nor smell him, and couldn't tell which way he was coming or going, but he clucked his tongue occasionally to let her know where he was, and thus she followed him out to the cooper's shed, and to a dark corner of it where beneath a workbench was a wooden box containing assorted old thingumajigs, whatchamacallits, and diddenfloppies, among the latter a pair of scissors. *I reckon that's what she's a-hankerin*

for, the *in-habit* said, and sure enough, when Hreapha presented them
to the girl she got a *hug,* a real *hug.* Thenceforward Hreapha could
take a nap without fear of being slaughtered in her sleep.

In the weeks afterward, as everything went to the dogs, so
to speak, Hreapha had to be careful whenever she was in the house
not to walk upon or disturb the paper dolls, who were breeding like
rabbits. The girl let Hreapha into the house whenever the frequent
thunderstorms occurred, having discovered that Hreapha shared her
intense dread of thunder, and the two fear-stricken females cowered
and quaked together. Ordinarily the man would not have allowed
Hreapha in the house so much, but he was too out of it to notice.

When it wasn't raining too hard, Hreapha spent a lot of time
guarding the chickens and the garden, and trying to keep the former
out of the latter. She despaired of explaining to the chickens that
the various succulent vegetables in the garden were intended for
the exclusive use of the poor sick master and the mistress. How do
you tell a chicken to leave be the vegetables that are intended to be
served with chicken? It took Hreapha days and days of shouting her
name at the hens and the two roosters whenever they attempted to
wander into the garden until finally the fowl seemed to decide that it
wasn't worth the bother, listening to all that hreaphering in order to
grab a bite of lettuce, and they kept out of the garden. Hreapha had
more problems with the occasional deer who came down to nibble
the veggies, and also the rabbits. But the poor sick master rose up
from his davenport long enough to teach the girl how to shoot at
and finally hit the rabbits. Your turn is next, Hreapha tried to tell the
deer, but they just backed off and waited for her to leave the garden,
which, eventually, went to the dogs, so to speak, what little was left
of it that the weeds didn't choke out. Hreapha had never been able
to understand the difference between a cultivated vegetable and a
so-called weed, many of which were just as edible and tasty as the
vegetables. Thus, while Hreapha was very good at protecting the
garden from mobile creatures, she could do nothing to protect it
from vegetative creatures.

Despite the neglect and assault, the garden managed to produce, in time, some edible produce. Especially the melons: huge

watermelons and cantaloupes that almost frightened Hreapha with their looming bulk, and which, once cooled in the springhouse, gave the man the only happiness he knew all summer.

Hreapha, who had never eaten any kind of melon herself, wondered if the melons could possibly be held to account for the latest development in the man's list of distresses: his inability to do his business. With only one eye open, Hreapha could observe that each morning the man staggered, dragging a foot behind him, out to the outhouse, where he remained forever, and from whence came the sounds of his grunting and straining, which Hreapha easily recognized because she too, like all creatures, suffered from occasional difficulty in emptying her bowels. She knew of certain grasses that could be eaten for the condition, but there was simply no way she could prescribe these to him. His inability to poop contributed further to his melancholy and his unpleasantness. And the only way he could alleviate his mood was by stepping up his consumption of the moonward beverage, so that in time Hreapha's *minding* could not determine whether he staggered from his drinking or staggered from his illness.

Eventually he began to fall down. Once he fell off the porch. Once he fell repeatedly trying to reach the beaver pond, and gave it up, returning to the house, where the girl drew many buckets of water from the well to fill a large tin tub for him to bathe in. Hreapha could not tell him, or her, that she had discovered the beaver pond no longer existed. The hideous rains had washed away the beaver's dam, and they had not yet been able to rebuild it. In the middle of one night Hreapha had gone to see if there was anything she could do to help, short of felling or dragging timber, and found a bobcat menacing the beaver family. The bobcat had already killed one of the kits and was trying to catch another one when Hreapha arrived and did battle with the cat. She had never fought a bobcat before and hoped she would never have to do so again. They are bigger than Hreapha and they claw and scratch something awful. But Hreapha inflicted sufficient bites all over the cat's anatomy to give the cat second thoughts about further disturbance of the beavers.

Mr. and Mrs. Beaver attempted by their body language and

assorted unintelligible snorts and squeaks to tell Hreapha how grateful they were that she had spared the other four kits from the snatches of the bobcat. Hreapha wished there were some way she could communicate to them her desire to help in whatever way possible with the reconstruction of their dam and pond. In her teeth she took hold of a long hefty stick and dragged it to the dam site, and the beavers perceived that she wanted to help, and for the rest of the night she worked alongside them. When she got home in the morning she was all worn out, but so was the man, who had fallen on his way to the outhouse and was just lying there resting in the outhouse path. He didn't seem to mind or even notice that Hreapha had to sleep all day, and that she returned after dark once again to the dam site.

The third night she set out for the dam site, Robin followed her with a flashlight. "Where are you going, B—?" she started to use the not-nice name the man had given her, but caught herself and said "Your name isn't really Bitch, is it? Did you ever have another name?"

"Hreapha," she said, matter-of-factly, not barking it.

"Oh?" the girl said, and then she did a wonderful thing: she tried to pronounce it. She didn't quite get the aspirate correct or trill the *r* as much as it should have been, but she did a good job on the plosive *ph* and the whole thing sounded almost like the way Hreapha herself said it. "I'll just call you Hreapha then, okay?" Robin said.

"Hreapha!" she said excitedly, and trotted on toward the beaver's place with Robin right behind her.

"Where are we going, Hreapha?" the girl wanted to know.

"Hreapha," was the only way she could pronounce "beaver dam."

"Will you protect me if we meet a bear or wolf?"

"Hreapha," was the only way she could tell Robin that she would protect her against any harm in this world but that they had nothing to fear from wolves, who didn't exist hereabouts, and as for bear, they were pretty scarce or at least she had not yet seen one.

At last they came upon the construction site for the new dam, where Mr. and Mrs. Beaver were busy as beavers, working with the help of their four kits. Since the beaver didn't have the impounded waters of a new pond ready yet, they had nowhere to hide when this human being showed up, and Hreapha could not explain to them that the girl had no intention of causing them any harm. So the family of beaver simply shrank back and trembled as Hreapha demonstrated to Robin how she had been grasping sticks and dragging them up to the dam site.

"What happened to the dam?" Robin asked. And then answered her own question. "Oh, did all that rain wash it away?"

"Hreapha," Hreapha said. And dragged another limb to the dam site. Fortunately many of the limbs and sticks and logs which had made up the original dam had not been completely washed away but had lodged against boulders further downstream.

"You're *helping* them build it back?" Robin said.

"Hreapha."

"You really are a good dog," Robin said.

Hreapha was pleased and proud. She was even more pleased and proud that Robin herself began to help, and was strong enough to drag larger limbs than little Hreapha could drag. Robin also observed how the beaver were picking up large rocks in their dexterous fingers to anchor the base of the sticks making up the dam, and Robin was able to do this work too. The kits were all four busy dredging up mud from the streambed above the dam and packing it against the sticks, so that step by step the water flowing down would distribute the mud among the sticks, chinking the dam and closing it up. The water began to rise, and as it rose the eight of them—two adult beaver, four baby beaver, a dog and a girl—added more sticks and mud to the top of the dam.

The dam was finished before morning! The new pond began to fill. "That was fun," Robin said to the beavers. "When the pond is filled, I'll come back, and you can teach me how to swim." Then she said to Hreapha, "I'd better get home. He's going to be mad I was out all night."

But he didn't even notice. Robin went into the house and came back out to report to Hreapha that he was sound asleep and snoring, even though the sun was well up in the sky. "Let's have breakfast," she said, and filled Hreapha's dish with the Purina Chow, and got her own bowl of cereal and sat with Hreapha to eat it. There were a few peaches she had found ripened on the old trees up in the orchard, and Robin sliced one of these atop her cereal. "This is almost good," she told Hreapha. "There's no real milk, and it's not my kind of cereal, but I can eat it. Are you okay with the doggy chow?"

"Hreapha," she assured her.

After breakfast they had a long and chummy chat. Or rather Robin did all the talking, and Hreapha was content merely to listen and to interject occasionally a mild *Hreapha* or a milder whimper, and at a few points a growl to indicate she understood the serious import of what Robin was saying.

"I think he's dying," Robin said. "Don't you?" Actually Hreapha's *minding* of him had not yet dared reach that conclusion, and she dreaded contemplating it, but already was beginning to feel not that she was losing a master but gaining a mistress, and a good one. "He talks about sending me to find a doctor, but isn't that silly? He says he'll tell me how to find a road that leads down the mountain if I will promise to get help for him. Do you know how to find the road?" Hreapha wished that dogs had at least been given the ability to nod or shake their heads as humans do to signify yes or no. But if she could really communicate, she was sorry she'd have to inform Robin that as a result of the recent severe rainstorms the whole east side of Madewell Mountain had been eroded into deep gullies and ravines that obliterated any trace of the old trail. Hreapha had recently attempted to locate the remains of the pickup and had discovered that even its burnt carcass had been washed far down the mountainside. And that precarious narrow ledge along the bluff leading to it had had sections of it knocked out by boulders in mudslides. Hreapha had had to make an elaborate detour along a rock-face that would be impassable by a human being, especially a young girl. Getting down off the mountain in that northern direction was unthinkable. Hreapha had not yet explored the southern direction, but intended to do so in the near future, because she was beginning to miss Yowrfrowr.

If the two of them were really having a good girlie talk, she ought to be able to tell Robin about Yowrfrowr, and she greatly regretted that she could not. Robin told her about a boy named

Jimmy Chaney that she had sort of had a crush on, and even asked, "Are there any boy doggies that you like?" But Hreapha could not tell her about cute and smart Yowrfrowr. Abruptly Robin asked, "Have you ever done it with another dog?" And when Hreapha could not vocalize her virginity, Robin said, "You know, *fucked*?" And then added, "I wonder what it's like. You know, *he* has never done that to me. I thought he was going to. I thought that was the main reason he kidnapped me and brought me up here. I was expecting it. I was sort of getting myself ready for it."

All of this talk about sexual matters did not embarrass Hreapha in the slightest, but rather gave her some strange and curious stirrings of desire. Her mother—and eventually in their long talks together Hreapha was to discover that among the many other things she and Robin had in common, for example, their fear of thunder and of spiders, not to mention their virginity, their mothers were somewhat alike, as Whuphvoff and Karen had both possessed a didactic nature—her mother had once given her a long explanation of the periodic condition she could eventually expect to experience, wherein her markings would begin to take on a faint olfactory signal easily detectable by the noses of any male dog within miles, informing them that she was in the mood for romance. Her mother had cautioned her not to permit such romance unless the marking's scent clearly indicated that she was "ready."

Hreapha's markings had never yet borne this aroma. She wondered what she would feel the first time they did. What would she do? Would the scent carry all the way to Stay More, three miles away, where Yowrfrowr could pick it up? Such thoughts could not fail to titillate her.

"Don't take this wrong," Robin was saying, "but I wish I had a kitty cat." Hreapha's ears snapped into better hearing position. "I mean, you're a really good dog, and I never had a dog before, and I'm awfully glad to have you as my dog. But I've really and truly always, always wanted a kitty cat."

Chapter eighteen

Talking with Hreapha was so much more fun than talking with that stupid doll, who had been the only one she could talk to for so very long and who just sat there and had to play-like listen. Robin had wasted so many hours saying things to that doll, pouring out her heart to it, when all along she could have had Hreapha, who was so attentive and appreciative and smart. Robin was convinced that if by some magic Hreapha could really talk, the dog could tell her what she ought to do, the dog could even tell her how to find her way out of here if she wanted to, and above all the dog could tell her how she ought to feel toward Sugrue Alan. Should she feel sorry for him? Should she truly hate him? After all, he was all she had in this world. Unless and until she could be rescued. Or by some miracle find her way out of here. For the longest time Robin had been almost happy sleeping in the featherbed with him beside her; sometimes her head was so close to his chest that she could feel his breathing and hear his heart beat and he was a lot more alive than Paddington had ever been. And she hadn't even needed to have a night light on, because she knew he was her protection. She hadn't wet the bed again, not once. In the summertime when the weather warmed up and some nights were almost hot, she didn't need her pajamas but she wore them anyway out of modesty and sweated inside of them. But when he became too ill to work in his garden, he no longer stank of his sweat although he stank of the whiskey that he kept on drinking, and he stank of his illness, whatever it was, and she had to scrounge over to the side of the bed to escape his stench. She hadn't slept close to him for a long time now. She knew that he was probably never going to be able to do anything to her. He never would fuck her. He was so sick now.

But the weird thing was, some days he seemed to be okay. Not only well enough to fix his own breakfast for a change but also to go out and try to do something, if he could. He would go out and chop wood until he was all worn out again, and she would have to help him back to the house, and then she would go stack the wood up into a neat pile. Among all the things he'd bought for her were a pair of work gloves so she wouldn't get splinters in her hands. They were getting lots and lots of stove wood. "I reckon it'll get right airish and crimpy up here come fall," he said. "And doggone dithery come winter. You'll need more firewood than you'll be able to cut yourself, tiny as you are." His saying that somehow made it sound as if he didn't think he'd be around in the winter, or if he was he wouldn't be able to cut any more firewood.

He was also concerned that when the snows came the chickens wouldn't be able to get out and scratch around in the yard hunting for bugs and worms to eat. There wouldn't be any bugs and worms in the winter! He confessed he'd made a mistake not to have brought more than one thirty-pound bag of chicken feed, which was all gone now. Chickens will eat just about anything (and Hreapha had a hard time keeping them out of her chow, as well as out of the garden) and ever since Robin's first experiments at baking bread, biscuits and cornbread had failed, the chickens had helped to eat the failures and they still ate all the leftovers, now that she had finally learned how to bake some decent bread. To make sure the chickens could have a food supply for the winter, Sugrue had planted extra corn—Robin had roasted or boiled corn-on-the-cob so many times she was almost tired of it—and they could dry the leftover ears and feed them to the chickens all winter.

Very early Robin had discovered that the chickens were flocking around behind and beneath the outhouse, and looking down into the hole she sat upon she was horrified to discover that they were eating doo-doo. For a while after that she could not eat either chicken or eggs, and she put their disgusting habit at the top of her mental list of all the things she couldn't stand about living here. But in time she realized that it was just a fact of country life, and if you stopped to think about it, it wasn't any worse than chickens eating worms.

She was glad to help store corn for the chickens to eat in the winter, and while she was helping Sugrue do it, he took a Mason jar and filled it with dried kernels of corn, and then took a handful and said to her, "I need to show you how to plant your corn next spring," and took her out to the corn patch with his hoe and showed her how to hoe up a furrow and plant it with the corn kernels. "Think you can remember all that?" he said to her afterward, and again she thought it sounded as if he didn't expect to be around in the spring.

One morning they were all just sitting on the porch when Hreapha jumped up and started barking, and they saw a hog raiding the corn patch! "Wooee," said Sugrue, "if that aint a razorback!" And for a sick man he was pretty quick and nimble in fetching his rifle and shooting the hog. "I ort to've let you shoot him," he said to her, "but if you'd've missed, we wouldn't've had no secont chance." Robin doubted she could have hit it, although Sugrue had made her practice with targets again and again and she was very good with the rifle, although the shotgun was still too much for her.

It was a big hog, and Sugrue's only shot had hit it right square in the side of the head. "This is sure enough a wild razorback. Aint seen one of these since I was a kid," Sugrue said. "Be damned if we aint got us a right smart of meat." She helped him drag the hog, which must've weighed more than him and her put together, to the cooper's shed, where they rigged up a pulley to hoist the carcass to a beam. And Sugrue insisted she watch closely, every step of the way, as he cut into the hog's neck ("Smack in the goozle," he explained) to make the hog's blood run out. "The moon aint right, probably," he observed. "You ort to kill your hog on the full moon."

They heated the big iron kettle of water that they used for clothes washing (the hardest of all Robin's many chores), and when it was boiling they poured it over the carcass and Sugrue dusted wood ashes all over it. "Got to get all that hair off," he explained. Robin used a dull knife to scrape and scrape on the hide to remove the hair, while Sugrue kept pouring on more scalding water and wood ashes. It was messy and it took them hours and hours just to get the hide scraped clean. They didn't even stop for lunch, which was a good thing, because when Sugrue started gutting the hog and made her pull the intestines out into a washtub she started to puke but didn't have anything in her stomach to throw up.

He identified all the parts of the hog's insides for her—the lungs, heart, kidneys, liver, stomach, and so on. He showed her how to separate the trimmings of fat to be made into lard and the trimmings of lean meat to be made into sausage. She thought about becoming a vegetarian, which she knew a lot of people were (her friend Beverly was), but she didn't like vegetables. She liked bacon and hated Spam and as they worked Sugrue kept telling her all the good things that could be made from this hog—spareribs and hams and pork chops. All afternoon they butchered the hog, and Sugrue was ready to drop. "I reckon we'll just have to wait till tomorrow to cure it," he said. "Bitch will have to guard it all night."

He went into the house and grabbed one of his bottles that said Jack Daniels Black Label Sour Mash Whiskey on it and he went to bed. And the next day he didn't feel like doing any curing, whatever that meant. She wondered if the hog had had some terrible disease that it had to be cured of. "That good meat is sure to spoil," he complained. "But I just don't have the stren'th to lift a finger." In the afternoon, he said, "Hon, do ye reckon you could fetch one of them bags of coarse salt from the side room?" It was a big bag but she fetched it. "Now," he said, "If you'll just listen careful, I'll try to tell you what to do. And then next year if you're lucky enough to kill another razorback, you'll know how to do it all by yourself."

He couldn't even go with her to the cooper's shed to supervise what she was doing. Hreapha kept her company but only for a while before falling asleep; she'd been awake all night guarding the meat (from what or from whom? Robin wondered). Robin spread the hunks of meat out on the shed's workbenches and started to cover them with the coarse salt. *Mix in molasses and pepper,* a voice said to her, and she turned, thinking Sugrue had finally come to help, although it was a much younger voice than Sugrue's. And Sugrue was not there. She wondered if she was imagining things, or maybe Sugrue was communicating with her through his mind. She went to the bedroom where he was sprawled out with his bottle, still conscious. "Did you tell me to mix some molasses and pepper with the salt?" she asked him.

"Why, no, I never," he said. "But come to think on it, that's what Grandpa Alan always done. We've got plenty of 'lasses out to the kitchen."

So she mixed the coarse salt with molasses and pepper and started smearing it on the meat. *Red pepper and black pepper,* the voice said. She wondered if she was suffering from overwork, but she went back to the kitchen and got the red pepper to add to the black pepper. It took her all the rest of the afternoon to finish covering all the hunks of meat with all of the salt mixture. She wondered if any other seven-year-old girl in history had ever cured a hog all by herself. Thinking of this, she realized that she was almost eight. She wondered if it might even be September already. She would be eight years old on September the twelfth. That's still pretty young for curing a hog by yourself.

"Now what?" she said to Hreapha, as if the dog could tell her what now. "How long do I leave the salt stuff on there?"

Pends on the weather, the voice said. *Reckon six or seven weeks ort to do her.*

"Hreapha, did you say that?" Robin asked, delighted with the possibility that perhaps there was some way the dog could talk to her after all.

"Hreapha," the dog said, which seemed to be negative.

She was tired and sweaty and dirty and had salt and molasses all over her. She went to ask Sugrue if he had any idea whether this might be September yet, but he was passed out. Or dead. She didn't care. She opened a can of beans for her supper (it had pork in it, which made her impatient for the new meat to finish curing), and then, when it got dark, she lit a lantern and headed for the beaver pond. Hreapha happily followed. Robin decided Hreapha wouldn't have to guard the meat, once it had been salted so much.

The pond had filled with water. Their beaver friends were enjoying a supper (or breakfast?) of alder bark. "Hello," Robin said, but they did not run; they remembered her and knew she had helped them rebuild their dam. She took off all her clothes, but felt no shame at all to be naked in front of the beaver or Hreapha, who were all naked anyway. "Can you teach me how to swim?" she asked, and walked out into the pond.

The beaver taught her how to swim. Maybe even if she wasn't the first nearly-eight year old girl in history to cure a hog, she was the first to receive swimming lessons from beavers, who are experts at it. She didn't possess their large webbed feet to paddle with, but she could imitate the strokes of their arms and front feet. It wasn't hard at all. And although the kerosene lantern helped her see what she was doing, she felt she could do it with her eyes shut. She was dizzy with pleasure and pride; not even her first spin at the roller rink had given her such a sense of escaping from humdrum reality. Hreapha jumped into the water too, and all of them swam and swam and splashed and flipped and bobbed. The beaver seemed to be trying to get her to dive underwater to reach their lodge, but she wasn't ready for that yet.

Suddenly a light appeared, not from the kerosene lantern. It was the light of a flashlight, and Robin's first thought was that some human being had finally found her and was coming to rescue her. Her excitement at that thought was mixed with a kind of sadness: if she were rescued and taken away from here she could never swim with these beaver again. Also she was a little concerned because she was naked, and didn't want them to see her.

But it wasn't a rescuer. It was Sugrue. The flashlight played over the figures in the water, and she could hear his voice behind it. "Just what in tarnation do you think you're a-doing?" he hollered, and she knew he was not only angry but drunk. Then she heard a rifle shot. He was firing at the beaver! Hreapha barked at him, and he fired at her too, but didn't hit her.

"Stop it!" she yelled at him.

"Get your little hide out of there!" he ordered her. She climbed out of the water, and he played the light over her naked body. "Bitch!" he yelled. "Bitch, you're supposed to be a guard dog, goddammit, and you've let a fox get into the chicken house! Come on out of that water." Hreapha climbed up onto the shore, and he immediately kicked her as hard as he could, knocking her back into the water with a big splash. "Stupid dog! I'll learn ye to mind me." Hreapha moaned and whimpered.

"You're a mean man, Sugrue Alan," Robin said to him. "I thought you might be nice, but you're just plain old nasty *mean.*" He slapped her. It really hurt, too, and she felt her eyes welling up with water but she was determined not to let him, or anybody, ever make her cry. "I hate your guts," she said.

"Just what do you mean anyhow, coming over here in the middle of the night and burning up all that kerosene? You won't have none of it left to get you through next year." His voice was really mad.

"I won't be here next year!" she yelled at him.

He grabbed her and started spanking her bare bottom. He spanked her so hard it made her jump around. He spanked her so hard she was going to be not just red all over her bottom but black and blue too. For the longest time she held back her tears but then she couldn't hold them any longer and she yelped and began crying. She really cried. It was the first time she had cried since she was three years old, and she was hurt more by the loss of that record than by the sting of his spanking. He had done so many bad things, starting with his kidnapping of her, and she had never cried. But now she bawled her heart out.

"Get your clothes on and let's get out of here," he said finally, his voice not quite as angry, as if he'd got it out of his system by battering her.

She decided that as soon as they got back to the house and he put that rifle back where he kept it, she would snatch it up and kill him with it. He made a mistake when he taught her how to use the guns. He would pay for that mistake, and pay for his cruelty toward her and Hreapha.

But she abandoned her plan to kill him. For three reasons: one, she would never be able to escape from this place if he were dead; two, he was dying anyway, and she understood even that this terrible nasty mood he was in was because he knew he was dying; and three, his terrible nasty mood was completely gone the next morning and he told her how very sorry he was that he had slapped her and spanked her. He told her that he was completely ashamed of himself and would do anything to make it up to her.

"I wanted to be your husband," he said to her. "That was my plan. But it aint never gon work out that way. So if I caint be your husband, leastways I can be your daddy. And help ye to get ready for all you've got to know and do to get through this life."

She needed a minute to think about that. And then she said, "I don't want you to die, Daddy."

Chapter nineteen

Hell, he'd been madder at himself than he'd been at her or the damn dog. For the longest time he'd felt pretty sorry for himself, that this peculiar affliction was ravaging his body, but that self-pity had lately turned into self-loathing. It wasn't simply that his body had let him down, completely, but that he still had possession of his brain, and his brain was letting him down worse than his body was. If he had the sense to come in out of the rain, he ought to be able to figure out some way to save himself, to get help, or get to somebody who could help, and save the girl into the bargain.

On one of the rare days (and why did his sickness come and go, come and go, like that?) when he was feeling well enough to put on his pants and shoes, he sneaked off from Robin and found the trail that led to where he used to park the pickup. He had done such a good job of covering up the trail, and the stretch of thunderstorms had also contributed, that he could hardly find it himself, but he found it, and, dragging one leg behind him like the mummy in those old mummy movies he'd loved as a kid, he traced the trail to where the bluff began and the path narrowed to just a ledge clinging to the side of the bluff. He took only one step out onto the ledge before feeling such vertigo he was lucky to back away from it without falling to his death. But he could see that farther along, the ledge was totally knocked out by boulders fallen in a mudslide. So that ledge, which he had traversed hundreds of times in stocking up the place, was no longer an option. He considered trying to climb down the bluff and going beneath it to reach the ravines that led to the gullies that led to the place where he'd burned the truck. But he realized that he was simply in no condition for such climbing and hiking.

On another good day he had the strength to try to braid Robin's hair, at her request. She said her mother often braided her hair, and she tried to show him how, and he tried his best, but couldn't really do it, and it made him mad. He offered to give her a haircut but she said she was never going to cut her hair.

On another good day he decided it was time to teach her how to line bees and find a hive of honey. He took his axe and crosscut saw, as well as his rifle, and she carried the four empty buckets, in one of them a bait of a corncob smeared with some of what little honey they had left. He'd only got one jar of honey from the store because he anticipated being able to find his own. Since they both had to give up such things as ice cream (he loved the stuff as much as she did, and missed it mightily), it would be good to have other ways of keeping the sweet tooth happy.

Dragging his leg behind him like the monster in those old Frankenstein movies, he led her and the dog for almost half a mile out into the deepest woods, where they set up that bait of honeyed corncob on a piece of bark in a glade. And then, as he explained to her, it was sort of like fishing: you just had to sit and wait. Wait for a bee to show up and discover the honey and then for the bee to head back for the hive to tell the other bees about it.

While they sat, and Bitch took a snooze, they got to talking about some things that was a-bothering them. He was in the habit of complaining, at least once a day, that his affliction must be God's punishment on him. And now when he said it again, she wanted to know what specifically was God a-punishing him for. Besides, of course, stealing a innocent little girl. As if that wasn't enough. Well, he thought back (he was having terrible problems with his memory these days) and told her near about every bad thing he'd ever done in his life that he might be paying the price for. Going all the way back to his schooldays, when he was the worst hell-raiser Stay More school had ever seen, and Miss Jerram had her hands full trying to deal with all his cussedness and wickedness. There was one time he used a baseball bat to break the arm of a kid he didn't like. Another time he actually branded his initial "A" with a red-hot nail onto the chest of a kid he "owned." The worst thing he'd done was to get even with some poor kids by killing their mule. And Miss Jerram when she found out about it made him dig a grave for the mule and give a speech at the mule's funeral. It had been humiliating.

"Miss Jerram," he related to Robin, "she. Wudn't. Bogzh. Fur-rup. Thog. Ervcrs. Since. Hard." He stopped because Robin was looking at him peculiar.

"What did you say?" Robin asked.

He suddenly realized that in addition to all his other misfor-tunes he was losing the power of speech. His tongue and his vocal chords seemed to be turning into rawhide. He grabbed his jaw and gave it a shake, but that didn't help much. "Ahrg. Riggin. Ahrg. Cain. Tawg," he managed to say.

"No wonder," she said. "That's a horrible story. What did you kill the mule with?"

"Stig," Sog said.

"You stuck the mule? What with?"

"*Stig,*" he said, and pantomimed the piece of timber that he had bashed over the mule's skull.

"That's horrible."

"Ahrg. Cain. Tawg," he complained and pointed to his frozen jaw.

"Then just hush up," she said, and sat there seeming like she was just a-thinking about what a bad boy he had been. But then she said, "Now I'll tell you about all the bad things I did. That I'm being punished for." And she started in to telling him all this stuff that she had done. She had once prayed that a certain girl would die, a girl who was very popular in school and the only one smarter than her. The girl hadn't died, but she'd come down with scarlet fever and missed most of her classes. Another girl who had annoyed Robin got herself pushed so hard while she was swinging in the swings that she shot right out of her swing-seat and broke her arm, and Robin denied to the teachers that she had done it, although she later bragged about it to the other girls.

"Keeb. Yur. High. On. Thatur. Kobb," he told her, but he had to sign-language his meaning by pointing first to his eye and then to the honeyed cob that was their bait.

Robin went on telling all the times she'd misbehaved or done something wrong, picking on other kids and being an all-around scamp and rascal. To hear her tell it, she'd been the holy terror of the school, just as Sog had been the holy terror of his, and he couldn't help wondering sort of wishful-like what it would have been like if they'd been in school together, if Robin had been in the second grade with him at Stay More schoolhouse and they could have conspired to make life miserable for old Miss Jerram. He wanted to tell her this, but realized he had lost the power of speech. He hoped that maybe the power would come back again, just as he had good days as well as bad days with this disease, whatever it was. He had promised Robin that some day he would tell her all about Stay More, all the interesting people who had lived there and the very few who still did, and for him to do all that telling he'd have to be able to talk good again. She'd already asked him the names of the families who had lived in Stay More so she could give these names to the families of paper dolls that she'd been cutting out and dressing up for a town she had decided to call Stay More instead of Robinsville, which was the name she'd already given a town back home.

If he couldn't talk plain any more, they were really sunk, because he was counting on being able to tell her stories about Stay More as a substitute for the fact they couldn't never again watch the TV or ever go to the movies or nothing.

"Hreapha!" said Bitch, and Sog looked around to see what the dog was barking at. But there wasn't nothing nowheres. "Bidge," he said. "Was gog yur?"

"Look," Robin said. "She's spotted a bee!"

And sure enough, the darn dog had pointed a bee alighting

on the honeyed cob. The three of them watched as the bee took its fill of the honey and then flew away. Sog tried to tell her that now all they had to do was wait a bit more and that bee would fly back to its bee tree to tell the other bees of its discovery and before long there would be a bunch of them going back and forth from the bait to the bee tree and all they'd have to do is try and follow them. "Urs ussuns waig orwell," Sog tried to explain, but all he could do was lay his hand on Robin's arm as a sign of staying more. They waited.

By and by, that good old bee-dog said "Hreapha" once again, and here come a line of bees making for the cob. They lit, filled up on the honey, flew off and up, circling around and then headed the way they'd come, and Sog got to his feet and motioned for Robin to get up too. But old Bitch was ahead of them and she took off after the bees, so they just had to follow her. Sog wished he still lived in Stay More so he could spread the word about this incredible dog who could line bees.

Sure enough, Bitch led them to this middling-size white oak tree with a bulge and a crack halfway up, and the bees swarming in and out of that crack. "Shud far!" Sog exclaimed.

The main problem with not being able to talk was that he now had to explain a crucial thing about bees to Robin but couldn't do it. Bees will only sting you if you're afraid of 'em. If you don't fight 'em or swat at 'em or nothing, but just act calm and still, they won't sting you. It was going to be hard to get this across to Robin but he tried his best with pantomime and going through all the motions of trying to get her to keep real still. He was able to say "Saw," which is what you say to a cow to keep her calm.

Bitch was sniffing around the trunk of the bee tree, and when she commenced barking again he figured it was just because she knew this was the right tree, but he took a look and there were some bear tracks around the base of the trunk! Bear! He knew how bears sure did crave honey, and he found claw marks on the trunk which seemed to indicate the bear had tried to climb the tree to get at the honey. Sog asked himself whether he ought to tell Robin that a bear had been here. No sense in scaring her, right now, but he had warned her that time she'd tried to run away that the bears or wolves would get her if she were out in the woods by herself. He knew there weren't any wolves in Newton County, maybe a few coyotes, but not any big bad wolves. But he'd seen black bears himself. Yes, I'll tell her, he said, and pointed at the bear tracks and said, "Mawr." He tried again, "Parr." But he couldn't say the name right. He motioned for her to stand a good distance back while he cut down the bee tree.

He hadn't hit the trunk more than a few licks with his axe when he felt the first sting. It sure don't do you a lot of good to know that you keep still to keep from being stung if you have to swing an axe. "Gahrdommid," he swore, and backed off and waited a while.

By the time he got the tree cut down, he'd been stung maybe a dozen times, but he knew from past experience that after a while the sting doesn't sting as much; the more you get stung the less you feel it. He'd heard stories about bee stings being good for arthritis, rheumatism and all kinds of other problems in the joints, and he figured maybe his foot might even stop dragging like the mummy's or Frankenstein's.

They got four buckets full to the brim with honey, but poor Robin herself got stung a few times in the process, and she didn't like it one bit. He gathered up the leaves of three separate plants—he didn't know which plants they were but according to the ages-old remedy it didn't matter which three so long as there was exactly three—and crushed the leaves together and applied them to her bee stings and to his, and the relief was almost instantaneous, but still she was pissed off. He wished he could speak and be philosophical. If he could be philosophical he could tell her that everything in this life worth getting requires being stung a few times. Thinking about this on the way home, he realized the main drawback of losing the power of speech wasn't that he wouldn't be able to tell her all those Stay More stories but that he wouldn't be able to tell her his philosophical thoughts about how the world was just no damn good, life was a joke, the world was full of meanness and wrongdoing and corruption and selfishness and evil and backstabbing and shoddy merchandise and wickedness and bum raps and disorderly conduct and weakness and malpractice and greed and moral turpitude and what not. It had been his plan to learn her to appreciate the isolation of this wilderness that protected her from all that badness and transgression. But how could he do it if he couldn't talk? Thinking of his bee stings and hers and the tried and true folk remedy he'd applied to the stings, he also thought of all the things he had to learn her about the old ways, the uses of plants, the phases of the moon, the reading of signs. What kind of teacher can't even talk?

On the way home he spotted the tracks of a wild turkey! "Darg eek," he exclaimed, and pantomimed the swagger of a turkey tom and flapped his arms to represent its wings, but he couldn't get across to her that somewhere out here in these woods their Thanksgiving dinner was a-running around loose.

When he got home after toting all that honey plus his axe and crosscut and rifle, even with her help, he was plumb dead on his feet and could only crawl into bed with Dr. Jack D's remedy. There he remained for several more days, thinking philosophical thoughts not only about all the stuff that was wrong with the world but how life itself was just one big joke that wasn't even funny, and the biggest joke was that if you ever got to finding anything good about life you'd soon enough discover that the only thing that mattered about life is that it comes to an end, by and by. There was this good old funeral hymn everbody used to sing, that Miss Jerram had got them to sing at that mule's funeral, which said that farther along we'll know all about it, farther along we'll understand why, but Sog wasn't too sure he'd ever be able to know all about it or understand nothing.

He didn't even have any notion what time of year it was. What was left of the garden was still producing some fine maters, as well as all the melons they could eat, and although some of the nights had got right crimpy the days was still warm enough to indicate that summer wasn't quite done by a long shot. But he figured that it must be at least well into September, and the next morning he woke up feeling tolerable he decided it was time for Robin's birthday.

He put on his overalls for the first time since he'd been a-bee-ing, and went out to the kitchen and stirred hisself around and set into making a birthday cake for Robin. He hadn't forgot how, and they had quite a few boxes of cake mix that all you have to do is follow the directions.

"What are you doing?" Robin asked him.

"Awr, og us ursings ur sprose," he tried to get around telling her what he was up to, and she left him alone.

While the cake was in the oven, he went into the storeroom and fished in some of the bags and brought out the pretty packages of birthday gift wrap that he'd stocked up on, and some ribbons and Scotch tape. Then he picked out from the hoard assorted little toys and games, as well as this one real nice dress that he'd bought her at the Wal-Mart, and a couple of pretty sweaters. That was more than he'd intended to give her at any one of her birthdays, but he might not even be around for the next one. He wrapped everything up nice and pretty. He sent Robin out to dig up taters, both Irish and sweet taters. And while the oven was still hot he put in a cut of ham off that razorback they'd slaughtered. The meat hadn't been smoked yet, but that wasn't necessary for just a cut of ham.

He served her a fine dinner and then afterward he brought out the cake, with candles lit on top and all. "Hubby bart deg tyoo," he tried to sing but gave it up and just set the cake on the table.

"Oh!" Robin said. "Oh!" she said again. "Is it my birthday?"

"Yur aid," he said. "Hubby bart deg."

And then he brought out all the wrapped presents and she had such a lot of fun opening them one by one. Too bad that dress was too small, and he realized that when he'd got all her clothes he hadn't even thought that she'd ever outgrow them. He reckoned that he had probably hoped she'd stay seven years old for the rest of her life. But now that she was eight, did he no longer desire her? That was a dumb question, since he didn't have no desire to speak of nohow.

"Oh!" she said, taking the wraps off a game. "A Ouija Board! I always wanted a Ouija Board!"

It was just a plain old game board with all this stuff written on it: all the letters of the alphabet and all the numbers, plus "Yes." "No." "Good Bye." There was a three-legged gizmo that was the only game piece, and Robin explained how you use it. Trouble was, you're supposed to rest your fingertips gently on that three-legged doodad, but his hands was so shaky he couldn't do it without jiggling the darn thing. And what it was supposed to do was answer any questions you might have, and he couldn't ask any questions without the power of speech. So they just had to make do with Robin's questions. They started off with easy questions, like "Is this September 12?" and the pointer thing crept its way over to the "Yes." So it really was her birthday, after all! If you could believe that pointer, What is the dog's real name? they asked the Ouija board, and it moved bit by bit to the letter H, the letter R, the letter E, the letter A, the letter P, the letter H again, and the letter A again. "Roffa," said Robin, which was what Bitch always said.

By and by, Robin asked the Ouija Board, "Will I ever see my mommy again?"

The board said, "Yes."

When she asked the Board, "Is Sugrue going to get well?" he wanted to stop her, but his curiosity got the better of him.

"No," said the damned board.

Chapter twenty

Her ambitious project for some time had been to procure a kitten as a birthday present for Robin. She herself had had only one birthday so far, the previous winter. Since it is the lot of most animals not even to know, let alone to observe, their birthdays, she had not expected that hers would be special. She had observed it simply by digging up her favorite bone, declaring *I am one,* and wishing herself a happy birthday. Of course she had realized the ambiguity of her words: not simply that she was one year old but that she was one fine dog, she was number one, one of the best, one of those, one to reckon with. She had been happily surprised later when Yowrfrowr had shown up in her yard, saying A pity I have no gifts for you but I do want to give you a birthday lick. And he had given her a birthday lick and then had tried to become more romantic than that, but the man had come out of the house and run him off.

Now with the approach of September she had wanted desperately to see Yowrfrowr again, and had given much consideration to exploring the environs south of the farmstead in search of any remaining trace of the old trail that Adam Madewell had used to reach Stay More when he went to school there. The *in-habit* had told her he could describe the route and which landmarks to watch for, but he couldn't take her or go with her, because it would lead beyond his haunt, that is, beyond the area of places that he was allowed to frequent. He also advised that she shouldn't attempt to hike the trail, which was a long and possibly treacherous journey that had broken some of his bones the last time he'd tried to use it, when he was ten. His warning didn't scare her sufficiently, because she had powerful motives: simply to enjoy canine companionship again, to tell Yowrfrowr of this particular situation she was in and Robin was in and the man was in, get his opinions thereof, and even, if nature so dictated, permit Yowrfrowr to assuage this peculiar nervousness she had been experiencing lately and the itching in her afterplace. But her principal motive, overriding the others, was this: she wanted to see if she couldn't take possession of one of those kittens that overpopulated the yard of Yowrfrowr's house. Hreapha had never bothered to count, but there were always dozens of felines on the premises, often openly and flagrantly engaged in procreation, and consequently no one would even notice if Hreapha removed one of the kittens, seizing the nape of its neck gently in her mouth as she had observed mother cats doing, and, carrying it thus, transporting it all the way back up to Madewell Mountain, and giving it to Robin, who wanted a kitten so badly. Could she do it? It was a challenge, and one that consumed many of Hreapha's waking thoughts.

But as Robin's birthday neared, Hreapha became frantic with the realization that such a journey would take at least one overnight and possibly two or three, and there was simply no way she could explain to the man, let alone to Robin the potential beneficiary, her disappearance.

As luck would have it, on one of Hreapha's frequent visits to the beaver pond to visit with her friends there and make sure they were all right, she encountered once again that audacious bobcat who had previously killed one of the beaver kits and had apparently not been sufficiently deterred by the whipping Hreapha had given it. Hreapha wasn't in the mood for further fighting; her body still ached and hurt from the time the man had kicked her into the beaver pond; but she resented the bobcat for not having learned its lesson in the first fight. So she attacked it again, and not only drove it away from the beaver pond but chased it for some distance through the woods. It was apparently trying to reach the safety of its den or lair when it stepped upon, or was attacked by, a copperhead snake. Copperheads are just as venomous as rattlesnakes, if not more so, and Hreapha had long learned to give them both a wide berth. The bitten bobcat staggered on toward its den, which was actually a nest of leaves in a hollow log, but just managed to reach the opening to the log when the venom took full effect and the bobcat crumpled and, calling out a sound that was like a dying calf's, expired. Hreapha nudged it with her nose to make sure it was absolutely lifeless.

The dying-calf sound came again, and Hreapha thought possibly the bobcat was still alive, but when she looked into the hollow log, there was a bobkitten, a lone bobkitten, saying *woo* again and again. Hreapha's first thought was to wonder if Robin would object to a kitten who said *woo* instead of *meow*. The bobkitten, oblivious or indifferent to Hreapha's presence, came out of the hollow log and attempted to nurse from its dead mother. Hreapha was touched. Poor kitty, she said. Where's your brothers and sisters? It occurred to her that a feline as large as a bobcat might not have a litter of more than one or two.

Hreapha waited until the poor kitty had discovered that it wasn't going to be able to get any milk from the dead mother, and then she gently chomped the nape of the kitten's neck, lifted it, and began the trek back home. The kitten remained motionless, as if paralyzed by the clasp of its neck in Hreapha's jaws. But when eventually Hreapha reached home and set the kitten down in order to announce her return and her gift, the kitten attempted to run away, and Hreapha had to chase and catch it and seize its neck again. She mounted the porch and scratched at the door. Because of the bobkitty in her mouth, she couldn't call out "Hreapha!" meaning *Happy Birthday,* but she could scratch the door and whimper, and finally Robin opened the door.

And you never saw such an astonished expression on anybody's face! "What have you caught, Hreapha?" she said. "Is it alive?"

To demonstrate its possession of life, Hreapha gently set it

down, and it immediately hollered *WOO! WOO! WOO!* and ran
under the davenport.

"GURFLAGE!" yelled the man. "Laud faint bub cut! Wul
sought my hide!"

Robin was full of questions which, alas, Hreapha could not
answer, the chief one being "What is it?" but also "Where did you
get it?" "How old is it?" "Is it a boy or a girl?" She got down on her
knees and peered under the davenport and studied it closely. And
began to answer her own questions: "It's some kind of kitty. Hreapha
must have found it somewhere. It's just a baby. And I think it's a boy.
Come on out, kitty. Here kitty kitty."

"BUB CUT!" yelled the man. "Glodge plairn fugadaze!"

"Can I keep him?" Robin asked.

"Wul hail far hit'sa wile beast," the man said.

Robin had succeeded in fishing the critter out from under the
davenport and was cradling it in her arms, where it began to purr.

"Hreapha," said Hreapha, that is, Happy Birthday.

"Thank you so much," Robin said. "It's the best birthday present I ever had."

Having determined, despite the man's atrocious mispronun-
ciation, that it was a bobcat kitten, Robin decided to name him
"Robert." She fetched one of her dollbaby's bottles, which had a real
nipple on it. She filled it with Pet Milk, and her new pet had its first
meal in Robin's arms.

"Floszh," commented the man. Then he slowly and painfully
rose to his feet and, taking one of his bottles, went off to bed, or, since
the feather mattress was being aired in the yard from an accumulation
of his markings upon it, his pallet on the floor.

"Thank you for the Ouija Board and everything," she called to
him, but he did not respond. He proceeded to guzzle the bottle.

Robert the kitten continued guzzling his bottle, and at length
fell asleep. Robin set him down on a corner of the davenport. "I'll
show you my other presents," Robin said to Hreapha. And she showed
her the dress and the sweaters and the toys, including the Ouija
Board, which she set up on the floor, suggesting, "Let's see if you
can play. Can you put one of your paws on this?" And she took one

of Hreapha's forefeet and set it upon a kind of miniature table with three legs. "Now I will ask a question, and put my fingertips here beside your paw, and this planchette will start moving until it finds the answer. Okay? I've already asked it how to spell your name and it spelled it out, H-R-E-A-P-H-A. So I know that's your real name, and you'll never be 'Bitch' again. Let's ask it: How many years will Hreapha live?"

Hreapha felt the planchette, as it was called, moving beneath her paw and she was prompted to bark. But she watched with fascination as the planchette moved to the numeral 1 and then to the numeral 9.

"Wow!" Robin said. "Nineteen years is a long life for a dog. Okay? How many years will *I* live?"

The planchette moved to the 8 and just stayed there.

"Oh-oh!" Robin commented. "This is scaring me. Does this mean that I'm going to die before my ninth birthday?" But the planchette was not absolutely motionless. It was moving but never departing from the 8, just circling it. Hreapha wished she could explain to Robin that that might mean it was doing the same numeral twice, that is, not 8 but 88. Robin would live to be eighty-eight years old.

"Let's ask it something else," Robin suggested, but she was clearly disturbed at the thought she might not live beyond this, her eighth year. "Would you like to find out who you will marry? Of course dogs don't have weddings, but would you like to know who your mate will be?"

Hreapha was not able to declare that she already knew, so she silently participated with her paw as the planchette spelled out the letters Y-O-W-R-F-R-O-W-R. Robin attempted to pronounce it: "Yowrfrowr! That's a cute name for a dog! Do you know any dogs named 'Yowrfrowr'?"

Hreapha moved the planchette to "Yes."

"Hey!" Robin exclaimed. "You can talk! You can answer yes or no questions. Are you and Yowrfrowr really, really good friends?"

"Yes."

"Does he live somewhere around here?"

Hreapha moved the planchette to "No." Of course it was

relative: "around here" could possibly mean Stay More, miles and miles away.

"Do you like Sugrue?"

That was easy. "No."

"He's not going to live much longer, is he? I was playing the Ouija Board with him when you came back with Robert, and we asked it if he was going to get well, and it said No."

The planchette was still resting on the "No," and Hreapha tapped it with her paw.

"Could we ask the Ouija Board how much longer he's going to live?" she suggested.

Hreapha was not comfortable learning so much about the future, but she consented, and they jointly "rode" the planchette as it moved to the 1 and circled it, meaning 11, then to the two and the three. 1,2,3. Maybe the planchette was just proving it knew the basic numbers. Did it mean that he was going to live for 123 days? No, it had circled the one, doubling it, so that would be 1123. That many days?

It was Robin who figured it out. "I think it is just trying to tell us the month and the day. Eleven twenty-three. The eleventh month is November. Sugrue will die on the twenty-third of November."

"Hreapha," Hreapha commented, meaning *I can hardly wait.*

But Robin said, "I don't want him to die. If he dies, we are going to be in trouble."

"Hreapha," Hreapha said, meaning, *That remains to be seen.*

"Okay, let's ask it who I am going to marry," Robin suggested. And she put her fingertips on the planchette along with Hreapha's paw. The planchette moved quickly to the letter A but stalled there and would go no further. They waited and waited, and then the planchette moved its way to the word that spelled "Goodbye."

"Well, goodbye yourself," Robin said to the Ouija Board, and put it back in its box.

In the weeks ahead, Robert grew so rapidly that both Hreapha and Robin had their hands full with his education and training. There is a natural antipathy between felines and canines and Robert did not like Hreapha, avoiding her and sometimes even hissing at her.

But they were bedmates, the two of them sleeping every night with Robin on the aired-out feather mattress, while the man continued to sleep on the pallet on the floor, which he frequently marked, requiring its daily airing out.

The nights were beginning to grow cold, so Hreapha appreciated that she was able to get under the covers with Robin, even if she had to share the covers with a creature who was so thoroughly nocturnal he couldn't sleep at night, and did most of his sleeping in the daytime. But Robin took him to bed with her every night anyway, and fell asleep herself with one arm around Robert and the other around Hreapha, whereupon, as soon as she was asleep, Robert would begin pestering Hreapha, hissing in her ear and nibbling on her flews, and trying to get Hreapha to fool around. By day, when Robin was playing with Robert (she seemed to have forgotten her paper dolls and her paper doll town), it was fun to watch the kitty rough-housing and running around, but at night the kitten was a nuisance. Hreapha endeavored to teach the kitten her own language, but the kitten wasn't interested and would not respond to any instruction or commands that Hreapha tried to give him.

One instruction that was imperative, and to which Hreapha devoted considerable time, with some help from Robin, was letting Robert understand in no uncertain terms that he was not to chew upon any of the baby chicks. Even though there was a great surplus of them, since both roosters had been busy fertilizing the hens, and the hens had sat upon and hatched countless eggs, and there were chicks of various ages all over the place. Robert loved to chase them, which was permissible, and to catch and play with them, which was all right up to a point, but Hreapha knew that if he ever killed one he would become hopelessly feral and bloodthirsty, and she did her best to prevent that from happening. Robert loved water, and his favorite swimming place was Hreapha's water dish, which made the water taste off.

One night, the last night of that autumn when it wasn't too cold to swim, and the moon was full so that a kerosene lantern wouldn't be needed, Robin got out the Ouija Board just long enough to ask Hreapha a yes-or-no question. "Should we take him to the beaver pond?" After some deliberation, realizing that Robert might grow up to get along with the beaver if he was introduced to them at an early age, Hreapha moved the planchette to "Yes" and they escorted Robert to the beaver pond. Since neither Robin nor Hreapha could communicate with the beaver in their language, they had a bit of a problem persuading the beaver that this kitten, who was their natural enemy, only wanted to use the pond for bathing purposes. But after a while they accepted him, or at least tolerated his frisky plunge into their pool. Both Hreapha and Robin joined him, although Robin shrieked with the coldness of the water. They didn't have to worry about the man coming and finding them.

The man spent nearly all of his nights, and most of his days, in a state of constant drunkenness, getting up from the pallet or the davenport only to grab his crutches—he had fashioned a pair of crutches out of saplings—and hobble off to the outhouse, the only exercise he got, which was futile, because he was rarely able to leave anything behind at the outhouse. He seemed to have forgotten that Hreapha existed, never speaking to her or trying in his garbled speech to give her a word, kind or unkind, and she realized eventually that he probably couldn't even see her; in addition to his other afflictions, he was going blind, or, if not blind, his vision was blurry and doubled: Robin told Hreapha that he had begun to think that there were two Robins, twins, or close look-alike sisters.

I have lived not because of you but despite you, Hreapha once said to him, but of course he couldn't hear her. She could not understand why she still felt any sense of duty or fidelity or any need to provide protection for him. It was probably just inbred.

But it was strong enough that she was torn with guilt when, eventually, she realized that she could no longer ignore the intensity of the new bodily feelings that overwhelmed her and left her markings with a musky new aroma. She was going to have to abandon him again, at a time when he might really have need of her. She would be leaving Robin too, and Robert, and all the poultry who depended upon her protection, but they did not disturb her as much as her forsaking him did. She went out to the cooper's shed and had a long chat with the *in-habit*, making sure that she understood his directions on how to find that trail that led to Stay More and how to stay on the trail if the trail no longer existed. Once again he warned her that she'd probably kill herself trying the trail, but he understood her desperation.

She wished there were some way she could explain her journey to Robin. Although she was smart enough to use the Ouija Board's "Yes" and "No," she was not smart enough to spell out words, to formulate language on the Ouija Board that would say, *Robin girl, I am going to have to go away for two or three days. You know about Yowrfrowr? Well, he has something that I have to have.*

There was nothing at all she could do. She had trouble enough explaining to her own *in-habit* that she was going to have to go away for a while. She cursed her body, she cursed her afterplace, she cursed her aromatic pee, but she went on peeing it, and then, one morning bright and early, all she could do was say to Robin, "Hreapha!" meaning, Goodbye for now, my dearest friend, I hope to see you again in a couple of days, three at the most.

And then to start trotting southward. Robin and Robert both tried to follow her, and she could only turn and yell, "HREAPHA!" meaning, I'm not going to the beaver pond. I'm going to Stay More.

And then to run so fast that they could not keep up with her.

Part Three
Without

Chapter twenty-one

They let him go, and he sure went. The first thing he done, which was the reason he'd come back to Harrison in the first place (you can bet your life it wasn't to see that crabby old grass widow he was married to) was to take his pickup to the used car lot and trade it in on a four-wheel drive. It was a trade-down, naturally, and he wound up with a piece of junk that reminded him of that bald-tired four-by-four his opponent had been a-driving, only his tires had good treads on them. So he could get to places that he hadn't been able to reach with two-wheel drive. Many a time he'd been required to either turn back, on some hairpin climb in Searcy County or Newton County, or else strike out on foot for the rest of the way, and usually only to discover after a long hike that the supposed abandoned house had fallen in completely or was still just a-setting there empty except for rats and mice.

You'd be surprised how many empty houses there is at the end of the road all over the Ozarks. It kind of made Leo sad, at the thought that families had once lived there, and children had played, and people had worked hard to squeeze a living out of their rocky acres, only to have it come to nothing. Leo wondered what had become of them. He knew most of 'em had probably gone to California, like everbody else. Or else they'd moved into one of the big towns like Springdale or Fayetteville or Harrison, and enjoyed the comforts of city living. It was a real shame they'd never been able to find a buyer for their house, and Leo found a few houses that was really in pretty fair shape, and he even imagined himself taking possession of one of them. In fact, Leo entertained himself as he roamed the highways and byways (he didn't much care for music or gospel preachers on the pickup's radio) by having daydreams of moving into one of those abandoned farmsteads.

Of course his ideal location wouldn't be up here on one of these godforsaken mountaintops but down along the river somewhere, and he'd found plenty of abandoned houses where the old road stopped at the river. For most of his life, until he'd more or less quit it in order to give all his time to the search for Robin, Leo had earned his living as a guide on the Buffalo River, taking rich sportsmen from Little Rock or as far away as St. Louis, KC and Chicago, out in johnboats to float the Buffalo and fish for linesides and goggle-eyes. He knew ever inch of that river and couldn't nobody direct the sportsmen to the best fishing spots better than he could. His customers always gave him a nice tip over and beyond the fee. Leo was constantly hoping that he'd find Robin safely living in some cabin at a dead-end along the river. If she was, and according to his daydreams after he'd shot and killed or taken prisoner that guy who'd stolen her, Mr. Bald Tires, why, he intended to return Robin straight to her mother, and then collect the reward and get his pitcher in the papers. And then he supposed he could just spend the rest of Robin's growing-up years giving her presents and being a nice grandpappy to her and admiring her.

The abandoned houses of the Ozarks was spread out all over northwest Arkansas and southwest Missouri, and Leo had already found quite a few of them in Missouri and intended to find quite a few more now that he had a four-by-four pickup. He was keeping track and whenever he found one of the places he had one of these here yeller high-lighters that he smeared around the little white empty square on the map that meant the dwelling was no longer dwelt-in (if it was black, it meant that it was occupied, but Leo had discovered a number of black ones that was empty too, so his maps was mostly out of date). There was just about the same number of empty houses up on the ridges and mountaintops as there was down along the river or off in some flat plateau somewheres.

It was the ones up high that made him need the four by four, and sure enough, as soon as he got the truck and headed south from Harrison (he could never forget that was the direction Mr. Bald Tires had headed), he found himself climbing a rough trail that led up a mountain near Gum Springs, south of Jasper in Newton County, a trail he couldn't possibly have climbed in his old pickup, the way it turned every whichaway and was full of washouts and mud holes and his pickup had a real work-out getting there. And when he got to the end of the road and stopped at the house, he saw at once the house wasn't really abandoned. There was chickens and pigs all about, and a garden patch. A man with a shotgun came out of the house, somebody Leo hadn't never seen before, and the man just pointed the gun at him and said, "Well?"

"Looks like a dead end, don't it?" Leo said.

"It's the end but it aint dead," the man said.

"You live here all by yourself?" Leo asked.

"Just me and the old woman," the man said.

"How old is the woman?" Leo wanted to know but that question was answered directly when the woman herself came out. She was old, all right.

"What does he want?" the woman asked her man.

"He wants to know if he can back up and turn around and get the hell out of here," the man said to her, and then he said to Leo, "Yes, I believe you can."

That was the second time he'd found people still living in a supposed abandoned house. The other time there'd been three women living together who'd pointed their rifle at him and driven him off. He figured most people who'd want to live at the end of the road wouldn't care for company.

But the third time he found people still on the premises of a deserted house, he wasn't turned away. It was in rough hill country over in Madison County, way up on the highest peak for miles around, and after climbing in low-lock for a mile over some terrible boulders, he came out into a field, and there was a young lady with her titties hanging out, why, she didn't have hardly nothing on but a too-tight pair of cut-off blue jeans, and a string of beads around her neck. He didn't know whether to wave or just pretend he never seen her. "Howdy," he managed to say as he drove up beside her. Her hair come pretty near to her waist. "Does this here road go anywheres?" he asked, conversation-like, without staring at her bosoms.

"You don't look like a narc," she said. "Boss. The house is right down there, Daddy."

He drove on, and the next thing he saw was another girl who didn't have nothing on. Not a stitch except some beads around her neck and a big floppy hat on her head. He decided not to speak to her. A little beyond her, he come to the house, which might've been abandoned not too long ago but now looked like people were sure enough living in it, and out in the yard of the house was a whole bunch of young folks, most of 'em naked as jaybirds, in mixed company besides, boys as well as girls.

When he stopped the pickup, one young feller with his pecker hanging halfway to his knees came over to him and said, "You're not the landowner, are you?"

"Who, me?" Leo asked. "Naw, I don't own this land." He could smell the smoke of mary jane in the air.

"Too much, man. Were you looking for someone?"

"Yeah, just a little girl."

"Your daughter? What does she look like?"

"Just my step-granddaughter, and she's seven going on eight, long blonde hair."

The young feller laughed. "Freaking, man. Nobody that young around here, man."

One of the stark naked girls came up beside the young man and wrapped her arm around him and said to Leo, "Daddy, I thought for a minute you were my father. But you're not. Cool." She was looking him over so much that he didn't think she'd mind him staring at her titties. And her bush. "What's your thing?" she asked.

"Thing?" he said. The only thing he knew about was what he'd once told Robin was his mousy, and it was a-starting to stir in a way he hadn't known for quite a spell.

"Are you just some farmer?" she asked.

"Naw, I'm sort of a fisherman," he said, if she was talking about job occupation

"Solid," she said "But there's not any fish around here." She giggled.

The young feller said, "Turn off your motor, man, and blow some good shit with us."

Leo wasn't sure just what that invitation involved, but he turned off the motor and got out of the pickup and soon he was in the midst of all those young people and somebody handed him a rolled joint of mary jane. He used to use the stuff regularly in the Navy, but lately the only times he did was when one of his sportsmen customers was lighting up along the Buffalo and passed the joint to Leo just to be polite, and he didn't smoke too much because he had to steer the johnboat.

But he smoked a lot that day. He smoked so much of it that he stopped feeling self-conscious on account of he was the only one with his clothes on and also the only one over thirty years of age. The smoking made him forget eventually that he wasn't under thirty, but nearly twice that, and before long he had also stopped being the only one who still had clothes on.

They invited him to crash, and he hoped they weren't talking about having him start up the truck and ram it into a tree or nothing. Some girl told him he was a gas, and he wondered if he had accidentally broke wind. Several people urged him to hang loose, and he was a little nervous about what they might be planning to do with him. "You're making the scene, Daddy," another girl said to him, and he wondered what he was supposed to do. They fed him some dish of rice and vegetables that was okay, nothing special, with home brew to wash it down. And after supper some of them got out their guitars and played rock and roll music, and he was invited to dance with some of the naked girls. Later one of the gals, a little on the hefty side, rubbed up against him and said, "You're mellow, man. Want to be my old man tonight and ball me?" He didn't like being reminded of his age, but whatever she had in mind he was ready for. Her name was Misti Dawn, and she showed him some real fancy fucking which must've been the fruit of lots of experience.

He stayed three or four days there with those young folks. He hated to leave, and they didn't want him to leave, but he had to remind himself that he had a mission, and he'd been neglecting it to enjoy himself. By the time he left he had even learnt what some of their language meant, "spaced" and "trip" and "way out" and "downer" and "happening" and all such as that. He had had plenty of mary jane as well as home brew and even something called acid which made him see things and scared him for a few hours. He was afraid if he stayed any longer he wouldn't want to leave. So he left.

But they traded him his ordinary clothes for some striped blue jeans with the first bell-bottoms he'd had since the Navy, and a fancy embroidered shirt, and they put what little hair he had in back into a pony tail with a ribbon around it, and that's what he was looking like the next time Louisa seen him.

"Where on earth have you been, and what on earth have you been doing?" she wanted to know.

"Outa sight," he said. And he stayed just long enough to see if the square world was still going round. The only development in the law's handling of Robin's case was that a couple who'd been in the parking lot of the roller rink that night, maybe fucking in the back seat of their car, had seen a suspicious man and had described him so well that a new police composite sketch had been made, replacing the one that Leo had done and not looking anything like that feller. The new suspect was actually identified as a known child molester recently released from Cummins prison, and there was a APB on him, with the state police and FBI concentrating on known places he had lived. That there FBI man who'd been so chummy with Robin's mother was spending all his free time with her, and the last thing Louisa said to Leo before he took off again was, "You might just get an FBI agent for your new son-in-law, so you'll have to watch your step, you old reprobate."

Leo looked over his maps and decided to see if he couldn't reach those places that he'd had to turn back from when his truck was just a two-wheel drive. One of them was up a mountain beyond the town of Snowball in Searcy County. The old Jeep trail climbed for a good two miles beyond the place where it left a good dirt road, and when Leo came in sight of the house he had a hunch or something that made him stop the truck and proceed on foot with the revolver tucked into the waistband of his bell-bottom blue jeans, with his embroidered shirt covering up the handle.

That way, he was able to catch 'em by surprise, and sure enough there was a old boy living there with a young girl, only she wasn't Robin, and she wasn't seven or eight but maybe thirteen. "How'd you find us?" the feller asked, and Leo knew that they was fugitives, and they was living here with a garden patch and a flock of chickens, and a spare room loaded up with food and supplies.

"I've just been looking everywhere for you," Leo said, which was practically the truth.

"Are you her father?" the man asked.

"Naw, I'm just her uncle, aint that right, sweetheart?" he said to the girl, and she nodded her head, playing along with his game.

"Trina, tell him I aint done nothing to you," the man requested of the girl.

"You know that's not true, Wayne," she said.

She held Leo's gun on Wayne while Leo tied Wayne up real good with some rope and put him in the back end of the pickup, and the girl rode up front with him. He figured he'd just take 'em both to the county seat at Marshall and hand 'em over to the sheriff. Making conversation, he asked, "How long has he been a-keeping you?"

"I don't know," she said. "I lost track. Maybe five or six years." She smiled real big, and said, "I'm so glad you found me. I thought nobody ever would. You're my hero. Could I give you a blow job?"

Leo slammed on the brakes and felt his old mousy unbending just at the thought. "That's real kind of ye," he said to her, driving on. "But I reckon I'd better take a raincheck on it."

As it turned out, when he'd delivered them to the sheriff at Marshall, the girl had been kidnapped five years previously, and the search for her had eventually been abandoned. Her kidnapper, Wayne Curtis, had a long rap sheet of child molesting and sex offenses.

Leo got his pitcher in the papers, with a story about how he'd actually been working on the famous Robin Kerr case when he accidentally stumbled upon the other one. But the reward offer had expired, so he didn't get nothing out of it except that raincheck, which he never got a chance to cash in.

The good deed gave him a right smart of pride and courage, though, and when he resumed his search for Robin he was filled with pep and renewed determination. As September rolled around, he was all set to give another try to a trail in Newton County that had turned him back in July. The country sure was pretty, what with the trees commencing to turn color, and all that red and orange warmed him up since the weather was getting cold and he had to wear his winter jacket. According to his map, there was this impassable Jeep trail that wandered all around the north end of a place called Madewell Mountain. He'd been able to climb less than a mile of it in his two-wheel-drive pickup before hitting a stretch that he couldn't negotiate. There was at least another mile or so of it to go to reach the white square that meant a uninhabited dwelling.

That was his destination now, and the hunch he'd played in finding that Trina girl was now hunching him over the steering wheel with shivers running up his hunched back. Something told him this was the big day.

But the damn trail just played out completely, far short of the goal. After getting stuck in one hole so rough and deep he had to get out and jack up the rear end and put rocks under the tires to go on a little ways more, he got into a gully that was really terrible and he couldn't go backward or forward, and spent two hours trying to jack the pickup up and get it out of there, without any luck. Since he couldn't go back the way he came, he figured he might as well just walk on, until he reached that house.

The trouble was, there just wasn't no trace whatsoever left of the trail. And the bluffs was steep and risky and the woods was deep and spooky, and it was beginning to get dark. He had a flashlight, and his revolver, and that was all he had to find his way to wherever he was trying to go.

Chapter twenty-two

She was so heartsick she couldn't eat. So she simply stopped eating. She didn't even bother to build a fire in the kitchen stove each morning, because Sugrue wasn't eating anything anyway. She built a fire in the living room stove just to keep warm. She made sure that Robert was fed, giving him his bottle with Pet Milk three times a day, and then tried gradually to wean him from his bottle by getting him interested in some of the canned goods: there were potted meats like deviled ham that he would eat. But there was nothing that she would eat. Not as long as Hreapha was gone.

She wondered if perhaps Hreapha had been eaten by a bear. Although the Ouija Board had once declared that Hreapha would live to be nineteen, which was really old, old age for a dog, there was a possibility that the Ouija Board was mistaken, just as a lot of things that require belief and faith are false: for instance, Robin had a hunch that there was no such thing as the Tooth Fairy, or, if there was, the Tooth Fairy had ignored the last two teeth she had left under her pillow. She had a third tooth almost ready to leave there, but had decided not to, out of fear it would prove beyond doubt that there is no such thing as a Tooth Fairy. And if the Ouija Board was wrong about Hreapha living to be nineteen, then it was also wrong that Sugrue was going to die. Some mornings he was able to get up and go out, hobbling on his homemade crutches, and although he couldn't do any work, and wasn't any good at talking, he was at least sobered up enough to listen to her.

When she told him she feared that a bear had eaten Hreapha, he simply said something that sounded like "Pigeon eat." More than once he said those words whenever she brought up the subject of Hreapha's disappearance. Was he trying to say that a pigeon had eaten Hreapha? Or perhaps that Hreapha had eaten a diseased pigeon which had caused her to get sick and die?

Although she accepted the possibility that the Ouija Board was wrong and that the Tooth Fairy did not exist, she refused to cease believing in spirits or whatever was unseen but clearly felt or known. She knew that there was some kind of invisible spirit who lived in the cooper's shed or spent most of its time there, and she had heard its voice clearly, that time she'd cured the pork. She was going to hear it again while doing the only work she would do during her time of sorrow over Hreapha: the smoking of the pork. One of the garbled things that Sugrue had said, whenever he said "Pigeon eat," was "Mokawg," and when several repetitions of mokawg failed to make any sense to her, he got his crutches and summoned her to follow him to the cooper's shed, where, on the dirt floor of the shed, he piled up an assortment of wood chips from the chopping stump and some of the accumulation of corncobs that they'd saved from their own corn on the cob and the chicken's winter supply of shelled corn. He built a fire and soon the interior of the shed was filled with smoke. He poked holes through the chunks of the razorback she had cured, and ran white oak splits through the holes and hung the meat from the joists of the cooper's shed.

He held up two fingers and then three fingers, "Toodaze. Freed-aze," he said, and hobbled on back to the house, leaving her to figure out that she was expected to keep the fire going by adding more of the wood chips and more of the corncobs. But was she supposed to stay awake and watch it for two or three days?

Dadblast it, this aint a smokehouse, you idjits, said that voice she'd heard when she was curing the pork. And then the voice began coughing. She thought that was funny, that an invisible spirit which had no body and no lungs and no throat to cough with, would be coughing at the smoke. It made her cough too, but she had lungs and throat.

"Are you really coughing?" she asked. "Or just faking it?"

I'm jist a-making out like it, he said. *Paw would skin ye like a hog if he knew you was smoking up his workshop thisaway.*

"He started the fire, not me," she said and pointed toward the house where Sugrue had gone. She wondered if the spirit could see her point.

He is a miserable cuss, aint he? Bad enough when he could talk plain, much worser since he caint.

"How old are you?" she suddenly wanted to know.

Me? I reckon I must be about three, four years older'n you, gal.

"Is your name Adam?" she bravely asked.

How'd ye know?

"Sugrue told me how this place had belonged to the Madewells, and they had a boy named Adam. Do you just live out here in this shed all the time?"

Why, no, I wouldn't rightly call it such as that. But you'uns has stuffed my room with all them boxes and bags and such that a body couldn't turn around in there.

"The storeroom was your bedroom?" she asked.

Not was but is.

"I can't see you, you know," she pointed out. "And I think maybe I'm just imagining you. Maybe I'm just going crazy because Hreapha is lost."

Aw shoot, that dog aint lost. She's just gone down to Stay More for a visit with her friends.

"Really? Whenever I talk about Hreapha, Sugrue always says 'Pigeon eat.'"

Her invisible friend Adam laughed. It was a boyish laugh that was more than just the kind of giggle that Jimmy Chaney made when he laughed. *Don't he have a lot of trouble talking, though? I reckon what he was trying to say was 'Bitch in heat.' He was just trying to tell you that she's having her time of estrus.*

"What does that mean?"

There was silence, and then he said, *Darn, you're a-makin me blush. It aint fitten to talk about, but you know what she-dogs and he-dogs do when they get together?*

She thought about that for a while, and then she smiled and said, "Oh. So maybe she's just gone to Stay More to see her favorite he-dog, Yowrfrowr."

That's the one, he said. *I had to tell her how to get there, because it's a long ways over the roughest country you ever seen, and I aint even so sure she could've made it.*

"I feel a lot better, knowing she hasn't been eaten by a bear."

Aint nothing ever going to eat that dog.

"I'm sorry we're smoking up your father's workshop, but I don't know what else to do."

Our smokehouse aint standing no more. It was right over yonder. She could not see the way he was pointing, *if he was pointing. So I don't reckon it will do no harm to Paw's shop if you just go on and smoke your hog in here. But you caint stay awake all night tending the fire, so I'll help ye with it.*

"Thanks so much," she said. And that night she put more chips and corncobs on the fire and watched to be sure it would keep burning, and then she bundled up in her thickest jacket and with a blanket and pillow made herself comfortable outside the cooper's shed but close enough to keep an eye on it. And she eventually drifted off to sleep, with Robert joining her under the blanket. Sometime late in the night or early morning she was awakened—maybe Robert did it—she was awakened by something and saw that the fire was dying out, and got up to add more chips and cobs to it.

She smoked the meat for nearly three days, until it was good and dark reddish-brown. Every time the fire was getting too low while she slept, she would be awakened again, but her new friend never spoke, although she occasionally called to him, saying "Hello?" This bothered her, and she wondered if he was tired of talking to her. Or if she had said anything to bother him. Eventually she decided that he wasn't really there, that she had just imagined him, that she had been talking aloud to herself.

When the smoking of the meat was all finished, and she had hung it up to keep in the storeroom, she returned to her neglected paper dolls. It was hard to play with her paper dolls when Robert was in the house, because he'd mess up her paper town of Stay More, which she had laid out so carefully and populated with dozens of paper dolls named Ingledew and Swain and Whitter and Duckworth and Coe and Dinsmore and Chism and so on. Now she wanted to put into the Stay More schoolhouse a paper doll named Adam Madewell, and she tried to imagine what he looked like. If he was three or four years older than she, he'd be twelve years old and in the fifth or sixth grade.

Late one cold afternoon Robin was standing on the porch of the house, admiring the pretty colors in the distant trees and in the yard, where a giant maple had turned bright red, when suddenly she heard, far out across the way, the name of her dog announcing her return home. Robin's heart nearly exploded with joy. And then she saw the dog, limping slowly across the field. Robin ran out to meet her.

"Hreapha!" Robin shouted gleefully.

"Hreapha," said the dog, and while there was happiness in the way she said it, there was also a kind of pain too, as if something was wrong with her.

Robin reached Hreapha long before Hreapha could reach her. And Robin knelt to hug the dog, but did so gently, astonished to see how hurt the poor dog was. "Oh, Hreapha," she cried, "what has happened to you?" And found herself astonished that she expected an answer, as if her friend could tell her the story of her adventure.

Hreapha could not even say her name. She could only whimper.

"Let's get you some food and water," Robin said, and tried to pick her up to carry her to the house, but Hreapha struggled and whined and had to be put down. So Robin walked slowly as Hreapha limped onward to the house, where Robert was so thrilled to see her that he forgot he hated dogs and jumped on her back and began

licking her. Robin drew a bucket of water from the well and rinsed
Hreapha's big plastic water dish, which Robert had been using as a
wading pool, and then held Robert back while she filled it so Hreapha
could have a drink.

For several days Hreapha did not feel like doing anything.
Robin made a pallet for her with an old blanket on the floor beside
the living room stove, which she kept running day and night. She
had a practiced swing with the axe, and was very good now at splitting firewood. Day by day the weather grew colder; there were even
dustings of snow. On one of her trips to the woodpile, Robin stopped
in at the workshop/smokehouse and said, "Hello? Adam? Would you
like to come in the house and keep warm?" She waited a long time
for an answer, but it never came, and made her realize that Adam
was just a figment of her imagination, whose voice had come to her
only when she was in desperate need of help.

She didn't need any help now. She kept everything going. She
had always been strong-willed but now she had to be stronger than
ever. Her appetite had returned with Hreapha's return and she did
a good job in the kitchen, although Sugrue didn't much care for
anything she tried to fix for him. She wondered if there was something in whiskey that was nourishing and a good substitute for food.
She learned all on her own how to make a good ham omelet, with
onions that had been dried from the garden, and it was so tasty she
had it several times a week. She always ate too fast, much too fast,
but simply assumed that was because her appetite was good. She
appreciated that there was no one to remind her to wash her hands
before supper, although she wished her mother was still around to
nag her about it, and she thought of her mother when she usually
washed her hands anyway. She wished her mother could be there to
praise her for being clean and to sample her cooking. After enjoying a scrumptious ham omelet, she followed it up with one of her
desserts: using the box of mix according to instructions, she made
perfect fudge brownies. A month earlier Sugrue had shown her the
location of a grove of pawpaw trees and they had brought home a
couple of sacks full of them to ripen, and there were still a few that
were ripening, and she had learned almost to like them as a kind of

inferior banana. No, she didn't need any help. She looked at herself in the mirror one morning and decided, "I don't look like myself." What she meant was that whatever self she had been thinking of herself as having was no longer there. Maybe her mother wouldn't recognize her. Whatever remained of her human self she now projected into her paper dolls, so that she became each of the citizens of her little town of Stay More and fabricated their lives for them, and did a passably good job of having them speak to each other. Hreapha and Robert always seemed to enjoy listening when she was talking in the voices of the citizens of Stay More as they lived through their lives. She wished her mother could listen to her talk about Stay More. Almost as much as missing her mother, she missed comic books, even more than she missed movies and television, and she took it for granted that she might never again see a comic book, so she would have to make up replacements for them.

The only drawback to her fabulous world of paper Stay More was that she had to do it all alone, even if Hreapha and Robert watched and listened. She really did not like playing alone. In fact she hated it. One day when Hreapha was feeling much better, Robin got out the Ouija Board again and got Hreapha to put her paw on the planchette and they asked a lot of easy, random questions, such as "Is there a Tooth Fairy?" ("NO.") And "Will Santa Claus be able to find his way to us out here in the woods?" ("NO.") And "What month is this?" ("N-O-V-E-M-B-E-R.") And "What day of the week is this?" ("T-H-U-R-S-D-A-Y.")

And then some questions like, "Did Hreapha find Yowrfrowr down in Stay More?" ("YES.") "Did they have a happy time together?" ("YES.") "Did Hreapha have a hard time reaching Stay More?" ("YES.") "Did Hreapha have a hard time coming home from Stay More?" ("YES.") "What happened?" ("C-O-Y-O-T-E-S.")

"My gosh," Robin said not to the Ouija Board but to Hreapha. "Were you attacked by coyotes?"

Hreapha moved the planchette to YES.

"You poor thing," Robin said, and thought about it and wished that Hreapha could give her details. "I guess you're lucky they didn't eat you." Robin had searched Hreapha's hide thoroughly, hunting for ticks (the best thing about the coming of cold weather was that the ticks and chiggers went into hibernation) and also for any wounds: she had found a few deep scratches and had used ointment from the first aid kit on the worst ones.

Robert didn't like being excluded from their Ouija Board game, so Robin decided to see if she could teach them how to play Hide and Seek. Hreapha caught on very quickly, although Robert was too impatient to wait while he was "it" to give the other two time to hide. There was no way to explain it to him, so they just had to play along with his finding one of them before they became hidden. Still, it was fun, and Hreapha apparently seemed to enjoy it a lot, it was the first fun she'd had in a long time.

While looking for a place to hide, Robin found a book or booklet about three times as thick as a comic book, called *Nudist Moppets*. Somebody had sure been looking at it a lot; it was all smudged and the pages were bent and crumpled and coming apart. It was nothing but pictures, hundreds of pictures of boys and girls without any clothes on. When the game of Hide and Seek was over, Robin curled up on the davenport to study the book. She didn't have much time before dark. She had made a decision never to light any of the kerosene lamps except in emergencies. The days were growing shorter and it was getting dark earlier, and she and Hreapha simply went to bed when it got dark, and even Robert was learning how to ignore his nocturnal habits and join them in bed.

Now she had just a little while to study all the pictures before darkness fell, and even without words it was a form of entertainment such as she had been missing for a long time. She had not held a book or booklet in her hands for ages. Most of the kids in the pictures were near her age, some of them older, some younger, and she could identify with them and even envy their freedom to sport and play and mix with each other without any modesty. Some of the boys had weenies that were not just hanging down but sticking out! Robin turned the page and found a picture in which one of the girls had her fingers wrapped around a boy's hard weenie. She tried to imagine what it would feel like to hold a weenie in your hand, especially if it was not limp like a hotdog weenie but hard and stiff.

Then she turned the page and got a real shock. The same girl who had been holding the boy's weenie had put it in her mouth! None of her friends had ever said anything about such a thing as that or what it was called or whether any of them had ever done it, probably because they didn't even know about it. Robin wondered how much the girl and boy were really enjoying it or whether they were just doing it because some man with the camera was making them do it so he could take their picture. Their faces both looked as if they were in heaven, and Robin wondered if it felt better for the boy or better for the girl.

Then it was too dark to keep looking at the book. She put it back where she found it, and she told Hreapha and Robert it was time for bed. She put more wood in the woodstove and turned the dampers so the wood would burn very slowly all night. It was going to be the coldest night so far, and Robin was glad to have her dog and kitty help her warm the cold sheets of the bed.

While she tried to drift off into slumberland, she found herself doing something that she had not done for years, although according to her mother she'd done it all the time when she was small: sucking her thumb.

Chapter twenty-three

Boy howdy but wasn't it a pure marvel how some mornings you could wake up without any sign or trace whatsoever of any bodily ailment? It was almost as if his fairy godmother—if she still cared for him at all—had passed her wand over him and taken away all his afflictions. Not only that, but the Lady had left him with the first genuine hard-on he'd had in recent memory. Not only that, but he hadn't bepissed the pallet during his sleep. Not only that but he had no urge to reach immediately for the bottle of Jack D. Not only that but he practically leaped up from the floor and did a little jig just to show that he could use his legs just fine. He felt wonderful…although previous experience had learned him to tone down his joy because it wouldn't last more'n a few days at the most, if that. Probably this was his last great bout of feeling fine before the final return of the disease which would wipe him out.

But as long as he was feeling so fine, he might as well make the most of it. He gave his pecker a pump or two just to make sure it wasn't a-fooling him, and then he headed for the bed, to enjoy at last the fruit of all these labors. The girl was surrounded by her pets, old Bitch and that darned bobkitten, all three of 'em sound asleep.

"Good morning!" he said loudly and cheerily, to demonstrate that even his power of talking had returned. All three of them woke up at once and all three of them stared at his revivified pecker. Bitch said "HREAPHA!" The bobkitten said "WOOO!" Robin said "That's a big weenie you've got."

"Hey Sugar," he said, "let's shoo these animals out of here so we can have us a little fun." And he gave Bitch a swat on her tail to make her jump out of the bed. Then he picked up the bobkitten to toss him off too, but the damn critter bit him! "Shit on a stick!" he hollered and flung the cat away. Then Bitch chomped him around the ankle; she didn't sink her teeth into his flesh but she held on and he couldn't shake her loose. "Damn it, Bitch, leggo!" he hollered, and tried to pull her loose from his ankle. Here come the bobkitten again, a-clawing its way up his back! "Git him off me!" he ordered Robin, who climbed out of bed and detached her bobkitten from his back.

By the time that he had got loose from the animals, Sog was dismayed to see that his erection had flopped. And Robin was laughing. He was mighty pleased to hear her laughing such a sweet laugh for the first time, but he felt she was amused by his drooping piece.

"What's so damn funny?" he said.

"They were protecting me," she said proudly. "You were getting ready to fuck me, and they knew it, and wanted to protect me!"

"You'll need all the protection you can get after I'm gone."

"You can talk right again," she observed. "You must be feeling well enough to go someplace."

"I aint going nowheres," he said. "But I'm not long for this earth."

"What does that mean?"

"This morning I'm feeling hunky-dory, but it's just a sign. It's a sign that my days is numbered. It's Mother Nature's way of tellin me that the worst is yet to come, and we'd better get ready for it."

He put on his overalls and marched out to the kitchen and fixed them a big breakfast of pancakes and bacon, having to slice up a bacon slab. "How come you aint been carving up the bacon slabs?" he asked Robin.

"You know I can't cut meat very well," she said.

"Time you learned!" he thundered, and before the morning was over he had learned her how to carve meat. He also learned her how to tie her shoes. Then he took her out to the chopping block and said, "You're pretty good with the axe, aint you? Well, just play like this here stick is the neck of a chicken and see if you caint cut it in two." She was real handy with the axe and could cut sticks just fine, but when he told her to grab a chicken and do the real thing, she had problems. She had trouble chasing down a chicken to catch. "Don't chase 'em," he advised. "Just sort of sidle up to a flock of 'em and reach down slow and grab one." It took three attempts before she could hold on to one and bring it to the chopping block. "Now," he said, "just hold its head down and pretend its neck is one of them sticks you just split."

"I can't," she said. "I'm sorry, but I just can't do it."

"You've got to," he said. "You'll never be able to cook fried chicken or roast chicken or chicken n' dumplings if you can't kill the damn chicken in the first place."

It took him a long time to persuade her to give it a try, and she botched the first attempt so he had to finish it himself to put the hen out of her misery. Then he insisted she try again with another hen, and he didn't care if they had to slaughter every damn chicken on the place until she got the hang of it. But she managed to kill the chicken the second time, although she still screeched and squealed while the headless body was flopping around in the yard.

He helped her with the work of plucking the feathers and scalding the birds and showed her the best ways to carve up the chickens. They had two fine big fat hens which would furnish them with plenty of good eating for a while. He was getting tired of pork himself.

While dressing the poultry, he realized that he had never bothered to dig up his sweet potato patch, so right after lunch he took Robin out there and showed her how to dig the yams. She wore her boots and her cute pair of denim overalls, but the tater-fork was just too much for her; she just lacked the body weight to force it into the soil. "Next year you'll be bigger and heavier and maybe you can work the fork into the earth. Also it helps if you do it after a rain when the earth is softened up." He went ahead and did the spading himself and let her dig the big sweet potatoes out of the ground, more than a bushel of them, enough to get her through the winter and spring. He took one of the mature yams and explained how she should save it for next year's crop, and how to poke nails in the side of it to suspend it in a jar of water until it rooted its slips. "Can you remember how to do that come next spring?" he asked.

"I think so," she said.

As long as he was feeling so healthy and strong, he decided it would be a good thing to fell a few more trees so Robin could have a supply of logs to chop for firewood. In another year she might be big enough to force a tater-fork into the earth but she wouldn't be big enough to cut down a tree by herself. He took her along that afternoon to watch him so she could see how it was done, if she ever got big enough to do it. With his crosscut he felled half a dozen oaks and maples not too big to drag back to the house, and she helped him drag them. It was a crisp autumn day, most of the color gone from the woods but the sky bright blue and the air not too cold. They found the tracks of bear, wild turkey, deer, possum, coon, porcupine and etsettery, and he learned her how to identify the tracks and even how to tell the difference between those of a buck deer and those of a doe. They also found some pecan trees, one of them a big one that had shed considerable amounts of its nuts that were just waiting to be gathered, and later on they could fill nearly a whole toesack with them. While he worked that day he told her helpful and philosophical things she ought to remember, that he'd been thinking about while he couldn't talk. Such as, everything in this life worth getting requires being stung a few times. But just as you can ease the sting of a bee by applying the crushed leaves of any three plants, you can always find something in nature to ease the aches and pains of life. Howsomever, there aint no cure for cancer, the common cold and whatever the fuck has been a-bugging me for the past several months. You have to take the bitter with the sweet. You can't get something for nothing. But be careful what you wish for because you're liable to get it and not want it. We all been sentenced to a life sentence in the prison of life, and there aint no parole.

But he realized that she wouldn't remember all that stuff. So that evening before it got dark he took the last paper sacks which she hadn't already cut up into paper dolls and he borrowed her scissors and cut up some rectangles like sheets of writing paper and he told her to write down these things so she could remember them: Time once gone caint never be got back again. Pawpaws make fair catfish bait. Life is like a dead-end road: it don't go nowhere and when it gets there it aint worth the trip. For a bad cough, just gather you a bunch of pine needles and bile 'em down with some molasses. People aint no damn good, and like medicine have to be took in small doses. Don't never drop your broom so it falls flat on the floor, and if you do drop it don't never step over it; if you do it means you won't be able to keep house worth beans. Disappointment comes in all shapes and colors; the least ugly is called pleasure. Laugh before it's light, you'll cry before it's night. If you sing before breakfast, you'll be crying before suppertime. If you hear the firewood a-singing and a-popping and a-cracking, it's a sure sign that snow's about to fall.

He went on and on, until Robin protested, "We're using up all the paper. There won't be any left for my paper dolls."

"Okay, I'll hush," he said. "I need just one last piece of paper, and I'll tell you what for. I've been feeling pretty good today, and like I say it's probably Mother Nature's way of telling me that the worst is yet to come. And when it comes, I may not be able to speak at all or even grunt. So I have to write my last words to you on this last scrap of paper, and here they are." He took the pencil from her and block-printed the letters: SHOOT ME. He showed them to her. "The time might come when I'll have to show this to you because I caint talk at all, and you'll have to do it. You can use the shotgun or the rifle or the handgun or whatever you want, but you're gonna have to put me out of my misery."

"I won't ever do that!" she yelled at him. "Don't you ever tell me to do that!"

He sympathized with her feelings and decided not to keep insisting on it right now. But soon he would have to force her some-way to agree to it. He had thought about this a lot. Why couldn't he just do the job hisself? Because, most likely, when the time came, he'd be too feeble and blind and shaky to handle any sort of firearm.

Thinking about this so much, he had recollected that he had shot and killed that hermit named Dan Montross, not knowing at the time that he was the grandfather of the little girl he'd kidnapped and not knowing that his motive for kidnapping her was pure: to raise the child away from the evils of the world. It would be right and proper, Sog had decided, that he hisself be kilt by the same means that he had kilt Dan Montross. It would also be right and proper as well as practical for Robin to do away with the man who had illegally snatched her away from the world.

There was so much to do, and so little time left. He had to take Robin up behind the house to the old orchard, help her pick a bushel or two of poor apples, which would at least do for drying and making cider and vinegar, and give her some hints on how to manage the orchard in the future, pruning it and grafting and such. She might even get some peaches and pears too if she took care of the orchard. Then he had to hurry. There was really just two more important things to do. He had to show Robin how to kill a deer and persuade her to do it, so she could have some venison. The meadow across from the house was often populated by a family of deer, and Bitch liked to get out there and mingle with them.

Late one afternoon he took the .293 rifle and Robin and they went to the meadow and he showed her how to stand and how to hold the gun, and they didn't have to wait too long before a young buck came out into the clearing, and he whispered, "Okay, aim for his chest."

"No," Robin said. "He's too beautiful to shoot."

By the time he was finished arguing with her, the buck had picked up their voices and run away. "Am I too beautiful to shoot?" he demanded. "Naw I aint, and you'd better believe that there are reasons for shooting something whether you like it or not."

The wonder dog, Bitch, one morning presented him with some junk she'd probably found in the cooper's shed in the same place she'd found the scissors. It consisted of an old rough corncob on a stick, a rosewood striker, and a quarter-sawn striker block. Sog recognized at once that the contraption was a frictionwood turkey caller. "Good dog!" he said, and reflected that Bitch would take better care of Robin than he hisself could ever do. "We're in business."

He persuaded Robin that turkey gobblers weren't beautiful at all. They was, in fact, ugly, especially their red wattle. He got Robin to practice with the caller, showing her how to make it cluck and yelp and purr and even make the quaver of young hens. And then he took the shotgun and led Robin off to the woods (she had to make Hreapha and the bobkitten stay behind) and sure enough before the day was done she had learnt how to call a gobbler and then shoot the sonofabitch.

"Hon, ask your Ouija Board if it's Thanksgiving yet," he requested, and she got out the board and they put their fingertips on the thing and it told them that Thanksgiving would be day after tomorrow. He helped her plan the menu for Thanksgiving: they would have roast wild turkey stuffed with apples and cornbread, mashed potatoes and gravy, and for himself (if he felt like eating; his appetite seemed to be going away again) a mess of greens: turnip, mustard, etsettery. His eyesight was starting to go again too. His goddamn eyeballs seemed to be vibrating inside his head. He had considerable difficulty seeing well enough to crack and shell the pecans, but he got enough of 'em done so they could have roasted pecans as a side dish with the turkey, and also a pecan pie for dessert. He had to get out his crutches again to help him move around in the kitchen.

He was proud of Robin, that she could do all those things, like roast a turkey. He tried to tell her so, but his voice was starting to disappear on him again. Too bad, because he still had so much to say to her. While he could still talk at all, he told her as best he could that he would tell her the location of a huge amount of money if she could agree to shoot him when the time came. Still she wouldn't agree. He was starting to lose his temper. He was truly pissed that she couldn't do this one simple little favor for him. He went ahead and showed her where the money-chest, the Sentry box, was buried under the front porch, but he decided to hold on to the key and offer it as a bribe when the time came that he needed to be shot.

He didn't know what time it was, or what day it was and even where he was at. She asked him, "Can Hreapha and Robert come to Thanksgiving too?" and that reminded him that it must be Thanksgiving. All his brains seemed to be turning into mush.

In one hand he clutched a quart bottle of good old Mr. Daniels from Tennessee (where his forebears came from too). Maybe this was the last bottle he'd be able to drink, though there was enough more in the storeroom to pickle Robin until her middle age if she ever developed a taste for the stuff. He laughed. Or tried to. In the other hand he held the key to the Sentry and the scrap of paper that said for her to shoot him. Those three things was all he needed in the world.

"Dinner's ready," she came and said to him, and helped him make his way to the table and sit down. There was a goddamn dog sitting in one of the chairs, and a fucking baby bobcat sitting in another one, and they both had little napkins tied around their necks. Or maybe he was just imagining it, because he couldn't see worth shit nohow. Robin was talking to him but he couldn't tell what she was saying.

The dog and the kitty was staring at him. He tried to pick up his fork to start in to eating, but his hand shook so he couldn't manage it. He wasn't hungry anyhow. All he wanted was some more of this here bottle in his hand, which he could leastways hold steady to raise to his mouth.

"We ought to say grace," he heard her say. He tried to remember who Grace was.

Nobody said her, so Robin came around and commenced feeding him, forking his food into his mouth until his mouth was filled and he tried and tried to chew and swallow, just to help out. But he couldn't, so he had to just spit it out, and it splattered all over the table.

It was time to go. Hell, it was long past time to go. He held up the sign that asked her to shoot him, and waved it back and forth in front of her face, and offered her the key, but she just shook her head and kept on a-shaking it.

He realized he needed to piss, and not only that, he needed

to shit. He grabbed his crutches and hobbled for the door, falling down before he reached it. She did her best to help him up. "You'd better sit down, Sugrue," she told him.

"Gotta go," he managed to say, which was his next-to-last words. He struggled on out to the outhouse, and she went with him. He got her into the outhouse and dropped his overalls and said to her the only thing that would make any sense besides "Shoot me." He grabbed the back of her head and said, "Sug my dig." And there really wasn't much that he remembered of this life after that.

Chapter twenty-four

Your own *in-habit* is always waiting for you whenever you meet up with it again, especially after a long absence. When she had come back from her long, terrible journey, her *in-habit*, which was now firmly and forever entrenched on these premises, had been happier to see her than even Robin had been.

But she had discovered a strange and important thing about others' *in-habits*. For whatever reason, someone else's *in-habit* will appear to you—no, "appear" is the wrong word—will make itself known to you only when you are in great need of it. That was certainly true of the boy *in-habit* who had helped her find the scissors and the turkey caller and had given her such detailed but ultimately useless instructions on how to find her way to Stay More. He was a wonderful *in-habit* and she felt as if she were his dog as much as she was Robin's and certainly much more than she was the man's. And yet when she returned from her long rough journey, he had not been around to greet her. She had "looked" for him around the cooper's shed, and had hreaphered for him a few times, but he seemed to have disappeared. Oh, of course, he was already and always disappeared, but his presence seemed to have evaporated. She had wanted to tell him that many parts of the trail he had used to get to Stay More simply no longer existed. She had also, since he seemed to be able to hear her as well as a fellow dog could, wanted to tell him that she was pregnant. It was an important announcement that she couldn't communicate to Robin or Robert or her friends the deer or her friends the beaver or her friends the chickens. She wanted someone to know, although she herself was not at all certain who the father was, dear sweet Yowrfrowr or one of the pack of coyotes who had raped her on her way home.

The trail to Stay More still existed in many places: she had watched for landmarks that the *in-habit* had told her to look for: a red bluff, a lone tall pine, a craggy gap through boulders, a steep slope of slate scree, a dark forest of hickory trees, a limestone ledge with a spectacular waterfall spilling over it and dropping fifty or more feet, a treacherous vertical path that she should skirt because she didn't have hands for holding to the limbs beside it, the dark luxuriant holler or glen surrounding the run-off of the waterfall, and then, nearing Stay More, abandoned logging trails, abandoned pastures, abandoned orchards, abandoned farms.

The last mile had been fairly easy, and even fun, although Hreapha realized that the entire route she had taken was simply not one that Robin could ever take, in order to escape her captivity, if that was her wish. Hreapha even doubted that Adam Madewell, if the boy were actually "around" today, could manage the journey that he had taken so often to reach the Stay More school. And she herself was nervous and disinclined to make the return journey when the time came. It would be mostly uphill going back.

She had grown increasingly hungry, having been on the hike for two days and a night. The first day and night out, although she had sometimes detected actual remnants of the path once worn by the *in-habit's* feet when he was a boy going to and from school, was confusing and difficult, and she had spent most of the cold night curled up in a cavern, not because she was tired yet or couldn't see well in the dark, but because she had heard the coyotes, who were mostly nocturnal, and she did not wish to encounter them. She had tried her best to refrain from peeing, because she did not want to attract the coyotes with her advertisement or give them a trail to follow. Even so, on the second day out, one of them had picked up her scent and begun stalking her. She had become so increasingly desperate for mating that she was tempted to allow the coyote to catch her, but thoughts of dear Yowrfrowr made her seek to escape the coyote. In running as fast as she could to escape him, she had slipped on the slate scree and tumbled down a steep slope and landed in a briar patch that scratched her up badly, even bringing blood. But she had escaped the coyote, and after getting her wind back she ran onward, finding herself lost in the hickory forest, with only a vague sense of direction and no visual or olfactory clues. She tried to tune in to her old Stay More *in-habit* but it had long gone to the Madewell Mountain house, where its presence was sending her such strong signals that she was tempted to turn around and go home, even if she had to mate up with a coyote along the way. She had nothing against coyotes; their breeding was just as good as, if not better than, her own. In fact, most of these local coyotes were descendants of the long-extinct red wolf, a magnificent dog. But she didn't like the idea of quick mating with strangers, and after all, coyotes did not speak her language, or rather they spoke a form of it that was not at all intelligible to her.

So she had gone on and managed to find her way out of the hickory forest. She had searched for but could not find the log which the *in-habit* had told her served as a footbridge over a little stream, so she had attempted simply to swim across in the frigid water, but she had been caught up in the current and thus discovered the fabulous waterfall by going over it! She had howled as she had fallen fifty feet to the pool beneath, had gone deeply underwater and struck herself on the bottom, losing consciousness. It was a wonder she hadn't drowned. But when she had come to, she had found herself on the bank downstream in the glen of the waterfall, bruised and thoroughly wet and cold, but still alive.

The rest of the journey had been fairly easy, although she was so sore she could hardly walk. And when, finally, she reached the dogtrot log cabin where Yowrfrowr lived with a thousand cats and a beautiful old lady, she could only weakly announce her name to him and then collapse at his feet.

I'll be jigswiggered! Yowrfrowr exclaimed. Will wonders never cease? I had given you up for permanently missing. Are you all right? And he licked her face.

I've just made a trip, she said, such as you should hope you never have to make.

For what reason? he said.

Why, to see *you*, silly, she said.

Oh, dear me, he said. I'm frightfully flattered.

Yes, dear you, she agreed. But she didn't feel like doing any more talking until she'd had some rest and possibly something to eat and drink. Yowrfrowr obligingly exhumed one of his favorite bones for her, and led her to the springhouse, where she slaked her thirst. She rested a while and then told him about some of her adventures on the hike down from the mountains, and told him also of her experiences at the old Madewell homestead, where her new mistress was a charming young girl named Robin, whom the man had kidnapped.

Good heavens, Yowrfrowr commented. You've been living with a felon.

She told him all the good things about the place, even including the nice *in-habit* who lived in the cooper's shed, as well as the beavers and their dam, and the recently acquired bobcat kitten. She wanted to make life up there sound as exciting as possible, on the chance she could persuade Yowrfrowr to go home with her. She told him that the man was very ill and would probably not last much longer.

But doesn't the girl want to escape and go home? Yowrfrowr wondered.

Probably, Hreapha admitted, but even if there was a way she could get out of there, and there isn't, she's having the time of her life and is starting to think of the place as her home. I have to get back to her as soon as I can, but I just had to see you. I have been dying to see you.

May I guess why? Yowrfrowr inquired, and that was all that either of them had to say for the rest of the day and night. They found privacy at a distance from the cabin, and there they went through the ritual of positionings, almost like a dance. She displayed her swollen afterplace to him, with her tail held to one side, then stood motionless while he rose up and clasped her around her flanks, inserted himself and began thrusting. Her mother, in describing the act she could eventually expect, had warned her in advance to expect to find herself tied or locked at the afterplace with her mate after he had deposited his discharge in her. Her mother had told her that the climax of mating was called 'getting off,' but you don't get off at all. You remain hooked together for a long time. And indeed, fifteen or twenty minutes passed before they could separate, whereupon they just lay snuggly cuddled and resting for a long time, talking about Stay More gossip and all the things that had happened on Madewell Mountain, until, after going to the springhouse for another long drink of water, they repeated the whole process.

Hreapha spent the night, and, in fact, another night after that one...or maybe two. She was not bothering to keep count, but it seemed they made love at least half a dozen times, until finally she had no desire remaining. But she had no desire to leave, either. Yowrfrowr gladly agreed to accompany her on a kind of sentimental journey to her old home, which she found completely abandoned and uncared for. No trace of her *in-habit* remained there, but she could not help reflecting that her poor master, if he had stayed there, might not now be in death's embrace. Conceivably, Hreapha could have lived out her life in this old place, happy with occasional visits to her beloved Yowrfrowr, without ever knowing of the heaven of Madewell Mountain. She began to talk to Yowrfrowr in earnest about the possibility that he might be able to join her permanently at the Madewell homestead. She stopped just short of actually begging him to go with her.

You make it sound so wonderful, he allowed. I am greatly tempted. But you must understand how devoted I am to my mistress, and how crushed and desolate she would be if I left her, even with all those uncompanionable pussycats she has.

I'll miss you for the rest of my life, she whined.

Godspeed and take care, he said.

And after she'd left him, she reflected that he might have gone with her if she were still in heat and if he had not exhausted himself servicing her. He also might have gone with her if she had asked for his protection against the coyotes. She hadn't even mentioned to him that there was a pack of coyotes roaming Ledbetter Mountain, which was the sister mountain to Madewell.

When she stopped to pee, she was relieved to note that her marking no longer bore the sexual advertisement. That was some small comfort in the hideous hike, mostly uphill, that lay ahead of her.

She had no idea how long it took her to get back home; certainly more than the two days and one night the downhill journey had consumed. It should have been easier because she had the guidance of her own scent on the trail as well as of her *in-habit* at the Madewell place, and if it hadn't been for the damned coyotes she would probably have got home without much more difficulty than she had had leaving it. She heard them before she smelled them, late on the second afternoon out. And then she saw them. There were five males, smaller than German shepherds, long legged, dark furred, pointy eared. They were good-looking, even handsome. They lacked Yowrfrowr's jovial bearing and shaggy casualness, especially his jaunty flopping ears, and certainly, when they began attempting to communicate their wishes to her, they lacked his elegance of speech.

Her first instinct was to run, but, tired as she was already from her uphill hike, she doubted that she would get very far out of their reach. So she stood motionless, cringing and snarling. Leave me alone, she said. I've already been bred.

They gave no sign of having understood her. Expressing their one-track minds in their guttural language, they began circling her, moving ever closer. Keeping her afterplace covered firmly with her tail, she breathed deeply, filling her lungs, deciding that she would not give in without a fight. But the wiser course would be at least to make an attempt to run away from them. When the alpha male raised a paw to begin mounting her, she bolted and ran harder than she had ever run, not uphill on the original path, but downhill, off into the woods. If only she could reach the waterfall again, she would gladly go plunging over the fall and into the pool, anything to get away from these lechers.

But they stopped her before she could reach the waterfall. The beta male and the gamma male jumped her and held her while the alpha male got himself into position to copulate. She struggled and bit viciously wherever she could find a piece of coyote to bite upon. But the alpha male poked and poked and got off without becoming locked, and then the beta and gamma males each got on and got off inside her. She had no strength to resist further when the delta and epsilon males each took their turn.

Eventually they just left her lying there on the ground. Their claws as well as their teeth had drawn blood on several parts of her body. It seemed that in their throaty voices they had debated with one another whether or not to kill and eat her, a fate from which she was saved when they caught wind of a passing deer and took off after it.

She was not able to move for another night—or perhaps two—laying in a thick pile of autumn leaves which offered only a little protection against the below-freezing temperature. Then when she finally could attempt to get to her feet, she could scarcely move. An entire day was consumed in covering less than half a mile of the trail. She found sufficient water to drink but nothing to eat. She saw an abundance of rodents and other small animals but lacked the strength to chase and catch one.

Thus she was truly starving and very cold when she finally reached the beaver pond, the first sign of home territory. Her beaver friends were solicitous about her welfare but she couldn't communicate her mishaps to them. She rested a while with them and then finished the journey home, exulting "HREAPHA!" when she came in sight of the house.

She was so very thrilled to be home again. She never wanted to leave. For days and days she was content simply to rest, keeping warm by the stove, sleeping for hours on end, enjoying Robin's company and even Robert's, and eating her fill of doggy nuggets. Apparently the homestead had survived intact without her during her absence, and even the chickens had not needed her supervision.

The man was obviously on his last legs, although he had a brief, mysterious spell of apparent freedom from his afflictions, beginning with an obvious intention to put his miraculously restored manthing to use, an intention which required intercession from both Hreapha and Robert. The moment of her seizing one of his ankles in her teeth to prevent him from assaulting Robin was the moment when she understood that her longstanding fidelity to him was at an end. But Hreapha was glad to get outdoors again when the man began giving Robin her final instructions. Hreapha watched sympathetically but fearfully as he taught Robin how to behead a chicken, and then as he tried to teach her how to dig sweet potatoes. Hreapha couldn't imagine why anyone would want to eat a sweet potato, but when it came to digging up things she was as good as a spade or fork and she demonstrated this ability to Robin by digging up some of the tubers for her. She also accompanied them to the old orchard, but being unable to climb trees there wasn't any help she could offer there. She kept her distance during their deer hunt, which she hated, and was terribly proud of Robin for refusing to shoot the young buck.

She had not had any "contact" with the *in-habit* since her return from Stay More, but as she was walking by the cooper's shed on her daily check-up on the henhouse, she heard a distinct *Psst!* requiring her attention. And there he was again, wherever he was. She could only hear his voice, *They's a right fine turkey caller my paw made out of rosewood and frictionwood which makes the most wondrous noises just like them wild turkey gobblers and hens, if you'd care to take it to those folks so's they could get 'em a turkey for their Thanksgiving.* Then he led her to the box in the cooper's shed which contained the pieces of wood and the corncob striker. Thanks so much, Hreapha said, and delivered this gift to the man, and heard herself called "good dog" by him for the first time in her life. She was sorry that Robin made her stay behind when she went off to use the turkey caller and shoot her turkey.

Hreapha had never eaten turkey before, but the smell of it when it was cooking in the old stove was certainly interesting, even savory. Hreapha understood how she was supposed to participate in this special occasion called Thanksgiving. She had no conception of any deity toward whom thanks should be directed, but she certainly was ready to thank Robin for working so hard in the kitchen to prepare this marvelous dinner, and she had no objection whatsoever when Robin wanted to tie a little napkin around her neck so she could climb up into a chair and sit at the table with the human beings…and with Robert, similarly attired.

The man was obviously in such bad shape he couldn't even feed himself, and when Robin tried to feed him he vomited the food all over the table. Hreapha's heart ached for the way he had ruined Robin's Thanksgiving. And then he began to shove that piece of paper in her face.

Hreapha was a very smart dog but of course she was not able to read the letters that humans use to communicate on paper. She knew the basic words of the Ouija Board such as YES, NO, and GOODBYE, but she could not decipher letters as such, and thus she did not know what was printed on the piece of paper which the man insisted on waving back and forth in front of Robin's face. It was something he was trying to say to her, something that he was trying to get her to do. Hreapha found herself breathing hard and feeling distinctly uneasy when the man got up from the table, fell down, was helped up again by Robin, and hobbled on his crutches in the direction of the outhouse. Robin followed, and so did Hreapha.

With the door to the outhouse not closed, and the afternoon light still strong enough to illuminate the scene, Hreapha could only watch with great curiosity and no little fear as the man dropped his overalls, took out his manthing, and forced Robin to put it into her mouth. Although in itself this did not strike Hreapha as exceptional (she had licked Yowrfrowr's genitals, and he hers), it was obvious that Robin hated it. She beat against him with her fists until he had to let her go, and then he collapsed upon the seat of the outhouse. Sobbing, with tears running down her cheeks, Robin brushed past Hreapha and rushed to the house, and Hreapha started to follow, but Robin came back at once, carrying in her hands the instrument she had used to kill the turkey. It had two barrels. Robin pointed the instrument at the man and the instrument fired twice, knocking Robin backward to the ground. Hreapha rushed up to her, but could only lick her face as Robin lay there for a long time crying her heart out.

Hreapha walked slowly to the outhouse and studied the man, who was sitting there with many holes in his body, through which blood poured. He may have been a bad man, a very bad man, but now he was not a man of any kind any longer. He was a corpse. Some part of Hreapha felt the loss of her master, but the ultimate measure of her smartness was that she understood that the man was now better off. And so were they all.

Chapter twenty-five

Readers who have been holding their breath in expectation that Sugrue Alan would cause some great harm to Robin Kerr—or vice versa—can now let out a long sigh. The bastard was terminated, and regardless of whatever mixed feelings were being felt by Robin, by that darling cur Hreapha, and by the devoted reader, I personally was glad, glad, glad, and I was making plans already to move from the barrel factory to the house, not that I preferred the house to the shed (shelter as such had no meaning for me) but I had deliberately stayed away from the house as long as Sog Alan was the occupant of it. And now the only house he occupied was the outhouse, which he would continue to occupy for years, actual years for heaven's sake, although it would be only his skeleton residing there. Of course his body was too big for poor Robin to move, and I was powerless to give her a hand—I didn't have a hand to give—and while she doubtless eventually (because of the smell, for one thing) thought of trying to pull the deceased off his throne and drag him to a burying spot, she realized that was simply beyond her strength. So she had to leave him there. She never used that outhouse again herself for the purpose of micturition or defecation, although there was, after all, an unoccupied hole, if she had been able to ignore the macabre. She simply squatted in the yard, as Hreapha did, as Robert did, confident that her privacy was not being invaded, oblivious to the simple fact that I could watch her, if I chose, because while I might not have possessed any of the handicaps of selfhood such as appetite, sleepiness, sensitivity to hot or cold, or the need to micturate or defecate, I did possess a certain sentience which gave me sight and hearing and speech. More about this later, but for now I was thoroughly aware of what was going on, and I did not avert my gaze when the little girl needed to go out, nor when the turkey vultures—or buzzards as we called them—soaring high overhead with their keen eyesight detected the carrion occupying the outhouse and made short work of removing the meat from the bones, so that in a matter of weeks there was not even an odor remaining.

This is not to say that Sugrue Alan, although his flesh became birdfeed, did not have any sort of funeral. One of my earliest memories of the jerk was when I was in the second grade at Stay More—no, not exactly *I* but rather my person, the person who went to California at the age of twelve and left me, whatever sentient form I had, to take his place as enchanted habitant of these premises (I like Hreapha's use of that term, *in-habit*, but it suggests that there might also be an *out-habit*), anyway, my person, while still living here and trekking eight miles each schoolday over that terrible terrain poor Hreapha had recently essayed, had been required by Miss Jerram, the teacher, to accompany all the rest of the pupils on a march up into Butter-churn Holler, to conduct a funeral for a mule named Old Jarhead, the work animal of a poor family of kids named Dingletoon, a mule senselessly beaten to death by a pack of punks led by Sog Alan. Miss Jerram forced the gang to dig a grave and bury the mule, and instructed various pupils, including Old Jarhead's owners as well as her murderers, to speak solemn requiems for the departed. Even Sog himself, miscreant and bully, was required to speak, and began, "I never done nothing in my life that I was sorry for," but paused and added, "until now." And spoke a sincere apology, which moved my person, seven-year-old Adam Madewell, to giggle, this causing him to be beaten up later by Sog and his cronies.

What my person—and I too, now—remembered most about that mule's funeral was the singing, at Miss Jerram's request, of a funeral hymn, a traditional dirge known to everyone at Stay More, which consisted of several verses and a chorus at the end of each:

Farther along we'll know all about it,
Farther along we'll understand why;
Cheer up, my brother, live in the sunshine,
We'll understand it all by and by.

The death of Sugrue Alan needed some sort of closure, a funeral or a service of some sort—no one in those days in that part of the world would have understood or appreciated the so-called "memorial service" held nowadays with its gaiety and laughter and jokes and digs amounting almost to a roasting rather than a commemoration of the departed—a ceremony of some sort to solemnize and ritualize the fact of Sugrue's death. Even I, at the age the "*in-habit*" was at the time of Sugrue's death (and still was, forever)—twelve—understood enough of human nature, without even the faintest notion of what psychology meant, to realize that the only way for poor Robin to climb out of her deep distress and grief would be to speak and sing some manner of last offices.

She was having a terrible time, and more than ever needed her mother and missed her terribly. Neither Hreapha nor Robert could console her; indeed, the very fact that they were animals seemed to highlight her awareness of being the only living human being on the mountain. It was almost as if she were the only person in the world. She certainly was the only person in the world of Madewell Mountain, and the only other person who had occupied that world had died at her hand. She was wracked with the ambivalence of having killed him as an act of mercy at his own request, but having been forced into that killing by his nastiness to her in his last moments. His attempt to make her "go down" on him did not in itself offend her—it wasn't pleasant but it wasn't unbearable—so much as his rudeness and desperation in insisting upon it. Was she able to understand that he had made the attempt not because he actually desired it, but

233

because in his reduced condition it was the only thing his poor mind could conceive of which might compel her to do his bidding and shoot him? Probably not, but she knew that he had ceased, in his last moments, being the Sugrue that she had known.

How did I know these were her thoughts? Well, my goodness, certainly you've fathomed that I possessed the ability not only to inhabit the premises but also to inhabit the consciousness of each of its inhabitants. How else could I reveal their thoughts and feelings to the most important, albeit temporary, inhabitant of this place, namely, you, the reader? Is it too much of a stretch for you to believe that I am the real narrator of this book you are inhabiting? Do you need proof? Okay then, I'll tell you what happened to Leo Spurlock, who you might have been expecting to show up at any moment, brandishing his revolver and ready to kill Sog Alan himself. Leo, you may or may not be happy to learn, got hopelessly lost on the north face of Madewell Mountain, spent a couple of frigid, scary nights in the woods, and like many lost people, moved unconsciously in a circle that brought him back eventually to his stranded vehicle, where a man driving an expensive type of suv was trying to get around him. He chatted with the man and assured him there was no way he could get on up the mountain, and finally persuaded the man to turn around and head back down the mountain, and even to give Leo a ride. The man was going to Harrison anyhow, where Leo was able to hire a tow truck to rescue his pickup from its miring on the hopeless trail, but he did not attempt any further progress up that vanishing trail. He was still searching other roads and other trails with his topographic survey maps, and still having adventures, albeit none as exciting as his encounter with those hippies and his rescue of that abducted girl. There. Enough of Leo. How would I know all that unless I'm performing for you some of the same services that I was performing for Robin?

But I had not yet made myself known to her again. She was in great need of me, and, like Hreapha, had come to the conclusion that I only showed up—maybe turned up is the better term—when I was greatly needed. I recalled fondly how she'd been searching for me previously, even inviting me into the house to keep warm, bless her heart, not understanding that I didn't need to keep warm, and not understanding either why I chose at that particular moment to remain withdrawn from her consciousness. I wasn't happy that she'd considered me only a figment of her imagination. It is so easy to believe that there isn't any such thing as us—call us *in-habits* as Hreapha does for want of a better term—or that we are only the products of a desperate imagination, an overheated need or yearning. We certainly don't come when we are called, or respond to any attempt to locate us or communicate with us, because we are, after all, intensely idiolectal: nothing could be more private and personal than a part of oneself that one perforce must leave behind when one leaves a place. I was just the residue, as it were, of Adam Madewell, but I possessed something he no longer did: habitation at this homestead.

The simple fact was that I didn't know what I could do for Robin, and I felt helpless. My joy at the removal of the bad guy was dampened by my awareness of her sorrow for having killed him. What could I say to her? *Gal, you done the right thing?* No, because for her to believe that, she'd have to accept it on her own, not because she heard it from a disembodied peer.

Several days after Sog's mercy-killing, if it may be called that, when the buzzards (and crows too) were busy at their feast, and I had moved from the shed to the house, Robin abruptly stopped crying and began to sing. The rest of us—Hreapha, Robert, myself—were surprised. She had rarely sung when Sog was alive, perhaps out of self-consciousness about her voice, which was, in fact, a very sweet soprano. What she sang was not important, probably a contemporary popular song—it was something about *Hi de ho, hi de hi, gonna get me a piece of the sky*—what was important was the sense that the singing was allowing her to vent her emotions, and that the time had come for closure.

When she finished, I remarked, *That's right perty. I reckon we can start in now to saying our goodbyes to the departed.*

Robin laughed and looked around as if she might be able to see me. "You're back," she said. "You only come when I need you real bad."

I don't reckon I come, one way or t'other. To come, you've got to've been able to've went, and I aint went. I'm just here. I just am.

235

"Well, I need you, that's for sure," she said.

You needed me real bad yesterday and the day before, I observed, *but I didn't have no notion what I could do for ye.*

"What do you mean, say our goodbyes to the departed? Do you think we should go out there to the outhouse and talk to him?"

I laughed. *Naw, I don't reckon the buzzards and the crows would let us git close to 'im. But it'd make ye feel a heap better iffen ye could hold some kind of ceremony. Not no funeral, because you aint a-fixing to bury him, but jist speak and sing something solemn, ye know?*

"Like read something from the Bible?" she said. "The trouble is, I don't have a Bible."

Let me see if I caint find ye one, I said. *Or if you'll jist listen careful, I'll tell ye where one's hid.*

By voice alone, since I couldn't point, I directed her to a little door in the ceiling of the kitchen and she was strong enough to raise the wooden ladder to the wall and with her flashlight climb up and push open the door. There was an attic space up there with mostly worthless dusty junk that Adam's parents had cast off, but in one dark corner, wedged between two ceiling joists and covered with boards, was one of Adam's mother's old castoff dresses wrapped around two books, the only books on the premises, which Adam's mother, blinded by trachoma and no longer able to read and not allowed to read in any case because Adam's father, Gabe Madewell, prohibited the possession of books for reasons we will later discover, had directed Adam to hide there.

One of the two books was a not-very-large but complete Holy Bible. The other was titled *Farmer's and Housekeeper's Cyclopædia*, subtitled *A Complete Ready Reference Library for Farmers, Gardeners, Fruit Growers, Stockmen and Housekeepers, Containing a Large Fund of Useful Information, Facts, Hints and Suggestions, in the various Departments of Agriculture, Horticulture, Live Stock Raising, Poultry Keeping, Bee Keeping, Dairy Farming, Fertilizers, Rural Architecture, Farm Implements, Household Management, Domestic Affairs, Cookery, Ladies' Fancy Work, Floriculture, Medical Matters, Etc., Etc. with two hundred and forty-nine illustrations.* It was published in 1888 and belonged originally to Adam's grandmother, Laura Madewell.

"You really are Adam Madewell, aren't you?" she said. "Or you wouldn't have known where these books were hidden."

Iffen it makes ye feel some better, I'm all that's left hereabouts of Adam, but he aint really here, so I caint say as how I'm him.

Starved for anything to read (the only reading matter in the house was a stack of back issues of *Police Gazette* which Sog had read and re-read and which Robin had found boring), Robin sat herself down upon the davenport with these two books and proceeded to forget about me. I didn't mind. I was happy to see that she had something to take her away from her miseries, and I enjoyed looking over her shoulder, as it were, as she skimmed through both books. The pictures in the latter book, mostly simple black and white wood engravings, were fascinating. And while Robin might never need to construct a spile or post driver or a hay elevating apparatus, she could certainly use such things as the instructions on grafting apple trees and making a simple smoke house out of a barrel, not to mention the many recipes.

While she pored over the two books, she wasn't unmindful of her primary objective: to find something suitable to read at the services. The problem with the Bible was that in search of inspirational or devotional readings she kept getting sidetracked into the stories or narratives which arrested her curiosity—Elisha and the bears, Joseph and his brethren, Moses and the princess, the plagues and The Passover, Queen Athaliah, and so forth. She was going to have a lot of fun on cold winter days reading the stories in the Bible.

"Well, I guess I'm ready," she finally announced, addressing Hreapha as much as she was me. But then she addressed me, "Adam, do you know any hymns we could sing?"

So I sang for her, in my own pleasant country countertenor, "Farther Along." I sang each of the verses, starting with this one:

Tempted and tried we're oft made to wonder,
Why it should be thus all the day long;
While there are others living about us,
Never molested though in the wrong.

Followed by the chorus, with its promise that someday we

might be able to make sense out of all this. Several of the six verses implied that we would have to meet Jesus first, when he came in glory and took us to meet our loved ones gone on before us, but the important thing was not so much inhabiting "that bright mansion" where we will meet Him but rather that we will learn answers to all our questions: why the wicked prosper, why the wrong are not molested, why we must leave home, why we must endure toils while others live in comfort, and so forth and so on. It is ultimately a hopeful and a reassuring hymn, and, as it turned out, Robin did learn the chorus if not all the verses, and thus was able to conduct a kind of memorial service for Sog, with three in her audience: Hreapha, Robert and myself.

She had, after all, come to think of Sog as her father, and she preached a little sermon to the three of us in which she declared that Sugrue Alan was not all bad, that he had some good qualities, like for instance he tried to teach her stuff, why just recently he'd taught her finally how to tie her shoes and cut her meat, and we ought to feel sorry for him because of how sick he'd been for several months now, and how feeble he had become, and she was sure that even if she could not forgive him for kidnapping her and taking her away from her home and her mother probably God would not hold it against him and he was probably going to heaven instead of hell. Amen.

"Okay, let's sing," she said to me. And I sang "Farther Along," she joining in for the chorus, hampered not by keeping the key but by the variation of our pronunciation, hers the plain and simple accents of a Harrison schoolgirl, mine those of a backwoods country boy. Poor Robert was a bit spooked because he couldn't tell where my voice was coming from.

When the hymn was over, she asked me, "Could you tell me a good part of the Bible to read out loud?"

Who, me? I said innocently. And then I added, *I'm mighty sorry to have to tell ye, but I never got a chance to look at that book.*

So she flipped aimlessly through the thick book, searching for something appropriate, but found nothing, just meaningless lists of names she couldn't pronounce. Finally she decided that it might be just as well to read something from the other book, the 1888 *Cyclopæ-dia*, so she let it fall open at random, and read aloud:

> **Bee stings.**—Take a pinch in the fingers of common salt, put on the place stung and dissolve with water, rub with the finger. If not relieved in one minute wet the place with aqua ammonia. Care should be taken not to get the ammonia in the eye. I have used this remedy for several years and it has never failed with me.

"This just goes to show," she declared, ceremoniously, "that he wasn't always right but sometimes wrong, because his idea was to mix up the crushed leaves of any three plants and put them on the sting."

Well heck, that's what I'd do, myself, if I ever got stung, I declared. *But the best thing is to try to keep from getting stung.*

"Besides I don't think we have any ammonia," she said. Then she said, "I can't think of anything else to say. So I guess this service is over."

But one final gesture remained. When the buzzards and crows and rodents and maggots had left nothing but a skeleton sitting in the outhouse, a skeleton who would have looked scary except for the big grin on its face, Robin took a bottle of Sog's favorite beverage, Jack Daniels Black Label, and, first tasting it herself but spitting it out, placed the bottle in the grip of one of the skeleton's bony hands.

Chapter twenty-six

What she really wanted to ask the ghost of Adam Madewell was if he knew whether Sugrue had a ghost too, and if so, was the ghost going to be around like Adam? But she was afraid of the answer she might get. What if Adam said that Sugrue was already busy at work haunting the place? If that were true, Robin surely would have to leave, which scared her even more, although she had given it a lot of thought and had an emergency plan ready: she would wrap enough food for several days in a dishtowel, and take a flashlight with fresh batteries and the .293 rifle with several bullets, and getting Robert to ride on Hreapha's back, she would just take off: heading south in the direction Hreapha had made her trip and hoping to come eventually to a path or trail or road of some sort. She'd have to wear her thickest coat, and maybe try to keep her hands in the pockets. There was already snow on the ground.

Why hadn't Sugrue thought to buy her some mittens or gloves? He had filled that storeroom—Adam's bedroom—with enough food and supplies and presents for her to last for a long, long time: he must have been planning to keep her for years. But he had neglected to get so many things that she would need, and hadn't even thought of

Kool-Aid and scissors and paper and books, and he hadn't seemed to realize that she would outgrow all the clothes he'd bought for her.

Thinking of Christmas coming, she decided to go ahead and open everything he'd bought, searching for gloves or mittens, and while this would spoil the surprise of opening things he'd intended to give her for Christmas or Valentine's or Easter or her next birthday or whenever, the whole idea of surprise and whatever fun is in the surprise means that there has to be another person involved, and there wasn't any other person any more. Even with Hreapha and Robert in the bed with her each night, she had moments of panic at the thought that she was all alone now. Anyhow, being all alone allowed her to go ahead and open all the boxes and all the bags, and see all the stuff that Sugrue had intended to give her for presents eventually. "Thank you, thank you," she kept saying to him again and again, as she opened the packages, which even included a box of ribbon candy intended for Christmas. Having learned to believe no longer in the Tooth Fairy, she was now prepared to accept this answer to her burning question, How could Santa Claus possibly find her this far off in the wilderness? She saw plenty of evidence that Sugrue had intended to be Santa, just as he had once been the Tooth Fairy. He had really got her some nice things, and she was sorry that he'd never be around to see her play with them or put them on...unless his ghost was here, and she surely had no awareness of his ghost being around, except for that ghastly skeleton in the outhouse.

Why didn't she just get rid of the skeleton, which wasn't too heavy for her to drag off its perch? It certainly wasn't because she was afraid to touch it, because after all she'd made sure that those finger-bones had wrapped around the neck of that whiskey bottle. And the skeleton as such didn't scare her. She remembered last Halloween when some of the kids dressed themselves in skeleton costumes, which she had thought were the least frightful of all possible costumes. What is scary about a collection of bones? No, maybe there were only two reasons she had decided to leave the skeleton there. One was that the outhouse had been Sugrue's favorite place, where he had spent an awful lot of time. Dozens of times when she'd needed to go, she had opened the outhouse door to find him sitting there reading a

Police Gazette and she could only say "Oops" and shut the door and wait for him to come out. But the other reason, the main reason, was that she liked the idea of leaving the skeleton there as a reminder that this man, Sugrue Alan, who had brought this world into existence, had kidnapped her away from her mother and friends and taken her to live in this place, was now no longer alive. She wanted to be able to glance in the direction of the outhouse at any time and see that reminder sitting there with that stupid grin and that stupid bottle of stupid whiskey in his hand.

Whenever Adam wasn't around—that is, whenever she couldn't detect that he was present, which quite often he was not—she just had to talk to Hreapha or Robert, or to herself. "I need to grow up fast," she said one day, to any ears that cared to hear it. Her own ears did: she was painfully aware of how little and helpless and innocent she was, and she wanted to become an adult as soon as she could. But the more she thought about it, and wondered how long it would take for her to become an adult, the more she understood that actually what she really, really wanted, more than anything else in the world, was just to stay the age she was right now forevermore. Just not ever change, just always be little and fragile and simple.

She knew she spent too much time thinking. And too much thinking wasn't good for her. She tried to avoid it by spending as much time as she could with her two precious books, the old *Cyclopædia* filled with all kinds of handy hints on how to live and manage a homestead, and the Bible filled with all kinds of interesting stories.

Much of the *Cyclopædia* was either over her head ("Farm Fences," "Making Our Own Fertilizers," "Caponizing,") or useless ("The Best Known Recipe for Corning Beef," "To Banish Crows From a Field," "How to Judge a Horse") but there were pages and pages of things she ought to know ("How to Keep Sweet Potatoes," "Winter Egg Production," "To Stop Bleeding," "Washing Made Easy," "Burns and Scalds"), and there were hundreds of recipes to be tried out, and she proceeded each day to try a new one: hominy fritters and potato cakes for breakfast, chicken patties and potato salad for lunch. There was something called "Sauce Robert," easy, with onions, which she couldn't resist making and trying out on her kitty, who liked it if it was poured over protein like chicken or ham. There were desserts galore she tried. There were sixty different recipes for pudding, but she had the ingredients for less than half of them, which was more than she could eat. Her favorite was called "Kiss Pudding," using mostly egg yolks (which was spelled "yelks" throughout the book). There was a simple recipe "To Cook a Rabbit," so with Hreapha's help she went out and shot a rabbit and cooked it according to the directions and it was delicious, although not that much different from chicken. One dish that was different somewhat from chicken was the pigeon pie. She used the .22 rifle to kill a few pigeons (remembering of course Sugrue's "Pigeon eat"). The recipe called for lining the bottom of the dish with a veal cutlet or rump steak, which she did not have, so she substituted ham, and it was just fine. She always shared her dishes with Hreapha and Robert, who greatly appreciated them.

She also took her mind off of thinking too much by playing with her paper dolls in her paper town of Stay More. The problem was that her paper dolls talked to her. Oh, of course it was probably just her own voice, but the paper dolls, those old country people of Stay More named Ingledew and Swain and Whitter and Duckworth and Coe and Dinsmore and Chism and so on, seemed to be talking to her in voices that weren't her own, that she couldn't even imitate, because they were country voices, like Adam's. They told her stories that she couldn't possibly have made up by herself, stories about floods and droughts and periods of darkness and periods of light, and an Unforgettable Picnic and the organization of a Masonic lodge—surely she couldn't have been making all of this up in play. But she distinctly heard their voices.

"Hreapha, can't you hear them too?" she asked, but her adorable dog just cocked her head to one side as if she were trying to listen, without acknowledging the voices.

For the longest time she had persuaded herself that the voice of the ghost Adam Madewell was just something she was imagining, although she couldn't imagine how she would have been able to know the particular way he talked and some of the words he used. But how could she explain his finding those two books for her? Did she just have a hunch to see what was beyond that little door in the ceiling of the kitchen and go up there with her flashlight and find those two books? Well, it wasn't impossible, but she was pretty well convinced that there really was a ghost named Adam who sometimes talked to her. And what about that business of singing the "Farther Along" hymn? She had heard Sugrue make some references to it, but he'd never sung it, so how did she learn the words and tune, unless she learned them from Adam?

She loved that song, and every day she sang it; she even sang it in bed at night when she was trying to go to sleep. She understood that "Farther Along" was a funeral hymn and ought to be reserved for funerals, but day by day the people in her paper town of Stay More began to die, of natural causes or illnesses or whatever people died of, including murder, and while she didn't actually try to bury the paper dolls she had a little memorial service for those who died and sang "Farther Along."

And when she got to that lovely verse which said, "When we see Jesus coming in glory, When He comes from his home in the sky; Then we will meet Him in that bright mansion, We'll understand it all by and by," she always began to wonder if this old house in which she lived might possibly be That Bright Mansion. She had never seen a mansion; Harrison had some fancy houses but not any mansions, which she knew were supposed to be very large and very imposing, neither of which this old house was. Still, she began to think that perhaps when Jesus came to meet her in this house, the house would be transformed into a mansion, just as pumpkins could be transformed into coaches in "Cinderella."

Robin was ready for Jesus. She took the Bible and, avoiding all those stories about unpronounceable names like Zelophehad, Ahinoam, Zedekiah, and Athaliah, began at the beginning of the New Testament and read the four gospels. It took her a week to read each one, but by then according to the Ouija Board it was Christmas, appropriately, because she could celebrate the first Christmas in her life in which the meaning of the day had real significance as the birthday of the nice interesting kind man named Jesus, who was called the Christ.

She had got out the Ouija Board again and with Hreapha's help determined that Christmas this year was only three days away. She took the axe and cut down a little cedar tree behind the house, and figured out a way to make it stand up in the living room, "planting" it in one of the wooden bails from the cooper's shed. "Adam, do you mind if I borrow this?" she asked, but got no answer. She decorated her Christmas tree with stars that she cut out of toilet paper tubes (although she never used the outhouse any more, she still used toilet paper) and colored with her crayons, which were in danger of being used up. Searching through the storeroom for the possibility that Sugrue might have bought more than one big box of crayons, she came upon a paper sack she'd overlooked before. In it were a half dozen ears of dried up yellow corn, and there was a note, hand-lettered on a piece of brown paper, which said, "THESE HERE IS POPCORN, FOR YOU TO POP ON THE STOVE AND EAT OR MAYBE MAKE YOU SOME STRINGS FOR YOUR CHRISTMAS TREE. SORRY THERE'S NOT NO ORANGES TO PUT IN YOUR STOCKING BUT I GOT YOU SOME RIBBON CANDY SOMEWHERE AROUND IN HERE. MERRY CHRISTMAS AND LOVE, SUGRUE." Before she shelled the kernels from the ears and attempted to pop them, she had to spend just a little time crying. Then when her tears were dry, she put some of the popcorn in a pot and popped it, and spent the rest of the day stringing it on coarse cotton thread (although Sugrue had never thought to have bought some scissors, he'd stocked a supply of other sewing things, like needles and thread). Thus her Christmas tree was garlanded with white fluffy strings of popcorn. It was the prettiest Christmas tree she'd ever had. She had a bit of trouble keeping Robert from climbing the tree, but she scolded him about it, and he left it alone, although when he thought she wasn't looking he took a swat or two at one of the dangling stars.

The next day she took the shotgun and the turkey caller and went off with Hreapha (she had to shut Robert in the house to keep him from going too, commanding him to stay off the Christmas tree) to find a turkey for Christmas dinner, although she'd eaten so many leftovers from Thanksgiving that she was really tired of turkey and didn't care whether she found one or not. The *Cyclopædia* had a great recipe for roast partridge and another recipe for a bread sauce for partridges, but she had no idea what a partridge was, apart from the "Twelve Days of Christmas" song. There was a pear tree up in the old orchard (which hadn't borne any fruit this year), and she looked there first for the partridge. "Hreapha, do you know what a partridge looks like?" she asked. Poor Hreapha looked very sorrowful not to be able to help, but Robin assumed that one bird was the same as the next to her.

The snow in the woods was deep in places, and they couldn't go very far. Robin didn't even bother with the turkey caller. She decided just to serve ham for Christmas and turned around and headed back toward the house. Suddenly a large bird of some kind flew up out of the leaves and landed on the limb of an oak, and she loaded the shotgun with one shell and aimed it and fired, and the bird was hit. She didn't know if it was a partridge or maybe a prairie chicken or grouse or quail or what.

But she plucked all the feathers off and washed it and stuffed it and prepared to cook it according to the *Cyclopædia*'s recipe for partridge. Christmas morning they woke early because of the brightness: it had snowed during the night and the sunlight was reflecting off the snow and brightening up everything ("In that bright mansion," she sang.) Still entertaining a shred of hope that Santa might somehow have found her house, she ran to the Christmas tree, but could only stand there pretending, "Oh look! A bicycle!" She realized there really wasn't any place she could ride a bicycle in this weedy wilderness. "Oh look! Skis!" she exclaimed and sat down to try them on. Hreapha and Robert observed her oddly. "Merry Christmas, Hreapha!" she said. "Here's a sweater I knitted for you!" and she pretended to put the play-like sweater on Hreapha. She noticed that Hreapha's belly was really swollen. "Merry Christmas, Robert!" she said. "Here's a toy mouse I got for you to chase!" and she wound up the make-believe toy mouse and set it free, but Robert wouldn't chase it. She was sorry that animals couldn't make-believe. She had gift-wrapped just a few of the presents that Sugrue had intended to give her, which were real, not make-believe, and she slowly opened them and thanked him for each one.

She could not help wondering what she might actually have received at Christmas from her mother (and maybe even her father too). She wondered how much her mother missed her, and thought that possibly her mother had even gone ahead and wrapped gifts for her even though she wasn't there. But she was proud of herself for putting together such a good Christmas without any help from her mother.

She'd left three of Sugrue's long socks (which she'd laundered) tacked to the wall beside the stove, and filled them with ribbon candy and popcorn balls made with sugar syrup. Hreapha's stocking also had in it some of the Purina dog chow (which was running low), and Robert's stocking had a can of tuna-fish, and the animals were really able to appreciate the edible contents of their stockings, except the ribbon candy, which they wouldn't eat.

Robin put the partridge (if that's what it was) in the oven to bake. The sun was so bright they went out to play in the snow for a while, and Robin decided to see if they could go as far as the beaver pond, to wish a merry Christmas to their beaver friends. She had to carry Robert because the snow was too deep for him, but it wasn't too deep for Hreapha, who managed to sort of leap in and out of it. They reached the pond to find it covered with ice, but there was an opening through the ice near the beaver's lodge, and when Robin called "Merry Christmas!" a few times the family of beaver came up through that hole in the ice and even attempted to walk on the ice, which was too slippery for them. But Hreapha barked her "Hreapha!" and Robert mewed his "WOO! WOO!" and they were all one big happy family for a little while until Robin began to get very cold, and they just barely made it back to the house before freezing to death.

She had to warm up and dry off at the stove for a long time before she could resume preparing the Christmas dinner. When it was ready, just as she had done at Thanksgiving, she sat Hreapha and Robert at the table and tied little napkins around their necks. She said a kind of grace, "Dear Jesus, I have got to know you pretty well by reading about you, and I do believe you're here with us on your birthday, aren't you? Thank you for being here, Jesus, and thank you for all this food and for keeping us warm and safe. If there was anything I could ask for, it would be that you would let Adam be here too. Happy birthday, Jesus, and Merry Christmas. Amen."

She waited just a few moments, and then called, "Adam? Adam! Don't you want to eat Christmas dinner with us?" There was no answer. She said, "Well, I'm being silly, because ghosts don't eat anything. Do they?"

And his voice replied! *I aint no ghost, you dizzy gal. Ghosts is dead people, I aint never been dead, though I'd felt close to it sometimes.*

"Merry Christmas, Adam!" she said.

Merry Christmas to you, Miss Robin. You've sure been doing it up proud the way my maw would've done, with them popcorn balls and all.

"I'm sorry you can't eat with us, but I'll set a plate out for you anyhow."

Thank ye kindly. Howsomever, that aint no partridge. It's jist a big fat bobwhite. I'll bet it tastes real good anyhow.

They had a nice fine dinner and everybody was happy and after dinner there was just one more thing Robin wanted to do for Christmas. She took a shovel and found the spot under the porch where Sugrue had said he'd buried the money box. She started digging it up. Hreapha stepped in and helped and was a faster digger than Robin, although her swollen belly hampered her and tired her out. They dug up the box and took it into the house, and Robin used the key which Sugrue had given her to try to bribe her into shooting him.

Just for the fun of it, and with nothing better to do for a couple of hours, she counted all the money, which was mostly in hundred dollar bills, four thousand and twenty of them. She might not ever be able to spend any of it. But it sure was nice to have that much, almost half a million.

"Thank you, Sugrue," she said. "Merry Christmas."

Chapter twenty-seven

Too bad the dinner was so meager. Robert got one drumstick and she got the other one, and Robin ate most of the rest. It hadn't been a very large bird to begin with. She had eaten all of the doggy nuggets that had been in her Christmas stocking, understanding full well that the supply of that particular kind of food was running out, and that the time would come when Robin might no longer be able to feed her.

But remembering the huge bird they'd had at Thanksgiving, she had looked forward to a similar feast for Christmas, and was disappointed and restless and famished. She wasn't simply eating for two now. She was eating for perhaps four or five or even six. For several days now, her appetite had been doubled, at least. There was no way she could tell Robin to please put twice as much Purina chow in her bowl. She could only whine and linger expectantly over the bowl, but Robin didn't get the hint.

There were times when she seriously considered eating Robert. It would not only furnish her with much-needed calories and proteins and all that but it would also rid the premises of a nuisance. The bigger Robert had grown, the friskier he had become, and he was constantly in motion, practically bouncing off the walls, and it got on her nerves, especially when she was trying to rest. She didn't care whether or not Robert or Robin understood that she was pregnant, but she had to get them to understand that she needed more rest and peace and quiet than usual. She liked to curl up beside the stove and sleep for hours, but Robert had other ideas: he wanted to play, he wanted to chew on her, he wanted to chase her tail (alas, he had none of his own to chase), he wanted to climb up to the back of the davenport, pretending it was a tree limb and he a mountain lion, and then leap upon his prey, *her*, and knock the wind out of her. She honestly could not understand the reason for the affection she felt for him, which kept her from eating him. Or maybe it was simply that she understood he wouldn't be very tasty.

Fortunately, but embarrassingly, ever since the man had ceased existing and thus had ceased eating many eggs, there was a great surplus of eggs, more than Robin could ever possibly use and more than the hens themselves wanted to sit upon and hatch, and thus, in the interests of self-preservation and to keep her stomach from growling at her (often she had awakened from sleep at full alert, thinking another dog was in the room), she had gone to the henhouse and sucked an egg or two. She was now regrettably a dyed-in-the-wool chronic egg-sucking dog, but she was almost tired of eggs. You really couldn't sink your teeth into their contents, so while they might be nourishing they weren't much fun to eat.

Shortly after Christmas the weather turned so terribly cold that none of them wanted to go outside, and the poor poultry were in danger of freezing. On one of the warmer days before Christmas, Robin had gone out to the woodpile and laboriously brought in all the wood she could carry and stacked it right in the living room. Then when the weather got so cold, she closed the kitchen door, letting the kitchen stove go cold, and did what little cooking she had to do on the living room stove. Eventually she had to close off the other two rooms, putting the feather mattress on the living room floor, so they lived entirely in that one room, going out only when they had to do their business, and making their business as speedy as possible. Although Robert had been what Robin called "housebroken" for some time now, meaning he didn't want to get scolded for doing his business in the house, there were a few days that winter when it was so hideously freezing outside that he stubbornly refused to go out for his business and did it under the davenport. Robin not only screamed at him but rubbed his nose in it, and Hreapha said "HREAPHA!" meaning, "Just say the word, and I'll gladly eat him,"

One day, when Robin opened the door to the storeroom to get some food, Hreapha dashed into the room and with her nose nudged one of the empty cardboard boxes toward the door.

Robin got the hint. "You want a box, Hreapha?" she asked, and picked up the empty box and set it in the living room. Hreapha nudged it closer to the stove, but not too close. Then she leaped up and pulled a pair of the man's trousers from a peg on the wall, and deposited them in the box. Then she likewise pulled the man's overalls off their wall-peg and put them in the box.

"Golly gee, Hreapha," Robin said. "Are you trying to pack up his things to send away or just get them out of sight? Maybe that's a good idea. I'm tired of seeing them."

Hreapha also got some of the man's underthings and stockings into the box, and then, when she had the "nest" thoroughly padded, she climbed into the box and curled up into a comfortable position, cushioned by the man's clothing. She hoped Robin would understand that she had built herself a nest.

And possibly Robin did. "Oh," she said, looking down at Hreapha. "Is this where you're going to have your babies?"

"Hreapha," said Hreapha.

But when the time came, she found that she couldn't remain in the box. Staying curled up in the box made her think too much and worry too much. She fully understood that what she was about to do was natural and part of her job. She did not worry a lot about whether she would be a good mother or not. But she couldn't help worrying about how all those babies were going to get out of her, and whether it would hurt her a lot. She got up. She sat down. She got up. She sat down. She couldn't decide which was better.

She paced the room. There wasn't really enough room to pace properly, but she had to pace and she walked constantly from wall to wall. "You don't want to go out, do you?" Robin asked, and held the door open for just a moment, but the wintry blast that blew into the room made her quickly close it.

What Hreapha really wanted to do was dig, yes. She wanted to get out into the snow and dig and dig and dig down into the earth. She didn't know why. Was she expecting the babies to be stillborn and wanted to have holes to bury them in? It scared her. She paced, and couldn't stop.

She began to shiver, but not because she was cold. Maybe she was shivering from dread. Maybe the living things inside her were doing the shivering and it was making her shiver too. She decided that what she really needed was some grass to eat, but all the grass was covered with snow.

She began to pant, as if she'd already been running for miles, but all the pacing she had been doing, wall to wall, had not tired her that much. She was not panting because of her pacing. But she kept on pacing, and shivering, and panting.

And then she stopped suddenly and helplessly threw up.

"Oh no!" Robin said. Robin put her hand on the back of Hreapha's neck, and that helped, but Hreapha went on heaving.

Leave her be, said the in-habit. *They allus do that, they allus puke right before birthing, just so's they'll have a empty stomach during the work. She'll be okay.*

Hreapha was so happy to know that the *in-habit* was going to be in attendance at the event that her fears left her for a while, long enough for her to climb into her box-nest and lie down. And then she felt the urge to strain, thinking at first that she needed to do her business, but then she was amused by that thought. It is my business, she said to herself, but not the business of pooping. The business of birthing. She liked the word the *in-habit* had used. Birthing.

Might be a good idee to build up the fire a bit, the *in-habit* told Robin. *Also have a towel or two handy.*

So Hreapha strained. And she strained. And she grunted and growled and strained. She really had a reason to be panting now, and between straining she did a lot of panting. Robin brought her a dish of water but she didn't want it. Not yet.

You jist might be a bit too young to watch, the in-habit said to Robin. *Why don't ye go sit on the davenport and I'll keep ye posted.*

"I want to watch," Robin said. Hreapha didn't want her to watch, and now even Robert had propped his paws on the edge of the box and was trying to peer into it. Hreapha didn't want anybody, not even the *in-habit,* watching. She snarled. "HREAPHA!" she said; go away.

But then she didn't care any more. She took a deep breath, bore down, grunted and kept it up for as long as she could.

Here she comes, said the *in-habit,* and sure enough she glanced at her flank and there was a pup, covered with slime and a double membrane which, she knew, she had to remove. She licked the membrane and seized it in her teeth and peeled it off her pup. The pup was a female and looked, Hreapha was pleased to note, more like Yowrfrowr than like herself. She was going to have a shaggy coat someday.

"He's beautiful!" Robin said.

She, said the *in-habit. It's a she-puppy. But jist hold your horses, they'll be more of 'em.*

To make room for another one, Hreapha had to tidy things up a bit: she ate the membrane, the placenta and the afterbirth, not that she was hungry at all at the moment and they certainly weren't especially tasty but they were edible.

And then she had to bear down and strain again for a long time before another one appeared. This one was male. She was getting tired, and wished it were all over, but there were hours and hours yet to go. The third pup seemed to be the hardest of all in terms of the time and effort before she could get it out. It was another female, who seemed to look more like herself than Yowrfrowr. Hreapha was too tired to eat the placenta and decided to wait and do it along with the next one. The fourth pup came fairly easy, another male, but Hreapha was exhausted and had to rest for a long time before she could even try to strain again to see if there might be a fifth one. She was so tired that she actually drifted off to sleep, aware that the four puppies were already nuzzling up to her teats and starting to nurse. That was the only pleasure she'd had for many hours and maybe that was what put her to sleep.

She woke because the fifth puppy wanted out. She didn't know how long she'd been asleep but perhaps it was long enough to give her the strength to strain again. She strained. Minutes passed. Did hours pass? It was dark outside. Night had come. She kept on straining. She strained so hard it made her dizzy. She felt herself drifting off again, not into sleep but into something dark and black and deep, but she fought her way back from there. She kept ahold of this world long enough to sigh and push out one more puppy. But she had no strength at all to lick the membrane from it. Even with the double membrane covering it she could see that this puppy, a male, did not look like his brothers and sisters. And also that he seemed to be stillborn. All the puppies had their eyes tightly shut but this one's eyes were not only closed but lifeless.

She heard the *in-habit's* urgent voice, *Wrap it in a towel! Wrap it and rub it! Rub it hard!*

That was all she could remember. When she came back into this world again, it was broad daylight; not only had the night gone but the morning too. She felt very sick, and needed to relieve herself, not to do any business but just to make much water. She tried to get up but there were five puppies clinging to her. There was blood all over the man's clothes lining her nest.

"She's awake!" Robin said. "She's alive and awake."

Them pups has started in to nursing again, the *in-habit's* voice said, *so ye ort to know they couldn't git no milk from a dead momma.*

"I think she needs to go," Robin said.

Go? Said the in-habit. Aw, ye mean to take a leak?

Robin pulled the puppies away from her, then helped Hreapha lift herself out of the box.

"I won't open the door for you," Robin said. "It must be below zero out there, and you'd freeze to death. Just use that corner." She pointed to a corner of the room behind the woodpile. There were wood chips there, so Hreapha wasn't too abashed to make her lengthy markings on them. But then she saw that some green stuff was oozing out of her afterplace, and then she had black diarrhea, and the sight of all that mess caused her to faint.

When she came to, it was night again. She was in her nest,

which Robin had cleaned up, and Robin had also cleaned her after-place. Her five puppies were not nursing, but just sleeping deeply, snuggled up in a pile with one another. It was very clear that the fifth one did not have Yowrfrowr as its father. But she loved it all the same, and gave its face a lick.

"She's awake!" Robin said. "But she's burning up." Robin's very cold hand was resting on her neck.

They're allus kinder hot for a few days afterwards, the *in-habit* said. *I reckon she'll be okay. But she's had a bad time*

"You know so much," Robin said. "Did you have a dog when you lived here?"

The *in-habit* laughed. *Yep, they was allus dogs on the place. But they was jist one of them, Hector, was my own mutt.*

"Hector's an odd name for a dog."

Old Heck used to want to go to school with me, but the trail was just too steep for him. So he'd just sit the livelong day waiting for me to come home after school.

The *in-habit* and Robin went on talking, and Hreapha drifted off to sleep again and even had dreams in which she led the whole pack of her five grown-up offspring as they chased a raccoon through the woods.

Hreapha woke to find the puppies nursing again, and she sighed and just lay there enjoying it, although she still felt very sick.

Finally she really had to go out. She was not going to do her business beside the woodpile and mess up the floor again. She scratched at the door and whined, and Robin said, "Are you sure you want to go out?"

"Hreapha," she said, and Robin opened the door and let her out. The first thing she did was dig down into the snow until she found grass, and got a mouthful of grass and chewed it and swallowed it. Then she did her business, and climbed the porch and scratched at the door. While she was waiting for Robin to open it, she glanced at the outhouse, where the white skeleton, the same whiteness as the snow, was just sitting there watching her. "Hreapha!" she said to him.

Days and days passed before the puppies finally opened their eyes and looked at her. Until then they were just helpless lumps who could barely move, and couldn't do their business for themselves but had to have their mother lick their afterplaces to clean them. Hreapha didn't mind. It was her job.

They couldn't even try to walk until two weeks or so had passed. And it was about that time that they made their first attempts at barking, so that Hreapha was able to determine what each of them wanted to be named. The firstborn male was named simply Hrolf. His sister, who had actually preceded him in birthing, was named Hroberta, possibly in honor of her godfather, the bobcat. The second male was named Hrothgar. And the second female was named Hruschka. But the third male, the fifthborn, did not make the same sounds as his siblings, possibly because his father was a coyote. So Hreapha had to accept that his name was Yipyip. Not only in name but in every other respect, he would stand apart from the others.

Robin was thrilled with the puppies, and was constantly picking them up and holding them (one at a time of course) and laughed to watch their clumsy attempts to walk and fight with each other. Robert sulked for a few days because of all the attention being paid to the pups, but eventually he discovered that they liked him and he attempted to join them in their play. He was especially fond of the one named Hroberta, and with Hreapha's permission he took naps with her. The pups slept practically all the time when they weren't nursing. But then, when they could walk, they discovered Hreapha's food dish and began chomping away at her doggy nuggets.

"Oh oh," Robin declared one morning as she poured some doggy nuggets out of the bag into Hreapha's bowl, where six hungry mouths were waiting for it. "That's all there is. There's not any more Purina Dog Chow. It's all gone."

Hreapha considered teaching her offspring how to suck eggs. But even the chickens were not laying many eggs in this horribly cold weather, when all the bugs and worms and other staples of their diet had gone into hibernation. There were only just enough for Robin.

Robin opened a jar of pickled pig's feet and put some of it in Hreapha's food dish. From previous experience Hreapha disdained it, but to her surprise she discovered her pups loved the stuff…after she took the trouble to pick the little bones out.

And when Robin opened a can of beef stew, Hreapha discovered that it would suit her just fine.

By the time the puppies no longer had to suckle milk out of Hreapha but could eat whatever Robin could furnish from cans or jars, the first signs of Spring were in the air.

Chapter twenty-eight

The imaginative reader, meaning you, has for some time now been caught up in the idyllic aspects of Robin's situation. Even before Sog was dispensed with, you had an awareness of the sheer lively entertainment that Robin was experiencing, almost to the point of making her forget the world she had been stolen from.

Thus it is my unpleasant duty to reveal aspects of her existence which were less than ideal. Sog's death was decidedly a mixed blessing; it left her figuratively without insulation against life with its unkind vicissitudes, just as the house itself literally had no insulation against the winter cold (in those days the so-called "wind-chill factor" had not yet been discovered, but the howling winds on Madewell Mountain often dropped the temperature well below zero). Despite my own antipathy toward Sog, I was willing to concede that preferably he should have been allowed to continue living for several more months or even a year if need be (for the record, his affliction was a malignant form of degenerative multiple sclerosis which would have been treatable with medical attention). Living a bit longer would have permitted him to fully prepare Robin for the life she was going to have to live without him. As it was, a day would not go by that she did not discover things she needed to ask him, or things she wanted him to do for her, or tasks that required his help.

If Sog had managed to hang on a while longer, he would certainly have chewed her out for her mismanagement of the household. He hadn't been at all fastidious himself, but he still would have jumped all over her. She quit sweeping the house, and not because of that superstition he'd given her, "Don't never drop your broom so it falls flat on the floor, and if you do drop it don't never step over it." Sog had often been required to nag her into washing the dishes; now that he was gone, she quit washing dishes entirely, except when she had to have one, and then she just wiped it with a dirty rag. She quit washing practically everything, including herself, her clothing and her bedding, using as an excuse the fact that it was too cold to go out to the well. One morning, when she just had to have some drinking water, she found the well bucket frozen tight to the ice beneath it, and couldn't pry it loose. She made do with snow melted in a pan on the stove. The stove periodically required having its ashes removed, and although she had a scuttle and a little shovel for that purpose she was negligent in using them, and the stove became inefficient to the point where all the inhabitants (except me) were unnecessarily cold.

She had no regard for the larder. She had no concept of budgeting the food supply, and thus had already run out of several things that she couldn't do without, least of all the Purina Dog Chow. She was going to run out of flour in a few more months, and then she'd really be in a pickle. And speaking of pickles, having happily discovered that Hreapha's pups loved Sog's pickled pig's feet, she gave no thought to rationing the stuff. And speaking of Hreapha's pups, although their thoughtful mother did her best to housebreak them, Robin did nothing to clean up the mess that they sometimes made, with the result that the living room in which all eight creatures were living and from which they were all loath to sally out into the subzero weather was a veritable pigsty, or (since the only evidence of actual pigs were their feet) a crummy dump, uninhabitable by anyone except an *in-habit*: fortunately, although I could see and hear I chose not to smell. At the age of twelve I was not especially neat and tidy myself;

in fact, I couldn't care less about orderliness, but even I was moved to remark to Robin one cloudy day, *This place aint fitten for dogs!* If Adam's mother had been there, blind though she was, she would have fainted. If Robin's mother had been there…well, of course, if Robin's mother had been there she would have immediately whisked her daughter out of the place.

Which reminds me that it has been a good while since we last saw or heard anything from Karen Kerr. Mention was made that she'd been spending a lot of time with the FBI agent, who, Leo's wife Louisa had remarked, might become Leo's new son-in-law. If it's of any interest, as a matter of fact the FBI agent, Hal Knight, did propose to Karen Kerr at Christmas, but she, while confessing her love for him, said that it would not be "seemly" to get married while she was still in mourning for Robin. I'm sure we'll hear more about her farther along.

As Hreapha was the first to detect, the signs of Spring were in the air, and it would soon be time for the whole pack of them to get outdoors, open the windows and doors and air out the house, and for Robin, even if I had to get on her case, to do a bit of cleaning.

In fact she was prompted to do so not by my giving her a talking to, but by the appearance in the yard of the first daffodils. Adam's mother had once obtained, after a visit to her sister in Parthenon, a peck of bulbs for tulips and daffodils, and had planted them ("naturalizing" is the modern gardener's term) randomly around the yard, where many of them had received unwitting fertilizer from the toilet habits of Hreapha, Robert, and Robin, as well as all the pups (not to mention the dozens of free-ranging chickens). Now, twenty-one years after Sarah Madewell had gone to California, leaving behind the bright flowers that she had been able to enjoy only through touch and smell (and Adam would never forget the sight of his mother down on her knees gently fondling the daffodils each early March), the bulbs not only continued to bloom but had greatly multiplied. Their coming up seemed to be, for Robin, a sign of renewal and hope. She gathered several to put into a vase for the kitchen table, and the sight of those bright clean yellow flowers in all that squalor tempted her to do something she hadn't done for months: give the house a thorough sweeping and dusting. That done, she was even inspired to go out to the henhouse and do an awful chore she'd neglected all winter, shoveling the chicken manure into the wheelbarrow and carting it out to fertilize the vegetable garden soil, as she had been advised by the *Cyclopædia*.

That done, she was even inspired to go into the barrel factory and straighten things up. *Hold your horses!* I exclaimed. *There aint no call to be moving things around in here.*

"Hi, Adam," she said. "I thought you'd moved into the house and didn't stay out here any more."

How confess to her that I was her stalker? *I generally keep an eye on whatever's going on around here,* I declared. *Don't matter whether it's the house or this shed or wherever.*

"It's so messy out here," she said, sweeping her arms around her.

But look what ye done, I pointed out, although I was unable to point. *You've put the bung flogger and the chime hoop maul on the same bench. That aint where they belong.*

"There's so much junk all over," she said.

Aint a bit of junk. Ever one of them tools—stave froe, jointer, swift, stoup plane, horse, chince, backing knife, croze and flagging iron has got a use, and if you was to lose ary one of 'em, you'd be on the spot.

"But what do *I* need them for?" she asked. "I won't ever make a barrel."

Naw, but you might could make a firkin.

"You're bad, Adam! Did you say 'fucking'?"

I blushed, as much as invisible cheeks can redden. *Aint you the feisty'un, though? What I said was* firkin, *which is what's called a small cask for keeping butter.*

"Where would I get any butter?" she wanted to know.

She had me there. I laughed at my own slip. And then offered, *Wal, ye never can tell, some old cow might come wanderin lost into the pasture some day.*

"That would be nice," she said. "Would you be able to teach me how to milk it and then how to use the churn to make butter?"

Why, shore. If you'll look at the corner over your left shoulder you'll see a right nice butter churn.

"Sugrue told me what it was."

That was the last thing I made afore we left. I mean the last thing that Adam made afore his folks up and took off for California. Can you turn it upside down and look at the bottom?

She did so, and there were the initials "AM" that Adam had burned into the wood with the branding tool.

"*You* made this?" she asked.

Adam Madewell made it well, I said with a giggle. *Recall I aint Adam, jist his leavings. What ole Hreapha calls a "in-habit."*

She was smiling. "So this '*AM*' is not just your initials, but it means you *are*."

I didn't yet follow her. At twelve I was slow in realizing that she had recognized and was referring to the first person singular present indicative of *be*. As in the Cartesian axiom. Am = *sum*. In all his years of living with those initials—and he was still very much living with them—it had never occurred to Adam that the initials were an assertion of his existence, his being. When Adam's twelve-year-old *in-habit* finally got the concept through his thick skull, his admiration for Robin was greater than ever: he fell in love with her, although what he had been feeling for her already amounted to slavish devotion.

That shore is real clever, I granted.

"So can you teach me how to make a fuckin?" she asked.

If you can learn to say the word proper.

"Firkin! Firkin! Firkin!" she said, and giggled.

My daddy never believed that I could make that 'ere churn, I related. *Matter a fact, I aint made it just yet. I'm not but twelve and Adam made that churn when he was twelve just before he left me behind, so you could even play like the churn aint been made yet. Not "am" but "aint." Wal, little lady, I'll tell ye: you'd want to make your firkin out of cedar, not out of white oak the way all these barrels has been made. I made my churn out of cedar. Cedar don't shrink when it dries. But you've got to cut the cedar in the fall, not the spring when the sap's a-rising. Come to think on it, there's a stack of cedar staves out to the barn that I already split with the stave froe.*

"Sugrue told me not to go near that barn," she said. "It could come crashing down on top of me."

Naw, it won't. Grampaw built that barn to last forever. Braxton Madewell had made the barn as well as he made anything, and the barn might still be standing years after I no longer inhabit the place.

"I could just tiptoe in there and grab them," she offered. "How many would I need for a firkin?"

A dozen ought to do it, I said.

Robin brought an armful of cedar staves from the barn. They had been seasoning for two decades and were thoroughly dry. "Now what?" she asked.

I sniffed one of the staves. *All the cedar smell is gone, so it won't give your butter a cedar taste.*

"What butter?" she asked, and laughed. "I can use it for a water bucket instead of a firkin. What do I do next?"

Them is churn staves. You'll have to saw 'em down to firkin size, if you can. That's the stave saw hanging on the wall yonder. She looked around but couldn't seem to find it. It was a damned nuisance for me not to be able to point. *See all them things a-hanging yonder by the window? Naw, to your right. That's it. The third one over is the stave saw. Now prop a stave here on this horse and see iffen ye can cut it in half.*

It was slow work. Robin simply didn't have the muscle for sawing, but she persisted, and managed after a long while to cut the stave in half. I might have become bored or restless during the long passage of time required for her to do all the cutting, but for the simple fact that just as I was free from appetites and susceptibility to the physical world, I was also free from the passage of time, its speed or dragging. But Robin's pets, seven in number now, grew tired of observing her and went off to play elsewhere. Or, more likely, they went off into the woods to rustle up their supper.

The shaving horse was just a little easier, not much. She had to sit on the horse, and draw the two-handled bucket shave toward her again and again along the edges of the stave, to shape it. She began intoning aloud a little work-chant: "Shave the stave. Shave the stave. Shave the stave." Why hadn't I ever thought of that? Or rather Adam, when he worked? Because he lacked her imagination, and her sense of words. I joined my voice to hers: *Shave the stave. Shave the stave.*

Shave the stave. She had to stop to laugh more often than she had to stop to rest.

But then, as I pointed out, it was necessary to sharpen the bucket shave. *Blades has got to be kept keen,* I told her. Sog had already shown her how to use the treadle whetstone, although she was always catching and bumping her knees in it and had hobbled for a week the first time she'd tried to use it. That had been for sharpening the kitchen knives and the hog butchering knives and occasionally her scissors. Now she had to learn how to keep the cooper's knives and shaves razor-sharp.

Paw allus tole me, "Ever a tool falls off the bench, don't never try to grab it. It'll slice your fingers off." It was something Robin would have to learn and remember because one always instinctively tries to keep something from falling. If a cooper's tool falls, you must let it fall.

I couldn't show Robin my right hand—I didn't have one—and I couldn't show her Adam's right hand, which was missing the index finger, from an accident in which he forgot that warning, grabbed for the backing knife as it fell, and not only sliced off the finger but hurled the knife against his leg, causing a deep gash that left him unable to walk at all for months and to walk only poorly thereafter. Only once again was he able to try to make the long hike to Stay More, and that, as we'll see, ended in an accident which kept him at home thereafter, which his father considered a blessing, for two reasons: one, his father despised education and books, and two, Adam was able, once he could walk again, to spend all his time helping his father in the cooperage.

Nor could I show Robin Adam's left thumb, which was severely callused from the hammering and driving of the hoops onto barrels. His hands in general were covered with hard skin, although not nearly as bad as his father's, which were grotesquely callused all over.

I did not want Robin to get any calluses, let alone cuts. But she was determined to make her firkin. The days were still short, and it grew dark before she had completed the task of dressing the staves, and I half hoped that her enthusiasm for the job might drift away overnight if she got interested in something else. But she returned to the cooperage early the next morning, and it was my painful duty to point out to her that while she had successfully shaped the staves she had not yet jointed them, that is, tapered their sides so they would fit together in a circle. It was hard to explain to a girl so young that *backing* a stave, which she had done, must be followed up by *jointing* the stave, with the upturned plane called a jointer. And first she had to sharpen the blade of the plane. By the time she had successfully reassembled the plane with the sharpened blade and was ready to use the long-jointer, I had to explain the gauge to her: a two-pronged wooden thingamajig which determines the angle of each stave to make them fit snuggly into an exact diameter of, in this case, ten inches.

This here's the most important job of all, I said, meaning to encourage her, but it seemed to dispirit her.

She did a fair job of angling the edges of four or five staves, but then her eyes moistened and tears began running down her cheeks and into her work. She returned the jointing plane to the bench and said, "Adam, I don't think I'm big enough to do this. Would you mind if I waited until I got bigger?"

Her words touched me. If *in-habits* could weep, I would've. Something in her words seemed to suggest a kind of resignation: she truly understood that she would have to go on living here until she grew older and bigger. Or even until she died.

But the twelve-year-old *in-habit* was somewhat scornful that she could not finish a job that she'd started. I pouted, *You was the one who wanted a firkin.* I realized the sexual suggestiveness of those words. I rephrased it, *You was the one who wanted to be learnt how to make you a little cask. But heck, I won't hold it again ye.*

"Thank you, Adam," she said, and went on back to the house, where she took advantage of her pets being out of doors to spread out her paper doll town of Stay More on the newly swept floor. But she took one paper doll house and three of the paper dolls and put them not on the floor but on the topmost part of the davenport. "This is the Madewells and their house, way up here on a mountaintop," she said, in case I was listening. "Someday soon you'll have to tell me all about them."

Any old time, I said.

Chapter twenty-nine

Stay More was a relief to her, it helped her get away from herself and her plight and her most recent failure. Maybe she never could build a firkin, but she could always build Stay More, not just the town itself but all the people in it. She lost herself in their lives. It was hard to feel lonely when there were all these Ingledews and Swains and Dinsmores and all of them let her make them and follow their feelings and their doings. So easily she took on their voices. So easily they softened her solitude.

She had the town (and the Madewells up on their davenport-mountain) arranged so neatly that for many days she would not let the animals come back into the house, for fear they would mess up her paper dolls in their paper houses. It was getting warm enough now that even though the nights went below freezing Hreapha's pups and Robert could snuggle up with Hreapha somewhere out in the yard or maybe the cooper's shed and keep warm until the sun rose.

And that good old sun started rising earlier and earlier and hotter and hotter. One morning Robin realized it was just too nice outside to stay indoors with her paper dolls, so she put on her light jacket and went out. The lovely daffodils had drooped and shriveled and would soon be finished with their flowering. Robin decided she might have to plant some flowers, if she wanted any more other than wildflowers. She went out to the garden spot and kicked out around the leaves that covered it. She was uncertain about that garden. On one hand her attempts to spade it up and plant it and all might require more muscle than she'd had to use in her failure to make the firkin, and she didn't need another failure so soon after that one. But on the other hand, she really did love corn on the cob and muskmelons and even the vegetables that weren't green, such as yellow squash and potatoes and onions and, yes, those big juicy tomatoes that Sugrue had grown which were so much tastier than the bland tomatoes her mother used to bring home from work.

While she was kicking around through the leaves, she uncovered some spinach and turnips that had survived the winter. She was amazed that they were still alive and growing, even though she wouldn't eat spinach and positively hated turnips. But later that same day, while she was poring over "The Garden" parts of her 1888 *Cyclopædia*, she came across the following, in a section on starting tender seeds such as tomatoes, squashes, and melons: "It is desirable in transplanting not to check the growth by disturbing the roots. A good way to avoid this is to scrape out turnips, fill them with good soil and plant in two or three seeds, setting them in a warm, light place, and keeping them moist. When the weather is suitable, place these out in the garden at the proper depth. The turnip will decay and the plant will thrive unchecked if properly cared for." It sounded like a lot of fun, so Robin took the shovel and went back out to the garden and dug up all the turnips, just a dozen or so, and took them to the house and scooped out their insides. The pulp was earthy and piquant and she was almost tempted to cook it and see if she could stand to eat it.

Where had Sugrue told her he was keeping the seeds? She searched through the storeroom (Adam's room once, and now again) looking for the little box that contained the packets of seeds, but couldn't find it. "Adam?" she called out. "Can you help me find the seeds?" There was no answer. She should have known better. She had learned that Adam would never "come" when called. In fact, she had learned that it was almost a guarantee he'd stay in hiding if she tried to find him or reach him or call him. It was frustrating. And it also made her think again that Adam was simply somebody she'd made up in her own head, the same way she made up all those paper people of Stay More. But how could she have even started on that firkin without his help? How could she have helped Hreapha give birth without his help? No, she *knew* that this place really was inhabited by Adam's—what was that word he had used?—his *leavings,* his *in-habit.* She knew she didn't have the imagination to come up with that name, *in-habit,* just as she didn't have the imagination to come up with *firkin* or even the name of Adam's dog, Hector. "Adam?" she said, louder. "Don't you want me to have a garden? Can't you help me find the seeds?" But there was no answer. She went on searching. The Madewell house had no closets or cabinets the way other houses do, so there weren't any places like that to search in.

She practically turned the storeroom upside down, moving all the boxes and bags and sacks. But the box wasn't there. The only place she hadn't looked was inside the Sentry money-box, and she opened the lid just to see if all her money was still there. And there amidst the money was the box of seeds! She certainly hadn't put it there. Or she certainly didn't remember putting it there. Had Sugrue's ghost possibly put the seeds in the money-box? The thought made her flesh crawl. But she had enough trouble with *in-habits,* she didn't want any trouble from ghosts. She knew that it wasn't impossible that she herself had absent-mindedly put the seeds in the money box, because she was often confused and distracted with all her responsibilities that cluttered up the world worse than all the actual clutter that was everywhere.

Anyway, she now had the seeds. She sat and slowly sorted them, setting aside any that she either wouldn't plant or wouldn't plant until she was old enough to develop a taste for that particular plant: green beans and peas and spinach and lettuce and cabbage and cucumber and beets and turnips and okra. To the other side she placed the packets for sweet corn, popcorn, tomatoes, squash, cantaloupe, wax beans, onions, carrots, and radishes. She couldn't find the seeds for the potatoes, but then she remembered the instructions Sugrue had given her for sprouting a sweet potato to make "slips," and how to cut up the Irish potatoes so that each had an "eye" that could be planted. She also added to the "using" pile the seed packets for some flowers: nasturtiums and marigolds and zinnias and petunias and sweet peas and morning glories and cosmos. The *Cyclopædia* didn't say anything about planting and raising flowers; it had a whole chapter on "Floriculture," but that was mostly on how to decorate with flowers after you've grown them.

There was one thick envelope in the seed box that simply said "wheat" on it. She couldn't remember that Sugrue had planted any wheat. She could remember a film she'd watched in school about gristmills and how they ground up wheat to make it into flour. She hadn't been thinking of flour as something that was grown but she suddenly realized that the big cloth sack of flour on the storeroom floor was the last one; they'd had several to start out with. When that sack was used up, she wouldn't have any more flour. She wouldn't be able to do any more baking.

"ADAM!" she called out. "Please help me. I'm frantic. Where did you get your flour? Did you grow wheat?" But again there was no answer. She decided to look up wheat in her *Cyclopædia,* but all it told her was how to harvest it and stack it into shocks. It didn't say anything about how you could make your own flour.

She took the scooped-out turnips and filled them with dirt and planted in each of them seeds of tomato, cantaloupe, and squash, as the book had said. She set them on the south window sills and forgot about them, until one day Robert knocked them all off, and she had to replant them and tell Robert that he was no longer allowed in the house.

It was lonelier for her at night, not sleeping with her kitty (who wasn't a kitty any more but a large cat), or her dog, and she started pining for Paddington again. And some nights she had to cry herself to sleep.

Thinking of Paddington, she wondered how long it had been since she had seen him last. So one afternoon, after she was tired of trying to spade up the garden (the *Cyclopædia* talked about plowing your garden with a cultivator pulled by a horse, ha ha), she took a break and put her Ouija Board on the floor of the porch and called Hreapha to play with her. Hreapha was such a devoted mother that Robin didn't see very much of her these days unless she made an effort to look her up, and often Hreapha took her pups out into the woods to run around and play and even hunt little animals to eat. Both Robert and Hreapha had learned to catch squirrels and rabbits and chew them up, which was a good thing, because Robin had nothing in the house to feed them with.

The first thing they asked the Ouija Board was how to spell the names of the five puppies. Although Robin had been able, from the sounds of their barking, to guess roughly what Hreapha's babies were named, it was good to find out how their names were actually spelled, and Robin was interested to note that they all started with "Hr" like their mother's name, except for the odd one, the one who didn't look at all like the others, and whose name wasn't spelled at all like theirs, Yipyip. While Hreapha herself seemed partial to the first-born, Hrolf, and Robert liked to play with the one named Hroberta, Robin had from the beginning felt more affection for Yipyip, possibly because he was so different from the others, and Robin herself, as long as she'd had other children to compare herself with, had prized the differences in herself, how she was distinctly her own person and would not like anything simply because other kids liked it, and how she was often at odds with everyone else. Yipyip preferred to go his own way. And of course he spoke his own language.

"Now," Robin said to Hreapha, "what I want to ask the Ouija Board is how long I've been here at this house. Have I been here a whole year yet?" She tried to explain to Hreapha—and to the Ouija Board—that she wanted to do something to observe the occasion (she vaguely recalled the word "anniversary" but wasn't certain about it), not that she wanted to celebrate, because she didn't intend to celebrate a year of being taken away from her home and mother. "Whenever it's a full year that I've been here, a whole twelve months, the earth has gone all the way around the sun. Does that mean anything to you?" She looked into Hreapha's eyes and caught a glimmer of understanding. Then Hreapha put her paw on the planchette and moved it to the "YES."

The Ouija Board told them that the anniversary would occur in six days. "So we ought to do something on that day, six days from now, to, not to celebrate but just to *keep* the day. Don't you think that would be a good day to escape, to try to find the way out of here?"

Hreapha's paw moved the planchette to "NO."

"No? Why not? Do you like it here so much?"

Hreapha's paw tapped the planchette as it was parked upon the "NO."

"Are you afraid to try to get out of here with your pups and Robert and me?"

Hreapha moved the planchette to "YES."

Robin pondered. At length she said, "Well, we can't stay here forever, can we?"

Hreapha tapped the planchette at "YES."

"That's not fair!" Robin said, realizing her voice was whining. "I can't go on living my whole life here and never seeing anybody ever again. I mean anybody *human*." When Hreapha made no response to that other than continuing to stare at Robin with her soulful eyes, Robin at length said, "Okay, I guess we'll keep the day of the first year by doing something special like planting the garden."

And that is what she did. She spent the six days until that day working until she was exhausted, spading up as much of Sugrue's garden space as she could possibly spade up. She wore her boots and stood up on the back of the tines of the spade and jumped up and down on them to force them into the soil. The third day it rained, so on the fourth day she discovered she could force the spade into the soil without jumping on it. By the sixth day, the awful anniversary of her captivity, she had enough of the soil turned over so that she could rake it and plant in it all the seeds that she had selected from the seed box. Unfortunately she did not know that some seeds must not be planted until after last frost, and these seeds did not take or the tender seedlings were killed when the last frost came a couple of weeks later. Worse than that, she had no idea how deep to plant seeds, and planted most of them too deep, although the potatoes she planted too shallow.

Robin was going to have to learn gardening by trial and error, and she was going to have to remember from one year to the next what mistakes she had made. She thought of her first year's garden as a worse failure than her attempt to put a firkin together, but that wasn't strictly true. She would, in time, reap what she had sown. The stomach is the best teacher. The harvesting in less than a month of the first radishes that she had planted were such a joy that she made a lunch of nothing but radishes, and was motivated to do something Sugrue had never been able to persuade her to do: keep the weeds out of the garden.

Her little garden plot covered less than a third of the space Sugrue had originally cleared for a garden, so she broadcast the wheat seeds over the other two thirds, and in time took an interest in watching the wheat come up and grow, and was informed by her *Cyclopædia* exactly when the wheat would be ready for harvest.

As the spring passed into summer and the hot sun bore down, Robin discovered that she really didn't need any clothes. So she stopped wearing them. They were getting too small for her anyway, and she remembered that stupid Sugrue had never realized that she would outgrow all the new clothes he'd bought for her. She had already decided never to cut her hair again, and it was down to her shoulder blades behind and to her nipples in front, and when the breeze came, as it often did, it blew her hair all around her face and shoulders, and she loved the feel of the breeze as well as the smell of it. She discovered that the breeze in her hair felt better if she washed her hair and made it fluffy, and this alone gave her the motivation to keep her hair washed.

She recalled with amusement, as if watching a movie about somebody else, the Robin Kerr who could not stand to go barefoot even when all the other kids were doing it at recess. Now when she ran around without a stitch on, that included the stitches of her shoes. Sometimes she stepped on something sharp that caused her to yell, and a few times she stepped on something sharp that pierced the sole of her foot so that she had to run to the house and get out the first aid kit and apply antiseptic ointment and maybe a Band-aid. But her feet learned to love the feel of the cool moist earth.

When work was done, she played. She went back to the practice of taekwondo, and perfected it, with her kicks and thrusts and jabs. "Come out, Adam!" she hollered, "and I'll give you a *chagi* in the nuts!" She knew that he was probably watching her. Probably he was even all excited to see a naked girl jumping around like that doing her taekwondo. In the evenings before dark when she was tired of reading the Bible stories or the *Cyclopædia,* she would get out the third book, the only other book in the house, the *Nudist Moppets,* and have some fun looking again at the displays and antics, and she understood full well that if men (including twelve-year-old *in-habit*s) got so much fun out of looking at such pictures, then Adam was probably getting more than an eyeful.

One day when he made no response whatever to her inviting him to come out and get his nuts kicked, she hollered, "Come out, Adam, and I'll give you a kiss!"

And sure enough, that brought him out. *Here I am,* his unmistakable young voice said, *but I reckon I don't need no kiss.*

"You've been ignoring me for months!" she complained. "Where have you been, anyway? Gone fishing?"

You ort to know I caint be living with ye, much as I'd keer to.

"But can't you answer simple questions? I wanted to know about wheat and flour and needed you to answer me. Did your folks grow wheat? Where did you get your flour?"

Down to Latha's store, where everbody else got it.

"You mean the general store in Stay More? But how did you carry it home? An eighty-pound bag of flour would be awfully hard to carry on that terrible trail."

I took a mule the long way around, on the trail that you came in on, what Grampaw called the North Way. It took a while, but I generally had to get a bunch of other things that Maw needed from the store. And I generally wanted to say howdy to Roseleen.

"Who was Roseleen?"

He was slow in answering, as if he didn't want to tell her. *I aint tole ye about her yet, but I reckon I will one of these days.*

"But you bought all your flour at the store. You didn't grow any wheat?"

Grampaw used to grow it out in yon meader, but it'd have to be

took to town to the mill, so it was easier jist to buy the flour. Mill's been
shut down for many a year.

"Well, I can't go to Latha's store, and I'm nearly out of flour.
I've got just enough to make maybe one more loaf of bread."

I notice you've planted a little bit of wheat. Adam laughed, as
if that were funny.

"So what can I do? Do you know how to turn wheat into
flour?"

I reckon it could be done, if you put your mind to it.

"Thank you, Adam," she said, but before he could go away
again, she added, "I'm sorry I said that about giving you a kiss. You
don't even have any lips, do you?"

Chapter thirty

Ma, are all people as little as Mistress? Hrolf was full of such questions, but she didn't mind answering them. She was glad to see that Hrolf was not going to merely accept the world as it was without wanting to understand it. The other pups—and they weren't exactly pups any more; in dog age they were already as old as Robin—rarely asked her any questions other than, When can we eat, Ma? She considered the possibility that the answers she gave Hrolf to all of his questions were passed along to his brothers and sisters, for Hrolf was the natural leader of the pack, as he had been the firstborn male.

She had explained to all of them, as soon as they were able to understand her, that Robin was their Mistress, the boss, the lady of the house, and they must not only refrain from biting her, chewing her garments or playing tug of war with them, disturbing her paper dolls and stealing her food, but also they should always obey her and worship her and be faithful to her unto death. Later, when Hreapha had begun to regale them with anecdotes and narratives, she told them stories about the man, the man who had set up this house and kidnapped Mistress long ago and then had died. Hrolf was full of

279

questions about the man and even wanted her to describe the "vehicle" that the man had supposedly owned as a means of transportation. Will I ever be able to ride in a pickup? he wanted to know. I doubt it, she answered, but there are things to do that are a lot more fun than that.

Like what? He wanted to know.

Chasing coons, she said. She explained that while he and his sisters and brothers weren't really coon hounds—or any other kind of raccoon dog, for that matter, they probably had instincts for chasing coons and foxes and squirrels, not for man's benefit but for their own.

What's a instinct? Hrolf wanted to know. Hrothgar's end stinks but mine don't.

Hreapha chuckled. You can't smell an instinct. It's something you're born with, something you don't have to learn, something that tells you what to do, makes you do what you do without even thinking about it.

Hrolf thought about that for a while, and then he asked, Is Adam an instinct?

No, he's an *in-habit*. You can't smell him either. And you sure can't see him, but you can hear him, can't you?

I sure can, Hrolf said. He talks to me a lot.

Does he? asked Hreapha. What does he talk about?

He tells me what a good dog I am. And that time when the thunderstorm came and scared the piss out of all the rest of you he told me not to be afraid because it was just noise and it wouldn't do me no harm.

You're his favorite dog, she said. You're mine too but don't tell any of them I said that. Thunder doesn't scare you, and even snakes don't scare you, but you'd better listen to me, boy, snakes can kill you if you mess with the wrong kind. Thunder can't hurt you but snakes can bite you to death.

I just don't like them thinking they own the place.

They don't own it, but you don't either.

Hreapha's biggest problem in the education of her offspring was trying to teach them that all of this vast wilderness in which they lived was not theirs to defend. There were even limits to how far they should mark up the immediate neighborhood—Adam's haunt—to establish their territory, and they had to know those limits, and if other creatures encroached upon their territory they had to be willing to share. Hreapha herself didn't like the encroachment, and she still remembered that incident of the hawk who had tried to attack the chickens (a story she had told more than once to her pups, at their request), but she did her best to instill in her brood a knowledge of the difference between harmful and benevolent creatures, while assuring them that even the most harmful creature doesn't consider itself harmful, that a rattlesnake is just doing its job with its instinctive behavior and theoretically has just as much right to be here as we do. Still, it is good to know the difference between a rattlesnake and a king snake, the latter not only unafraid of the former and immune to its poison but also not poisonous itself. In fact, Hreapha was seriously considering giving Robin a baby king snake for her next birthday, which was coming up soon. It would make an excellent pet.

The present she'd given Robin for her previous birthday was getting rather stale. Robert spent less and less of his time around the house these days. Possibly, Hreapha realized, he was out searching the forest for a female. Or he was certainly searching the forest for food, since Robin was not able to feed him anything any more. They had made clear to him that he was not ever even to think about eating one of the chickens, and he had certainly become so friendly with the beaver family on his many visits to the beaver pond with Robin and the others that he would never consider recognizing his mother's instinctive appetite for beaver. Robert was sometimes gone for weeks. He'd always come back, with no stories to tell or any sign of having been in a fight or an adventure of any kind. The young dogs were always glad to see him, despite their instinctive aversion for felines. And Robin always picked him up and held him and listened to him purr, and Robert still loved her, but he wasn't truly a pet any more and it was time Robin had a new one.

The young dogs were quickly growing almost as large as Robert was, and he was practically full grown. Hreapha realized that soon she would have to honor her promise to take them hunting for something larger than the squirrels and rabbits they were constantly catching for supper in the nearby forest. Hrothgar especially needed some excitement. Early in life he had developed a compulsion to chase his tail and even to inflict bites upon it, and she needed to provide some exercise for the lad.

All of them had a regular chore which gave them a certain amount of useful activity; Hreapha called it the garbage detail. Trash and empty tin cans regularly accumulated in the house, and Robin, who wasn't a very neat housekeeper, usually just tossed them out the door. Hreapha taught her brood how to dig holes at a distance from the house and bury the garbage and then cover it up.

I don't get it, Hrolf had complained, the first time his mother introduced him to this accomplishment. What good does it do me, since I don't even get to eat anything from the cans any more?

Hrolfie, we must always do anything and everything we can to make life easier for Mistress.

Why can't she bury her own garbage? I've seen her using a shovel.

Listen, boy, and don't ever forget: she is *Mistress* and we must honor her and worship her and sacrifice for her and please her.

Whether he passed that message along to his siblings or not, there weren't any more complaints about their chores.

Hreapha did have a bit of a problem teaching them something that basically ran against their instincts: that they must never harm deer, especially not fawns. She taught them that fawns have no scent, and because the coloring of their coats looks like the leaves and stuff in which they sit, they often cannot be seen. Their mothers deliberately leave them all alone out in the open, because the mothers don't want their own scent to draw any predators. So if Hreapha's young dogs should happen upon a fawn, they should treat it like a copperhead or rattlesnake and stay away from it.

That's not fair! Hrolf protested. They really look good to eat! My instincts tell me to eat them!

Listen, the reason you are not merely a dumb dog but an intelligent canine is that you can use your head and convince yourself that fawns are too innocent and beautiful to be eaten, regardless of what your instincts are telling you.

Hreapha considered capturing an orphaned fawn and presenting it to Robin as a ninth birthday pet, but she decided to wait until Robin's tenth, or even, if a king snake were presented for the tenth, the eleventh. By the age of eleven Robin would fully appreciate the young deer and would know how to provide a home for it without completely domesticating it...just as Robert's long residence in the company of a human had not, apparently, taken away his wildness.

So it was decided, eventually, practically on the eve of the birthday (again determined with help from the Ouija Board), that Robin's ninth birthday present would be a baby raccoon. The woods of Madewell Mountain were not exactly teeming with raccoons—a coon needs at least two hundred acres to itself—but they were *out there*, and Hreapha had entertained her pups endlessly by speaking of the *out there* and all it contained. She would never tell them of the many trips she had taken with the man to the large towns far away, because she didn't want them to feel deprived of something they might never experience in their lives. And she hadn't yet told them about the tiny village of Stay More. Only Hrolf had been curious about the identity of his father, and Hreapha was surprised that he had even learned the concept of "father" without yet knowing anything about reproduction. She had answered his questions by describing what a beautiful beast Yowrfrowr was, and not simply beautiful, but intelligent beyond all comprehension.

Where does he live? Hrolf wanted to know. Why can't I go visit him?

Someday you can, she told him. But it's a long ways off, and nearly impossible to get to.

Often, at night, if they listened carefully, they could hear the distant calling of the coyotes, a sound which always excited Yipyip, who would prance around speaking his name whenever he heard it. Hreapha had explained to them that a coyote is an attractive but uncouth dog and that a pack of them prowled the forests *out there*. Hreapha hoped that the coyotes would never come around here, and she hoped it would be a long time before her young dogs would have to fight them. Just as her own mother had done for her, Hreapha had taught her pups all the skills of fighting, and they sparred with each other constantly and sometimes with her. Hrolf wasn't the best fighter. In a tussle between Hrolf and Yipyip, the latter was usually top dog. So Hreapha knew that if the time ever came when her dogs had to fight the coyotes, the coyotes would probably win.

Raccoons are vicious fighters, and the first time Hreapha took the dogs coon hunting they not only failed to kill any of the quarry they encountered, but they themselves, Hreapha included, came away scratched and bloody. And the coons had an unfair advantage in that they could climb trees. Hrolf once remarked, If God had allowed dogs to climb trees, we would be the lords of the earth.

Where did you hear about God? Hreapha wondered.

Mistress talks about Him, Hrolf said. He's the one who made me and you and everything.

But the second time they went coon hunting, knowing what to expect and even practicing in advance, they tracked a coon until it came to a clearing, without a tree in easy reach, and all six of them pounced upon it at once, killed it quickly, and ate as much of it as they could separate from its fur. They decided that coon is much more palatable than possum or squirrel. The latter, after all, is just a rodent, while the raccoon is cousin to the bear. Speaking of bears, they had occasionally come across some bear scat, and learned the scent, and they knew that there was a family of black bear somewhere *out there,* but Hreapha knew they would have to wait a long time before they were big enough, strong enough, and smart enough, not to say brave enough, to go bear-hunting.

The raccoon was enough for now, and kept their bellies full for days. On their way home from the feast, Hrolf picked up another raccoon scent, or thought he did, and while none of them had any appetite remaining, out of curiosity he traced the scent to a hollow tree, explored it, and came running back to report, Ma, there's some baby coons in that tree!

There were three of them. They were very young, their eyes not yet open, and Hreapha, understanding that their mother had just been killed and eaten by ravenous dogs, knew that the babes still had to be suckled for weeks before they could manage on their own. They were orphans. Their father was probably still in the vicinity, perhaps watching at this very moment, and while raccoon fathers help in the rearing of their young they would only eat any young who lost their mothers. Hreapha had not intended to give Robin *three* birthday presents, but she couldn't very well choose which one to take and leave the other two. So she instructed Hroberta and Hruschka to gently lift two of them by the nape of the neck, and she took the third herself, and thus they carried the three baby raccoons quite a distance back to the homestead.

"Hreapha!" Hreapha said to Robin, that is, "Happy Birthday!" And each of the other dogs wished her a Happy birthday too. "Hrolf!" "Hroberta!" "Hrothgar!" "Hruschka!" "Yipyip!" It was quite a chorus.

"Good heavens, what are they?" Robin wanted to know, which reminded Hreapha of Robin's first response to the sight of Robert. Baby raccoons appear more like the mature coon—just a smaller version—than baby pups resemble dogs. Their distinctive facial markings are already clearly in place. Hreapha realized that perhaps Robin had never seen a raccoon before and had no idea what they were. It didn't matter. Creatures don't have to have names to be appreciated.

Robin attempted to nurse the raccoon kits with the same doll baby bottle she'd used on baby Robert. "I've only got a couple of cans of Pet Milk left," she said.

Adam's voice became present: *It aint a good idee to hold 'em like that,* he told her. *Upside down they might choke on the milk. Hold 'em right side up, on their bellies.*

"What are they, Adam?" she asked him.

Baby coons, he said. *I used to have one. Raised it till it was full growed, but it was so full of mischief my dad took it away off into the woods and let it go. Or maybe he kilt it.*

Whether because the Pet Milk was used up, or because it wasn't right for the kits in the first place (raccoons can't drink cow's milk, Adam told her), two of the kits perished before a week was out. Hreapha instructed her pups to bury them. The third one struggled on, opening its eyes and managing to crawl around and even to grasp one of Robin's fingers. But it was sickly for a long time, until Robin could get it to take some mashed up apples (Robin had done a good job of getting the orchard to produce this year, with just a little help from her book and from Adam). Maybe the sugar in the apples was all the kit needed, and it began to perk up. Robin gradually added to its diet some Osage oranges, or "horse apples" as Adam called them: the huge fruit of the bois d'arc. And before long, it (or she, for it was clearly a female) was well, and eating anything they could find for it.

Robin named the baby raccoon Ralgrub, explaining to Hreapha (who in turn explained it to her brood) that it was "burglar" spelled backward. The facial markings, she said, resembled a mask worn by burglars, who are people that sneak into buildings to steal things. As she grew up, Ralgrub would often do that; sneak into the house and steal things.

Ma, when it's my birthday will you give me a baby animal? Hrolf wanted to know. Something I can eat?

Don't you ever think of anything except your stomach? she chided him, but instantly realized that wasn't kind. Of all her young, Hrolf was the most interested in things beside his stomach. Tell you what, she added, if you're a good boy and behave yourself, on your birthday I'll take you to visit your father.

Really? he said. Really truly promise cross your heart?

She had let it slip out, and couldn't take it back. The slipping out was probably an indication of how much she herself wanted to see Yowrfrowr again. She had hoped that he might want to see her—and his offspring—and might somehow be able to leave home long enough to search for her. Whatever markings she had left along the trail were long evaporated; she had told him the general location of the Madewell place, and if he wanted to, he could find it. But he was devoted to his mistress and wouldn't leave her.

Hrolf, we'll just have to see. Your father lives in a place called Stay More. It isn't too awfully far from here, but it's almost impossible to reach. You once said, If God had allowed dogs to climb trees, we would be the lords of the earth. No, we wouldn't. God would have had to allow you to take wing and fly. The only real way you could get to Stay More easily would be to fly there. If we could fly, I'd take you there tomorrow. But we have to go on foot, and Mistress herself couldn't possibly do it. Ask Adam to tell you about that trail. Or to tell you what it was like when he could use it to get to school. If he tried to use it today, he'd be out of luck.

Part Four
Within

Chapter thirty-one

I was out of luck the last time I tried to use that trail when I was a kid. I had used it so often through the third grade of school that I could have used it blindfolded, which is what my morning use of it had amounted to, anyhow, since I'd always had to set out from home well before sunup in order to make the journey before time o'books, which was eight o'clock. I made that journey so many times in the dark that I might as well have closed my eyes. I'll never forget the very first time I made it, the only time I wasn't alone. Grampaw took me. I was six years old, and it was August during the war years, and I had heard Grampaw and Paw arguing the day before over whether I was to be allowed to go or not. Paw had quit going to the school before he'd finished the third grade and had not been promoted to the fourth, not because he wasn't smart and not because he was a troublemaker, but simply because he could not—or would not—learn how to read. He had no use for it, he always said. There was no earthly reason why a feller had to know how to look at a bunch of squiggly marks and tell what words they stood for. Words, if used at all, was meant to be spoken, not figured out of some squiggly marks. He was not going to let me start school either, despite my mother's tears, she who'd never been known to shed any. But Grampaw, who lived in a shed (long gone now) behind his cooperage, and was still very much in charge of the homeplace he'd built as well as the cooperage, told my father, "For you to keep that boy out of school because you failed at it yourself would be like me keeping you away from coopering because I was fourteen before I could hammer and drive a barrel myself."

And it was Grampaw who came into the house before the others were awake and shook me and told me to get dressed. He had a coal-oil lantern, and I followed single-file along after him, barefoot because I had no shoes, as he led me on the narrow trail which I hadn't even known existed. He told me he'd blazed that trail himself when he'd anticipated going for the doctor to assist Grandma in her labor for the birth of my father. The job had taken him three weeks with axe and shovel and he was prouder of it than he had been years earlier making the road up the north side of his mountain that had allowed him to get his team and wagon in and out, up the steep winding road and back again. He'd had to practically carve the cliffside into a ledge wide enough for the wagon wheels (a ledge eventually fallen away and constricted into the narrow path that Sog Alan had been required to use). Every week he—and during my growing-up years, my father in his stead—drove a wagonload of finished barrels, lashed together to keep them from falling off the wagon, across that precarious ledge and down that crooked road and onward for many miles to Harrison, where he sold them, making just enough money to buy whatever was needed to live on until the next shipment of barrels could be made and loaded and hauled. He told me that making that original road—he'd called it the North Way—had been much easier than making the trail we were now using, the South Way, which, although it was not wide enough for a wagon and team and scarcely even wide enough for a person as big as Grampaw, had taken not just an awful lot of physical effort but considerable trial-and-error surveying of the best possible—in some places the *only* possible—route. He told me he'd jokingly said to Grandma, "Laurie, I reckon it'll be a real tribulation for you to birth that baby but most of the labor was mine." There was one spot on the trail so steep that he related how he'd had to tie a rope around the doctor's waist to haul him up—although now you could hold on to the branches of shrubs and trees on either side to raise and lower yourself. In such places, I had to keep my hands free by gripping in my teeth the bail of the dinner pail my mother had filled for me: hard-boiled eggs, a big tomato, a roasting ear, some cornbread and a bit of meat, probably possum.

"I hope ye've been taking heed of where you're at," Grampaw said, when the trail finally emerged onto one of the Stay More roads, "because you'll have to handle that trail all by yourself on the way home. Leastways you won't be needing no lantern that time of day." And then he delivered me to the schoolhouse, an awesome building because of its length and the windows of its one room and the belfry on the roof and most of all because it was painted white—I'd never seen a white building before. Grampaw said he hoped I'd have a good time and learn a few things, and then he left me.

The truth was, I had been following in his footsteps most of the trail without paying much attention to any landmarks or turnings in the trail. And that first day of school was such an ordeal that it left me all shook up—Miss Jerram was easy enough and did her best to make the first day of the first grade tolerable, but being thrust into the company of so many other kids after an isolated early childhood took more social skill than I could muster, and I was left feeling like what some of the kids called me: a "furriner." Because I wasn't from Stay More or from the immediate environs, and nobody had ever seen me before or heard of me, I was a furriner. And thus an outcast from the beginning. I was determined never to go to that school again…if only I could find my way home.

Trying to negotiate that treacherous trail without Grampaw was a fittingly sad conclusion for a sad day. I lost my way more than once. Climbing up steep places that had been relatively easy climbing down seemed to take forever. At one point, in the exertion to reach the top of a steep climb, my teeth lost their grip on the bail of the empty dinner pail, and it fell and clattered down to the rocks below, and I had to climb carefully down and retrieve it. In all modesty, what I was required to do at the age of six makes Robin's ordeal at the age of seven pale by comparison. Hreapha, having made the trip herself (although she couldn't have climbed in the places that required hand-holds), understood how precocious I was. She also understood why I was never able to allow my dog Hector to accompany me on that trail. And she understood why her own promise to Hrolf to take him to visit his father was so fraught with peril.

It was past suppertime when I finally reached home. "Dear Lord in heaven, I'd done given ye up for gone!" my mother said, hugging me to her.

"I was jist fixin to go out huntin fer ye," Grampaw said.

"How was school?" Paw asked. It was a rhetorical question, nearly mocking, but I didn't know that. I told them I would just as soon stay home.

"Didn't ye learn nothing?" Grampaw asked.

"I learnt that most folks live in houses that aint on mountain-tops and where you can see other folks' houses," I said. And then I wanted to know, because I had never been told, "How come we live up here in a place like this, anyhow?"

"What I've always wondered," my mother remarked. "What I'd sure care to know."

"Hesh, woman," my father said.

"Boy," Grampaw said to me, "this here's the highest house in all the country. And it's smack dab in the midst of all the fine white oak you'd ever need to make your barrels. And if you caint see no neighbors from here, so what? I never gave a hoot for no neighbors."

But he woke me again before dawn the following morning and handed me the dinner pail my mother had filled the night before, and then he remarked, "There's a full moon still up. Just as well, cause you don't need to carry a lantern with you."

I tried to protest, but he said, "Shhh! You'll wake your folks."

So by moonlight I made my way back over that awful trail. At least this time I paid more attention to the turnings it took and the landmarks whose silhouettes loomed in the moonbeams, so that I could find my way home. And during morning recess, Miss Jerram took me aside and asked me where I lived and how I'd managed to get from there to the school, and she also complimented me on learning the ABCs quicker than the other first-graders.

I told Grampaw he didn't have to wake me to get me up for the journey to school. I could wake my own self. And when winter came, Miss Jerram gave me a pair of shoes that fit. "I just found 'em somewheres," she said. They made a big difference when the trail was covered with snow. I knew how to read before springtime came. Paw was real glad when school let out for the summer, because he had plans for me to help him in the shop, sweeping up shavings, tending the forge, arranging the tools and, eventually, sharpening them on the treadle whetstone.

I loved working in the cooperage with Paw and Grampaw (whose days, I didn't yet realize, were numbered). They didn't talk much, but I overheard enough to understand a few things: they were the only full coopers in all the country. The woods were filled with men who cut down white oak trees, sawed them up into stave bolts and hauled them down to the Parthenon Stave & Heading Company, where they were fashioned into staves, not for making into barrels there on the spot, but instead just being bundled and hauled out to the places in Harrison and Pettigrew where they were shipped by rail to big cooperages elsewhere. Paw and Grampaw had many disagreements and sometimes loud arguments, but one thing they were agreed on was their refusal to sell the stave bolts alone, even though, in the years after the war, they could have got as much as a dollar apiece for white oak stave bolts.

"Start to finish," was Grampaw's motto, passed along to my father, and eventually to me. In fact, much of the white oak timber they were harvesting had been planted by Grampaw when he was a young man, so a finished white oak bourbon barrel, carefully charred on the inside, made well by Braxton Madewell & Son (& Grandson) was indeed a product created from start to finish. (But to be completely finished, I once observed to Grampaw, we ought to distill the bourbon meant to fill it. He was not amused by the remark.) Ironically, in the last year of his life, he could not work completely from start to finish; there was no market for his finished barrels, and his middleman had gone out of business, with the result that he could only try to sell the staves themselves, not the finished barrels. He was driving a wagonload of staves to Parthenon, too many of them for the wagon to bear, when the wagon slipped off the bluff near our house. He never recovered from his injuries.

By the second grade, two important things had happened in my life. One was that my skill at lettering had reached the point where I made a bold suggestion that my father and grandfather debated for only a little while before accepting: using an iron rod heated to red hot in the forge, I could brand the barrels with the word MADEWELL. My father might have been illiterate but he could read his own name and he took pride in seeing each of the barrels branded on its head with those letters, a job that required little of my time, usually on weekends when I wasn't in school. I loved the smell of the oak burning as the hot iron sank into it. My clothes were impregnated with it.

Which is what led to the other important thing. My seatmate in school—as in all the country schools of that time the pupils sat two by two at desks made of wood and ornate cast iron with folding seats and lifting tops—was a shy little girl named Roseleen Coe. I wish I could say she was just as cute as Robin at that age (the age Robin was kidnapped) but in fact Roseleen was just moderately attractive: not homely by any means, but a long way from possessing Robin's beauty. And she was terribly shy; Miss Jerram had to wring the least word out of her, and she never, ever spoke to me, her seatmate. I think Miss Jerram had assigned us to the same desk because we were not inclined to speaking, and we were both poor, both unkempt, both dressed shabbily, both shoeless (except in winter, and that second winter I gave Roseleen the shoes Miss Jerram had given me the previous winter, because I'd outgrown them and they would fit Roseleen, although I learned she had only a comparatively short way to walk in the snow to reach home).

The first words Roseleen ever spoke to me were to ask, "Do you live in a smokehouse?"

When I'd overcome my astonishment that she'd actually spoken to me, I said, "Why, no, matter of fact I don't. How come ye to ask that?"

"One time our house burnt down and we had to live in the smokehouse till we got another'n built," she related. "And you smell like we did."

"Oh," I said. "I've been branding barrels and the oakwood smokes when it burns and the smoke gets all over me."

"Adam and Roseleen," Miss Jerram said. "What are you two a-jawing about?"

"Nothing," I said, and we hushed up.

But after school Roseleen caught up with me and said, "I'll walk with ye a ways." I didn't mind. After being silent so long toward each other, we rushed to say everything in the short time we were together, until I reached the place where my rugged trail left the main road. Her main question was why I was branding barrels, and I had to explain the work that my paw and grampaw did and how I helped by burning our name into the barrelheads. How many brothers and sisters did I have? None. How many did she have? Scads. How far away was my house? Miles and miles. How far away was hers? Just down the road yonder. Was she any kin to Gerald Coe, the Stay More boy who'd died a hero at Iwo Jima? Yes, he was her own cousin. Where did I get my funny name? I said that I'd been told that in the olden days it was either Maidewell or Madwell, but somewhere along in there they didn't know how to spell. Did I know I was the best speller in the second grade? Or the third too as far as that goes? That I could "spell down" practically anybody? Why, no, I never knew that. It's true. You can. And I think you are just swell. I like you a whole lot too.

"Come go home with me and eat supper and stay all night with me," she said.

Having never heard such an invitation before I did not realize that it was just polite and perfunctory, a commonplace way of saying goodbye that isn't meant to be taken literally. I didn't know how to reply. I didn't know that I was expected to return the invitation at once by saying, "I don't reckon I can tonight, but why don't you come go home with me and eat supper and stay all night with me?" which would allow her to counter it by saying "Not this time, I reckon, but I'll be looking for ye."

All I could think to say was, "Really?"

That caught her by surprise. She had to think about it for a while before saying, "Well, yeah, if you really want to."

"I'd really like to," I said. "But my folks are looking for me, I reckon."

"So I'll see ye tomorrow at school," she said. And she kissed me on the cheek, and walked away.

In the third grade she kissed me on the mouth.

The summer before the fourth grade I had a bad accident in the shop when I grabbed for a backing knife that fell off the bench, and I cut off my first finger and I gashed my leg something terrible. My mother wanted to see if they couldn't get a doctor to come, or at least take me to see one, but my father said I could just take off from work for a while and see if it didn't get better. I never could walk too well on my left leg after that.

And I was out of luck the last time I tried to use that trail, which was the morning of the first day of the fourth grade. I had missed Roseleen all summer, and I had no idea if she even knew anything about my accident. Surely she must have wondered why I didn't ever come into Stay More again to shop at Latha's Store. Surely she was just as eager as I was to see how far we could go. Surely she had delightful memories of how far we'd already gone.

My father and mother both didn't want me to attempt to go back to the school with my very bad leg and the fact that Grampaw was practically bedridden with rheumatism and Paw needed my help more than ever in the shop.

But I couldn't put off seeing Roseleen any longer, and besides Miss Jerram had promised us that the fourth grade would be really special, when we'd really take up the study of geography (and it was going to be her last year, before a soldier she'd met during the war took her away from Stay More). So I begged my mother to fill my dinner pail for me, and I got up before dawn and dressed. I was no longer wearing overalls; but a shirt and trousers, and I felt grown up. But I had covered less than a mile of the trail, hobbling with my bad leg and practically having to drag it behind me as Sog Alan would be required to drag his leg so often toward the end, before I began to have serious doubts about my ability to complete the journey. Only my vision of Roseleen kept me going. And that vision was not enough to sustain me when, attempting the most hazardous and vertical drop of the trail, I lost my grip on the branch I was clinging to—or perhaps the branch broke under my weight (I was a real big boy now) and I plummeted to the rocks below. It was some kind of miracle I didn't break every bone in my body. I broke only four of them, in my wrist, arm, ankle, and skull. The cracking of the skull gave me a concussion that left me unconscious for hours, and when I came to I could scarcely move. I drifted in and out of consciousness for the rest of the day, sometimes having dreams of Roseleen, even very sexual dreams of Roseleen, and managing only, at one point, to crawl far enough to reach my dinner pail and eat its contents. That was probably around suppertime. When I did not return home for supper, or at any time during the night, my folks figured that something must have happened to me, and the next day my father went out upon that trail himself, the first time he'd ever used the trail his father had blazed to allow a doctor to come for his birth, and he found me and carried me on his shoulder the rest of the way into Stay More, where Doc Swain set my broken bones.

I was never able to go to school in Stay More again. I never saw Roseleen again…until…but that will have to wait.

Chapter thirty-two

It was the longest stretch she'd ever listened to the *in-habit* and it left her convinced he really was there, not just a voice in her own head. It was very timely too, because more and more lately she had been bothered by the inescapable idea that she was just inventing the whole world inside her mind, that nothing actually existed except her mind. Even before all of this began, when she still lived happily at home with her mother, she had noticed the strange developments that whenever she thought about something, or was hoping for something, that that something came to pass, it occurred, it appeared as if by magic, the magic that was in her head, as if she had just *made* it happen. This left her feeling powerful and it made her wonder if she had the ability to perceive things that other people could not. But it also, now, left her doubtful of the existence of other people, or even if other people had ever existed at all except in her creation, the way she created the paper inhabitants of Stay More. The last living human being she had seen, a year ago, was Sugrue, and she had done away with him. Although Adam was *here,* she could not see him nor touch him nor kiss him, and it was so easy to think that he was only the most remarkable product of her lively mind.

One of her favorite lines in the Bible, in the very second chapter, was "And out of the ground the Lord God formed every beast of the field, and every fowl of the air; and brought them unto Adam to see what he would call them: and whatsoever Adam called every living creature, that was the name thereof."

It was so easy, when she was feeling lonely, as God must have felt, to think that she might really be God herself, and that she had created Adam out of the dust and told him to name everything. Sometimes she tested the idea: "Adam, what's the name of that little tree over there?"

Why, that's a sassafras, I reckon. It aint good for much. Slack cooperage, maybe, but we don't make slack barrels, just tight ones. Course, you could make tea out of the small roots.

"Adam, what name have you given to that big bird pecking on that tree trunk over there?"

I call it a woodhen, but I've heared Grampaw call it Lord God Peckerwood on account of it's so big. It's actual named a pileated woodpecker, I don't know why. Maybe because of that red crest.

"Adam, what did you decide to name this big spotty spider?"

That there is jist a orange garden spider, but don't she make a perty nest? I had one I named Mirandy and she made a web that was ten foot acrost, and I've watched her catch grasshoppers in it. Look at them there cocoons, big as hickernuts! They won't hatch till after Christmas but the babies will stay in the cocoon till May or June.

And She saw everything that She had made, and, behold, it was very good.

When she turned nine years old her new motto was, "Let's be real." Having for some time now decided that Adam simply could not be pure imagination, although her imagination never ceased to amaze her, she was not surprised that two important things happened because of him. The first was that he helped her make flour, something she couldn't possibly have figured out how to do on her own. And something she desperately needed. She had run out of flour a long time back. It had been ages since she'd been able to make any bread or biscuits or cakes or pies. She could still make cornbread with the cornmeal (which was also about to run out), but that was it. She had broadcast the wheat seeds Sugrue had left, and harvested enough of the wheat, stacked into shocks as the *Cyclopædia* directed her, to result in almost two bushels of wheat, after she'd followed Adam's instructions for making a primitive winnowing fork (out of sassafras) to throw the threshed grain into the air and separate the wheat from the chaff. (Here her other book, the Bible, was more helpful than the *Cyclopædia.*)

Adam told her that down the trail toward Stay More, very near a large waterfall, in a glade or glen into which he had fallen during his last attempt to reach the Stay More school, were several caverns once inhabited by Bluff-dweller Indians. He had explored those caverns and had found an Indian mortar and pestle which he had brought home and shown to his folks, but his father had said "We aint got no use for such as that," and Adam had put them away in the barn somewhere. Robin searched the barn and found them in one of the stalls.

Pounding the wheat by hand with the Indian mortar and pestle was a lot of work, taking hours and hours, and then Adam said it would have to be sieved, and he helped her fashion a sieve from a tin can with nail holes punched in the bottom, which was slow but it worked. In the box of kitchen gadgets Sugrue had brought from home was one of those old tin hand-crank flour sifters, and when she got through using that she discovered that she had enough flour to make at least one loaf of bread, and maybe a pie.

But when she got up one morning to light a fire in the kitchen stove so she could bake that loaf of bread, she discovered that she was out of matches. There had been several boxes of Diamond "Strike Any-where" Kitchen Matches, but she had used one or two whenever she wanted to light a fire or a lantern or even a candle, and now she was all out! And winter was coming on and it was cold in the house!

"ADAM!" she yelled. "How can I start a fire?"

This time, thank heavens, he came when he was called. *Put on your coat, silly,* he said. He could say that, not ever feeling cold or hot himself.

"I have to light a fire in the stove!" she said. "And I'm all out of matches!"

I don't have ary a match, he said.

"You don't have ary a anything!" she mocked his language. She had once asked him what "ary" meant, and he said he figured it was just a way of saying the old-time "ever a" or "e'er a".

"How did you make a new fire when you ran out?" she asked.

We didn't never run out. It's terrible bad luck to let a fire go out, and it never happened to us.

"But didn't you ever make a fire without matches? The way the Boy Scouts do or whatever? Rub a couple or sticks together or something?"

What's Boy Scouts? he wanted to know. *Naw, but one time I lit the forge in the shop with a kind of bow drill like the Indians made. Let's see if that there bow drill aint still anywheres about.*

But it wasn't. They searched through all the stuff in the shop and even with her coat on she was getting very cold. Many days later she remembered that Sugrue had possessed a pocket lighter that he lit his cigarettes with, and she went to the outhouse and searched in the remains of his disintegrating trousers on the floor, managing to say "ew" not more than a couple of times, and found the Zippo lighter. But that was many days later, and now she was cold and eager to get the oven ready for some bread.

Listen careful, Adam said, *and I'll try and tell ye how to fashion a bow drill. It aint near as hard as making a firkin.*

It took some whittling of an Osage orange branch, the type of tree that left those big inedible (except by Ralgrub, who loved them) horse apples all over the ground, the tree that got its name from the fact the Osages who'd lived and hunted hereabouts (years after the Bluff-dwellers had died out) made their bows and arrows out of it. She made the bow drill's bow out of that, and also the spindle. The bearing block she made from an oak barrel stave which she drilled with the bung-borer, an augur Adam said was used to make the bungholes in barrels.

The idea was fairly simple, and all she needed now was something for a little bundle of tinder. Adam said the fluff of cattail was the best thing, but that not being within hiking distance, she substituted the fluff of a milkweed pod (*It's called butterfly weed,* Adam explained, *and it's good for all kinds of things*). The idea was to wrap the bow's string around the spindle and saw back and forth to set the spindle spinning in the hole of the bearing block until it charred and then the hearth board began to smoke as the char dust ignited into a coal, and the red coal was dumped onto the milkweed down of the tinder bundle, which you blew upon until it burst into flames.

Although the idea was fairly simple, it took Robin most of the day to make it work. By the time she got the tinder bundle burning and carried it into the house and put it in the kindling in the stove, it was too late to make the bread that day, but at least if she kept the fire burning and never let it go out completely for the rest of the winter, she'd have no problems. She was proud of herself for making fire. She understood how the very first people who lived must have felt when they learned how to make fire. But she understood she'd never have been able to do it without Adam.

She left the woodstove in the living room burning all night. It was a cold night, but she did not let the animals into the house. There were too many of them, and while Ralgrub was still young and practically helpless it wouldn't be fair to let her spend the night in the house if none of the others could, and it wouldn't be smart to let all those dogs into the house. "You understand, don't you, Hreapha?" Robin said, and Hreapha was content to spend the night in her usual spot, a hole she'd dug in the earthen floor of the barrel shop, out of the wind. As for Robert, he never came around at night any more anyway. Wherever he spent the night, he was all worn out the next day, and spent the whole day sleeping on the porch.

Robin slept alone now, and usually it didn't bother her too much, but occasionally she felt lonely. She'd not forgotten Paddington, and ached to have him with her. Sometimes, even, she recalled how nice it had been to go to sleep lying snuggled with Sugrue. One evening she spoke aloud, "Adam, would you like to sleep with me?" But, as so often was the case, she got no answer. It didn't matter. Even if he had answered, and said he'd be glad to sleep with her, she wouldn't know he was there. She wouldn't be able to feel him. She'd just have to pretend that they were snuggling up and keeping each other warm...but no, his body wouldn't be warm because he didn't have any body.

Sometimes he occupied her dreams. She had never seen him by day nor even made any attempt to imagine what he looked like, but he was clearly visible in her dreams, a tall boy of twelve in overalls with an unruly shock of brown hair and a very nice face. She could almost touch him. In fact, she did touch him in her dreams. It seems she kissed him, and hugged him. He was very bashful, and blushed a lot. When she wasn't dreaming about Adam, usually her dreams went bad, and involved being lost in the woods and pursued by animals that wanted to eat her, or fires or tornadoes. Her ninth year included a lot of nightmares, from which she sometimes woke up screaming or crying for her mommy. She also knew that when she read the horror stories in the Bible—the beheading of John the Baptist, Absalom accidentally hanging himself, Moab making lime out of the king's skeleton (did she need any lime for anything?), the murder of the daughter of Jephthah, and David killing Goliath not once but twice—these stories would give her nightmares, and she tried to stop reading whenever she came to one of those parts of the Bible. The few times she had really nice dreams, often involving Adam, were mostly just before waking in the mornings, so that she had trouble waking up and wanted to go back to sleep and return to the dream.

Often in her ninth year she repeated her invitation, "Adam, would you like to sleep with me?"

Finally when warm weather had returned she got a reply. *Gal, I don't never sleep.*

"Oh," she said, and thought about that. "There's no bed in your bedroom," she observed. But he didn't seem to spend any time in that room anyhow. She couldn't imagine how anybody, not even an *in-habit*, could stay awake constantly all the time. "Don't you ever get bored?" she asked.

What's bored? Bored is when you caint find something to keep you curious. So long as there's anything going on in the world, I'll never be bored.

"But what's going on in the world? Nothing ever happens around here."

She heard his scoffing laughter. *You just aint looking for it. Or you caint see it. Or caint hear it. Or caint taste it or smell it or feel it. Why, there aint a moment goes by that something wondrous don't occur.*

"Like what?"

Like a orange garden spider building her web. Or like the wind a-slewing through the cedars. Or the sound of them dogs afar off a-hrolfing and a-hrothgaring as they chase their game. Or the lightning bugs all over the meader at dusky dark. Or the fine smell of oak wood fresh cut. Or the sweet breeze that puffs from your nose when you're a-sleeping.

"So you watch me when I'm sleeping?" she wanted to know. Her breath caught and she felt uneasy.

Iffen I don't have nothing better to watch. Which aint too often.

"And you watch me when I go to the bathroom?" She didn't mean bathroom, because there wasn't one, and she didn't mean when she was taking a bath, although she did mean that too, except that she didn't take a bath very often.

He did not answer, which she took to mean that he did. But somehow her sense of modesty, what little was left of it, wasn't offended. Being watched by an invisible *in habit* isn't nearly as embarrassing as being watched by someone who has real eyes. And since she rarely wore any clothes any more when it was warm, and had outgrown all her clothes anyhow, her going naked made her less and less self-conscious about it. In fact she felt more self-conscious when she had to dress against cold: when it was cold she had to try to squeeze into an outgrown coat or else wear something of Sugrue's that was too big for her. She had thought about taking the scissors and the needle-and-thread and cutting down some his garments to make them fit her, but she wisely realized it would be better to just wait until she grew into them, and meanwhile she went without clothing in warm weather and made do with whatever would fit or wrap around her in cold weather. None of her shoes fit any more, and all of Sugrue's were much too big for her, but she wore them if she had to walk in the snow. Otherwise she went barefoot all the time.

Chapter thirty-three

As she had planned, Hreapha gave Robin a snake for her tenth birthday. It wasn't easy. She wasn't at all certain that Robin would even appreciate the gift, because a snake, even a baby snake, is not in the least cuddly and cute. But she discussed the matter with the *in-habit*, and while he was amused at the idea of giving someone a snake for a birthday present, he knew there might be obstacles to overcome in the way of fomenting a bond between Robin and her newest pet. King snakes, he said, were known to live to a ripe old age, sometimes twenty years or more, and would Robin want to keep a slithery reptile on the premises for that long a time?

But come to think on it, he allowed, *maybe it's high time she learnt that pets don't have to be furry and cuddlesome.*

Hreapha offered to present the snake to Robin as a birthday present from them all, including the *in-habit*, who was not physically able to present Robin with birthday gifts, and had not yet done so.

By the way, Hreapha asked him, when is your own birthday? It's not right for us to honor Robin each year and ignore your birthday.

I aint got ary, he said. *Ole Adam has one, which is right before*

Christmas, but I'm jist his remainder, don't ye know? I don't never get no older, so I don't have birthdays.

Do you mean you'll be twelve all your life? Hreapha asked him.

The *in-habit* chuckled. *All my "life" aint exactly the way to put it. But I'll never change a whit.*

That August, without leaving his haunt, that is, within barking distance of the house, the *in-habit* helped Hreapha find a rotting stump where a mother king snake (*Ort to be called a queen snake, I reckon*) had laid a clutch of nearly a dozen eggs in a pile of loose damp stuff. The oblong eggshells were white like chicken eggs, but not brittle; they were tough and leathery.

How do you know the eggs are king snakes' and not rattlesnakes' or copperheads'? Hreapha asked.

Them pizen snakes don't lay no eggs. They just have live babies the same way you do.

Hreapha told all her offspring about the plan for Mistress' birthday, and asked them to take turns watching the snake eggs to see when they hatched.

Shoot far, exclaimed Hrolf. What if the mother snake comes around to keep a watch on her eggs?

The *in-habit* explained that snake mothers don't ever pay any attention to their eggs once they're laid, nor do the baby snakes ever get any attention from their parents. *Pore things is all on their own.* He also explained how the baby snake has a tiny but sharp "egg tooth" on the tip of its snout which it uses to slit the eggshell so it can escape.

Of the dogs, only Hruschka would have nothing to do with the eggs, for she had a morbid fear of snakes that she would never overcome. Hreapha herself was on watch when the first hatchling emerged, so tiny, hardly bigger than a worm, and totally helpless. How do they nurse? Hreapha wanted to know.

They sure don't drink milk, not that I know of. By and by they'll be able to catch little critters and eat 'em, but for now your best bet is to see if you caint find some baby mice to feed 'em. Or little lizards. Or tree frogs.

Hreapha instructed her dogs to help in rounding up sufficient lizards, frogs and baby mice to feed the newly hatched snakes. They left the snakes alone with their food overnight, because snakes don't like to be disturbed while they're feeding.

Hreapha then had to decide which one of the several hatchlings to capture and present to Robin. Do we want a male snake or a female snake? she asked the *in-habit*. And how can I tell them apart?

Iffen I had fingers and thumbs I could tell ye, he said. *And you don't have fingers nor thumbs neither. Ralgrub has got 'em, and I could try to explain to her how to sex a snake, but maybe you'd better just take your chances on getting a female.*

Why a female?

Hreapha could hear the *in-habit* hemming and hawing. Being the smartest of the animals hereabouts did not endow her with the ability to understand right away what would eventually occur to her: that a snake, being symbolically phallic, would be even more suggestive as a male. Especially to a ten-year-old girl who was just a year or two short of puberty, and who spent all the hot summer in a state of nakedness like all the other creatures on the place (except possibly the *in-habit*, and Hreapha decided that invisible clothing didn't count anyhow). Robin was as totally lacking in self-consciousness about her nakedness as she was about her singing. She had a lovely voice, and she sang all the time, although more often than not she did not sing any actual words of a song, but just pure tones in some kind of melodic chant. Her voice must have carried to the far reaches of the haunt. Except for Hrolf, who seemed to appreciate it, and of course Hrolf's mother, the other dogs found Robin's singing objectionable, and usually ran off into the woods to get away from it.

If Hreapha had given full thought to the sexual allusions of snakes, she'd have gone ahead with her plan to give Robin a fawn for her birthday. But she'd already gone to the trouble to prepare a cage of sorts for the new pet: there was a discarded two-gallon glass jar in the trash that the garbage detail would have buried, but Hreapha rescued it, and rolled it with her nose out to one of the stalls in the barn, where she managed, with help from Hrolf, to get it into a vertical position. Now that the bunch of baby snakes had been more than adequately fed as a result of all the dogs' round-up of tiny rodents and reptiles and amphibians, to the extent that they were beginning to crawl away from their nest, Hreapha selected the prettiest hatchling, to the extent that snakes can be pretty, and, hoping it was female, transported it gently in her jaws to its new home in the glass jar in the barn. For the next few weeks the dogs regularly dropped assorted baby mice, lizards, and frogs into the jar, until Robin turned ten.

Ma! hollered Hrolf one morning. That snake has done turned itself inside out!

The *in-habit* was summoned to inspect the damage, which wasn't damage after all but simply, according to the *in-habit*, a shedding of the skin, and the snake would shed its skin once again before Robin's birthday. The *in-habit* explained to them all that it was the only way the snake could grow. It had to shed its skin to get larger. And they were feeding it so much that it was getting large fast. It looked already like a miniature version of the six-footer it would become; it had the same markings: black with white and yellow crossbands that forked on the sides and ran into each other. It was indeed a pretty creature.

The day arrived for Robin's birthday, and the *in-habit* persuaded her to use one of the last boxes of cake mix to make herself a birthday cake. Hreapha overheard their conversation.

"That would be selfish," Robin said. "Making a birthday cake for yourself."

How's that any more selfish than anything else you do for yourself that you have to do because there's nobody to do it for you?

All the inhabitants, including the *in-habit*, were invited to the birthday party, and each was given a piece of the cake. Ralgrub and Robert especially enjoyed the cake, and the dogs, although they didn't have sweet teeth, dutifully ate a piece each.

Robin cut one more piece and held it up to the air. "This is your piece, Adam, but I'll just have to eat it for you." And she ate Adam's piece.

Mmmm, moaned the *in-habit, that was sure scrumdiddlyumptious. And now if you'll kindly foller your dogs out to the barn, they've got a real present for you.*

"Oh, really?" said Robin. She heeded the invitation and followed them out to the barn.

"Hreapha! Hreapha!" exclaimed Hreapha, that is, Happy Birthday! And just look what we've got for you!

"Eeek!" exclaimed Robin. "It's a snake!" And she backed away from the glass jar.

Hit's a shore-enough king snake, said the *in-habit. The masterest snake there is. Won't do you no harm, but it'll slay any pizen snakes that try to come around. Some folks call it a chain snake on account of them markings that look like links in a chain.*

"What kind of birthday present is a *snake?*" Robin demanded. "I can't pet it."

Pet it all you like, said the *in-habit. Go ahead, stick your hand in the jar and take aholt of it real gentle-like. I guarantee she won't bite you.*

"She?" said Robin. "Is it a girl snake?" Robin slowly and cautiously put her hand into the jar and took hold of the snake and lifted it out of the jar and cradled it in her arms the same way she would cradle any other infant. The snake squirmed and wiggled to get loose from her grasp, but it soon settled down.

I can tell ye how to find out, the *in-habit* said, and he instructed her in a procedure called "popping" whereby she turned the snake over to locate its afterplace and then pressed or "popped" in a certain place to see if it had the snake's equivalent of a penis. It didn't. *So I reckon it's a female, sure enough,* the *in-habit* said.

"Then how can you call it a 'king' snake?" Robin wanted to know.

You got me there, he said. *I never heared tell of no queen snake, though, but it appears that's what you've got.*

So Robin decided to name her snake The Queen of Sheba, explaining there was a woman of that name in her book called the Bible who had brought rich treasures to King Solomon.

They all called the snake Sheba for short, and everybody lived happily ever after.

No, that wasn't true, Hreapha realized. Sheba was going to live for many, many years, and in no time Robin had made friends with her, so much so that after Sheba's eighth shedding of her skin they could release her from the glass jar and she wouldn't try to run away and they didn't have to feed her any more. She kept the whole haunt free of mice and rats, even to the extent of depriving Robert of part of his food supply, so that he had to roam farther and farther into the woods for his supper, although on at least two occasions he saved Sheba's life, once by killing an owl that attempted to prey upon her, and the other time by killing an opposum also bent upon making a meal of Sheba. Sheba had a number of natural predators, including skunks and coyotes. She established her throne in the stall of the barn where she'd grown up, and she could usually be found there, where Robin often visited her and enjoyed picking her up and holding her and even wrapping her around her neck or waist. King snakes—and in this case a queen snake—are constrictors, and they capture and kill their prey, including the poisonous snakes, by wrapping themselves around the prey and squeezing it to death. Sheba's squeezes on Robin were gentle and sensuous.

Hreapha understood that sex was the most important part of every creature, that all creatures lived in order to mate, and thus mating had been intended to be a main source of pleasure. She herself never again came into heat—something had gone wrong during her first and only experience at birthing, and whatever internal triggers or switches consume and devote the body to procreation were no longer operative in her—but she still enjoyed observing the manifold manifestations of love in all other creatures, including her own offspring. Recently Hreapha had witnessed an act that she had been suspecting for some time: Robert was not merely a constant companion and mentor to his protégé Hroberta but had also become her lover. Hreapha didn't mind; she thought it was cute. And it couldn't result in Hroberta's pregnancy and overpopulation of the premises. But when Hroberta's sister Hruschka also went into heat, she simply disappeared. Hreapha could only assume that Hruschka, who was the quietest and shyest of her offspring, was neither willing to discuss her feelings with her mother nor willing to have one of her brothers or Robert put her passion to rest, so she wandered off in search of succor elsewhere in the world. Hreapha wondered if she might have managed to reach Stay More and even unknowingly mated with her father, Yowrfrowr. Or, more likely, she had encountered the pack of coyotes who roamed these hills. Or perhaps she had headed north and found other dogs somewhere. They were all sad to lose her, and they hoped that she might come home after she had been bred, but she never did.

Her three brothers began to pester their mother to allow them to attempt to find Stay More, not just to search for Hruschka but also to meet their father. Hreapha had promised to take Hrolf on his first birthday to see Yowrfrowr, but the birthday had come and gone and Hreapha had never been able to overcome her fear that the journey was no longer possible…although it wasn't inconceivable that Hruschka had somehow accomplished it. But now she had another motive for making the attempt, in addition to all her other motives, not least of which was her desire to see dear Yowrfrowr again.

So, in the early springtime, not long after the dogs' second birthday and thus, she told them, worth considering as a belated birthday present, she took them to see if they could find Stay More. Hroberta wanted to go too, but Robert dissuaded her. Of course Hreapha explained her destination and itinerary to the *in-habit*, who in turn explained it to Robin.

"Don't go, Hreapha!" Robin said to her. "I'll worry about you. It's dangerous. Have you forgotten the last time you tried it?"

"Hreapha," she said, that is, No, I certainly haven't forgotten, but that time I was all alone and this time I have my three big boys to help me.

Leave her to give it a try, the *in-habit* urged Robin. *They can allus turn back if the going's too rough.* Then in parting he said to Hreapha, *You'll just have to find some way to skirt around that there drop-off in the trail where it goes straight down near the waterfall.*

Which indeed proved to be their downfall, in both senses of the word.

But before they even reached it, they encountered another obstacle: the coyotes. There weren't five of them, or not the same five who had raped Hreapha, but only four. The four of them circled Hreapha and her three boys, and the eight dogs went through the formalities of sniffing each other's afterplaces. She did not recognize, or could not recall the specific scent, of any of them. They were especially curious about the scent of Yipyip, and he was equally curious about them.

He looked at her. Ma, am I any kin to these guys?

She did not say, as she was tempted to, One of them might be your father. Instead she said, They're coyotes, and you've probably got some coyote in you.

In their guttural language the coyotes began conversing among themselves, perhaps debating whether to attack. Yipyip listened with great interest, and almost seemed to understand them, which Hreapha couldn't do.

Ma, Hrolf said to her, would you mind if I took a bite out of one of these bastards?

Not until they bite first, she said. Her boys were full grown and had their father's muscular build, and she knew they could hold their own in a fight with these bastards. As her own mother had done for her, she had taught all her offspring the full array of martial skills: each of them was an excellent fighter, although none of them had had a full chance to put their skills to the test. They hadn't yet encountered a bear.

One of the coyotes, possibly the alpha male who had inherited the position from the leader of the previous pack Hreapha had encountered, spoke at length to Yipyip, who listened with excitement and then turned to her and said, Ma, they're inviting me to go hunting a bear with them. Can I?

What could she say? He was too old even to be asking her permission. It's your decision, she said. Don't stay too long. Then she addressed the alpha male, You'd better take good care of him, and let him come home when he's ready.

But she wasn't at all certain the alpha male knew her language. She could only watch as the pack loped off into the woods with her Yipyip in their midst.

Hreapha resumed the journey and they came at last to the head of the waterfall, the place where she had attempted to swim across the little creek and had been caught up in the water and swept over the falls. She had told this story several times to her offspring. I recognize it, Ma! Hrothgar exclaimed, and before she could stop him he leapt into the water and attempted to paddle his way across it, and was seized by it and carried over the falls, and, as his mother had done, plummeted fifty feet down to the pool beneath, where he disappeared underwater. Hreapha and Hrolf crept warily to the edge of the precipice and peered over, waiting to see Hrothgar emerge from the water, but he did not. "Hreapha!" she wailed down to him.

"Hrolf!" howled his brother.

They waited a long time but Hrothgar did not come to the surface. They searched all along the cliff for some way to get down to the pool. They found the remains of the trail, in the place where it was nearly vertical, the place where Adam had fallen on his last attempt to reach the Stay More school, a place that was nearly impossible for humans and completely impossible for dogs.

There was no way that Hruschka could have gone down there. She must have gone northward, or, as Hreapha herself had done the first time she'd tried to reach Stay More, taken the road that ran along the east side of Madewell Mountain.

Hreapha and her one remaining boy returned sadly homeward, their heads held low and their tails drooping. They waited a long time, months and months, to see if either Hruschka or Yipyip might come home, but they did not. Nor, of course, did Hrothgar.

Chapter thirty-four

My heart went out to Hreapha. It went out to all the survivors but especially to her, the mother, who had lost three of her progeny and was disconsolate for a long time. Eventually I got them all together—Hreapha, Hrolf, Hroberta, Robert, and Robin, as well as Ralgrub, Sheba, and Dewey, the fawn that Robin got for her eleventh birthday—and told them something that I had been keeping to myself: how Grandma Laura Madewell had lost three of the children she'd had after my father, Gabriel, was born. I did not wish to malign either Laura or Hreapha with the comparison, but they had much in common, especially that their mates were so much alike: Braxton Madewell wasn't as well-spoken as Yowrfrowr but he was very like him, even in his shaggy, droop-eared appearance. I told my audience about the romance of Braxton and Laura, pointing out how similar it was to that of Yowrfrowr and Hreapha, with one important exception: that the latter two were not permitted to live together. There were some marvelous parallels, even including the fact that Laura had hiked a long way from her home, in a place called Boxley, in order to be with Braxton and try to persuade him to move to Boxley, and just as Yowrfrowr was too devoted to his mistress to leave her, Braxton was too devoted to his, the oak-forested mountain. Gabriel was their first born male, as Hrolf was Hreapha's...but I would save for another day spelling out the many similarities between Gabe and Hrolf. Laura would have two other boys, and two girls. One of the girls ran away from home—like Hruschka? Eventually there was only one remaining, Gabe, my father—like Hrolf?

In the earlier part of my childhood I knew Grandma Laura well. She was a small woman, as Hreapha was small, and her white hair was the color of Hreapha's. What I remembered most about Grandma—and this held my audience, who began to drool—were the buttermilk biscuits she made, light as feathers, which practically dissolved just as you sank your teeth into them. Robin wanted to know if she'd got the recipe out of that 1888 *Housekeeper's Cyclopædia,* which she'd brought from Boxley to Madewell Mountain as part of her small dowry or trousseau or whatever. No, the secret of those biscuits was something she'd learned from her mother, a Villines, and which she passed on to her daughter-in-law Sarah, my mother, but which my mother could never make as nicely as Grandma Laura could.

In-habits, who retain all their senses, including taste, but possess no need to eat nor any hunger, can only endow with rich memory such an experience as biting into Laura Madewell's biscuits. Even if Robin discovered, as she was busily investigating recipes all on her own, a way to make perfect biscuits, and assuming her rather crude home-milled flour would permit her, her biscuits could never do for me what Grandma's did, what Proust's madeleines did for him.

But remembrance of biscuits past was distracting me from my main point, the tragedy of Laura's loss of her children, which corresponded to Hreapha's loss of hers. I would not go into the details of how each of them lost their lives, although the stories had been told me by Grandma herself: the important thing is not that one of your children dies in a waterfall and another one runs away from home but that some vicissitude robs you forever of the pleasure of their company. Farther along we'll know all about it.

That little narrative and sermon were for the benefit of the whole company (including you), and were delivered in the elegiac accents of a twelve-year-old country boy who had been left behind by that actual part of himself who against his will had been removed from these beloved premises. I was only a simulacrum, no, an *eidolon* in the classical Greek sense, a *presence*, and my presence was needed more these days not by Robin but by Hreapha, and I spent countless hours (what is a mere hour to an *in-habit?*) in the latter's company, not merely consoling her for her loss but honoring the promise that farther along we'll know all about it.

I hate it here, Hreapha said to me one day when she was feeling despondent. I wish I were anywhere else.

Is that a fact, now? I rejoined. *How can ye be certain that anywheres else would be any better?*

I can't, she said. But it just wouldn't be *here*. Here is so dismal.

I reckon I may of felt that way sometimes. Or Adam did, I mean. Until it was time to leave. Until they was a-fixing to take him away. And then he got right mastered by the thought of leaving.

I told Hreapha the story of Adam's last day on Madewell Mountain, of Gabe loading the wagon with just the bare essentials of their possessions, just what the wagon would hold in addition to the three of them—or the two of them, because at the moment of departure Adam kissed his mother and said, "You'uns have a good time in Californy. I aint a-going." And ran away into the woods. No, not ran, because with that game leg of his he couldn't even walk very fast, but it was fast enough to get away from his father, who had been busy loading the wagon, and by the time Sarah told Gabe that their son had gone off into the woods, he was too far behind to catch him. Still, Gabe plunged into the woods in pursuit, yelling over and over again, "AD! AD! AD!"

Adam knew he was being stupid. He didn't manage to get so far off into the woods that he couldn't hear in the distance that voice, "AD! ADAM MADEWELL, YOU BETTER JUST STOP AND GIVE A THOUGHT TO WHAT YOU'RE A-DOING!"

But Adam was so determined not to leave Madewell Mountain that he spent the whole night in the woods, cold and hungry. He discovered the unburied corpse of his dog, Hector, whom his father had shot days earlier. (This part of my story moved Hreapha out of her megrims.) Early in the morning he went back to the house to make certain that his parents had in fact departed. He searched the kitchen for something to eat, but his mother had left nothing behind. Days earlier, his father had taken the remaining livestock—the cow, the pigs, the goats, the chickens and geese—to his brother-in-law in Parthenon. Gabe Madewell had planned after reaching Harrison to sell the wagon and the mules for whatever he could get and pay a family in Harrison who were planning to drive a truck to California and would have room for the Madewells. Adam assumed they were already on their way to that Promised Land. Up until the day of the departure he had almost persuaded himself that the only good reason for going to California was that he might find Roseleen there; he had heard that the year before her parents had joined the endless migration of Arkansawyers (or "Arkies" as they were called) to California. But on the day of the departure he had had to choose between Madewell Mountain and California, and he knew that the latter, for all its fabled splendors, was simply no match for the former.

Now, even if he was only twelve (which, after all, Robin herself wouldn't reach for another year), he planned to live here by himself, fend for himself, make do, subsist, exactly as Robin was doing so many years later. His father had taken the firearms, but Adam had a slingshot he'd left in the cooper's shed, and he also had some fishing tackle and he could make a spear or two, and catch enough game to cook on the nice old kitchen stove that had been left behind. He didn't even have the advantages that Robin had, not just of firearms but of a stock of edibles (albeit hers were practically gone now) salted away by Sog Alan, so Adam had to start from scratch in fending for himself. It was a daunting prospect.

But right away he killed a squirrel with his slingshot and fried it on the kitchen stove, having just a little difficulty with the recipe because all the previous times he had killed squirrels with his slingshot his mother had done the cooking. He overcooked the squirrel but it was still edible, and something for his stomach.

"Better piss on that fire, and put it out," said Gabe Madewell, and Adam wheeled around to see his father standing there. His father was holding his rifle loosely in one hand. Adam was instantly scared, wondering, What's the rifle for?

"I figured you'uns had done gone," he said.

"You didn't figure your maw would let me go off without ye, did ye? Why, I didn't hardly make it to the foot of the mountain afore she commenced a-bawlin at the top of her lungs."

"So you've made up your mind to stay?" Adam said hopefully.

"Naw, not a chance. The wagon's still at the foot of the mountain, where we had to camp out last night. I've hoofed it back up here to get ye. Now unbutton yore britches and piss on that fire and let's go."

Adam would not piss on the fire. "I aint leavin, Paw," he declared.

"Well, we aint goin nowheres without ye. Yore maw won't allow it."

"Then bring the wagon on back up here."

"Boy, you aint yet learnt why we caint do that? When your grampaw died, this place died with him. This place aint fit for nothing. I caint run the cooperage without your grampaw, and you aint much help, and besides there just aint much of a market no more for homemade barrels, nor even stave bolts. I've told ye all that, time and time again."

"Come and look, Paw," Adam requested and led his father out to the cooper's shed where, in one corner, Adam had hidden the cedar churn he'd recently made. "Look at that, Paw," he said. "I can make anything, and if you'll just give me time I can make a barrel ever bit as good as you can."

Gabe Madewell laughed, but he fondled the churn and admired it and allowed as how it was pretty good made. "But nobody uses churns no more," he observed. "You can buy your butter at the store real easy." He tossed the churn aside, and Adam heard it crack as it fell. "It'll be another two or three years afore you're big enough to make a barrel, and no telling but what there won't be no market at all for homemade barrels." He took the boy's upper arm in a tight grip, the muscular vise-like grip of a cooper, and led him out of the cooperage. "I never should've dragged your maw up here in the first place, but your grampaw needed me, and now he don't because he's dead. And now it's time to make your maw happy and get the hell out of here."

Adam broke free from his grip. "God damn it, Paw, I'm not leavin. You caint make me."

His father just studied him for awhile. When he spoke again the coldness of his voice sent shivers through the boy. "Ad, you know I had to put ole Heck away because we couldn't take him with us. Now I could just as easy put you away too, if we caint take you with us." He raised the rifle and pointed it at his son.

Adam was shocked as well as scared but he managed to put a little courage into his words, "How you figure to explain that to Maw?"

"I'd just have to tell her I couldn't find you nowheres. I'd just have to say we'd have to get on. Them folks in Harrison that's a-taking us to Californy won't wait for us. We've done already put 'em a day behind. Now take your pick, Ad: get yourself down the mountain with me, or there'll be only your ghost to stay here."

Adam turned and gazed at the homestead. Would his ghost really be able to stay here? He had spent a number of idle moments pondering the matter of death, especially when his grandfather had died, and he had considered whether or not it is possible to survive death in some way. Is there some part of yourself that can go on after you're gone?

He knew it was possible that his father didn't really mean it, that he had no intention of killing him but was just tricking him into leaving by that threat.

"Give me a minute, Paw," he requested, and walked away from his father, back to the cooper's shed. He reached down to the earthen floor of the shed and clawed up a handful of dirt and put it into his britches pocket, to take to California. From his other pocket he took his handkerchief and held it to his lips. "Adam Madewell," he whispered, "be always here. *Be always here.* Never leave, Adam. Stay more forever." He spread the handkerchief over the toppled cedar churn, and then he straightened up as his eyes began to fill with tears, and he limped out of the cooper's shed and rejoined his father, and they walked together as fast as his limp would allow down the mountain to where his mother and the wagon were waiting.

The wagon has halfway to Harrison before he realized that he had never pissed on the fire. He smiled at the thought. Maybe the house would burn down. But maybe the fire would just die out.

"So you left yourself here on purpose?" Robin said. It wasn't a question so much as a statement of fact. And it was as good a way as any of stating the truth, namely, that Adam Madewell had created me, had made me and bade me become his proxy, to inhabit these beloved premises after he was gone. I looked at Robin, aware that she was almost seeing me, aware that she had been listening to the story along with her dear dog.

"*You,*" she said, "never did go to California."

Nope, I never did, nor will I ever.

"Does Adam know you're here? Do you somehow talk to him?"

Naw, I caint reach him. Nor vicey versy.

"You don't know what he's doing in California? Or even if he's still alive?"

I reckon he must still be alive and kicking, or else I wouldn't be, myself. But I'm sorry to say I aint got the least notion what-all he's up to.

The lad in his awkward way had stated an accurate but perplexing fact: *I,* Adam Madewell, already forty years old, was indeed living and working in Rutherford, California, having endured some experiences about which we'll at least have a synopsis farther along, but I had no awareness at all that the little ritual I'd performed upon leaving Madewell Mountain had actually had the magic effect I'd intended, of creating not a second self but an ersatz self, free from time and appetite, forever keeping the home fires burning (literally, in view of his showing Robin how to make a fire). It would have been so nice if somehow I could have contacted him from time to time to ask how things were going. Or if he could have followed my progress through life, my fortunes, literally, in California. But we were as two brothers who went their separate ways and never corresponded. I suppose that is simply an inescapable condition of all *in-habits* everywhere.

How then, you're wondering, can I, the mature, learned, and even, I hope, occasionally entertaining adult Adam, switch places, or at least first-person pronouns, so readily and glibly with that backwoods hobbledehoy or his lively understandable spirit? Because, as I've hinted before, this story, at least for now, is all in the past tense, of which I am master. This does not mean that I could omnisciently witness everything that was happening on Madewell Mountain at the time of the story, but that from this retrospective of the present, *now*, I can reconstruct all of it for your benefit at least as adroitly as Robin had been reconstructing with her paper dolls the entire history of Stay More.

Alas, she had outgrown the paper dolls. Or lost interest in them. Or found other things to play with. She had not destroyed them, and when I asked her, *How come you aint played with them little paper people for some time now?* she shrugged and said she had run out of paper.

Which was true. Robin was running out of everything...except determination and resourcefulness, which, with my help, would get her through. She ran out of sugar. She ran out of toothpaste. Sog Alan had stocked up several dozen tubes, but Robin despite a general laxity in her personal grooming liked to brush her teeth at least once a day (which was a good thing because she was not going to get any care at all from a dentist), and the toothpaste was all gone. She vaguely remembered something she'd learned in school about using baking soda as a substitute for toothpaste, and there were enough boxes of baking soda to last her until she was able to devise or invent some other dentifrice (at fourteen, having taking an interest in geology after Hreapha gave her a chunk of crystal quartz for her fourteenth birthday, she would discover a small deposit of chalk on a cliff side, and discover that chalk makes a splendid dentifrice).

But you can live without toothpaste. It's hard to live without soap, and now that was all gone too. Nothing to bathe with, nothing to wash the dishes with, nothing to clean your clothes with (although she rarely wore clothes, it was nice to keep the bedsheets and pillow-cases laundered). The *Cyclopædia* had a recipe for hard soap with three ingredients, sal-soda, unslacked lime, and rainwater, only one of which she possessed (although she knew from the Bible that lime could be made from a skeleton), and although I had watched Grandma Laura and my mother making lye soap I had only the vaguest idea of the process or the ingredients, and thus was of no help to Robin. Often I, the *in-habit*, could only say I was sorry I couldn't help, or didn't know what to advise her.

Robin's body was getting dirty. It was also changing, as I couldn't help noticing and admiring. She was already as tall as I was, and I in my innocence began to wonder if she would eventually outgrow me entirely. I already knew that she would soon become as old as I was, and thereafter she'd get progressively older than I. As her childish body had grown, it had softened and rounded, especially in the hips as her pelvic area broadened, her waist was more accented and narrow, her arms were rounder—her body was taking on the classical feminine vase shape. She was no longer a child, at all. Most delightfully her nipples were beginning to project, and the area around them was swelling into a conelike projection on her otherwise flat chest, although, curious to young Adam's ogling *in-habit,* one breast seemed to be developing more rapidly than the other one.

Having the advantage of invisibility, the *in-habit* could indulge his desire by gazing upon her ripening body to his heart's content, and even to his part's content.

Chapter thirty-five

There was only one mirror in the house, a half-length wall mirror with its edges fading and rotted-looking, but she loved to stand in front of it, even if she badly needed to wash off some of her dirt (if she could only figure out how to make soap), and examine what was happening to her body, how she was not just growing up but filling out. When she went to the mirror, she liked to allow Sheba to wrap herself around her neck and upper body (she'd measured with the yardstick, and Sheba was nearly six feet long now), which Sheba herself seemed to think was her favorite place in all the world, wrapping around her and gently squeezing. Her blonde hair was a mess. It came down to her waist and she hadn't been able to shampoo it since the soap ran out a long time back. Studying herself and Sheba in the mirror, although she loved her nakedness, she wished that maybe sometime she could dress up in a really nice fancy dress, but all the dresses Sugrue had bought her were ridiculously small now.

She caught sight of her fawn Dewey watching her. She often let him into the house, and even let him sleep with her, along with Ralgrub, the three of them all snuggled up. Dewey was cute beyond belief, with those big innocent eyes and big ears and his head too big for his little body. But now, as she studied his reflection in the mirror behind her, he seemed to look too fuzzy, and she knew he wasn't that fuzzy. His speckled coat was smoother than that. She thought at first there was something wrong with the old mirror, but then she backed away from the mirror as far as she could back, and studied her own reflection with Sheba wrapped around her. She looked fuzzy too, or blurry, and maybe it wasn't the mirror's fault. She moved to the window and looked out at the yard and the trees all around and the garden and in the distance the blue mountains rolling off to infinity, and all of it was kind of hazy.

"My eyes are going bad!" she yelled. "Adam, god damn it, I'll have to start wearing glasses!"

I caint imagine you in spectacles. Where do you plan to find ary?

To use one of his favorite expressions, he had her there. Her chances of getting glasses were more remote than her chances of finding some soap or some sugar. She was learning to substitute other sweeteners for sugar; the previous spring, when the sap was rising in the trees, Adam had shown her how to take the bung augur and drill a hole in the trunk of a maple tree and catch the sap in a bucket and boil it down into a kind of dark but very sweet maple syrup. And then of course each autumn she took Hreapha and the other dogs out to "line" bees, as Sugrue had shown her, and find honey, and although she usually got stung (and had to treat the stings with three kinds of crushed leaves), she had more honey than she could eat, and also plenty of beeswax, which she liked to chew; it was almost as good as having some chewing gum.

Most recently, while she and Hreapha were at a bee tree, she saw again the footprint which Sugrue had taught her to identify, a track so much like a human's footprint: a bear's. She still hadn't seen a bear, and she wasn't completely convinced this was not the footprint of a human. She was only a little frightened, because no wild animal could ever scare her any more, not since she'd made friends with Sheba. "Hreapha," she said, "I think I'd like to have a bear cub for my twelfth birthday."

"Hreapha," her sweet dog said.

And one day she was sitting on the davenport chewing some beeswax, feeling restless and itchy, unable, as she often was, to sit still on the davenport. As she often did, she began squirming around, bouncing, and twisting and wriggling and throwing a leg over the arm, and swinging her feet, and cocking her head this way and that and then making faces to herself, and laughing, all signs that her mind was busy at work. She suddenly realized that the texture of beeswax was such that it might make the base of soap, if only she had the other ingredients, whatever they were. Her *Cyclopædia* had mentioned beef tallow, which of course she didn't have and could never get, unless some old beef came wandering into the yard; she also didn't have the *Cyclopædia*'s other ingredients such as gum camphor, borax, bergamot and sal soda. But Adam had mentioned his grandmother using lye to make soap.

"What's lye, Adam?" she asked the air. He didn't answer, as usual. She let the matter drop for a little while, and went on flouncing her body around on the davenport, giving full thought to the practicality of making soap, if she could figure it out. After a while, she said, "Tell me what lye is, god damn it." That had become her favorite swear-expression lately; she had memories of how Grampaw had said it and how Sugrue had said it, and although she read her Bible regularly and knew that you aren't supposed to take the Lord's name in vain, she didn't think there was anything vain about it, and she was always careful that "god" was not capitalized.

Keep your shirt on, gal. Naw, I don't mean your shirt, 'cause you aint wearin ary, but don't get your back up. Gentle down. You been a-squirmin and a-fidgetin around on that davenport like a bunch of blister beetles was a-chompin on ye.

"Tell me how to make lye, gol dang it."

Lie? You mean like a whopper or just a windy?

"The kind of lye that was used to make soap, silly."

Never heared tell of no silly soap.

She sighed. "Adam, you are impossible. I have got to have some soap. You said your grandmother made soap with lye. Did she have to buy it at the store?"

Naw, they just made it out of wood ashes.

"Wood ashes? We've got gobs of those."

You'd have to make you a ash hopper. Let me see if I caint remember what it looked like.

He could remember. And he told her how to make it, at least a crude makeshift funnel sort of thing out of slats of wood—old staves, but not the staves she was saving to finish that firkin whenever she got around to it. He said that as best as he could remember, they'd lined the hopper with paper to filter the water through the ashes, and of course there wasn't a scrap of paper left in the house that she hadn't made into dolls. She thought of using pages torn out of those issues of *Police Gazette* that Sugrue had kept and which she never cared to read. That did okay to line the hopper, and then she filled it with all the ashes she could get from the kitchen stove and the living room stove. She poured water on top, and behold, lye dripped into the bucket (the same bucket she'd used for collecting maple sap), and she realized her firkin, when she got around to finishing it, would do a better job.

"Now I need to know, what's 'tallow'?"

Taller? Why, I reckon taller's just the hard fat that comes from beef.

"Seen any beef lately? Can you get tallow from chicken fat?"

I misdoubt it. Say, maybe you could get it from hogs.

"Seen any hogs lately? Which reminds me, it's been a long time since I had any meat from that pork I smoked a few years back. We had the last of the ham last Christmas."

But Sugrue had taught her to save all her bacon grease, which he said was the best thing for frying chicken in, and she had several jars of it. She decided to see if you couldn't get tallow out of bacon grease.

She built a fire under the big iron kettle that was used for washing clothes (which she hadn't used since she ran out of soap), and put some water into it and brought it to a boil. All her friends were gathered around, watching her as if she were preparing something special to eat: there was Dewey, and Ralgrub, and Sheba, and Hreapha, and Hrolf, and Hroberta, and Robert, and of course Adam too was somewhere around. Making a ceremony out of it, she dumped in the bacon grease, the lye, and several big chunks of beeswax, and took a wooden stick and began to stir. She stirred and she stirred, feeling like a witch stirring a cauldron and wondering if she ought to add magic ingredients or at least something that would perfume it and take away the greasy smell. At least she had plenty of energy for stirring, the kind of energy that had gone to waste bouncing around on the davenport. But after an hour of stirring, the whole mess just looked like dark gravy and didn't smell anything at all like soap.

One more failure in her education. But at least she was learning something. She reflected that if she were in Harrison she'd be in the sixth grade, about to graduate from Woodland Heights Elementary, but she wouldn't have learned a fraction of all that she'd learned up here at Madewell Mountain Elementary. She went to bed not brooding about her failure but wondering just what she'd learned from the experience.

The next morning she went out to dump the contents out of the kettle, reflecting that she'd probably not need the pot for washing anyway, if she didn't have soap. But she discovered she *did* have soap! Overnight the dark gravy had hardened. She took a knife and cut into it and brought forth a cube of honest-to-god soap! It wasn't nearly as hard as store soap. But it was soap. Soap!

She cut all the hardened soap into rectangles and squares, and stacked them up in the house, and then scraped out all the remainder in the kettle to be used for flakes of dishwashing and clothes-washing soap. Then she filled the kettle with water, built up a fire to boil the water, dumped in all her filthy towels and sheets and rags and the few items of clothing she wore from time to time, and began to sing as she worked:

> Here we go 'round the mulberry bush,
> The mulberry bush, the mulberry bush.
> Here we go 'round the mulberry bush,
> So early in the morning.
>
> This is the way we wash our clothes
> Wash our clothes, wash our clothes.

This is the way we wash our clothes,
So early Monday morning.

Come to think of it, maybe it was Monday. It might as well be. One nice thing about not having a calendar is that one day was just as important as another, or as unimportant as you wanted it to be.

She finished the job of washing all the clothes, and hung them out on the clothesline to dry in the sunshine. It felt so good to have everything fresh and clean...except herself, which was next. In the kitchen she filled the galvanized tub with hot water from the stove, enough for her hair as well as her body, and she climbed in, discovering she couldn't really stretch out the way she had been able to in earlier years, and got her body and hair thoroughly wet and rubbed her homemade soap all over herself. It didn't smell very much like bacon grease; maybe that was what the lye was supposed to do: bleach out the greasy smell.

She was so happy to be getting clean and so delighted by the feeling of the bar of homemade soap running over her body that she became not just overjoyed but intensely excited, so much so that she had to slide the bar of soap down to her groin and move it around there for quite a while. The sensation of the wet slathery bar of soap, her own handiwork, rubbing against her poody lifted her higher and higher in her feelings. She gasped. She knew that Adam was probably watching her, but he had been watching her for so long that she felt not the least bit self-conscious; on the contrary, the idea of his watching made all of this even more exciting.

"The soap works," she said to him, wherever he was. "Oh, the soap *works!*"

She felt tingly as well as soapy all over, and the tingle spread from her hair to her toes and changed from being just a tingle to a ripple, and then a tremor, almost as if an electric current was starting to pass through her body. She jiggled the bar of soap against herself so rapidly that she was sloshing water out of the tub. She'd never felt anything like this before. She felt a sense of certainty that something she couldn't avoid was about to happen, a sense of expectation and anticipation that was all the more thrilling because it also scared her just a little. But it didn't stop her. She was all out of breath and the sweat of her body was mingling with the water of the bath. She searched for a word to name what she was feeling, but all she could come up with was *reach*. She was reaching for something, and the reach was about to happen.

And then it happened! It was as if she'd been turned inside out or, like Sheba, shed her skin, or like Adam taken leave of his whole body: she shivered and shook uncontrollably, not reaching anymore but getting there, and *there* was the most awesome and intense feeling she'd ever had. It went on and on for nearly a minute and left her exhausted but happier than she'd ever been. She could only lie perfectly still in the water, marveling at what had happened. She felt so good and so peaceful that she might have easily fallen asleep and drowned herself, but the bathwater was beginning to grow cold, and she climbed out. Realizing all her towels were hanging on the line, she shook the water from herself like a dog and then went outside to dry herself in the sunshine. She resumed her song, with her own words:

> That was the way we washed ourselves,
> And that was the way we reached ourselves,
> That was the way we reached ourselves
> So early in the morning.

"Adam, sweet honey, is there a mulberry bush anywhere around here?" she asked.

As was often the case, there wasn't any immediate answer. But couldn't she hear his breathing? Or rather his panting? He seemed to be breathing real hard. What was he doing? Had he been running around his haunt? Did he really run? What did he do for exercise? Finally, with his voice still out of breath, he said, *They's only one mulberry I know of, but it aint a bush. It's a full-growed tree yonder on the east edge of the meader.*

"Why are you panting so, Adam?" she asked. "What are you doing?" But there was no answer.

For most of the summer thereafter, Robin took a bath nearly

335

every day. Imagine that. Usually when the weather was warm she bathed by swimming in the beaver pond, but she had learned long ago that the beaver didn't like for her to use soap in their pond, so she didn't use the beaver pond very much any more, except to visit it to say hello to her friends.

Toward the end of that summer, not long before she was going to have her twelfth birthday, there was a drought. She didn't know that word, although she'd encountered it several times in the Bible, but she knew that it was getting harder and harder to draw the water from the well for her frequent baths. And then the well dried up entirely! Adam instructed her on how to roll one of the shed's barrels up to the corner of the house where it could be connected to the downspout to make a rain barrel. But it didn't rain. Not for the longest time. The spring at the springhouse dried up too, which not only removed that source of water but made the springhouse useless for cooling leftovers or keeping anything cool. It was very hot, as well as very dry. The animals didn't suffer too much; they could always get a drink from the beaver pond, which was too far for the chickens to hike, so she had to haul water in buckets from the beaver pond to keep the chickens from dying. Robin wouldn't drink the pond water herself without boiling it first, but that at least gave her drinking water.

Baths were out of the question, and she missed them terribly. For a little while she tried simply to soap her poody, but without water to wash the soap off it wouldn't work, and she couldn't reach at all again. In frustration she tried to make herself reach without the help of the soap, and was shocked to see that her fingers became covered with blood!

She had probably done something terribly wrong. She couldn't ask Adam to explain it to her. He probably didn't know, anyhow.

The bleeding went on and on slowly day by day. She wiped it up with rags. She needed water to clean herself, but had none. The beaver pond was beginning to dry up, and what would she do if there was no water at all anywhere? And no rain came? How would she live? How would any of them live? The beaver too would die.

"Adam!" she cried. "I think I'm dying. Please help me!"

I'm here, he said. *I reckon I'm allus here.*

She frankly confessed to him what she had done to herself, although she knew he had probably witnessed it anyway. She was really and truly sorry that she had done it. She should have known better. She should have realized that anything which felt so good must be wrong. She had done a terribly wrong thing, and now she was bleeding, and the bleeding wouldn't stop, and she needed to see a doctor, but there was no way she could do that. Was there nothing Adam could do that would help? Or tell her how to stop the bleeding? Or something? Anything? Adam? *Adam?*

You've got me all afeared now. I caint imagine what could be wrong with ye.

Chapter thirty-six

His mother told him that, yes, there was a possibility that Mistress was dying, but that did not excuse him from his responsibility to assist in, and perhaps even direct, the task of locating and taking possession of a bear cub for Mistress' twelfth birthday. It was an awesome obligation which had given him much thought, search, practice and discussion with his lieutenants, only one of whom, Ralgrub, had anything to contribute, because she claimed that she was cousin to the bears and understood their habits and their ways...not to mention that she was the only one of them other than Robert who could climb trees.

What if they went to all the trouble to capture a bear cub and bring it home and even put a red ribbon around its neck as a birthday present, and then Mistress died of whatever was ailing her and causing all that blood? What would they do with the bear cub then? Just set it free, and say, Sorry, pal, but we don't need you after all? Well, of course they could eat it, but Hrolf didn't have much appetite these days, what with having to eat the chickens as they died. The drought was killing off the chickens, although Mistress each day brought a bucket of water from the beaver pond just to give the chickens some water, but that wasn't enough to keep them from dying, and his mother had decreed that it was now permissible to eat a chicken if it was clearly dead, and Hrolf would be just as happy if he never saw another chicken again, he'd eaten so many of them.

Hrolf realized that the only way to get out of the responsibility of bringing home a bear cub would be for Mistress to die before her twelfth birthday. He hated to see that happening, but she was bleeding, and it wouldn't stop.

It was a long hike to the beaver pond for a sip of stagnant slime. And then the beaver pond went completely dry. The beaver disappeared, without a word to anyone. Nobody knew whether the beaver had simply died or had gone elsewhere in search of water. Hrolf's campaign to teach the beaver how to communicate in dog language had not been successful. The beaver were too ignorant, or too stubborn, or perhaps even too proud, to attempt to master the easy rudiments of dogtalk. And thus they had not said anything to anybody before departing. Hrolf considered it one of his failures. He had been proud and triumphant in his campaign to teach dog language to all the other creatures of their acquaintance, except of course Sheba, who had her own mysterious language that was unfathomable. But Ralgrub spoke a passable tongue, and Robert from a very early age had been quick to pick up on the language, although he never had learned to bark and still said "WOO! WOO!" as his primary exclamation. Hrolf had taken it upon himself to stress to everyone the superiority, nay, the *nobility*, of canine communication, and his efforts to dogize the other creatures, at least in dogese, were rewarding. They were all noble.

Thus, when he gathered them around him, in the presence (the omnipresence) of the *in-habit*, Adam, he knew that they could all (except Sheba) understand him when he declared, Friends, we're going to have to go on an expedition. Our main objective is to find water, somewhere, anywhere. But our secondary purpose is to honor Mother's request to find a bear cub for Mistress' forthcoming birthday. I'll take with me only the following: Mother if she wants to go, Hroberta and Robert and Ralgrub. And Adam.

You'uns know I caint leave the haunt, Adam declared.

Sorry, I forgot Sir, Hrolf said. He'd never called the boy "Sir" before, but he felt it was needed in this context.

Why can't I go too? Dewey asked in his still fumbling form of dogtalk. Dewey wasn't a mere fawn any more, but a young buck. He was growing up, and before long he'd start sprouting antlers.

Well, I suppose you could, Hrolf allowed.

I can find water as good as any of the rest of you can, Dewey boasted. And I bet I could find a bear even better.

All right, Hrolf said. Let's go. Adam, Sir, would you explain to Mistress where we went, and that we may be gone more than a day or two. Don't mention the bear cub.

The expedition set out, the six of them romping abreast across the meadow but changing to single file as they reached the dry beaver pond and the old path that was known as the South Way. I'm real proud of you for doing this, son, Hrolf's mother said to him.

Ma, we'd all die of thirst if we didn't.

But they were perishing of thirst by the time they'd gone a mile or so through the forest. They hoped that the creek which fed the waterfall would slake their dehydration, but they discovered it was bone dry, as was the waterfall itself. Peering over the precipice, Hrolf could see a dog's skeleton in the dry bed of what had been the pool at the base of the waterfall. He realized that must be poor Hrothgar. He nudged his mother aside to keep her from peering over the precipice.

I can't go another step without a drink, Hroberta declared.

They all sat around panting and moaning in the torture of extreme thirst. And before the sun set on that day of the expedition, Hrolf said apologetically, I'm sorry I brought you'uns out here. But we can't go back. There's nothing to drink anywhere.

Woo, Robert said, there's got to be some way to get off this fucking mountain and find a creek.

Ralgrub said, Whatever creek you found might be dry too.

As night fell, several of them chewed on grass to get just a little moisture.

The next morning, it was Dewey who found the spring. It wasn't much of a spring, and hard to reach, a trickle seeping out from beneath a rock on the cliff side, but it was genuine water. Each of them had to wait their turn (Hrolf insisted that his mother go first) to dip their tongue into the seep and lap a bit, and then wait a minute for more water to seep out for the next creature. Hrolf was sad to realize that even if he got Mistress to bring her bucket to this place, it would take hours or days for the bucket to fill.

But they'd each had enough water to sustain them through another day of searching. As they traversed the forests of Madewell Mountain, and Ledbetter Mountain too, everywhere they saw the effects of the drought: the carcasses of birds, animals, and reptiles who had perished. They came across the bodies of whole families of mice, squirrel, rabbit, possum, porcupine, skunk and coon. Some of the creatures were sprawled out full length on the ground as if they had used the last of their strength to try to reach water somewhere.

It was Robert who found the bears. There was a cave mouth mostly concealed by leaves and brush, and he burrowed through the camouflage, went into the interior of the earth, and came back in a little while, saying, Come and look! There used to be a little stream of water in there, but it's dried up now. There's a dead bear sow lying beside it, with one of her dead cubs. The other cub looks like he's still alive.

They all went into the cave to investigate. It was much cooler in there, which was a relief, but the cave's stream of water was nothing but drying mud. There was a stink from the bodies of the dead sow and the cub. The other cub was unable to move, and his eyes were closed, but he was still breathing. He was scrawny and pitiful and his black fur was matted and grungy.

Ma, I'm doubtful that he would be much of a birthday present, Hrolf observed.

We'll have to take care of him one way or the other, as long as he's still alive, she said. First we have to figure out how to get him home.

They tried nudging the cub into a walking or crawling posture, but the cub could not keep himself righted. If they could get him out of here at all, the first thing they'd have to do would be get him to that little trickle of a spring and get him to drink as much water as he could.

Hrolf's mother took charge. Dewey, she said, would you mind lying down on top of the bear sow and rolling around?

For heaven's sake, *why?* Dewey wanted to know.

So you'll get her scent on your own body. So the cub won't be so afraid of you.

With a look of disgust, Dewey lay atop the dead sow and squirmed around, getting her scent onto his own hide.

Now, Hrolf's mother said, let's see if we can't get the cub up onto Dewey's back. Lie down, Dewey, and when we've got the cub on your back, stand up, but don't bump the cub on the ceiling of the cave.

They all cooperated in tugging and pushing the cub into position along Dewey's spine, with the cub's paws on either flank.

When Dewey stood up, he yelped, Yeoww! He's sinking his claws into me!

Good, Hrolf's mother said. He's trying to hold on. Let's get out of here.

Hrolf and Hroberta walked on either side of Dewey to make sure the cub wouldn't topple off, and thus they made their way slowly back to the cliff side where the tiny trickle of springwater had been found. There, Dewey knelt and they gentled the cub off of Dewey's back and led him to the spring. But he would not drink.

Maybe he was still nursing, Hrolf observed. Maybe he hasn't learned how to drink.

No, Hrolf's mother said, he's too old to be nursing. He's probably weaned. Let's hope so. Our next step, if we can get him to drink, is to find something for him to eat.

Hrolf's mother crept to the spring and lapped up a mouthful of water and put her mouth to the cub's mouth and spewed or sprayed the water into the cub's mouth. The cub shook his head in rejection of the dog-smelling water. But Hrolf's mother kept at it, and finally got the cub to swallow some water. Then she put her paw on the cub's head and forced his head down to the spring's trickle, and the cub got the idea and began to lap at the water.

When the cub had drunk all the water he could hold, they each slowly took a drink, and then they got the cub up onto Dewey's back again and headed out in the direction of home.

Ralgrub, Hrolf's mother said, what would your cousin like to eat, do you think?

Mast, Ralgrub said.

Come again?

Mast. Acorns and nuts.

Eww! said the dogs.

Okay, gang, let's round up some mast.

The drought had cut back the trees' production of fruit, and few of the nuts had yet fallen this early in the fall, but both Ralgrub and Robert were able to climb some trees and knock down a few acorns and nuts. The hickory nuts were hard to crack, but the pecans cracked easily enough in a dog's powerful jaws, and Hrolf's mother directed them to masticate enough nut meat to make a mess that might appeal to the cub despite its scent of canine saliva. As it had at the spring, several attempts were required before they could get the cub to eat the masticated nutmeats. And in the process all of them grew powerfully hungry themselves. Ralgrub could eat some of the mast herself, but for the others there was only the carrion of drought-slain animals, which, if they could find a freshly deceased bird or rodent, sufficed. Lucky Dewey could survive on twigs and brush and what little grass had survived the drought.

The food and drink restored the cub's spirits to the point where he could put up resistance to being abducted. He began to growl in his whiney little voice, and more than once attempted to escape from Dewey's back, but the vigilant expedition crew kept him in place. Before they reached home they had to stop again to gather mast, masticate it (Hrolf wondered if *mast* got its name from being masticated), and feed the cub, although no further water was found for any of them. After the second time they fed the cub, instead of resuming his perch on Dewey's back for the continued journey home, he snarled and climbed a tree. The dogs impulsively barked at him, their instincts being to bark at anything which is treed, and that didn't help. Ralgrub and Robert had to go up after him, and perhaps Ralgrub knew enough of bear language to assure the cub that they were all his friends and had no intention of eating him, and besides, didn't he want the comfort of Dewey's back, which smelled like his mother? Somehow Ralgrub and Robert got him to come back down out of the tree and resume his perch on Dewey.

As they neared home, Hrolf conferred with his lieutenants about how they would keep the cub until it was time to present it to Mistress on her birthday. They didn't know just when her birthday was, and the exact date didn't matter, but they did have to decide on a day, and maybe they should wait a few days to give the cub time to fatten up and regain some of his health and strength. While Ralgrub had the manual dexterity to tie a red ribbon around the cub's neck when it came time to make the presentation, she could not tie a rope around the cub's neck to restrain him until the birthday. They needed some place to keep him until the presentation.

Hrolf's mother suggested using the abandoned beaver lodge, a brilliant idea. They coaxed the cub into it, left him with a small but adequate supply of mast, and closed the opening to the lodge with sticks and brush. Ralgrub attempted to have a chat with the cub before they left it, to tell the cub they'd soon be back and would soon be delivering the cub as an offering to a goddess, a beautiful human girl whose twelfth birthday would be greatly enhanced by the cub's presence. Whether the cub understood any of Ralgrub's words was doubtful, but he promptly curled himself up and fell asleep in his new temporary home.

The beaver lodge was just outside the haunt of the *in-habit*, and as soon as they stepped across the line on their way home, the *in-habit* met them, or at least his voice did. *Well, howdy, did you'uns find any water anywheres?*

No, but we found a bear cub, Hrolf told him. We're keeping him in the beaver lodge.

Won't be ary bit of use, lessen you find some water.

They all sighed. Hrolf was tempted to say to the *in-habit*, You're lucky you don't have to drink anyhow. But that would be catty, and he was a noble dog. Instead he asked, How's Mistress?

She aint a-bleedin no more, the *in-habit* said. *She's just fine, aside from being real thirsty, but she's been missin you'uns something terrible.*

They all went home to kiss and lick and be hugged by Mistress. Although she said she was just fine, she was obviously suffering from lack of water. So were they all. There was a nearly tangible or smellable pall in the air, a sense of impending doom. Hrolf decided that if they were all going to perish from the drought, as all those creatures in the forest had perished, he would be noble to the end, and with his last breath he would be guarding the bodies of his mother, Mistress, and the others. Or, come to think of it, probably Dewey and Sheba would be the last ones alive. Sheba didn't seem to need any water, or at least she could go for a long time without drinking, and Dewey seemed to be able to get the moisture he needed out of bushes and leaves. Hrolf didn't like the idea of being survived by others, and he would try his best to stay alive. The bear cub was an inspiration to him. If the cub had somehow survived after his mother and his sister died, Hrolf could do likewise.

Knowing that bears are mostly nocturnal, Hrolf went back at night to the beaver lodge to sit outside the closed opening and try to teach his noble language to the cub, so he could tell the cub of the kinship he felt for it as well as the encouragement he'd received from the cub's example in surviving the passing of his family. But the only dogtalk the cub was interested in learning were swear words, coarse exclamations that sounded like he was trying to say Shoot far! and Up yours! and Your mother! Hrolf shook his head and decided, This is one cantankerous bear.

Hrolf's mother decided which day would be Mistress' birthday, possibly in consultation with Mistress herself and that device they used which was called a Ouija Board. Nothing else was planned for the birthday. The supply of flour Robin had ground from her wheat was insufficient for making a birthday cake. Ralgrub went into the storeroom while Mistress wasn't looking and filched a red ribbon. Ralgrub had already told the cub how handsome he would look with a red ribbon tied around his neck, and all the other promises and expectations that she and Hrolf had bombarded the cub with appeared to be the reasons the cub was willing to leave the beaver lodge readily and walk the distance to the homestead with his canine and feline escorts. Adam joined them when they stopped so that Ralgrub with her dexterous fingers could attempt to tie the red ribbon around the cub's neck. *That sure is a mighty fine bar,* Adam complimented Hrolf. *Let's just hope he aint too rambunctious.*

Hrolf could see Mistress waiting for them. She was standing on the porch of her house, with Sheba wrapped around her neck and bare chest. She was shading her eyes from the sun and squinting but the squinting wasn't because of the sun; it was because her eyes were going bad. As they approached across the meadow and into the yard of the house, they were finally close enough for her to recognize them, although she couldn't recognize the beribboned bear cub they had in tow. Her squinting eyes finally lit up in recognition of the new animal, but then her face darkened, as if a cloud had passed over it. Indeed, Hrolf looked up at the sky and saw the clouds, and then he heard the rumble, and then the boom. Hrolf was the only one of them all, except possibly the *in-habit,* who was not frightened by the sound of the thunder. The rain began before they reached the porch, so they ran joyfully the last of the way. Shoot far! Hrolf yelled. Water! They all reached the porch, and the cub was very reluctant to climb the porch steps into human company, but the downpour began and prompted him into the porch's shelter.

Happy birthday, gal! the *in-habit* spoke for them all, although they were each trying in noble dog language to say the same thing. "Hrolf! Hrolf! Hrolf!" he shouted blissfully, joining his voice to the chorus all around them. He didn't know which made him happier, the downpour ending the drought, or his accomplishment of his mother's decree to obtain for Mistress a bear cub for her birthday.

Mistress was beside herself with joy. She held her arms up to the heavens to feel the rain and she splashed it onto her face as it fell and happily drank it. Then she dropped to her knees and attempted to hug the cub, who would have none of it, who said Piss off! and shied away from her.

"Oh, Paddington!" she cried.

Chapter thirty-seven

I had distinctly mixed feelings about that bear cub. While I agreed with the others that the acquisition of a twelfth birthday present for Robin was almost as wonderful as the coming of the rain (which went on and on until the well filled and the spring ran and the beaver pond brought its builders home), I had many reservations about bringing such an obstreperous beast into the menagerie. During the time Adam had lived there, that is, the same number of years Robin had now been alive, he had never seen a bear. I had seen their plantigrade tracks here and there, but I could only imagine, from stories my grandfather told me about them, what they looked like. I had heard plenty of these, such as the tale about the bear hunter who always shot his bear just enough to irritate and not cripple it and then ran for home with the mad bear hot on his heels and waited until they'd reached the cabin before shooting the bear dead; that way, he didn't have to worry about lugging home a five-hundred pound carcass. I had plenty of respect for and fear of the largest of all local wild creatures, but I had never encountered one. Now the beast that Robin unwisely chose to call by the same name she'd called her little stuffed animal (and she'd told me all about *that* Paddington) was very young and very cute ("adorable" was her word for his deceptively mild and cuddly appearance) and bore no resemblance to the fearsome hulking monster I'd imagined, but would in time come to lose his cuteness, and become a thoroughly ferocious, virile and lumbering fellow. I was, quite frankly, jealous of what he would become.

In my present maturity I've learned a few things apart from the appearance and behavior of adult bears: the name Paddington was cribbed from a mythical (and adorable) bear in the stories of Michael Bond, who gave the animal that name because he happened to live near Paddington Railway Station in London. And, unlike the other creatures in Robin's menagerie, *this* Paddington should not have been made into a pet, because wild bears, being solitary creatures who don't do mutual grooming of one another, don't understand the idea of petting. Thus, for a long time Paddington resisted Robin's efforts to take him to bed with her. She did not know that his assorted screeches and snarls were obscene and hostile in dogtalk, but she was hurt that he refused to snuggle up with her in bed or even on the davenport. And I, at twelve, was at a loss to explain anything to her or to help her.

She, at twelve, had already outgrown me. That in itself was unsettling enough, although of course she didn't know it, being unable to see that the top of my head came only to her hairline, and I wasn't going to tell her that she was taller than I. She seemed to be leaving me behind in her growth, not just physically but intellectually and emotionally.

The *in-habit*, meaning me, was certainly capable of crying, laughing, coughing, sneezing, and, to use that quaint participle created out of the verb, coming (although I preferred Robin's *reaching*). This might be the proper place to confess that Adam Madewell as he turned thirteen and then fourteen out there in Rutherford, California may have sometimes remembered the self that he willed himself to leave behind on Madewell Mountain, and in such moments of remembrance or at least in his dreams wondered if the *in-habit* was having a good time jacking off, as he'd learned to call it in California.

What frustrated me more than the inability to actually have sex with Robin was the inability to *do* anything physical for her. She needed someone to cut down some trees for her: each winter she had to get her firewood by dragging in limbs of deadwood, usually the result of the ice storms that came nearly every winter. She needed someone to help her spade the garden, although year by year as she grew older and stronger she was able to spade more and more of it by herself. There was so much work to be done around the place, chores that Adam had regularly performed when he lived there but which his puny *in-habit* could not handle. If I'd been able to lift a finger to help, the first thing I would have done, years earlier, would have been to give Sog Alan's skeleton a burial, but it was still there now, sitting and grinning in the outhouse, although Robin was old enough and strong enough to dig a hole to bury it if she chose. She had the decency, if that is the word, to put one of Sog's hats on the skeleton's head, so he wasn't completely nude, although the result reminded me of Donatello's *David,* that is, it simply called attention to the rest of the skeleton's nakedness. Sometimes she went and spoke to it, and of course I eavesdropped, as I pricked up my ears at her every word and gawked at her every act. "I hope you're satisfied," was something she often said to it, the skeleton. Just the other morning she said to it, "I think that sometime around now I'm supposed to start eighth grade at Harrison Junior High, but I can't, because you wanted a little girl to fuck, although you never did, or never could."

But back to that bear. Another mistake people make when they attempt to "tame" a bear is to feed it. Feeding wild bears simply turns them into greedy, lazy parasites. Robin didn't have an awful lot around the house that the cub would eat, but she apparently reasoned that since she'd seen bear tracks around the trees where'd she got her honey, bears must be fond of honey, so she spooned up a dollop for Paddington and sure enough he was crazy about the stuff, so much so that before she could stop him he had swiped the honey bucket from her and was dipping his cute little nose into it. And before she could stop him he'd eaten it all. And before she could stop him she learned that she couldn't stop Paddington from doing whatever he damn well pleased. And he seemed to get angry with her for not being able to furnish a perpetual supply of honey.

He would never look her in the eye, even when she tried to

make him do so. He might look overhead or sideways or down or behind him, but he would never look her in the eye. It was easy to believe that Paddington might simply be shy, but I don't think this was the case. I think he had some peculiar notion that as long as he didn't look at you, you weren't there, or you couldn't see him. And therefore he was safe from you. It wasn't simply Robin he refused to look at. He wouldn't make eye contact with *any* of the other inhabitants of the place, even including, for heaven's sake, the *in-habit*, me. Did he know I had eyes? Could he see my eyes? It always bugged him if I ever tried to look him square in the eye. Maybe, I decided, he was afraid that making eye contact would allow us to "read" the mischief that was brewing in his mind. I've heard that many rapists can't make eye contact with their victims.

Almost a month had gone by since the episode of Robin's bleeding, and during that month, although she felt itchings and longings, she did not again attempt to touch herself down there, out of fear. But the time came when she simply had to try it again. With soap and plenty of water. And wouldn't you know it? She started bleeding again, without even reaching. Wouldn't she ever learn? She got out the supply of rags (Sog's ripped up shirts) she'd laundered from the previous experience with bleeding. We all assumed that whatever wound she'd suffered had not healed completely. So she was having a relapse. Again, I didn't know what to do. Adam out there in California would turn fifteen years old before he learned that fertile females bleed each and every month, year around, and it is a non-threatening condition called menstruation. He learned quite a few of the slangy synonyms as well, one of which, "on the rag," referred literally to Robin's method of dealing with the problem. But Adam *In-habit*, age twelve, had never heard or imagined that such an affliction would curse all womankind periodically from puberty to menopause, and in his isolation on Madewell Mountain he had been ignorant of all the quaint Ozark superstitions, such as that a menstruating woman must never take a bath and must always bury rather than burn the contaminated rags. Robin went on bathing during her periods, now that there was a plentiful supply of water, and with that water she washed and rinsed her bloody rags, month after month until sometime in her fifteenth year it finally dawned on her that her recurrent bleeding was not caused by her fondling of herself but rather had something to do with being ready for reproduction. She would even attempt to explain it to me, three years her junior by that point and still as ignorant as ever.

Which raises an interesting question. If *in-habits* never change and never grow old, but always remain the age they were when they were installed with their real self's departure, are they capable of learning anything? Wouldn't the acquisition of knowledge imply a change? Oh, as we'll see, I learned as much from Robin as she ever learned from me; we grew in wisdom together, but she would eventually outgrow me in every way. I would always be essentially a boy; she would become a woman. It was fun to watch. I had been able for years before her coming to take pleasure in the mere act of observing the development of an acorn into an oak sapling and thence into a sturdy tree. Robin's maturity came faster and more spectacularly.

Was she happy? I like to think so. She did not often dwell upon the world she'd left behind in Harrison, or have intolerably painful yearnings for her mother (Karen Kerr had married Hal Knight and reluctantly moved to Little Rock to live with him, despite her fear that Robin might any day return to her old home and find Karen gone from it. Karen and Hal Knight became the parents of a little boy, Robin's half-brother, Richard Knight, but Karen's new motherhood, while it eased some of the pain of her loss, did not stop Karen from remaining always active in an organization, called The Robin Kerr League, devoted to the prevention of child molestation and the recovery of kidnapping victims). Of course Robin no longer pined for Paddington the First, now that she had a breathing, snorting Paddington the Second to entertain her. She missed being able to go roller skating and bicycle riding and having a sparring partner for taekwondo, although eventually she'd teach Paddington how to stand up and take it. Sometimes when she had nothing better to do (which was rare) she would fantasize about, and make mental lists of, all the things she would spend her money on if she had an opportunity to spend that nearly half a million dollars. She'd get herself a fabulous wardrobe out of the kind of women's catalogues her mother used to receive in the mail. She would buy *huge* quantities of all the foods she hadn't had for years: spaghetti, ice cream, pizza, hot dogs, milk shakes, Kool-Aid, Coca Cola, Pepsi Cola, Dr. Pepper, Seven-Up. She would of course have to have herself fitted for eyeglasses, but she would buy the most attractive and expensive kind, maybe seven pairs so she could wear a different one each day of the week. But all of these expenditures would only make a tiny dent in her fortune. She needed to buy something that really cost a whole lot. What?

One afternoon when she was trying to teach taekwondo to Paddington (he always fell on his butt when he tried to kick a *chagi*), she heard a rumble up in the air, and thought for a while it was only thunder, but as it grew and changed in tone to a rhythmic drone, she looked up and saw a helicopter.

She knew what it was although she could not remember what it was called; she had seen photographs of them during the Vietnamese war. Forgetting that she was stark naked, or having been so long out of the habit of clothing herself that it didn't even occur to her, she started waving her hands overhead to attract the attention of the pilot. Was this her rescue? Did she really want to be rescued? Even if the helicopter landed in the yard and offered to take her back to the world, would she be willing to leave all her friends? Of course not. But maybe she could tell the helicopter people to let the world know that she was okay.

The pilot and one other man in the helicopter finally caught sight of her and waved back at her. The other man put two of his fingers in his mouth and made a shrill wolf whistle which she could barely hear over the sound of the helicopter's rotors. Then he made a circle of one thumb and forefinger and took the index finger of his other hand and poked it through the circle and thrust it in and out. The pilot blew her a kiss. Then the helicopter drifted on away and never came back.

I have tried to imagine, or to learn, what might have been going through the heads of those guys. Supposedly during those years there was a hunt for marijuana growers in the Ozarks that involved using one or more helicopters for surveillance. Is that what those two men were doing, hunting for patches of pot? Then what did they think, finding a homestead on a mountaintop at which no marijuana was growing but at which there was plenty of evidence of habitation, including a lovely young nubile nude, waist-length blonde hair barely concealing her breasts, with a rapidly-growing black bear cub in her company? Maybe those guys were smoking pot themselves. Why didn't they land? I suppose we shall never know.

But that helicopter gave Robin a bright idea for how she would spend her money, if she could. She would buy one of those aircraft and hire a pilot to fly her over Harrison and all the rest of wherever she wanted to go. She would take Paddington with her, to see what he could see. She sang:

> The bear flew over the mountain
> To see what he could see.

It was an entertaining fantasy to which she often returned whenever she played "How I'll Spend My Money."

Around Thanksgiving, Paddington, having fattened himself up on mast and forbs, decided that the best den for his hibernation would be Robin's bed. Actually black bears don't truly hibernate, at least not that far south, but they go into a kind of dormancy that amounts to the same thing, except that they can be easily awakened. Robin didn't try to wake him. She just snuggled up through those cold winter nights, and put herself to sleep each night imagining what she'd have to do to get ready for school in the morning.

Had she been at Harrison Junior High in the eighth grade, she would have had to submit two practice letters for the Language Arts class, one addressed to her Congressman, the other to her best friend; for Social Studies class she would have had to submit a report on the native Americans who inhabited the Ozarks; for Science class she would have had to be prepared for a test in the winter positions of the constellations; and she would have skipped Algebra class because her homework wasn't done and she needed to practice several a cappella lieder for the concert choir. Of course she would not have been able to do any of these things because she had missed so many years of school leading up to them.

Likewise, I could easily identify with whatever yearning for school had befallen poor Robin. In Rutherford, California, there was a public elementary school just a few blocks from the little house in which Adam lived, but he had not attended school since the fourth grade in Stay More and now he should have been in junior high but was several grades behind, and his father's stubborn resistance to the whole idea of education continued in the face of the fact that Adam's hike to school *there* would have been immeasurably easier than his hike to the Stay More school, and he could have ridden a bright yellow school bus to St. Helena. California law prohibited him from holding down a job at the age of twelve, so his father's idea of having Adam beside him at work as a journeyman cooper was a vain dream. The Madewells had, upon arrival in California, been detained and interviewed by a state agency responsible for resettlement of migrants, principally Okies and Arkies. (Eventually, having fallen in love with cinema and having made a hobby of watching it, Adam saw a movie called "The Grapes of Wrath," greatly identifying with Henry Fonda as Tom Joad, and he was inspired to read the novel on which the movie was based, and while he didn't think that Steinbeck had a very good ear for the speech of Ozarkers, he was inspired by the novel to read many other novels.) Because Gabe Madewell was not just a farmer but a highly skilled cooper, he was not sent to the fields to be a picker but found a job in the barrel works of a Rutherford winery called Inglenook. Back home in Stay More, the dominant family (for whom Robin had cut many a paper doll) was named Ingledew, and Gabe Madewell always believed that perhaps the Inglenooks were Ingledews from Stay More who had gone to California and couldn't spell their name, as he could scarcely spell his own and had to have somebody fill out his application forms for him. Actually the name, which was famous as a label of wine, was bestowed in the 19th Century by a Finnish fur trader named Gustave Neibaum, who had bought a "Nook Farm" on which to grow grapes and called the winery after an "inglenook," a nook or cranny beside a fireplace.

In the years the Madewells settled in Rutherford, wine-making in California had fallen on hard times, and the Inglenook vintage itself was inferior to the great wines that Gustav Neibaum had produced, equaling the best of Europe (and in fact winning awards at the Paris Exposition of 1889 at which the Eiffel Tower was dedicated) and continuing until the 1930s to win awards as the best American wine.

When Gabe Madewell went to work as a cooper for Inglenook, there were only two other men in the cooperage, and they used redwood staves to make the wine barrels. French wines have always been racked in oaken barrels. Gabe Madewell had been accustomed to making 50-gallon whiskey barrels of oak; he had just a little trouble learning to make the standard 59-gallon French Bordeaux barrel out of redwood. In time, he would persuade his superiors to switch to oak, which would eventually become the standard. In later years, Adam liked to think that his father was the "inventor" of the American oak wine barrel, which lends its distinctive flavors to even a jug of the cheapest grocery store wine. Whether or not Gabe Madewell actually deserved the credit, the aromas or flavors of wine, such as coconut, caramel, vanilla, fresh toast, dill, nuts and butter, or spices like clove and cinnamon are not inherent in the grape but come from the oak barrel. Adam was destined to become the foremost expert in these aromas.

If Adam couldn't work beside his father making barrels (at least not until he turned sixteen), what could he do with himself? Rutherford was just a village, not much larger than Jasper, Newton County's tiny seat, but it didn't even have Jasper's supermarkets or movie theater or newspaper. For major shopping, people in Rutherford had to go into the city of Napa, fifteen miles away, and Gabe Madewell would not be able to buy a car and learn to drive it until he'd been there for a few years. Meanwhile, Adam, hobbled by his bad leg, led his blind mother to one of the two grocery stores in Rutherford and helped her shop, a wonderful thing she'd never done back home.

The two things he remembered most about his first year in Rutherford: attempting to describe to his sightless mother the items on the shelves and in the cases of the grocery store (she had not dreamt you could buy meat in a store), and, one Saturday, limping four miles (the same distance he'd hiked to the Stay More school but over far more hospitable terrain) to the town of St. Helena, where there was a movie theater. Adam had never seen a movie before, and it would be several years before his father would buy a television.

The experience of that movie (although he cannot remember its title or cast or plot) made him almost glad he no longer dwelt on Madewell Mountain.

Chapter thirty-eight

She had grown at last into Sugrue's clothes. Not that they really fit, but with the pants cuffs rolled up and the shoulder straps taken in as far as they would go, a pair of Sugrue's denim overalls would hang from her body, at least during cold weather, which was the only time she ever wore clothes, together with one of Sugrue's thick sweaters, which made her wish she had something knitted of her own. The winter of her twelfth year was very cold, in fact the coldest of all the winters she had been there, and she really envied Paddington his ability to sleep through most of it, at the same time that she was grateful for the warmth of his body and the softness of his fur under the covers on the worst winter nights. The howling winds outside left long icicles hanging from the eaves of the house, and tree limbs snapped all over the forest, and she was moved to permit all her friends to move into the house temporarily, even Sheba, who, Robin had learned, actually did hibernate every winter. For that matter, so did Ralgrub; on the awfullest day of winter Robin put on Sugrue's thickest jacket, and his boots that were much too large for her, and trudged out through the snow to the barn to lift Sheba out of the pile of leaves in which she was coiled into winter sleep, and reinstalled her on a pile of leaves in the corner of the living room. Then she went back out in the snow for a considerable distance to the hollow tree where Ralgrub had settled into hibernation. The raccoon woke up when Robin tried to lift her out of the tree's interior.

"Sweetheart," Robin said, "it's absolutely freezing, and it's going well below zero tonight and you won't survive. Wouldn't you like to come in the house?"

Ralgrub moaned and squirmed and chittered but allowed Robin to carry her into the house, where she was given a new den among the debris in the storeroom, Adam's room, which was the coldest room in the house, but much warmer than outdoors, and of course Adam didn't care what the temperature was.

Better than growing into Sugrue's clothes was growing into Adam's age, and Robin didn't have to feel younger or inferior to him any more. He might know an awful lot that she didn't know about how to live in the country and how to take care of a homestead, not to mention how to make a churn and firkin (and she was determined during her twelfth year to finish that firkin), but now he wasn't any older than she, and he certainly wasn't that much smarter than she, and she bet she knew a lot of things he didn't know. Maybe his ignorance of sex was just the result of growing up among people who considered anything sexual as unmentionable or forbidden. He'd told her that *Hereabouts, it aint fitten to say 'bull.' You have to call 'em 'topcow' or 'brute' or 'cow-critter.'*

"By the way," she'd said, "when is that cow you mentioned going to come wandering into the pasture, so I can make some butter in your churn?"

Haw, he'd laughed. *Why don't ye jist ask Hreapha to get ye a cow for yore thirteenth birthday? That'd be sure to do the trick.*

"For my thirteenth birthday," she'd declared, "I want an elephant."

What's an elerphant? he'd asked.

"Huh?" she'd said, but sure enough he had no idea what an elephant was. For that matter she'd never seen a live one herself, but she'd seen pictures of them, and she certainly knew what they were and what they looked like. Poor Adam really had a lot to learn.

And the thought of that gave her a worry (she was to discover throughout her twelfth year that she spent entirely too much time worrying, about all kinds of things): if Adam stayed twelve forever and she kept getting older and older, wouldn't she become—what was that word? *condescending*—wouldn't she look down upon him? How long could they remain friends before she started thinking of him as just a kid? She certainly wasn't a kid any more. Not only could she wear Sugrue's clothes, but her hips and thighs were fully developed, almost like a grown woman's. Although she was spreading out down there, her face, neck and shoulders were slimming, losing the last vestiges of baby fat. Her breasts kept growing and the nipples were darkening, and she was only mildly disturbed by the hair that was sprouting in her armpits and around her poody. She remembered that her mother had had hair in those places, although she could hardly remember what her mother had looked like, or her teachers, and she really wanted to see other women so she could confirm or disprove her suspicion that she was turning into a very beautiful woman. Her fingernails were dirty and needed trimming badly (although she chewed off the ends of her thumb-nails, possibly a bad habit), and she sometimes was tempted to cut her long, long hair but had taken a vow never to do it.

What she really wanted was a brassiere. Although she thoroughly enjoyed the freedom to run around naked in warm weather (and even in the winter when the living room stove was hot), she liked the idea of having a bra, something that she and her girlfriends in the second grade could only distantly aspire to. She considered that she might look kind of funny, running around in a bra and nothing else (she had no similar cravings for a pair of panties), and since it was highly unlikely that a bra would come wandering into the pasture like a cow, she ought to put the thought out of her mind, which was too crowded with other thoughts anyhow, although most of her thoughts were just as useless or senseless as having a bra. For instance, she gave too much thought to the fantasy of going to college eventually, which was completely stupid in view of the fact that she'd never be able to finish high school. She wasn't exactly sure what "college" was, but Miss Moore had told the class what to expect when they finished twelve grades. Robin liked to have fantasies (which were harmless enough even though they wasted brain energy) about using a chunk of her money, if she ever got out of here, to go off to some nice college somewhere, maybe even—what was the name of that best one which Miss Moore used to talk about? yes, Harbard—going to Harbard and wearing smart college clothes and learning all kinds of fabulous stuff, especially about her chosen subject, wildflowers. She adored imagining college. It would be so different from elementary school. Everything she learned would be worth learning.

In her twelfth year she began to have an intense hunger for knowledge. She wanted to get ready for college, somehow. If she'd been home in Harrison she would have gone to the public library and read each and every book in it until she'd read them all. She had nothing to read except the Bible (which she'd already read all the way through twice and was now on the third reading) and the *Cyclopædia* (which she could cite or recite from memory, even the parts on rural architecture, live stock management, the dairy, and Ladies' Fancy Work). When February came and Paddington woke up and smacked his lips and grunted what sounded like a bunch of cusswords, she took him out to watch the daffodils blooming. He promptly ate a few. She led him off into the woods in search of nuts and acorns. There weren't many; other animals had already got most of them. She saw some pig tracks, and realized that sometime soon she was going to have to try to find, and kill, and butcher, and smoke, another hog; it had been so long since she'd had bacon she couldn't even remember what it tasted like.

Often that spring she took Paddington out and away from the house, telling the other animals to stay behind because she was teaching Paddington the things his mother would have taught him, how to recognize what was edible and what wasn't. Their hikes deep into the woods in search of food for Paddington also turned into nature walks for Robin; the beginning of her realization that books weren't the only source of knowledge. Paddington would never leave her side, except to chase and swat at a butterfly, or to wander off while she was down on her knees looking at some liverwort or tiny wildflower. Often he would look at her quizzically and snort a noise that sounded like he was asking her a question, "Ma, what's that there little critter with those stripes down his back?" Robin realized that whether he thought of her as his mother or not he was expecting her to teach him the ways of the world or the ways of the wild, and she couldn't explain to him that she herself was just as woods-ignorant as he was when it came to naming things. If he or she wanted the name of something they'd have to ask Adam, but she knew that there was an area called the "haunt" that limited the space Adam could traverse (she almost thought to call it "reach") and she had already taken Paddington beyond the haunt.

The main difficulty she had with Paddington was that often she found a wildflower or plant of some kind that she wanted to study, but he wanted only to eat it. Once, in a crevice on the side of a gorge, she found a really marvelous little flower that looked like an elf's penis standing under a hood to protect it from the rain. Beetles were crawling into it, and gnats were being caught by it and swallowed inside the chamber in which the elf's penis was standing. The idea of a plant that could eat bugs really captivated her attention, but then Paddington came along and ate the flower before she could stop him. "Hey, that had bugs in it!" she protested. Whether it was the bugs or something else—maybe the plant was trying to teach him a lesson not to eat any more of them—he immediately got a stinging pain in his mouth and all the water he could drink wouldn't make the sting go away. He was miserable for a long time. "Did you learn anything?" she asked him.

Whenever they went on a nature walk after that, she searched and searched for another one of the flowers, which she had come to think of as "elfsdick," but it was a long time before she found another one, and she watched to see if Paddington would recognize it without any word from her, and sure enough when he saw it he made a big show of leaving it alone. She carefully dug it up (it had a big root like turnip) and took it home to show it to Adam and ask him if he knew if elfsdick would be a good name for it. He laughed and said, *Sure, but we allus called 'em jack-in-the-pulpit.*

She became fascinated with all the wildflowers and even had visions of sitting in a classroom at Harbard listening to a very smart man giving lectures about wildflowers. In her restless search for more and more varieties that she had not found before, she took Paddington deeper and deeper into the woods, in every direction from the house, but she always made sure to remember things that they passed, a big rock here, and a lone pine tree there, so that she could find her way home. But on one of their nature walks, Paddington flushed some kind of large rodent, maybe a woodchuck, and began chasing it, over hill and over dale, with Robin following as fast as she could. By the time Paddington had chased it into its den or burrow, she had neglected to observe any landmarks along the way, and when she tried to get her bearings after persuading Paddington that he'd have to give up the critter for lost, she herself was lost. She realized she didn't know where they were, or which way to turn. She had a very poor sense of direction.

"Paddington, do you have any idea how to go back the way we came?" she asked. "Do you know which way we should even turn?" But his reply, a kind of growling which sounded sort of like the way Sugrue used to snore, was not much help. "Well god damn it," she said, and began walking just to see if he might make any attempt to correct her direction. He did not, but just followed along. She tried to run away from him, but he snorted sounds that were clearly the bear equivalent of "holy shit" and "smoley hokes," and caught up with her and knocked her down. One of his claws raked her back and drew blood. "Now look what you've done!" she said, showing him the blood. She wiped at it and slapped him with the wiping hand. "Bad bear!" she said. He whimpered and hung his head.

She walked on, not even able to see very well the direction she was going, because of her poor eyesight. She began to feel panicky, having no idea which way to go. The afternoon came and passed and it began to get dark. Although the day had been very warm, as darkness fell it grew cold, and her bare body was chilled. She kept on going, although the woods seemed to get deeper and darker. She never found any sign of an old trail or path, although she wondered if maybe she walked long enough and far enough she might come eventually to some path that might lead to a road, or even to somebody's house, and she might finally find a way to get home, home meaning her old home in Harrison. But the thought of that gave her a bad scare. She couldn't take Paddington with her. She couldn't take any of her animals. She had a flash image of a possible scene where she tried to introduce Sheba to her mother, and her mother screamed.

No, she didn't want to find her way home, not to *that* home. She wanted to find her way home to *her* home.

Paddington caught a chipmunk and ate it for his supper. She had nothing for hers, and she was getting very cold as well as hungry. But she kept on walking, hoping that she might find something familiar, or any of the landmarks she passed earlier. She did not. And then it was full dark. She was afraid of stepping over a bluff, and her fear of falling made her stop. She was so tired. She lay down and pulled Paddington to her and they snuggled up. His fur kept her from freezing. "I guess we'll just have to try to sleep," she said to him. But he didn't seem to be in the mood for sleep. He snarled a few of his cusswords and was restless, and when she tried to hold him close to get warm he pulled away from her and stood up and began to growl. He sounded like a grown-up bear might sound. And she realized there was another animal nearby that Paddington was growling at. The other animal made a hissing and then a distinct "woo" sound that she recognized.

"Robert!" she said. "Is that you, Robert?"

It was a bobcat, but it wasn't Robert. It was a bobcat who wanted to eat Paddington, and was getting ready to pounce. Robin grabbed a stick and clubbed the bobcat over the head. The first blow stunned it, and while she couldn't see very well in the dark, she kept swinging the stick down where the bobcat had fallen, and kept on hitting with the stick and hitting with the stick and finally she must have killed the bobcat. The thought of having killed it made her sad, because it was one of Robert's cousins, but it was either Paddington or the bobcat and she was not going to let anything harm her cub. He was making a kind of woofing sound that expressed his thanks to her for doing away with his enemy. They settled into sleep.

She was starving the next morning, and when Paddington caught a rabbit for his breakfast she was tempted to take a few bites of it herself, but did not, and of course had no matches or anything to start a fire to cook the rabbit. But for his breakfast dessert Paddington found in a glade a patch of wild strawberries, and she picked as many as he did, or more. They were delicious.

With something in her stomach, she had the energy to resume the aimless search for a way home or a way off the mountain, whichever came first, she really didn't care, although she hoped it would be home. She hiked determinedly onward. Eventually she came to a small creek, and Paddington slaked his great thirst, and she decided it would be okay to drink the water too. Then she made another decision: using her head, she figured out that the force of gravity made creeks continue *downward* from the source, and therefore if she just followed this creek she might come eventually to a larger creek and then to a river, and if she followed the river she was sure to come to a town or a place where people lived.

So she followed the creek, even as it tumbled down boulders and meandered through the forest. Her eyesight was not good enough to detect the place the creek suddenly disappeared, and she was on the verge of disappearing with it when Paddington swatted her, knocking her down again, and again drawing blood. "You bastard bear!" she hollered at him, but the she saw why he had knocked her down. She had almost stepped over the edge of a high bluff, where the creek turned into a waterfall that fell a long way down. She had mistaken the gurgling sound of the waterfall for Paddington's constant babbling comments on the world. She peered over the edge but her weak eyes could scarcely see to the pool far down below where the waterfall splashed. All around the pool in every direction was a great glen or holler, with caverns opening into the bluff-faces. It was a magnificent woodsy place, and she looked for some way to get down to it. She crept cautiously all along the top of the bluff, first in one direction from the creek and then in the other direction, but she could not find any way to get down...except, finally, she discovered a kind of vertical gorge that looked as if human beings had cleared away the brush in order to make a descent. Was this possibly the place where Adam had fallen and broken his bones? Was this the same place where, every day from the first to the fourth grades, he had to climb down to get to school and then climb back up to get home from school?

It was an awesome drop...and an even more awesome climb if there were any way to get down. Studying it, and realizing there was no way she could possibly get down there, at least not without a rope, she had a renewed respect and admiration for Adam, and she began to be more determined than ever to find her way home, so that she could tell his *in-habit* what a wonderful boy Adam had been.

It occurred to her to back away from that drop and search for any signs of the trail that had once led from here all the way to the house, the so-called South Way that Braxton Madewell had once blazed for the benefit of the doctor who would come for the birth of Adam's father, Gabe. Sure enough, there were places where Adam's daily hiking of the trail had left a faint but discernible indentation in the earth: a path, a way.

With Paddington eagerly following her, as if he too sensed that they were finally heading home, she happily climbed that South Way on and on, up through the hickory forest, up a long and slippery slope of some kind of gray slatey rock, up through a crag of boulders to a towering lone pine tree. At that pine tree she lost the path and a long search would not reveal any further trace of it. She walked this way and that. She saw wildflowers of every color and every shape but could not stop to study them, and Paddington saw butterflies of every color and every shape but could not stop to swat at them. She found no more evidence of the trail.

And that day too waned and the dark came and they were lucky to find a kind of cavern to shelter them from the cold.

Chapter thirty-nine

She didn't even notice the first night Robin failed to return home. She knew that Robin and the bear were in the habit of going into the deep woods almost every day, and for a while it had given her some unshakeable feelings of jealousy that Robin was paying so much attention to the bear and neglecting her other animals. When was the last time Hreapha had received a pat on the head or even a kind word? But after a while it no longer bothered her. She knew that it was a phase Robin was going through, not just of getting through her crucial twelfth year but also of pretending to be Paddington's mother and teacher, just as Hreapha herself had been mother and teacher for her brood. It had been a long time since any of Hreapha's offspring had truly needed her or even asked her a question, and the last time she had even been made to feel useful was when they'd gone out to locate the bear cub and Hreapha had given some important advice, especially about getting Dewey to absorb the dead bear sow's scent so that the cub would ride home on his back. At the same time that Hreapha could feel worthwhile for having made the coming of the bear cub possible, and thereby having discharged her birthday duties to Robin for this year, she could understand that the more animals were on the premises the less time Robin would have for Hreapha. It didn't matter. Hreapha was happy as long as she could find something to eat. The fact that Robin had not been able to feed her anything for a long time, except occasional scraps from the table—a leftover biscuit or the dregs in some canned goods (and Robin was down to her last few cans)—was also part of the reason Hreapha was slow to notice that Robin was no longer around the house, nor was Paddington.

Still, she didn't do anything about it, not until after Robin had been gone overnight for two nights. And then she simply remarked to Hrolf, Have you seen Mistress?

Come to think of it, not lately, he answered. I'll ask around.

She was proud of Hrolf that he had become practically overseer of the demesne. He was not only Top Dog but also Top Critter save for Robin herself. And Hreapha wasn't envious to admit that Hrolf was probably the smartest of them all, smarter even than herself. Robert was craftier, Ralgrub had more manual dexterity, Dewey was faster, Sheba was more cunning, and Hroberta was sexier, but Hrolf possessed not only brains but leadership qualities.

Thus when he reported back to his mother that nobody, not even Adam, had seen Robin or the cub for two nights, she asked him, What would you suggest?

Let's see if we can't pick up their scent, he suggested. Hreapha gladly accompanied her son as he went off sweeping his handsome nose over the ground (she reflected that the older he got the more he looked like his father) for quite a distance around the haunt until finally he stopped and said, There, take a whiff of that.

It was the faintest trace of the bear's odor, and they followed it for a long ways off into the woods, far from the house, catching along the way a few traces of Robin's scent too. But their quest eventually played out, and they changed their direction and went for a long distance without picking up any further smells of Paddington or Robin. They continued into the afternoon exploring the southern and eastern flanks of Madewell Mountain. Hreapha was pleased to note that they encountered no traces of the coyotes, who had probably deserted the environs entirely during the great drought. She wouldn't have minded seeing her son Yipyip again, but she was glad to know that they didn't have to share the mountain with the wild dogs.

Circling back northward toward the house, Hreapha found that they were in a ravine that seemed very familiar to her, and trying to place it without any olfactory clue she finally realized from some obscure crevices of her memory that this was the place where she had rounded up those chickens that had got loose when the man was trying to transport them from the truck to the house. Yes, if she went *that* way she'd find the route she'd driven the chickens to make them arrive at their new home. But she did not go that way. Something gave her a hunch to go the other way, which involved some difficult climbing along the side of the bluff, with Hrolf having just as much trouble as she did, until they reached another ravine or gorge which contained the burnt steel remains of the man's truck. Hreapha's heart leapt up: if she could somehow climb the bluff from this point, she'd locate perhaps the end of the road that led northward down the mountain.

As they tried to climb, Hrolf exclaimed, Shoot far, Ma, we'll never make it up there.

Son, she answered, if we *do* make it up there, we'll be on a road that could take us eventually to meet your father at last.

Why didn't you say so? he said, and with a burst of energy clawed his way to the top of the bluff, with her right at his heels.

And sure enough, there was the trail that the man had driven his truck over so many times to bring all the food and drink and stuff up to the mountaintop, the trail that Hreapha had taken when she had run away from him and had found her way back to Stay More. As she loped happily down the trail, she realized she ought to have told the *in-habit* not to expect them back before nightfall.

Much of the trail had been obliterated over the years by hard rains, but she and Hrolf managed to follow the traces of it and in time reach the foot of the mountain where the trail met up with a road. They had headed only a short distance along that road when they heard many sounds of the names of their kindred being announced, and Hreapha clearly recognized one of them: "Arphrowf!"

She had scarcely returned her own name, "Hreapha!" when

she caught sight of her former brief friend, the good old country lady that she had chatted with on her first and only trip past this place. Now Arphrowf was practically surrounded by other dogs, all of whom resembled her.

Don't I know you from somewheres long ago? Arphrowf asked.

Yes, I stopped by here and we chatted one day about five or six years ago, Hreapha said.

All of them took turns sniffing one another's afterplaces. Hrolf was delighted to discover that two of the dogs were comely young bitches. While he was shamelessly flirting around with them, Hreapha brought Arphrowf up to date on what had been happening since last they'd chatted.

Well fan my brow! Arphrowf said. You don't mean to tell me that such things has been a-going on right up yonder on the mountain top! Why, I'd of come to visit!

You'll recall you told me you'd never been up there because it was too far and snaky for you? Well, let me tell you about Sheba…

And Hreapha told her all about the friendly harmless queen snake, and the friendly bobcat who was in love with one of Hreapha's daughters, and the friendly raccoon and the fawn grown into a friendly deer.

Can you beat that? Arphrowf exclaimed. In all my born days I never heared tell of such marvels.

And then Hreapha told her about the bear cub and the fact that the girl-now-woman, name of Robin, had been missing for two days with the cub and Hreapha was searching for them with the help of her handsome son there, Hrolf.

Them there's my lovely young'uns, Arphrowf said, indicating the several other dogs. 'Pears like your boy is taking a shine to 'em.

Indeed it was difficult persuading Hrolf to leave when it was time to go. Arphrowf said, I declare, don't you'uns be a-rushin off. Stay more and spend the night with us.

In fact, it was getting on to dark, and Hreapha decided it might be better to tarry here among friends until daybreak before resuming their journey to Stay More. Her sense of fidelity to Robin was only mildly disturbed by the thought that Robin and Paddington would have to wait another couple of days before Hreapha resumed looking for them. It was more important, now that a way had been found, to get to Stay More and see Yowrfrowr again.

So they spent the night. Sometime after dark settled in, the door of the house opened and a man stepped out, or staggered out, clumsily carrying a large bag, which he upended, spilling dog chow nuggets all over the place. He yelled, "Supper's ready!" and went back into the house.

Blame if he aint drunk again, Arphrowf observed, as they congregated with the other dogs to chomp up the nuggets. Oftentimes it's all I can do to keep from biting him. She explained to Hreapha that the mistress of the house had died a couple of years previously (Pore thang prolly worked herself to death) and the man had taken to drink and was allowing his small farm to go to the dogs.

Yessiree, me and my young'uns has to run the place for him. The cattle is allus getting loose and it's all we can do to herd 'em back home. We'd even milk 'em if we could.

You wouldn't happen to have a spare cow or two, would you? Hreapha asked.

Laws a mercy, we got spare everything, Arphrowf complained. We got more cows than we'll ever know what to do with.

The next morning, Hrolf seemed to be more than willing to leave, although one of the bitches, a cutey named Alfalfa, didn't want him to leave and whined piteously as they departed.

As they loped down the long road that led toward Stay More, Hrolf remarked, Ma, I sure am all tuckered out.

'Tuckered?' she said. Did you pronounce that correctly? And she laughed.

When they finally approached Stay More, Hreapha was apprehensive that perhaps Yowrfrowr might have died of old age or his mistress might have moved away. But even before they reached the dogtrot cabin at which he lived with the old woman (and countless cats), Hreapha had picked up not only his scent, but another scent that was disturbingly familiar to her, and which took her just a little while to identify.

Hrolf picked up the other scent too, and said, Ma? Is that who I think it is?

I think it is too, she said, and soon her suspicion was confirmed, as she beheld not only her long lost daughter Hruschka, but her brood of grandchildren too. The yard of the dogtrot cabin was positively overrun with dogs and cats living in a kind of peaceful coexistence that made the menagerie of Madewell Mountain seem mild by comparison.

Hruschka was as shy as ever. Ma, is that *you*? she asked timidly.

Yowrfrowr was embarrassed, which Hreapha had never known him to be. He pretended ignorance. Hreapha, old girl, he said. What a surprise! Are you and my wife perchance related?

Yes, and you and your wife are also related. She's your daughter.

No! he said, pawing at the air. Then he turned to his wife. Hruschka, were you aware of that fact?

Sometimes I've had a hunch, she said.

Hreapha nudged Hrolf to come and sniff his father. And this is your handsome son, she said to Yowrfrowr.

The two males circled and sniffed each other, and Yowrfrowr declared, What an unmitigated pleasure! My boy! And such a rugged specimen! Well, come and meet your new brothers and sisters.

Or are they my nephews and nieces? Hrolf wanted to know.

It was all very complicated, Hreapha realized, but she was surprised to discover she felt no jealousy toward Hruschka, in fact she felt very happy for the girl, and was eager to sniff and examine each of her grandchildren.

The family reunion continued happily until the old woman, Yowrfrowr's mistress, came out of the house and said, "Xenophon, I declare if you don't attract strays the way shit attracts flies! You tell your new friends to get out of my yard. There's too damn many of you already!"

I'll walk a ways with you, Yowrfrowr declared, as he led Hreapha and Hrolf away from the cabin.

Goodbye, darling, Hreapha called to Hruschka, I hope to see you again sometime.

She's been spayed, Yowrfrowr related to Hreapha. For that

matter, I've been emasculated myself. Drat, we've all been unsexed. Mistress' grandson took us all in his truck to a Harrison veterinarian, where the operations were performed. Isn't that hideous? The lucky felines escaped such a fate and will go on propagating all over creation. But I suppose they're not as conspicuous, nor as ravenous, as all of us dogs.

If there are so many of you, Hreapha said, your mistress won't even notice if I borrow you for a few days.

Borrow me? But don't you understand, I'm no good for coitus any more…although I must admit, ever since the operation I've felt much calmer and more contented.

I'm beyond coitus myself, she said, and then she explained what she really wanted Yowrfrowr for: to help her find Robin and the bear. It took her a while to explain the whole situation, and to bring him up to date on what had been happening on the mountaintop since last she had seen him. He was considerably impressed at her recital of the expansion and variety of the menagerie, and confessed that he had always been eager to see the Madewell place, especially since his wife spoke so fondly of her memories of it. Truth be told, since their brood had been born and grown now into their second year, he had urged Hruschka to take him on a sentimental journey back to her birthplace, but Hruschka had had such a terrible experience finding her way down off the mountain, including a plunge over a waterfall, that she was reluctant to attempt the journey.

Hrolf and I have found a new way to get up there, from the north, Hreapha declared. Come go home with us.

Hhmm, hummed Yowrfrowr. It's a magnificent temptation. But it would just be a visit, you understand. I can't join your menagerie.

You couldn't anyway, not unless Robin asked for another dog for her next birthday, Hreapha said. And she wants an elephant.

Elephant? said Yowrfrowr. Did I hear you correctly? My ears are going bad in my old age.

Yes, that's what she says…although I warn you, she has a weird sense of humor.

An elephant, eh? Of course they don't grow in these parts. But I've heard of them. Mistress' son-in-law, Hank Ingledew, has told the story of his experience as a boy, many years ago, visiting something called a 'circus' that came to Jasper, and encountering there an enormous elephant. As the story goes, the elephant used its long snout to fling Hank through the air, and Hank said to the elephant, "If Godalmighty made you, He orter make one more and quit."

Most of the way back up to Madewell Mountain, Yowrfrowr romped on ahead of her with Hrolf, the two of them talking and laughing up a storm, and while she was happy to see father and son becoming so chummy she hoped they weren't having any laughs at her expense.

When they finally attained the upper reaches of the mountain, near the spot where the man's burnt car had crashed, Yowrfrowr remarked, It has been a long time since I caught the scent of bear, so correct me if I'm wrong, but isn't *this* a bona fide bear scent?

She sniffed at the place he indicated but could scarcely detect any scent at all. Of course, Yowrfrowr's nose was much longer than hers, which was one among many reasons she wanted his help in searching for Robin. Hrolf also sniffed at it but shook his head.

Not only is it distinct, Yowrfrowr declared, but it's heading *that* way. And he indicated a westward route up through the forest, in the same area where Hreapha had been diverted by the sight of a deer with two fawns when she was supposed to be guarding the man's truck, and had been punished for wandering away from it. The distant memory gave her a peculiar sense of freedom to be now following Yowrfrowr up through the same woods where she had followed the deer and fawns.

Yowrfrowr's unerring nose led them a long way, until Hreapha herself could detect the scent, and was sure that it was Paddington's, not, as she'd feared, some other bear's. They went on, and emerged from the forest at almost the crest of the mountain, where the old orchard of the homestead met the woodland, and there, under an apple tree, both of them sound asleep, were Robin and Paddington!

"Hreapha!" she shouted exultantly, and woke them. The bear leapt up, snarling, and rose in front of Yowrfrowr to his full length, with his claws bared and raised, and his voice cursing to high heaven

in a grinding roar that sounded much worse than any of the man's
snores had ever been.

"Hreapha!" said Robin and embraced her. "And Hrolf!" She
embraced him too. "But who is *this?*" she pointed to Yowrfrowr, who
was trying to defend himself against the menacing bear.

"YOWRFROWR!" Yowrfrowr barked at the bear, who in return
said some obscene curses in his own language.

"Y'all hush!" Robin said to them. "They'll hear us down there.
Look, there's a house down there and it looks like people live in it. But
I'm afraid to go meet them. Looking like this, without any clothes.
And what if they try to take me away, back to Harrison?"

Hreapha was slow in understanding what must have happened:
Robin and Paddington, lost and like anyone lost, moving in circles,
had made a huge circle that had brought them finally to the rear
of the Madewell place, the northwestern side at the orchard, from
where the house could be only distantly seen, and Robin with her
poor eyesight, not even recognizing her own orchard from that angle,
had not yet recognized that the house was her own.

Hrolf told Paddington to shut his yap. The bear cub, who was
hardly a cub any more, understood that Hrolf was the boss.

"Hreapha Hreapha," Hreapha said quietly to Robin, meaning,
You silly thing, that's your own house down there. Why don't you
go see?

But of course Robin couldn't understand her, and looked
fearfully toward the house. Fortunately, they were within the haunt,
and thus it was not long before Adam *In-habit* made his presence
known, saying, *Boy howdy and jumping grasshoppers, I had done give
you'unses up for lost.*

Yowrfrowr was spooked at the voice and the presence of the
in-habit, although he had encountered a number of *in-habit*s in Stay
More, left behind by the many citizens who had abandoned the town.
Hreapha introduced them to each other, explaining to Adam that
this was the selfsame Yowrfrowr she had told him so much about,
the father of her children.

Right pleased to meet ye, Yowrfrowr. I've heared so much about ye.

Hreapha said to the *in-habit*, Could you please explain to Robin that that's her own house down there? She's confused.

I think she's a-figuring it out on her own, the *in-habit* said. *On account of I'm here, and so it must be in my haunt.*

So they all walked joyfully down out of the orchard and to the house, where the others were waiting for them. And there they all lived happily ever after.

And these are the birthday presents that Hreapha arranged for Robin to receive in the years to come:

For her thirteenth: not an elephant, of course, but something pretty big and far more useful—a cow.

For her fourteenth: a pet rock, a chunk of crystal quartz which she named Sparkle.

For her fifteenth: a pair of mourning doves.

For her sixteenth: an opossum.

For her seventeenth: an armadillo.

For her eighteenth: …but let us, Hreapha will urge, be patient. As she will be.

Chapter forty

Dear Hreapha's characteristically optimistic notion of that standard catch phrase, "happily ever after," was not meant to imply any finality or even perpetuity in the ongoing saga of Robin's adventures. The whole concept of "ever after" for a dog is limited mostly from one meal to the next, and the concept of "happily" can apply to anything which induces the wagging of one's tail. Hreapha's tail wasn't very long but she wagged it often, and in those years to come she would have countless occasions to keep on wagging it, although of course there would be, in the great balance of things, a number of sadnesses, hardships, deprivations, disappointments and general malaises.

Earlier I proffered the caveat that we should not be lulled by the excitement of Robin's life into feeling that her experience was totally idyllic. Her larder was empty and she had run out of such basic amenities as salt and kerosene and was essentially living directly from nature and from whatever her garden could provide. On the positive side, she was spared some of the grief that most girls suffer during adolescence, particularly in social relationships. For example, never would she feel slighted and lonely because her boyfriend ignored her whenever he was with his pals. Never would she be hurt because her boyfriend took out on her his anger or rage from fighting with his parents or peers. Never would her desire to belong and be popular compel her to have her body tattooed and to pierce various parts of it, including her tongue, for adornment. Her social calendar, her dance card, as it were, was filled with lovely interactions with her zoological garden, which, as Hreapha's birthday list has already indicated, constantly grew from year to year.

Alas, Robin mostly lost interest in me, perhaps feeling she had outgrown me, which in fact she had, not just physically but intellectually. If she thought of me at all, it was as a kid brother. The only time she ever called upon me or solicited my help was once in her fourteenth year when she finally decided to finish that firkin she'd abandoned years before and she needed from me a brief refresher course on the use of the cooper's tools. I was more than happy to oblige. She not only completed the firkin successfully, but, since the fractured churn of mine she'd been using to make butter was malfunctioning, she decided to start from scratch and see if she couldn't make a churn entire, and I was pleased to guide her. Indeed, by the time of her seventeenth birthday she had made an active hobby of cooperage and was even riving her staves from the oak forest with axe and saw, and actually completed a not substandard barrel before she was eighteen.

During those years of her adolescence, she missed out on all the things that were happening to her generation's delight in movies, music, literature and culture in general. In music alone, she never had the experience of hearing all the fabulous new songs and rhythms, just as she was also denied exposure to the great classical composers. But it may be observed that what she missed, she invented. Art, after all, is the expression of that which the ordinary mortal cannot express. Her solitude forced Robin into extraordinariness, and she filled the air with her own music, her own attempt to translate into pure sounds those universal emotions—exultation and despondency, the yearning and seeking and the glory in finding—out of which all music, classical and popular, springs.

Her health was quite good, in fact remarkable, but of course there were no communicable diseases for her to catch, not even the common cold. In her fourteenth year she had the usual problems with complexion: pimples, blackheads, pustules, and blotches, with no one to explain them to her (since I at twelve had not yet experienced these dreads the way that Adam in California would endure acne but grow out of it) and there were times she worried her complexion would be permanently disfigured. She continued to be (as she always would be) a chronic worrier, and sometimes her tension gave her stomach-aches or headaches, although she had long since discovered the very best outlet for tension was simply a quick (or leisurely, depending on her mood) *reach,* having eventually convinced herself that it was not the reaching which brought about the monthly bleeding.

She had remarkably few dental problems. In her sixteenth year she had a yeast infection, but in time it cleared up. It may safely and incredibly be said that she never had anything wrong with her that demanded a visit to the doctor or dentist.

A visit to an ophthalmologist might have been desirable, but the only real inconvenience her myopia caused her was in her shooting: it became impossible for her to bag game with the rifle, and her use of the shotgun was limited to things within easy view. In her thirteenth September a wild razorback hog, which she could not have caught in the rifle's sights, happened to discover her sweet potato patch and was so busily preoccupied with rooting up and munching the yams that it didn't notice Robin sneaking within range. She fired pointblank and enjoyed ham and bacon again for a whole year or more, although she had run out of salt with which to cure it and had to condescend to accepting my instructions on how to extract salt from hickory ashes, cow parsnips, and pigweed. By her fourteenth year she had run out of everything that Sog had originally stocked, except for a few jars of pickled pig's feet, and of course the huge supply of Jack Daniels, which, by the way, she had begun imbibing on occasions. One summer she had an unusually severe problem with chiggers, those maddeningly itchy mites, and I happened to mention to her that whenever the chiggers had caused great distress in my family, we treated the bites with small applications of Chism's Dew, as the local moonshine was called, a jug of which my mother kept strictly for such medicinal purposes (ironically, although their lives were devoted to making whiskey barrels, neither Braxton nor Gabe Madewell ever touched the stuff). Robin wondered if Jack Daniels might effectuate the same result as Chism's Dew, and tried it, pouring some on the bites on her long lovely legs, and sure enough it did the trick, killing the chiggers, and as long as she had the bottle open she poured a small amount into a glass, diluted it with water, sipped it, and made a variety of grimaces which diminished on the second sip and disappeared on the third. She finished the glass and poured another, and, as the saying goes, acquired a taste for it. She learned it could greatly enhance her music.

Out in California Adam acquired a taste for the wine that went into the barrels which gave the wine the many flavors of the oak. Although California law prohibited Adam from going to work in the cooperage until he was sixteen, his father circumvented that restriction by taking Adam into the cooperage after hours, when Gabe Madewell, eager for the time-and-a-half they paid him for working overtime, often toiled at the cooper's trade, sometimes late into the night. There, as Adam grew older and stronger, he learned the advanced labors and tricks of coopering, until, by the time he was sixteen and allowed by law to become officially employed, he was no longer an apprentice cooper but a journeyman. Still, despite being able to do anything his father could do as well as him, he was only his father's assistant, constantly under orders and instructions and criticism from his father, who, when their arguments grew bitter, reminded him that he might have been left a corpse on Madewell Mountain, a notion that Adam sometimes dwelt upon, thinking he could still have inhabited the place as a ghost and not knowing that he was definitely inhabiting it as an *in-habit.*

The Inglenook Winery was in a great stone chateau, with the cooperage in one basement of it, and some nights when his father had no immediate task for him to do, Adam would wander into other parts of the chateau, where he discovered the sampling room and could help himself to different tastes of wine, always careful, of course, not to consume so much of it that his father would notice. Thus at an early age he learned how to avoid drunkenness.

The topography of Napa County bears some resemblance to that of Newton County, enough to have kept Adam from being hopelessly homesick. To the west of Rutherford rise the Mayacama Mountains, the highest point, Mt. Veeder, being the same height, 2,500 feet, as the loftier mountains of Newton County, and another peak, Mount St. John, still wild enough to remind Adam of his explorations of Madewell Mountain back home. To the east could be seen a muscular mountain called Stag's Leap, the very name of it suggesting an affinity to Stay More's Leapin Rock, from which at least four people had been known to commit suicide (and Robin in her now-outgrown paper doll period had emulated that tradition by having four paper dolls fall from the top of the davenport to their deaths, each followed by her ad libitum descant of "Farther Along.")

Every available slope and terrace of the valley was covered with vineyards, all lovingly cultivated, the neatness of which presented a striking contrast to the wildness of Newton County. Whenever he could, Adam would get out into the countryside and wander limpingly among those vineyards, or hike up into the semi-wilderness of Mount St. John, where he found an abandoned house to explore, and a quicksilver mine. East of Rutherford the Napa River flowed, with a swimming hole that Adam visited on hot summer afternoons, although the other kids there teased him and mocked his Ozark pronunciation and vocabulary, and came to call him Arkie. There was also a large reservoir called Lake Hennessey, unlike anything Adam had seen before, since Newton County does not have a single lake. Nor does Newton County have a single mile of railway, and there was a track of the Southern Pacific Railroad running through Rutherford, which carried the huge cargo of wine off to market. Adam liked to visit the Rutherford Depot, a plain building in a long shed, and watch the loading of the big tank cars with wine or the loading of cartons of bottled wine into boxcars. Studying the train's schedule and behavior, Adam learned how to climb aboard unnoticed and ride the train five miles down to Yountville, which wasn't as big as St. Helena but possessed more shops than Rutherford and had a building that became Adam's refuge during those years when he awaited the legal working age of sixteen: a public library. The kindly librarian, a young woman from San Francisco who told him it was all right for him to call her Frances, said to him at closing time one day, "You know, if you like, I could issue you a library card and you could take some books home with you."

"I reckon not, ma'am," he said. "Paw don't allow no books in the house."

"That's too bad," she said. Then she asked, "Why aren't you in school?"

"Iffen I was let to go back to school, ma'am, I'd just be in the fourth grade, and I'm too big for that."

"Oh. How old are you?"

He told her he was fifteen and she kept on asking him questions. He told her his whole story so far, how he'd hurt himself trying to get to school in the wild mountains of the Ozarks, how he'd lost the index finger of his right hand working in his father's cooperage, and so forth. He even told her how he'd been coming to Yountville to visit the library by climbing up on the freight train. She told him she admired his desire to give himself an education, and she wondered if he needed any help picking out books. He told her he'd just been picking them out at random, but he hoped eventually to read every book she had.

"Who are your favorite authors, so far?" she asked.

"Arthurs, ma'am? You mean the folks who wrote the books? Tell ye the truth, I never paid much attention to that, just the titles."

And from then on she told him some authors she thought he would like. Joseph Conrad. Mark Twain. Thomas Hardy. Did he know, by the way, that Ambrose Bierce, who wrote some fine satirical fables and some short stories shot through with savage irony, had lived just up the road at St. Helena? Yes, she said, and after Adam finished reading some of Bierce's tales, she would be happy to drive him up to St. Helena some Sunday and show him the house in which Bierce had lived. Also he ought to know that the splendid Scottish author Robert Louis Stevenson, before he became famous, lived with his California bride in a squatter's shack up the road on Mount St. Helena.

Among the hundreds of books that Adam read at the Yountville Public Library were Stevenson's *Silverado Squatters*, based on that experience, as well as his *Treasure Island*. He also enjoyed Daniel Defoe's *Robinson Crusoe* and W.H. Hudson's *Green Mansions*.

A railroad guard caught Adam climbing down from the freight train on one of his trips to Yountville, and that put an end to that mode of transportation. Desperate, he tried walking the five miles from Rutherford to Yountville, but with his bad leg the hike hurt him and tired him, and he told Frances he was going to have to quit, and why.

"It won't be long anyhow, ma'am," he said, "afore I'll turn sixteen and be let to go to work, and my paw has plans to start me in to a-coopering at the place where he works."

"Until then," she said, "you know I have a car and I can come and get you any time you want me to."

She not only did that, and took him to see Ambrose Bierce's house, and to the site of Stevenson's squatter's shack as well as for Sunday drives all over the countryside, but she taught him how to drive, and eventually she taught him how to make love, that is, in his sixteenth year she taught him what he needed to do for her in order to get her ready and willing, and she taught him what he ought to try to do so that either he could hold off coming until she was good and ready or else how to be patient enough to make her come too. He'd had no idea that females actually came. It surprised him and filled him with wonder. He asked her if there were any books which explained it; she let him read a novel by D.H. Lawrence which belonged not to the library but to Frances herself. He'd had no idea that authors could actually write about things like that, and he acquired a taste for it, the way he'd acquired a taste for the Cabernet Sauvignon that all the local wineries made. She let him read some of the other books that were in her own private library, books by Henry Miller, and a recent novel by J.P. Donleavy, and his favorite, by some Russian named Nabokov about a girl and a man. He had nearly as much fun reading all those books as he did in the act itself, which they continued doing whenever they found the opportunity, especially on Sundays at her little house in Yountville, where sometimes they spent the whole afternoon doing it. Frances was a thin woman not nearly as tall as Adam, and her favorite place to be was on top of him, where he bore her weight easily and marveled at her velocity and shaking. When Adam was seventeen, his father found out about Frances. His mother had already known, or at least she had met Frances, and being blind could not see her and determine that she was older than Adam and believed him when he said that Frances was his girlfriend and he hoped to marry her eventually. His father was not blind, not physically; his soul was blind, but his eyesight was good enough to detect that Frances was an older woman, and when Adam finally introduced Frances to his father, the first thing Gabe Madewell said was to ask her how old she was, and she told the truth, which surprised Adam: she was thirty-one.

Later his father said to him, "How come you caint get yourself a gal your own age?"

"Tell me where I'd find one," Adam replied.

Not that there weren't any girls in Rutherford, or St. Helena, or Yountville, who were his own age. But they were all in high school, where Adam would never go. Usually he saw girls his own age at the movies in St. Helena, where Frances often took him, which he enjoyed more than anything next to sex and books. Frances had not only told Adam all the best books for him to read, for the improvement of his mind as well as for fun and pleasure and excitement, but she had tried to tutor him in a few things he might have taken in high school if he had gone: geometry, Spanish, U.S. and World history, and biology. He was always resistant to learning anything that he could not put to practical use, but it is fair to assume that by the time he would have graduated from high school he already possessed a greater store of learning than most high school students, and had a knowledge of social relationships and sex that went far beyond anything ever acquired in high school.

But when he proposed to Frances, she laughed. "Why do you want to ruin a good thing by doing something like that?" she asked.

That was about the time the little Russian fellow started coming into the Yountville library on Saturdays at the same time Adam was there. The Russian was a dapper, well-dressed man in his fifties with slick dark hair and very bushy eyebrows. He spoke with an

aristocratic accent and for some time after he began coming into
the library Adam worried that the man might be pursuing Frances,
even though he wasn't as tall as she, in fact he was an inch short of
five feet, and Adam himself had already shot up beyond six feet. But
when he confronted Frances with the notion, she laughed and said,
"Oh, no, he's just a very courtly and nice gentleman. André isn't after
me, he's after some books he can't find in the St. Helena library. Have
you noticed the car he drives? He's very well-to-do."

Since Adam was so fond of Nabokov, he was not against
Russians. This man's name was Tchelistcheff, which, Frances told
Adam, could be pronounced as Shelly-shef. He was a winemaker,
a research oenologist, working for BV, as everyone called the large
Beaulieu Vineyards. In fact, André had years before developed the
Cabernet Sauvignon which became the valley's principal wine, and
was of course Adam and Frances' favorite beverage. They sometimes
consumed too much of it.

Eventually, since they shared the library every Saturday, Frances introduced Adam to André. Frances said to André, "Adam is my
protégé in the realm of letters but in the realm of work he's a master
cooper."

"Oh, indeed?" said André Tchelistcheff. "Where is your workshop?"

"In the oak woods on a mountain in the Ozarks, sir," Adam
said. "But if you mean the place I'm employed, it's Inglenook."

"You make barrels for Inglenook?" André said.

"Yes, sir."

"I did not know they make their own barrels. We order ours,
and it is huge bother to wait for them most of the time." And then
he asked, "Where is Ozarks?"

Adam explained that he had only been referring to his grandfather's shop in the forest on Madewell Mountain, in the state of
Arkansas, which he had left five years before.

"Madewell. Is good name for cooper. Will you show me your
work?"

And that was how Adam became friends with André, the
great oenologist, who, when he was taken to inspect the Inglenook

cooperage, demonstrated the same discrimination that made a *San Francisco Chronicle* writer once say of him, "His palate was so refined he could tell by taste whether a wine came from Rutherford dust, Oakville dirt or a furrow in between." After Adam introduced André to his father at the shop, André later whispered to Adam, "Let me see can I not distinguish your work from your father's," and after inspecting several of the finished barrels he did indeed select one and say, "This one you make." Adam had a habit of burning his initials "AM" inconspicuously onto a stave of each of his barrels, but André had not noticed that or used it as a clue to distinguishing Adam's work from his father's. "Miss Frances said what is truth. You are *master* cooper," André said. "But she spoke one mistake. She said you are *her* protégé. I would like you should be *my* protégé."

And that was how Adam escaped from his father's control, and, in time, from his father's house.

Part Five
Whither with her

Chapter forty-one

In her sixteenth year she decided to make contact with the world again. Or, she thought, what ought to be called the *other* world, since the world in which she lived, not just Adam's haunt but her own haunt that went far beyond his, was plenty of world for her. But it had been seven or eight years—she had lost count—since she had pulled the trigger on Sugrue and thus had her last sight of another human being. She had plenty of company from nonhumans; in fact, she had too much company from Paddington, who adored her and could barely (ha! *bear*ly!) let her out of his sight, but sometimes she considered the fact that being the only human being in her world made it too easy to feel that she was the only person in the world, an incorrect and dangerous thought, a thought that allowed the more incorrect and dangerous belief that she had simply created the entire world in her imagination. She was proud of her imagination, whether it simply took the form of giving names to her pair of mourning doves, Sigh and Sue, or, as she had been doing for some time, rewriting the Bible in her mind to make the stories more interesting. She wrote a new version of creation showing that God created woman first and Eve had to wait a while for the man to show up. She attempted to tell what happened to Lot's daughters after they had birthed their babies, and she told the story of David and Goliath from the giant's point of view. But recreating the Bible shouldn't be permitted to allow her to feel that she was in competition with God for creating the whole world, and she needed to get out into that world and see for herself that it contained human beings she had not created.

There was no longer any problem, really, in getting out. Over the years her explorations of the countryside, with or without Paddington or one or more of the dogs, and sometimes with Ralgrub and her offspring, had shown her several possibilities for escape. She had been as far south as the great waterfall which fell into the magical glen Adam had told her so much about, in which he had explored and found Indian relics. She had seen the treacherous place where he had fallen trying to get down, and she knew that even if she had a rope she wouldn't want to try to get off the mountain *that* way. But her wanderings had also led her to the place where she found the crumpled, blackened remains of a vehicle, and she guessed it had been Sugrue's truck, and climbing the bluff side above it, with Hreapha and Hrolf, who seemed to know where they were going, she had discovered the end of what little remained of the trail on which she had been brought to Madewell Mountain so long ago. She knew that if she followed that trail she could find her way down off the mountain. So momentous was the discovery that she was tempted to try it right then and there, but she was naked, as usual, and decided that if she ever encountered another human being, she would have to be clothed.

Thus, when she finally embarked upon her journey to the *other* world, it was only after substantial thought and preparation. She even considered cutting her hair, which now reached nearly to her knees, but instead she simply gave it a thorough washing and braided it into two long pigtails which she wrapped around the top of her head into a kind of crown or turban, held in place with small wooden pegs. She trimmed her fingernails with the scissors and used a knife to clean carefully under the remaining nails, then she did the same for her toenails, which had practically become claws. She considered using Sugrue's razor to remove the hair from her legs and under her armpits but she decided that would be hypocritical if she allowed the bush of golden hair to remain around her poody, and besides, her clothing would cover her legs and armpits (and of course her poody). She donned Sugrue's best shirt and his overalls, also freshly washed, and scarcely needed to roll up the trouser cuffs, since his clothes now fit her well. His shoes were too large, but she didn't mind going barefoot; in fact, she preferred it. She remembered how once long ago she and Beverly had gone into her mother's bedroom and put on her mother's make-up, what fun it had been to pretend to be grown-up, and now that she actually was grown-up, she wished she had something to use in place of lipstick. She took the juice of pokeberries and stained her lips with that, although it wasn't very neat, and rather purply.

Then she called for Adam and attempted to keep the condescension out of her voice, which was hard, because he was such a child, just an awkward, ignorant, backwoods kid. "Well? What do you think?" And she held her arms wide.

Holy moses, he said. *You shore are dolled up fit to kill. Are you a-fixin to git married?*

"No, I'm 'a-fixin' to see if I can't find Stay More."

You don't mean to tell me. What for?

"Just to see what it looks like."

Last time I looked, they wasn't hardly nothing there to speak of.

"But I need to see whatever's left of it. I won't be gone long."

We'uns will all miss ye. I'd admire to go with ye, but of course that's right far out of my haunt.

"I'm taking Hreapha with me. I need you to explain to the others, particularly Paddington, that I haven't abandoned them, I've just gone away for a day or so, however long it takes to get there and look around and get back."

You might have to tie a rope and collar on Paddington to keep him from a-follerin ye.

"I'll just sneak away. But I need you to tell me how long I can leave Bess without milking her."

Well golly gee, I caint rightly say. I never heared tell of no cow that was left alone and unmilked unless she was dry anyhow.

"*Think* about it, Adam. Use your head. And let me know, soon. I'm in a hurry to get started."

Adam needed a while to think about it. Or at least he took a while. She wondered if maybe his feelings were hurt, the way she'd spoken to him. Or possibly he simply didn't know what to tell her but couldn't admit it. From the time, three years before, on or around her thirteenth birthday, when Hreapha and the others had appeared herding the cow across the meadow and to the barn, Adam had told her all he knew about the care and keeping and milking of cows. He hadn't been able to *show* her how to squeeze the teats but he had verbally described it so well that after several attempts she learned to do it, and ever since had enjoyed plenty of milk and cream and butter, with a surplus that kept the animals, especially Robert, happy. She had milked Bess for ten months of each year, nearly every day. It had never crossed her mind that there might ever be an occasion when she'd go away and not be able to milk her. Adam—or his voice—finally returned to tell her that he didn't honestly believe it would hurt Bess any to leave her unmilked for a couple of days, or even three days at the most, although it wouldn't be such a bad idea (Adam always pronounced that "i-dee") to just tie Bess to her stall in the barn so that she couldn't get out into the pasture and eat grass. That way, she wouldn't store up too much milk. But Robin was sure she could return after a night or two away.

"Goodbye, Adam," she said. "That's a word that I haven't used in a long time."

Was he sniffling? *Promise me ye'll come back. Don't let nobody take ye away and keep ye.*

"Don't worry about that."

And you be keerful on that trail. It's bound to be the hardest hike you ever made.

Robin had fashioned herself a sort of backpack, in which she had some provisions—sandwiches, a couple of tomatoes, a couple of apples, a couple of boiled ears of corn. The backpack also contained, just in case, one hundred bills in the denomination of one hundred dollars each.

She turned to Hreapha and beckoned for her to follow, and

the two of them started out. It was not easy. Adam was right that it was the hardest hike she'd ever made. It took almost an hour simply to reach the end—or the beginning—of the trail that led down the mountain, the place where Sugrue had burned his truck. To reach it, there were places where she had to boost Hreapha to get her up the sides of bluffs and out of ravines and gorges. She herself slipped and fell more than once. And even after they reached the remains of the trail, the trail itself was washed out in places and in other places extremely rocky and rough, and it wound back and forth, back and forth, as it crept down the mountain.

When at long last the trail reached the foot of the mountain and met the dirt road at a T, and the dirt road actually had the imprint of car tires in it, Robin started singing, a swelling chant of exultation at having escaped the mountain. She blinked back tears of joy. At the same time she was fearful of actually meeting somebody for the first time, of a car coming along, of her being exposed and spotted and approached and caught. Also she wasn't sure which direction on the dirt road she should take. Her inclination was to turn left but Hreapha said "Hreapha!" and nudged Robin's leg in the direction of turning right. From the turning Robin could see a pasture in which grazed several cows of the same color and coat as Bess, and she asked, "Is that where you got Bess?" and Hreapha wagged her tail. The owner of the cows must live nearby, she realized, but it wasn't Stay More, not the place she wanted to go. So she heeded Hreapha's guidance and took the road to the right, to the southeast.

Along the road that flanked the east feet of Madewell and Ledbetter Mountains, a one-lane dirt road that climbed and dipped and twisted and turned, Robin noticed a few, a very few, houses or other buildings, not one of them in use. And she encountered no traffic, no people, and the only creature she saw was a skunk crossing the road. Still, she felt a constant sense of excitement in anticipation of soon seeing an actual person.

It was late afternoon when Hreapha said "HREAPHA!" and bounded on ahead out of sight, but she soon came back, in the company of several other dogs, one of them the big shaggy fellow that Robin recognized as Yowrfrowr, and another dog that Robin also recognized but hadn't seen for many a year: Hruschka, as well as an assortment of dogs that appeared to be Hruschka's offspring. They were all announcing their names and busily chatting with Hreapha in dogtalk. Robin patted them one by one, and then she followed them as they led her to their home.

Robin had never seen that particular kind of log cabin before, consisting of two separate log cabins joined in between by a kind of breezeway where the people (and the dogs?) could lounge around in the open air out of the sun or rain. At the moment the only loungers were cats, and they were all over the place, in the breezeway and around the yard. Robin loved cats and wished she could go closer and admire them, but she was very nervous because obviously somebody lived here and she might soon be meeting one or more live people, and she hadn't even given any thought to what she would say. She was scared, really.

The dogs were barking and even the cats were meowing, and soon the door leading onto the breezeway from one of the cabins opened, and an old woman stepped out. Robin's eyesight couldn't clearly perceive her, but she must have been eighty at least, with snow-white hair.

"Xenophon, what in tarnation is all this commotion?" the woman said, and Robin realized she was addressing Yowrfrowr. The dog continued repeating his name. Robin savored the moment of having heard a human voice for the first time in years, and although the woman was speaking sternly to her dog it was a very kind voice. Then the woman caught sight of her, and spent a long moment just studying her. Finally she said, "Why, howdy, there."

"Hello, ma'am," Robin said.

"You're a gal," the woman said. "For a minute I thought you were a man, dressed like that. Come on up here where I can get a good look at you."

Robin approached the breezeway, and up close could see the woman clearly. Despite being very old she still seemed to Robin to be one of the most beautiful women she had ever seen although of course Robin hadn't seen any women at all for nine years. "Is this Stay More?" Robin asked.

The woman laughed a young laugh. "Not *this,*" she said, sweeping her hand over her home. "The village is on down the road a ways. You must've just passed it and not noticed it, there's so little left of it."

"I didn't come that way," Robin said. "I came from *that* way."

"On foot?" said the woman, and looked down at Robin's bare feet. "You must've got lost at Parthenon and took the wrong turn. I can't imagine anybody coming to Stay More from *that* way, which used to be called Right Prong. But here now, I'm being chatty and rude. Pull you up a chair and rest your feet and I'll get you a tall glass of lemonade."

Robin couldn't believe it, but soon she was holding in her hand a glass with *ice* in it and filled with lemonade, which she hadn't tasted in so long she'd forgotten there was such a thing. The old woman had a glass too and raised it and said, "To your health," then added, "You sure look pretty healthy, I'd say. How old are you?"

"Sixteen," she said. "And I feel *very* healthy."

"And *tan,*" the woman said. "Do you spend all your time out hiking the back roads?"

"No ma'am, today's the first time I've ever been on a back road on foot."

"Really? Where are you from?"

Robin started to say "Harrison" but realized that was totally false. "Madewell Mountain," she said.

The woman looked at her. "That's just up yonder a ways, not too awfully far at all. But here I'm being chatty and rude again and haven't even told you my name. I'm Latha Dill."

"Oh. You used to be the postmaster of Stay More."

"Long ago, before you were born, when there was still a post office."

"And you used to run the general store, where Adam got his flour and stuff."

"Adam?"

"Adam Madewell."

The woman was looking at Robin very intensely. "The Madewells went to California, oh, maybe thirty year or more ago.

It's still called Madewell Mountain, and you say that's where you're from, but how did you happen to know Ad Madewell? Are you some kin to the Madewells?"

"No, I'm just a good friend of Adam's."

"Oh, so you're really from California, then?"

Robin realized that she was going to have some trouble explaining it all to this nice old lady. She doubted the woman had ever heard of an *in-habit*, or would even believe her if she tried to explain what an *in-habit* was. So she decided not to try. "No," she said, "actually I've never really met Adam. Could you tell me what he looked like?"

"I think you've been out in the sun too long, young lady, and you need more ice than what's in that lemonade." She went into the cabin and returned shortly with a dishtowel in which she had wrapped a bunch of ice cubes. "Here. Hold this to your forehead."

Robin obligingly held the bundle of ice to her head. It felt wonderful, although she had nothing wrong with her head that needed cooling off. "Where do you get ice cubes?" she asked.

"From the fridge, of course," the woman said.

"Oh. You have electricity?"

"Sure. Don't you?"

"No. I haven't seen an ice cube for about nine years."

The woman was smiling. "Whereabouts on Madewell Mountain do you live?"

"The top."

"Oh, then you live in the Madewell place, I reckon."

"That's right. Have you been there?"

"Not since I was about your age. I was born and grew up on the east side of Ledbetter Mountain, out Left Prong yonder, at the old Bourne place, where Brax Madewell's trail comes down off the mountain. That was the way your Ad used to get to school. Did you know that?"

"Yes, the trail goes up through a glen with a high waterfall."

"That's right. Have you been in that holler?"

"I've seen it."

"Well, Brax Madewell built his house up there about the time

I was born. Him and my daddy were friends, and Daddy took me with him once to visit up there. It sure is shut off and out of the world, isn't it?"

"It sure is," Robin agreed. "But I've got many friends, including my dog Hreapha, who's sitting there with your dog Yowrfrowr."

"Yowrfrowr? Is that what you call Funny? His name is Xenophon, or Fun for short. *Yowrfrowr*! The woman laughed, and the dog jumped up at the sound of his real name and came to her. She scratched him behind the ears. "Yowrfrowr, huh? Is that your real name, boy? It's certainly what you say all the time."

"And 'Hreapha' is what my dog says."

As if to confirm it, Yowrfrowr said "YOWRFROWR" and Hreapha said "HREAPHA." Not to be left out, Hruschka said "HRUSCHKA" and each of her offspring announced their names too.

The woman went on laughing, and eventually she stopped laughing and asked, "What are the names of your other friends?"

"Oh, there are so many of them, but their names aren't always the sounds they make. There's Robert the bobcat, and another one of Hreapha's pups named Hroberta, who is Robert's girlfriend, believe it or not." The woman started laughing again, and Robin laughed with her, realizing that she had almost forgotten how to laugh. She went on, "Then there's Hroberta's brother, Hrolf, who thinks he's the lord of the place, and Ralgrub the raccoon and her three children, and Sheba the king snake, or queen snake, and Dewey the buck deer, and Paddington the bear, and Bess the cow, and Sparkle the pet rock, and a pair of mourning doves named Sigh and Sue, and most recently we were honored with the presence of a clever opossum named Pogo."

The woman was really laughing now, and could barely stop to say, "I remember Pogo in the funny papers."

"He's not *still* in the funny papers?" Robin asked.

"No, the artist who drew him, Walt Kelly, died seven or eight years ago."

"That's too bad. Well, my Pogo is just like the Pogo that used to be in the funny papers."

The woman named Latha laughed some more, then stopped

and said, "My stars alive, that's quite a crowd of friends you have. But isn't one of them named Sog?"

Robin's skin prickled, and she thought she might be shivering, not from the bundle of ice cubes. "Do you mean Sugrue Alan?" she said. "Did you know him?"

"I knew him quite well. Too well. Until he disappeared, he was one of my few remaining neighbors. Not a near neighbor. He lived on the other side of Stay More. But I knew him all his misbegotten life, until he disappeared. How's he doing these days?"

"He's dead," Robin said.

"Oh. I wish I could say that's too bad, but I can't. Did you kill him?"

"Yes."

"Good for you. *Good* for you, Robin Kerr. Did this happen recently?"

Robin was almost certain she hadn't mentioned her name to the woman. "No, I shot him when I was eight. But he asked me to. He was pretty bad sick."

"Sick in the head primarily," Latha said. "You must stay all night with me and tell me the whole story. But the first thing I want to know is: how badly did he hurt you?"

Robin thought about that. "Physically he never hurt me. Not much. He slapped me once, that's all."

Latha waited, then asked, "How often did he…did he molest you?"

Robin took time wording her reply. "I know that's what he probably wanted me for, but he didn't. He couldn't. Something was wrong with his, his, his *dick* is all I know to call it. It wouldn't get hard."

Latha's laugh was gentle, not mocking. "My," she said, "you'll really have a story to tell me. But let's go start supper. Is there anything in particular you'd like to eat?"

Robin needed just a moment. "Could you make spaghetti?"

"Sure. With meat sauce?"

And for dessert they had real ice cream. And they talked and talked and talked, late into the night, Robin telling the whole story of the kidnapping, captivity and the killing of Sugrue, as well as life on Madewell Mountain (although she still couldn't bring herself to include the *in-habit*). The inside of Latha's cabin was very neat, and the woman had a telephone and a television and a bookcase, and the kitchen was really up-to-date, with appliances she had never seen before, including something called a microwave. Robin slept on a wonderful bed and in the morning Latha gave her some real woman's clothes to put on, after her bath in a real shower: blue jeans that fit and a knit cotton top, and even a new pair of sneakers. After a breakfast with a real banana and some blueberries to put on her cereal (and Robin was almost sorry to discover how much she liked coffee), during which they talked and talked through the third cup of coffee, Robin asked, "How did you know it was Sugrue who did it?"

Latha explained, "I read the newspapers and watch television. I saw your mother on TV twice. I just had a hunch it was Sugrue because he disappeared at the same time, and because I knew him well. But I had no idea he'd taken you to Madewell Mountain. Now then. Let's go look at the Stay More you have imagined so much."

Chapter forty-two

Yowrfrowr really wanted to go with them, but he explained to
her, My rheumatism, if that's what it is, makes it increasingly weary-
ing for me to get around. So I'll just sit here and lick the place where
my balls used to be until you get back. Have fun.

She debated with herself whether to stay with him or follow
Robin and Yowrfrowr's mistress. Since her first loyalty, despite her
great love for Yowrfrowr, was to Robin, she chose to amble along
behind them as they hiked down into the remains of the village.
She enjoyed listening to their conversation, as the woman named
Latha would pause to point to a building or house and relate its history, and since Hreapha was so good at *minding* Robin, she could
absorb all of Robin's feelings and reactions to the sights and sites of
Stay More. "We probably won't encounter a soul," the woman said,
"but if we do I'll just say your name is Sally Smith and you're a high
school student from Jasper doing some research on the history of
Stay More. Okay?"

They detoured over a low-water bridge across the creek, which
was nearly dry this time of midsummer ("That's Swains Creek or
what's left of it," the woman said), and reached the schoolhouse,

a modest white clapboard building with a well in the yard and a single outhouse. The woman, who said she'd attended school here herself long ago, explained that the single outhouse had been only for girls; the boys, including Adam, had simply "used the bushes". They went inside the schoolhouse, which still had all its furniture in place although it hadn't been used for a quarter of a century. "The first-graders sat down there," the woman pointed, "and the eighth graders sat back here, with all the other grades in between. Right there's where your Ad probably sat last, but he suffered a bad accident in the fourth grade and had to drop out of school."

"I know," Robin said. She sat down at the desk where Adam had probably sat, whose top was attached to the back of the desk seat in front of it. "He really loved this school, but I don't think he missed anything after dropping out."

"How do you know so much about Ad?" the woman asked, sitting down at one of the other desks. "The way you talk about him, I'd think you went to school with him. Did he leave a diary behind?"

"A diary? No, he left behind something a lot better than a diary. I don't know how to tell you this, but…"

Hreapha sat too, on the splintery pine boards of the schoolhouse floor, and listened raptly as Robin attempted to explain to the kindly old woman the existence of, the nature of, and the habits of, an *in-habit*. Hreapha studied the woman's face carefully to see what degree of disbelief she showed, but the woman, whom Hreapha was beginning to *mind* as well, had taken on the expression of a studious schoolgirl sitting at her desk listening to a teacher explain the most difficult of lessons, and while the expression contained elements of perplexity it was also filled with wonder and delight.

And Robin must have *minded* the woman too, because when she was finished she said, "You believe me." It wasn't a question.

For a while the woman did not say anything but stared at the room's blackboard as if waiting for the teacher to diagram an *in-habit*. Finally she said, "Goodness gracious." And a little while later she simply took a deep breath and said, "If that doesn't beat all creation." Then the two women got up from their desks and left the schoolhouse, and re-crossed the low water bridge.

That put them square in the middle of what had been the village, and there was really nothing left except the big two-story house, which, the woman explained to Robin, had been built by Jacob Ingledew, the founder of Stay More who had later been governor of Arkansas after the Civil War. The house had a porch with fancy balusters running the whole length of the front. "My grandson Vernon owns it," the woman said, "as he owns most of everything around here, but he doesn't live here. At the moment he's renting it out to some college professor named Larry, who is probably sound asleep in there amongst the cockroaches. He has what they call a drinking problem."

"Which Sugrue had," Robin said. "And which I'm going to have if I don't lay off all the whiskey he left behind."

"I think you probably know when to stop," the woman said. The woman pointed out where the big Ingledew general store had been, only its cement porch floor remaining, and where the big gristmill had stood, and where Doc Swain's house and office had been. "Did Sog tell you about Doc Swain?" the woman asked.

"Yes. He was my favorite paper doll," Robin said.

"He was my favorite person," the woman said. "Well, right there is where he patched up your Ad after he fell off the mountain."

"You keep calling him *my* Ad," Robin said.

"Well, isn't he?"

They walked on up what had been the main street of the village and the woman pointed out where the bank had been, The Swains Creek Bank and Trust Company, the stone of its edifice now demolished and used to form a dike against the occasional rise of Swains Creek's waters. Across from it was the only other remaining building in town, a three-part house also with a porch all along its front.

"Now that was my store and post office," the woman said. "And also my house for many years before I moved out to the dogtrot, which was my husband's home. After the post office closed and I moved out, it remained dusty and empty for many years, except for the old oak post office boxes, which are still in there. Recently my granddaughter Sharon moved in and fixed it up a bit. But let's not talk too loudly, or she'll hear us and come out."

Robin asked, "Is she alone?"

"Yes. She had a very unhappy marriage which ended several years ago, thank heavens."

"That's interesting," Robin said, "that she lives *here* and that man lives down *there,* and they're the only people in town. Do they ever speak to each other?"

The woman laughed. "Rarely. In fact, Larry was her boyfriend for a while, in Chicago, where he taught, and he followed her here, but...oh, Robin, it's such a long story you don't want to hear it now."

"If I still played with my paper dolls, I could make up a great story for them."

"You certainly could. But you don't have to do it with paper dolls. You could *write* it."

"I don't have any paper left."

The woman put both hands on her hips. "Now *that* is inexcusable and I won't allow you to leave without a supply a paper." They resumed walking up the road, and Hreapha happily followed, with an inkling of where they might be going. "There's only one other place to show you," the woman said. "And it's another half-mile or so up this road, the Parthenon Road, if you can walk that far."

The old woman didn't seem to mind walking. Probably she had a lot of practice, and had no infirmities like her Xenophon's rheumatism. Hreapha reflected sadly that her lover Yowrfrowr might not live forever. For that matter, she herself was an old dog now, and she brooded that Yowrfrowr probably no longer considered her attractive. Well, certainly he no longer had any desire for her, not her fault or his.

They came to the man's house, and a wave of nostalgia swept over Hreapha. "This was where Sog lived," the woman said, "before he pretended to go off to California but instead kidnapped a seven-year-old girl and took her off to live on a mountaintop. Look, the note he left is still on the door: 'GONE TO CALIFORNIA.'"

Hreapha was a little surprised to see how the house was falling apart now that it had been abandoned for so long. Time and the elements had removed all familiar scents and sights, and even the holes she'd dug all over the backyard had filled with silt. She could not detect any trace of her own *in-habit* at all, and decided conclusively that she must have taken it with her to Madewell Mountain.

"So this is where you grew up," Robin said to Hreapha.

"Hreapha," she said.

"You're much better off now," Robin said.

"Hreapha," she agreed

"And so are you," the woman said to Robin. "Now let's get on back home."

That afternoon, as the two women sat in the dogtrot of the cabin (and Hreapha did not trot but sat), sipping their lemonades and taking in the breeze, Robin asked, "How do you manage to keep so many pets?"

And the woman returned the question, "How do you?"

"Well, I don't have to feed them, much. They feed themselves."

"My very generous and wealthy grandson Vernon, who is virtually my sole means of support apart from Social Security, regularly stops by to visit and always brings several boxes of canned cat food and dog food."

"Is he also not married?"

The woman laughed. "No, but he's been living for years with a woman, his cousin Jelena, and if you'll stay with me for several days I'll tell you their story too."

"I'd really love to stay, but I do have to get home. You have such a nice house. And you and I are alike in so many ways, especially because we've learned how to live alone."

"We certainly are alike, you and I. In fact, you remind me of myself at your age. Except you are much more beautiful."

"I doubt that. When you were my age, you must have been the most beautiful woman on earth."

"I doubt that. But why can't you spend a week with me?"

"I've got to get on back home and milk the cow, for one thing."

"Oh, when you first said 'home,' I thought you meant your former home in Harrison. You have no plans for returning there? Even though your mother remarried and lives in Little Rock now?"

"Really? No, I haven't given any thought to going back to Harrison. I could never give up my friends, not even Adam, whom I was becoming too supercilious toward."

"Does the *in-habit* know words like 'supercilious'? Where'd you pick that up? Do you have books to read up there?"

"The only books I have are the Bible and a manual on farming and housekeeping, which Adam's mother left behind, and one of those books must've had 'supercilious' in it."

"It's too late for you to start your journey home today," the woman said. "So you'll have to stay at least one more night with me."

"Okay. I'll be very happy to do that."

"If I can find the number from Information, could I persuade you to call your mother and tell her you're okay?"

Robin did not answer. Hreapha *minded* her and got an electric blast of panic, which was somewhat surprising. Didn't Robin want to make any contact with her own mother? Finally, Robin said, "Please." That's all she could say for a while, and then she was able to add some more: "Please don't let anybody know where I am. Don't you understand?"

"Sure, Robin, I understand. Even if you told your mother that you want to stay on Madewell Mountain, there would be so much publicity over the news that you're still alive that you'd be mobbed with tourists." The woman laughed at her own exaggeration, then added, "Still, I think it might mean the world to your poor mother if somehow you could let her know you're alive and well."

"I'll think about it," she said, but before she said anything further on the matter, she and the old woman went inside the cabin to begin preparing their supper, and except for a brief moment when Robin reappeared to give Hreapha a nice dish of dog food, Hreapha didn't see her again until the morning. Hreapha spent a good part of the night just visiting with Yowrfrowr, Hruschka, and their children. One of Hreapha's grandsons said to her, "Granny, Pa says there's all kinds of critters living with you up on the mountain. Is that true?" And Hreapha regaled her grandchildren with stories about the menagerie, particularly the additions that had been made since Yowrfrowr had visited. She told them about some of Pogo's hilarious antics. Later, when all of them slept, Hruschka didn't mind that Hreapha slept snuggled up next to Yowrfrowr, whom she might never see again.

In the morning, early, Robin and the woman came out of the house. Robin's backpack was bulging with things the woman had given her. The woman asked, "Can you manage to take some kittens with you? I've got plenty. More than plenty."

"Oh, I'd love to," Robin said. "But one is all I could manage."

"Take your pick."

Robin picked out a very young, cute, female calico kitty, and nestled it into the open top of her backpack. "Thank you so much for everything," Robin said to the woman. "Especially for the books and the paper and the pencils. I've already written on the first sheet of paper. Would you like to read it?" And she handed the woman a sheet, which the woman read aloud.

> "Dear Mommy, I want you to know that I survived my kidnapping, and I am alive and well and happy and the man who did it is dead. Some day, not soon, I hope to see you again and tell you all about it. But for right now, I want with all my heart to stay where I am, so I can't tell you where it is, and I hope you won't try to find me. Please know I'm just fine and I love you very much. Robin."

Robin said to the woman, "If you can ever find her address, and have your grandson or somebody mail that from Harrison so it has a Harrison postmark, do you think that will help?"

"Thank you," the old woman said.

"No, thank *you*," Robin said. "Thanks beyond words for everything. Thanks also for showing me how nicely you can live all by yourself. I hope you will stay alive forever because I want to see you again."

"And you take care of yourself because I want to see you again too. Are you sure I can't persuade you to take some oranges and bananas with you?"

"If I did, I might develop a hankering for them," Robin said, and both women laughed.

The women hugged each other for a long moment, and then Robin said one more thing, "Remember your promise never to tell anybody where I am."

Hreapha licked Yowrfrowr upside his handsome face, and he returned the lick, saying, Take care, old girl.

And then they were on the road home. Hreapha's sadness was relieved by the gladness of going home, and apparently Robin was joyful too, because they were hardly out of sight of the dogtrot cabin before Robin began singing, not any of her songs or hymns with words but just those pure tones of hers that were so beautiful, rising and falling and revealing the colors of her heart. Hreapha felt like singing herself.

But going back up the mountain was much harder than coming down the mountain. Halfway up, Robin had to stop for a long time, panting and trying to get her breath back, and she said to Hreapha, "I don't know if I can make it. Maybe you ought to go on ahead without me."

"Hreapha," she said, meaning, I wouldn't hear of it.

So they sat for a while beside the trail and Robin got her lunch and the kitty out of the backpack, shared the lunch with Hreapha and the kitty, who, she said, she had decided to name "Latha," and then she showed Hreapha the various other things the woman had given her: a package of writing paper, several pencils, a ballpoint pen, three thin books with paper covers, two packages of spaghetti noodles, a cylinder of Morton's salt, six packages of yeast, as well as a dress, a pair of panties, a brassiere, a bath towel and washcloth, a hair comb, etc., etc. No wonder Robin was winded, trying to backpack all that stuff up the mountain.

"Wasn't she the nicest person you could imagine?" Robin said. "I never could have dreamed up anybody like her. None of my paper dolls, not even Doc Swain, was as good as her. I left her some money. On the bed where she'd find it. Ten thousand dollars."

After lunch Robin was ready to resume the climb, although she had to stop several more times before reaching the end of the trail. While they were resting again, they were startled by the appearance of a small but strange creature which Hreapha had not often seen but recognized as an armadillo, which looks like an opossum wearing armor.

"Good heavens! What's that?" Robin asked.

"Hreapha," she said, meaning, an armadillo.

"Okay, you might as well get me one for my next birthday."

"Hreapha," she said, meaning, It is done.

When they finally emerged into the pasture, the first of their friends to greet them was Bess, who mooed loudly. Bess's udder was utterly swollen, and Robin took off her backpack and squatted to milk Bess right there, allowing the milk to run out on the ground. Robin explained to Hreapha, "Adam said the first milking after a delay wouldn't be fit to drink, but we need to relieve Bess."

Adam was the second of their friends to greet them. *So how did Stay More suit ye?* his voice asked.

"I had a wonderful time," Robin said. "I stayed two nights with Latha Bourne Dill."

You wouldn't fool a feller, would ye? Is she still going strong?

"Adam, tell me something. What did she look like the last time you saw her? She wasn't white-haired and stooped then, was she?"

Why, no, I reckon she must've been close to fifty but she still had a full head of dark hair and I relished her, I thought she was ripsniptious, I mean swelldifferous, I mean she was a real sight for sore eyes.

"That's good, because she told me she thought you were the best-looking boy she'd ever seen. She said you were a 'dreamboat.'" Robin waited, then said, "Adam? Did you hear me?"

I'm abashed, he said quietly. *I caint imagine what would've give her that notion.*

"Oh, I wish I could *see* you."

I've got a gimpy leg and a missing finger, he said. *I'm a freak.*

"But your face must be lovely. Latha told me that Roseleen Coe thought you were a prize, and it broke her heart when you had that accident and couldn't come to school any more. By the way, Latha showed me that schoolhouse, and I sat in your desk."

That was Roseleen's desk too. I'm happy to know it's still there.

"Latha also said that when Roseleen left with her family for California, she said for Latha to tell you that she would always see you in her dreams, but Latha never saw you again herself."

Who knows, maybe Adam ran into Roseleen out in California.

Chapter forty-three

Indeed he did, but not for a number of years, and I hope to reach their vital meeting somewhere in this chapter. We have left Adam still a teenager, about to become the protégé and assistant to the great oenologist (who preferred to spell it simply "enologist," either form deriving from the Greek for wine, *oinos*) André Tchelistcheff, whom Adam began to worship and eventually to emulate, even to his detriment. For example, while T (as Adam and Frances began to refer to him to each other) taught him patiently and meticulously how to discriminate among the subtle tastes of different wines and of same wines of different age or quality, he also taught him how to smoke cigarettes, practically to chain-smoke, although strangely this did not affect his acute senses of taste and smell. Once on his doctor's orders T attempted to give up smoking, and Adam dutifully gave it up along with him, but they both quickly discovered it ruined their taste discrimination, and they just as quickly resumed their constant nicotine habit. T told him that when he'd first come to work at BV for the legendary Georges de Latour, T had insisted on being allowed to sample everything in the winery, and De Latour had identified each of the samples, "This is Sauvignon Blanc," or "This is Riesling," and so forth through all the wines. "But I could not tell one from another," T said, "not because I lacked the judgment but because they were all the same!"

When Adam first went to work for T, California wines were still cheap and undistinguished. Americans for the most part preferred sweet wines—ports and sherries—and they considered good table wine to be "sour." Beaulieu Vineyards, under T with help from Adam, gradually changed all that. At the time Adam met him, André Tchelistcheff had already left the day-to-day winemaking business and spent most of his time in his small research lab, the Napa Valley Enological Research Laboratory, located up the road at St. Helena, conducting experiments and seeking to improve the quality of the wine. Adam was not merely a lab assistant; T taught him how to conduct experiments, chemical analysis and complicated tests upon different types of oak for the barrels, as well as different methods of "toasting" the oak. Nominally, Adam was the master cooper for BV, but actually he spent more time in T's St. Helena laboratory, and he eventually became the leading expert on the composition of oak barrels. T had amassed a large library on wine and wine-making, most of it written in French, a language he insisted that Adam teach himself (with Frances' help and with daily conversation from T, who said, "When I think about wine, I think in French, not English"). Neither T nor Adam were above mucking in the vineyards themselves, especially if frost threatened and help was needed at night setting out the smudge pots, whose kerosene smoke always reminded Adam of the fuel used in the Ozarks for illumination and starting woodstove fires.

Adam's refined senses were constantly detecting something that reminded him of the Ozarks. Especially his sense of sight. On their rambles together, T showed Adam a one-room white clapboard building that had once been the Rutherford schoolhouse, which reminded Adam almost painfully of the Stay More school. T had a son named Dimitri, several years older than Adam, who had gone to school there. The author Nabokov also had a son named Dimitri, the same age as T's son, although T had never read nor heard of that other marvelous Russian-American, who had many things in common with T, even the fact that they were both from aristocratic families who had lost everything in the Russian revolution, and T had also fought with the White Russian army against the Reds. Adam continued to buy and read each new book by Nabokov as it came out, until, by the time of the great writer's death, he owned all of his novels that had been written in or translated into English. Otherwise his library consisted only of various wine books T had given him, or cast-offs from the Yountville Library that Frances had given him.

He continued living with Frances for several years. His father evicted him from his own home, not because of his relationship with Frances but because of his relationship with T, which Gabe Madewell bitterly begrudged him, since Adam was no longer obliged to his father for employment and thus Gabe could not continue his long-standing habit of criticizing everything Adam did. That habit had been the core of their father-son relationship, and breaking the habit cold turkey threw Gabe Madewell into a depression so irrational he would no longer tolerate the visits Adam tried to make occasionally to see his mother.

So Adam had moved in with Frances, and they lived as com-mon-law man and wife (the acronym POSSLQ was just coming into vogue) for several years through Adam's twenties, until Frances, nearly forty and beginning to lose her looks, insidiously stepped up her consumption not just of the splendid wines Adam brought home from work but also of more potent beverages such as vodka, rum, and scotch. For a while Adam appreciated that her regular intoxication left her completely free-spirited and uninhibited. But then she lost her library job as a result of her drinking, and while Adam could easily afford to support her so that she didn't need to work, the absence of regular employment gave her more opportunity for drinking. Once she asked him, "Do you still want to marry me?" and he had to say in all honesty that he hadn't given it any further thought. Whenever he came home from work, she was too far gone to speak coherently to him, let alone prepare meals or make love. He had his own car, and drove her to Napa city in the evenings to attend meetings of A.A., but that organization was not able to remove her thirst, which had gone beyond her control or his.

One year during his twenties, Adam was sent to France, at

the expense of Beaulieu Vineyards and at the suggestion of T, who wanted him to study first-hand everything connected with the making of French wine barrels, from forest management to stave production to the actual methods of cooperage. Adam was thrilled, and not at all nervous, since he had learned to speak French so well. The problem was that Frances wanted desperately to go with him, and he couldn't take her. Not that he (or BV) couldn't afford it, but he was going as a businessman, not a tourist, and she would be in the way, and in the back of his mind he kept saying to himself *I'm giving up Frances for France* and indeed he hadn't been in Merpins, his first stop after Paris, for two nights before he was sleeping with a tantalizing *femme* named Felise, who not only relaxed him after a busy day but began to accompany him as *aide et secrétaire* as he toured the *tonelleries* of France. Felise was his constant companion for three months as he absorbed everything there was to be learned about French cooperage, most of what was to be learned about French wine, and a good deal of what was to be learned about French lovemaking. About the latter Felise knew things that wanton Frances couldn't have dreamed. For example, while Frances had shown him when he was only fifteen how a "French kiss" was done, Felise introduced him to *maraichinage,* the prolonged caressing of each other's tongues, sometimes for hours, and usually to the point of orgasm. When it was time for Adam to return to America, he invited Felise to come with him; short of proposing marriage outright he made her an offer she couldn't refuse, but she refused it, with the revelation that all along, she had been hired by a major *tonellerie* to entertain and assist him.

And when he got home, there was a note from Frances saying she'd gone back to San Francisco to live with her sister. Thereafter he dwelt alone for several years, except for occasional dates with women he met in the bars of St. Helena, until on one of his annual two-week vacations, he decided to visit San Francisco, which he had not yet seen. He had the address of Frances' sister, and he intended to see Frances again and apologize in an effort to relieve the guilt that had been nagging him since his return from France. The sister would not let him in the door. "So you're the famous Adam Madewell," she said. "I have heard so awfully much about you. I thought of phoning to see if you'd want to attend the funeral, but I didn't." She told him which cemetery to go to and he put a dozen red roses on her grave. He wanted simply to drive on back home, but he spent a couple of nights in town, went to a Giants game, rode the street cars, visited the Palace of Fine Arts, and toured Haight-Ashbury, still inhabited by the counterculture. On a crowded sidewalk outside the Psychedelic Shop he bumped into a woman who cursed him, then grabbed him and said, "Man, you *still* smell like oakwood smoke."

It took him too long to recognize her, with her long beribboned dirty-blonde hair, her floppy hat, the bangles and beads and all. "Well swoggle my eyes!" he exclaimed. "If it aint *Roseleen!*"

"My, my, I'd hardly know you, you're so *tall,* and you're even better-looking than, like, you ever was. Man, I always thought you was the best-looking feller I ever knew, you know? And I've loved you all my life, man." She tried to sell him some crystals. He offered to take her to dinner. They went to an Italian restaurant, where, over the second bottle of wine, they told each other all about themselves. The reason he still smelled like oakwood smoke was that he'd been conducting a number of experiments on the optimum amount of charred "toast" on the inside of barrel staves. Roseleen had been married twice and had a daughter living with her father over in Fillmore. "It aint Stay More but its Fillmore, you know?" she said. Roseleen was "into" Zen Buddhism, if he wanted to hear about it. He didn't. Would he like to crash at her pad? He would, if only to finally consummate the passion he'd felt for her when he first learned what passion was. As it turned out, she wasn't spectacular, or even particularly adept, in bed. As she struggled to reach orgasm, she began to grunt, "Fuck me! Oh, *fuck* me, man!" and he suspected that the orgasm she reached was pretended. Later she said, "Man, that was like what I used to like dream of you doing to me like when we was only like ten years old, you know?"

"Me too," was all he could say.

At breakfast the next day, she said, "Do you ever think about going back to Stay More?"

"All the time," he said.

"But you haven't, ever?" she said. "Me neither. I'd sure love to,

Do you have a car? Let's just like jump in your car and take off, okay? Man, let's me and you just go like right home to Stay More."

Oh boy, was he tempted. But whatever passion he'd felt for Roseleen Coe in their childhood was just a distant memory, indelible and remote, elusive as the fragrance of vanilla in oakwood. It made him sad to think that he'd probably changed as much as she had, maybe for the better, but still not the same Ozark boy he'd been. Frances and T had both kidded him sometimes about certain words he still used: he said "ary" and "I reckon" and "dusty dark" but for the most part his manner of speaking was much more sophisticated than it had been. Roseleen had lost all trace of her Ozark accent too but had replaced it with a kind of coarse hippie talk. "I dig but I don't groove," she said when Adam tried to tell her why he couldn't take her back to Stay More.

But in the months ahead, while he was overcoming a serious case of gonorrhea he had probably contracted from Roseleen, he allowed his mind to fantasize that trip with her back home, if only just as a lark. He had been truthful in telling her that he thought constantly about going back to Stay More, but he had never admitted it, even to himself, and now that she had raised the subject, he couldn't shake it loose. It would keep on bothering him until he did something about it.

André Tchelistcheff retired once again, as he had been doing periodically ever since Adam had met him and as he would keep on doing until he retired to that great Vineyard in the sky at the age of ninety-three. But this time, he had another reason: Beaulieu (the name means "beauteous place") had been sold to Heublein, the liquor giant, who had also swallowed up Inglenook and Italian Swiss Colony and would eventually absorb Almadén and Glen Ellen. Heublein had bought the Regina Winery and turned it into a vinegar plant, and T loudly speculated that it might do the same to Beaulieu. "Or if we not make vinegar, what we make tastes like vinegar," he said. He also advised Adam to get out. More than that, he offered to help Adam get set up in his own cooperage, an independent cooperage that would sell its barrels to all the Napa Valley winegrowers. Adam recalled that the top price Braxton Madewell got for a barrel was five dollars, the top price Gabe got was ten; now an American oak barrel was selling for hundreds of dollars (a French oak barrel for twice as much), with no end in sight to the rising price, the steepness of which was largely responsible for the increase in the price for a bottle of good California wine. Thus, with some backing from T and with the assurance of steady customers among the wineries of the region, Adam founded the Madewell Cooperage, whose name, it was widely assumed, boasted of the workmanship put into the product. In fact, the making of oak barrels was becoming increasingly automated, from start to finish, free from human hands, and much of Adam's start-up expenditure was for fancy machinery. Adam himself never again built a barrel from scratch at his giant cooperage. He spent most of his time at his large desk (made of oak, naturally), with paperwork or customers, or inspecting the products of his assembly line. Occasionally he sneaked away to the Napa Valley Research Laboratory, where T kept on tinkering, and where Adam could continue his own research and his search for the best possible oak and treatment thereof. Then the University of California, Davis, which operated a branch at nearby Oakville devoted to enology and viticulture, offered Adam an adjunct professorship. When they learned from his resume that he hadn't even finished grade school, they changed the title to adjunct research specialist, but the job was the same: teaching one evening course each semester in the history, making and use of oak barrels. He certainly didn't need the salary, and taught the course purely for pleasure. The students, including several women, were eager and hardworking, and they would go on after graduation into vineyards and cellars all over California. A few of the best Adam would hire for Madewell Cooperage. He enjoyed his students as much as they enjoyed him, and in time he would become so fond of one of them, named Linda, that he would ask her to marry him.

He was in his mid-thirties and she hadn't quite reached her mid-twenties. Her father owned a vineyard in Sonoma County, and Adam was invited there for Thanksgiving, Christmas, and for Linda's birthday, and he got along well with her parents and siblings. The wedding was planned as a big event for the fall to coincide with the grape harvest and be part of its celebration. But first, that summer

419

before he tied the knot, he had a little thing he wanted to do, and he did it. He thought of it as strictly business, but he wasn't fooling himself: somewhere in the back of his mind, homesickness was lurking. He was going to visit the Ozarks in search of the best possible oak for his barrels. He had searched the oak forests of Iowa, Minnesota, Ohio, Pennsylvania and Wisconsin for the best-grained and best-fragranced standing oak, and his cooperage used staves from all those places, but most of his staves were cut from the big river oaks along the Mississippi near Perryville, Missouri, and he maintained a constant nagging suspicion that mountain oaks would have better flavor than river oaks. In the back of his mind was even the idea of getting up to Madewell Mountain and reclaiming some of its magnificent wood.

Surprisingly Linda didn't ask to go with him. He was prepared to talk her out of it if she did, as he had talked Frances out of France or talked Roseleen out of Stay More. He knew he couldn't use "business" as an excuse because Linda herself was just as fascinated with oakwood as he was. But he didn't need any excuses. *Have fun*, was all she said. He said, "I reckon I'd like to take just one good look around the Ozarks before I settle down forever in California."

"I don't suppose you're planning to search for some childhood sweetheart you don't want me to know about," she said.

"Yeah, maybe that's it. Only she never wore a dress nor had long hair nor even a cute little nose like you've got. She was just a *place,* for heaven's sake."

He let her have the fancy German sedan and he took the sports-utility vehicle, as they were just becoming known in those days. In fact, his was a top-of-the-line English model with powerful four-wheel drive, which he assumed he'd need if he ever decided to climb Madewell Mountain. He drove up into the Rockies and across the plains, taking his time and studying a few stands of oak en route, spending a couple of nights on the road before finally reaching the place he'd spend the third night, Harrison, Arkansas. Although it was one of the principal trading centers of the Ozarks, he'd only been there once before in his life, when his father had put them into the back of a rickety truck headed for California. He spent the night at the Holiday Inn and had a decent supper and breakfast at their restaurant, where someone had left the *Harrison Daily Times* at his table, which he read while eating. Crossing the state line into Arkansas had thrilled him, entering Harrison had been a triumph, picking up this newspaper and seeing the names of his people (even if he saw no familiar names) gave him a sense of controlling his destiny.

The main local news concerned the continued search for an abducted girl, only seven, last seen in a roller skating rink, and the subject of a massive search by the state and local police as well as the FBI. The girl's mother, Karen Kerr, had agreed to the organization of a national support group named after her daughter for parents of missing children. Adam wondered how he would feel if his daughter were kidnapped. He wondered how he would feel if he had a daughter. Linda had not yet broached the subject of whether they'd have children.

He drove to the dying village of Parthenon, which still had a post office in a humble stone building, where he made inquiries. There were no Madewells still living in the area. Adam's mother's sister, Aunt Effie, had died. The man who had owned the Parthenon Stave & Heading Company was still alive and in his eighties, and Adam visited him and was taken to the site of what once had been a school, the Newton County Academy, where only one ruined building remained, the former gymnasium, a dilapidated old stone building being used for the storage of what was thought to be worthless oak staves. He and the man went inside, and Adam staggered at the sight of thousands upon thousands of oak staves, neatly stacked and turning gray as they aged. He lifted one at random, scratched it with his thumbnail, and inhaled an oaken fragrance that he had not smelled since the age of twelve and which he'd been searching for ever since.

The man told him that most of the staves had been deposited there by Braxton or Gabriel Madewell, and since Adam was their heir, he was free to help himself. He gave the man the address of Madewell Cooperage in California and wrote him a check to cover the cost of hiring a convoy of trucks to deliver the staves.

The business part of his trip, to all intents and purposes, was accomplished.

Did he want to visit Stay More? It wasn't a matter of *did he* but rather *could he?* He'd found that childhood sweetheart in San Francisco and knew her only in the Biblical sense.

Could he drive his powerful SUV up Madewell Mountain? He could try, although he discovered he was sweating and nervous.

His progress up the steep trail was halted when he encountered a pick-up truck mired squarely in the road. The owner of the truck, who said his name was Leo Spurlock, told him there was probably no way to get on to the top of the mountain, not even on foot.

Adam had a bad leg. Worse, he had a great fear that if he succeeded in reaching the top of the mountain and finding the place where he'd willed a part of himself to stay forever, he would never want to leave again. He just couldn't do it.

So he returned to California. André Tchelistcheff was honored to be asked to serve as his best man at the elaborate wedding, held in the glowing, lovely vineyards of Linda's family, a Madewell barrel serving as altar.

Chapter forty-four

She was a woman now. Latha had said so. She remembered how, long ago, the Woodland Heights Elementary had wanted her to skip a grade because she was so advanced over the others, and now she felt that she was not merely seventeen, she had grown entirely out of adolescence and if anybody asked her how old she was (if there was anybody anywhere to do such a thing—like Latha) she would have to say she was well along into her twenties. Maybe close to thirty. Yes, she was at least as old as her mother had been the last time she'd seen her. And much better than her mother in so many ways. Prettier. Smarter. Funnier. Shapelier. Friendlier. Sexier (God, *yes*). If only she had a man (not a boy but a man) to demonstrate it with. At her birthday party, when the dogs had presented her with the petrified but soon relaxed Armageddon, her armadillo, she had worn the dress Latha had given her, an old-fashioned country calico dress that Latha herself had worn in her twenties, and it made her look much older than seventeen, and she enjoyed being clothed for that one day, and finally understood for herself why human beings are the only creatures who wear clothes, not so much for bodily protection but rather because what is hidden is more tantalizing than what is revealed; that humankind, blessed with greater imagination than animalkind, needed to play a kind of constant hide-and-seek with the body itself, as all human creative work, which animals cannot do, is the expression of a hiding and a seeking and a finding, especially stories, and even music, yes, musical notes hide themselves and find themselves constantly (what else is melody?), as she demonstrated in her birthday descant. Then she said, "Adam, do you think I look more appealing in this dress than I do stark naked?"

He was slow in answering, as usual. Sometimes she didn't know whether his slowness was just a matter of being an ignorant twelve-year-old, or because the older she got the more reserved he was toward her, and now the five years that separated them was actually like ten or more. Finally, he said, rather wistfully, *Tell ye the truth, hit don't matter too awful much, one way or th'other, since I caint have ye, anyhow.*

"Have me?" she said. "Do you really *want* me?"

Again he took a while pondering or formulating his answer. *I've always wanted ye. But come to think on it, I reckon I'd want ye more in that 'ere dress than I'd want ye as you generally are, a-running around all over creation a-wearing nothing but a smile.*

"There!" she said. "That's what I figured. Clothes can be naughtier than skin, if they stir up your thoughts."

My thoughts don't need no stirring up.

"You're clothed, aren't you?" she asked him. "What are you wearing?"

Just my same old overalls.

He pronounced it "overhauls." She pretended to be staring down at him. "Don't look now," she said, "but you forgot to button your fly."

There was almost a visible stirring in the air; she could imagine him trying to button himself. *Darn ye!* he said. *That weren't funny.*

An idea occurred to her, but they were surrounded by all their friends, including the innocent new kitty, Latha, and the latest haunter, Armageddon, who hadn't made up his mind (actually, as she'd soon learn, it was *her* mind) whether he (or she) liked birthday cake or not. "Adam," she requested, "sometime before the day is over, as one more birthday present, even an immaterial one, let's you and I get together for a private conversation. Would you do that for me?"

He didn't answer, and she wondered if her tone had once again been too supercilious for him. She finished her own piece of cake and offered seconds to all the guests, but only Ralgrub and Pogo wanted more. She thanked Hrolf for leading the expedition to procure Armageddon. Then she went into the storeroom and got a fresh bottle of Jack Daniels and opened it. She offered it around, but nobody wanted any. Paddington would have been glad to have some, but she hadn't seen her bear for quite some time, and his absence was the only shortcoming in her birthday celebration. While she was relieved to be free from his constant devotion, she hoped that she hadn't hurt his feelings by locking him out of the house. She was sorry that he had never acquired the ability of the other animals to understand her; he had never grasped what she had tried to tell him: that he was too rough, and sometimes his claws raked her. Probably, she had consoled herself, he had simply wandered off across the mountain in search of a female bear who could love him in a way she could not. But giving up *this* Paddington had been far more difficult for her than giving up the original stuffed Paddington that she had loved so much. Now she drank what would have been Paddington's portion of the Jack Daniels, in his memory or honor or whatever.

After a while she needed to pee and she stumbled out to the yard but instead of lifting her dress and squatting there she had an impulse to use the outhouse, which she hadn't done for nine years. One of the two holes was still occupied by the skeleton, who was still holding his own bottle of Jack Daniels, and when she sat down over the other hole and began to tinkle, it was somehow more embarrassing, or more daring, to be doing it in the presence of Sugrue's skeleton than it would have been to be doing it in the presence of all the live creatures who inhabited these premises. She knew she wouldn't have done it if she hadn't been drinking so much. "Excuse me," she said to him, rather tipsily, "but maybe I'm getting too old to squat in the yard. Tee hee." Then she asked, "How've you been?" And she said, "Latha Bourne was asking me how've you been, and I had to tell her you were dead. She seemed to think that was good news. She's doing just fine, herself, despite being past eighty. I had a real nice visit with her. She gave me some nice things to bring home with me. She gave me three books, or she let me pick them out, telling me just to take whichever three I wanted and she could have her grandson Vernon replace them if she still wanted copies, although I left behind ten thousand dollars of your money. I picked *Mythology* by Edith Hamilton, which is very interesting and a lot of fun. Also I took a handbook on wildflowers, which has been very helpful in my study of my favorite subject. And finally just for fun I chose a book called *Lightning Bug*, which is a novel-book but has some interesting stuff on fireflies, and I've also started studying bugs a lot lately, even spiders, and you'd be surprised if you ever stopped to count the different kinds of bugs that are running and flying around all over this place. Latha also gave me a little bottle of cologne, because she doesn't ever use it any more. It's called "Tabu" and I'm wearing it right now. Can you smell it? Hey, it's my birthday, did you know? I'm seventeen, ten years older than when you first took me. There's not a single present left for me in all that stuff you left behind, except your whiskey, and I suppose there's enough of that for me to have a birthday bottle from you for the rest of my life. I'm all finished peeing but I'll just sit here a while with you, and bring you up to date."

She kept on talking to Sugrue's skeleton for a very long time. She told him how much she had tried to live according to his precepts, such as everything in this life worth getting requires being stung a few times, and be careful what you wish for, and don't ever sing before breakfast. When her mouth got dry, she borrowed the bottle he had in his bony fingers, and opened it and took a swig now and then. She actually got drunk, which she'd never done before and would never do again, because among other things she would have a hangover the next day that she never wanted to have again. She drunkenly told Sugrue that she wished he still had some flesh on his bones. She told him that if he did, she'd be glad to suck his dick, to get it stiff and hard so he could put it inside her. What she really wanted, more than anything, was a man. "If you had stayed alive," she said to him, "and if only you'd been able to wait several years and give me a chance to grow up, you and I could have really fucked. Let me tell you how we would have done it…"

She was busy describing a hot sex scene to the skeleton when a voice said, *Scuse me for buttin in, but didn't ye say you wanted to have a private conversation with me?* She jumped, her butt actually rising above the outhouse hole, then she realized it wasn't Sugrue speaking to her. The voice went on, *Leastways I could answer ye, which this here skeleton caint do.*

"Hi, honey," she said. She'd never called him that before. "Have a drink with me." She held out the bottle to him, but of course he couldn't take it. "Could you just pretend?" she asked. "Are you any good at play-like, Adam?"

Iffen I wasn't, I'd sure be up salt creek.

"That's what I wanted to talk to you about. So why don't you play-like you're having a big swallow of this fine whisky?"

Okay. Glug glug glug. Umm, mighty fine hooch, ma'am.

"Don't call me 'ma'am.' Let's get away from Sugrue. We don't want him watching."

Watching what, ma'am? But his ghost can foller us wherever we go.

"Really? Does he have a ghost? Have you seen it?"

He's all over the place. All the time. Like me, he never sleeps, ma'am.

"Please don't call me 'ma'am.' It makes me feel old. If Sugrue's ghost is everywhere, why haven't I seen it?"

I wish I could tell ye on account of he's just shy, or just invisible like me. But that aint it. Y'see, us in-habits outrank ghosts, I mean we're more powerful than them, so I've let that there ghost know that I don't never want him to show his hide—or his spirit.

"Do you mean there's nowhere we could go that he couldn't see us?"

Out to the barn, maybe. He don't never go near that barn, cause he's afraid it'll fall on him, but me and you know that 'ere barn'll still be a-standing there when me and you both are ghosts.

She'd been keeping Bess in the barn for some time now, and knew it was safe, but she didn't like the idea of ever becoming a ghost.

If she became a ghost, she'd really have to associate with Sugrue again. She wondered if ghosts could ever have sex. But she went out to the barn, and she assumed that Adam was somewhere behind or beside her. The kitten Latha tried to follow, but she shooed it away. Then in a dark corner of the barn, she said, "Now, Adam, if you're so good at play-like, would you like to pretend you're giving me my first kiss?" She held out her arms.

Silence. Then his voice said, *When you was still my age, I used to kiss ye all the time, specially when you was asleep. You may not know it, but you've been kissed many a time before.*

"Kiss me now. So I'll know it." She continued holding out her arms. She closed her eyes, to aid her own make-believe. And behold, verily it seemed that a pair of warm lips pressed against her own, for a long moment. She whispered, "Put your tongue in my mouth," and she opened her mouth and her tongue seemed to feel a wet tongue sliding along it, all the way to the back, and then rolling around inside her mouth. Her knees buckled and her whole body trembled with desire. "Kiss my neck," she requested, tilting her head. And behold those splendid lips of his kissed her in several places from her collarbone to her earlobe. "Oh, *Adam,*" she said. She unbuttoned her dress so that the top of it would fall below her breasts. "Kiss my breasts," she asked. His kisses there turned her knees to jelly. Fortunately they were standing amidst the hay that she'd cut and stacked for Bess' winter feed. She reflected that it was Adam who had taught her how to cut hay and how to stack the hay, and she wondered if he had even anticipated this use that they would put to the hay. She pulled him down with her into the soft hay. She asked, "Is your dick hard?" Silence. Had she said the wrong thing or in the wrong way? She waited, and then apologized, "I didn't mean to embarrass you."

I jist don't much care to hear you call it that, on account of that's what Sog called it.

"What do you call it?"

Actually, I don't call it nothing. But if you've just got to mention it, I reckon you could call it my dood.

She laughed. "Oh, goody! What if I called it your doody? Then it would rhyme with my poody, which it's supposed to fit."

Call it whatever you care to.

"But you *do* have a doody?"

Sure as shootin.

"And is your doody stiff right now?"

Iffen you're so good at make-believe, why don't ye take aholt of it and see for yourself?

She closed her eyes again and took a deep breath and reached down between them. It was her duty to feel his doody. And there it was! He must've already unbuttoned his fly. Good heavens, but it was *big*. Much bigger than that limp weenie that Sugrue had had. She wrapped her fingers around it and used her index finger to explore the smooth knob on the end of it. In the back of her mind she knew that she was just imagining all of this, that this was just play-like, and she knew also that she had had so much to drink that she could imagine she was flying away if she wanted to. But she did not want to fly away. She wanted to lie here in Adam's arms and she wanted Adam to put that walloping doody inside of her. "Your turn to feel me," she told him. And he did, timidly at first, lifting the hem of her calico dress. She was wearing the pair of silk panties Latha had given her, and she let Adam feel her through the silk for a while and then she took her hand off his doody so she could remove her panties. "Adam," she requested, "why don't you take off all your clothes?"

I aint never done that in all the years I've been here.

She sniffed. "It's a wonder they don't stink if they've never been washed."

Aint you a barrel of laughs, though? Okay, there, do I look any better now?

Adam had just a little hair on his chest and around his doody. She was fascinated, as she was with jacks-in-the-pulpit, with the two large lumps clinging to the root of his doody, which her girlfriend Kelly had first taught her to call nuts, or balls. She cupped them in her hand; they were not hairy but downy. She wondered if he had a special name for those too, and she asked him, and he coughed and said them was just his cods.

She had an overpowering urge to creep down and take his doody into her mouth and see if it was more fun to do it because she wanted to do it and not because he, like Sugrue, had made her do it. So she did. Adam gasped and she could feel his fingers in the back of her hair. She understood that what she ought to do is not suck it as you would suck a thumb or a nipple but move it in and out of your mouth over and over. So she did. She took her mouth off long enough to ask him, "Do you like that?"

He confessed, *I used to allus imagine ye a-doing that whenever I… when I was… when I didn't have nobody to…when I was trying to…*

He didn't have a word for that, whatever it was that happened to boys when all of a sudden their doodies throbbed and spewed out a lot of fluid, the equivalent of what she had called *reaching*. So she used that word to supply the end of his sentence, "…when you were trying to make yourself reach?"

Yep, if ye wanter call it that, and if you keep that up, I'm sure enough a-going to.

Instead of understanding that he wanted her to stop or slow down, she speeded up and, recalling a scene from *Lighting Bug* that was so exciting she had memorized it, she was swallowing and unswallowing his doody as rapidly as she could bob her head and her head was bobbing so rapidly it shook her whole body, and he grabbed her hair and tried to pull her away but she hung on for dear life and buried her lips at the root of his doody and waited until the last spurtle had dribbled down her gullet. It was so real, the taste of him, all that warm liquid in her dry mouth, that she knew she could not possibly be just making-believe.

He lay there panting and she waited a long time to see if he might reciprocate what she had done for him, but either because that would be beyond the thoughts of a twelve-year-old or because he didn't even realize how good it would make her feel and that she could come too, he made no move to do it and she lacked the words to ask him. She said to herself, "For heaven's sake, woman, you're in charge of this whole thing for yourself, so do whatever you feel like doing." But she could not will him to do that. By and by, they began to talk again, about nothing important, or about the barrel she was going to try to make in the shop, or about the saxifrage plant she'd found, which he called alumroot, with small but lovely white flowers and large glorious hairy leaves. He talked about the uses of alumroot, but then he said, *It's got hard again, if you got any more idees.* And she certainly had one idee, which she'd intended all along: just to do it the way it is supposed to be done, with her legs spread and him above her. She cried out when the mighty dood pierced her poody. All he knew to do was to thrust, in the same way but faster and faster, which was fine but not the best, and she wrapped her legs around his waist and used her hands on his butt to show him the best.

What convinced her beyond doubt that she had not merely created this whole thing in her imagination or make-believe was that she never once touched herself. When she finally and triumphantly reached, it was entirely from what he was doing to her and for her. And he let her know that it was happening again to him too, and she could actually feel herself filling up with his fluid. When they were both recovered and stopped breathing so hard, she remarked, "This has been the best birthday I ever had."

Through the rest of the autumn and the relatively mild winter and on into the spring, they did it whenever they felt like it. He helped her make her own barrel in the cooper's shop; it was so much more complicated than just making a firkin, but it was a real barrel. Twelve-year-old Adam had not ever made an entire barrel himself, only a churn, so in a sense she was making it for both of them. Of course they often had to interrupt the making of the barrel to make love in the cooper's shop, on the earthen floor or even standing, or sometimes with her sitting on the toolbench and him standing between her legs.

She never again had to use her hands on herself. She was so filled with longing and love that she was inspired to use the paper Latha had given her to begin writing stories. She wrote one story about what was going on down in Stay More between Latha's granddaughter and the man named Larry, who lived in separate houses but finally got together. She wrote another story about the skeleton Sugrue. She wrote a witty story about Robert, her bobcat. One story which she couldn't finish although she even read it aloud to Adam and asked for his suggestions, was about what happened to Adam when he went to California and grew up and became rich but did not live happily ever after. She had better luck writing about things that she knew from her own experience, and the best of all these stories was about a seventeen-year-old woman and her passionate affair with a twelve-year-old boy.

But despite the believability of this story, and of her own experience upon which it was based, it was not "real." It lacked tangibility, or palpability or whatever you call the actual contact of living flesh.

For a long time she had been thinking of asking Hreapha to get her a horse for her eighteenth birthday. A horse was powerful and she could ride it all over the mountain. Her lover Adam agreed with her that a horse would be a mighty fine thing to have. He could ride it behind her...although he could never ride it beyond his haunt.

But as the summer came and her eighteenth birthday loomed, she realized it was not a horse she wanted or needed. More than anything, what she most desired to have was a living, breathing, visible *man*.

Chapter forty-five

Woo. The bad news about the babe Latha was that she was a night sleeper. The tough shit about all these so-called *tame* cats was that they took up the habits of humans, who for some stupid reason liked to sleep away the best time of day or rather night, namely dark, when everything is happening, man. For ten fucking years now he had had to put up with it, even pretending, early on, that he was asleep himself, just so's he could cuddle up with them under the blankets, when all the while, for hours, he'd have rather been perched on a rock ledge in the moonlight, watching the world go by and ready to pounce or score or just hang easy and let it all happen. He'd hoped, when Latha signed on with the crew, that she might join the night shift along with himself, Ralgrub and her boys, Pogo, and now the other new one, Ged, or Alma Giddyup or however the fuck you pronounced her long name. (He wasn't sure about Sparkle, who seemed to sleep all the time anyway.) But no, Latha, a real bearcat who didn't take long at all to grow out of kittenhood into ripening puberty, was always asleep when he came pussyfooting around, midnightish, with action on his mind. If he had any hope of banging her, he'd have to do it at night when his wife was asleep and he could sneak away.

433

Hroberta had never been able to accept the simple law of nature that no self-respecting wildcat stud is monogamous. He'd never forget the first time he'd slipped away from her and was gone all night, coming home in the morning soaked with the fragrances of a dame, *of his own species,* mind you, and Hroberta had torn into him and chewed him up and then went and told her brothers and her mother, his sweet old mother-in-law, and they had ganged and jumped him and chewed him up and left him for dead. Woo.

He ought to have learned a lesson, but there is simply no going against nature, which dictates that wildcat dudes must mate up with anything they meet up with. Meet up with, mate up with, that had always been his motto. How else would he have mated up with a dog in the first place, for godsakes? Hroberta probably liked to think that he thought she was charming and alluring and desirable, but actually she had just been a handy hump, and a bit too big for him at that. Females of his own species were less than a third the size of males, which means that a female bobcat is not much bigger than a so-called *house*cat, which unfortunately Latha was determined to become, spending all her nights curled up at the head of the Queen's bed. By the way, that was one of the differences between cats and dogs: dogs wanted the foot of the bed. In his childhood and youth, about which he often had sentimental memories, Robert wanted the head of the bed, where he just pretended to sleep while he had thoughts of a rock ledge in the moonlight.

The dogs thought that because the Queen loved them and provided them with a home and took good care of them and petted them, she must be God. Robert knew that since she loved him and provided him with a home and took good care of him and petted him, *he* was God.

The dogs, and some of the other animals too, especially Paddington before he took it on the lam, were always "marking" what they thought was their territory, pissing all over the place. Robert didn't need to do that because he *knew* that all of the territory was his. The only marking he did was to spray his special atomizer on anything he desired, such as Hroberta or a passing chicken or the davenport.

There were other differences: the dogs always came running whenever the Queen called them. Robert (and he hoped now Latha too) let it be known that he was immune to verbal summons. Whenever the Queen talked to them, the dogs, particularly his sweet old-lady-in-law, would tilt their heads and act as if they were listening. If the Queen tried any of that language-stuff on him, Robert would just yawn in her face. The dogs were always doing things for the Queen, getting her new pets for her birthday and fetching things and even, woo, digging holes for her. In the beginning Robert had brought her a dead mouse but she didn't like it, so he hadn't brought her anything since.

And now she wanted them to bring her a man for her eighteenth birthday. Man, a *man*. Right. Big deal. He understood what she needed one for, not to patch the roof or plow the garden but to plow *her* garden, which he himself at one time had attempted in a fumbling roundabout way to do, not knowing she was years short of puberty but driven by his motto, meet up with, mate up with. (When they'd acquired Sparkle for the Queen's fourteenth, that dazzling hunk of crystal quartz, he'd made at least a shot, albeit futile, at humping it too. Woo.) What was apparently a secret to everyone else—where the hell had ole Pad gone—was no secret to Robert: Robert knew for a fact that ole Pad had gone off in search of ass.

Had they forgotten that it had been Robert who had found Pad in the first place, in a cave down the mountain? That particular cave was a lair for bears, and Pad had wandered off and revisited his childhood home and discovered there a comely sow who quickly made him forget whatever fun he'd had in the Queen's menagerie.

Robert had watched them balling, enjoying the show without being detected, a thing he was good at. If you needed any skulking done, Robert was your cat. He didn't have a dog's nose that could smell a turd a mile away, but he had in the roof of his mouth two little holes that led directly to whatever olfactory power his brain possessed and whenever he held his mouth open to allow the various vapors to congregate inside, he could discriminate among the most subtle pheromones. That, coupled with his limitless territory and his ability to climb trees and go anywhere, made him the perfect snoop, sleuth, tracker, *bloodhound* if you will. So if they wanted to find a man for the Queen, who better to ask?

In fact, unbeknownst to the rest of the stay-at-homes, he had ranged widely all over the countryside and already knew the whereabouts of all the eligible men. That time when they'd all gone out on the bear cub hunt for the Queen's twelfth, and everybody was perishing of thirst, and Robert himself had complained, Woo, there's got to be some way to get off this fucking mountain and find a creek, he was actually just pretending, just to conceal his knowledge of the countryside. He'd known damn well how to get off the fucking mountain, in any one of several different directions. Otherwise he'd literally have perished of thirst, because next to ass, water was his favorite thing in all the world. He couldn't live without it (and he nostalgically remembered swimming in his future mother-in-law's water dish when he was just a kitten). Frequently during that bear-cub expedition he had sneaked away from the others to a few sources of water known only to him. So all right, he was sneaky. He was born that way. He was also born a loner and didn't give a shit for the clubbishness of all the Queen's other critters, including especially this latest, Ged, who you couldn't even give a friendly poke because she had hard plates all over her pudgy body. And he'd never got along with Sheba; who wants to be friends with a bitching *snake* anyhow? Even though he'd saved her life twice by killing an owl who tried to eat her and again by chasing off a possum (not the same one who became good old Pogo), he resented Sheba for her inroads on his food supply, sometimes beating him to the mice that were his staple food. Come to think of it, he didn't even like females in general, as a rule, except when he had the hots for them. He liked the *smell* of the Queen, he liked to nuzzle her armpits and lately he was nuts about that warm woodsy Tabu stuff she was wearing, but any kind of strong scent just drove him wild anyway, him who was so wild to begin with.

So, being so unsociable, he didn't like the idea of this jam session that his brother-in-law Hrolf called to discuss the acquisition of a human male for the Queen's benefit, but he went anyhow, just to avoid further unpleasantries with his old-lady-in-law.

You don't fool me, Hreapha said to him. I know that you've been around, and you've smelled a lot more men than I have.

Yeah, Moms, he replied, but they're all old farts.

You're an old fart yourself, she said.

Which was true, maybe. He'd lived at least half of his expected life span, which somehow hadn't dimmed his libido. The babe Latha had called him a "dirty old cat," and he didn't like being thought of as such. But presumably the Queen needed some manflesh that was still fairly fresh, somebody if not her own age at least not a dirty old man, as all of the eligible males Robert had sniffed probably were. This past year the Queen had become so desperate for fresh manflesh that she'd taken up imaginary banging with that fucking *figment* who supposedly lived here. Among his other idiosyncrasies, Robert was the only one of them all who refused to believe in the existence of the so-called *in-habit*, a harebrained notion if ever he'd humped a hare. Sure, Robert had heard the voice, and it always spooked him, it really creeped him out because he couldn't smell any saliva or halitosis producing the voice, but he was a dogmatic cat and couldn't accept the idea of invisibility. It might be fun, and it certainly was comforting, but it don't put no groceries in your belly. Just to try to understand or sympathize with the Queen, Robert had tried to imagine the sexiest possible babe, of his own species, mind you, and he had tried to get it on with her, and it hadn't worked at all, man. Woo.

So he was glad that "Adam" was excluded from the jam session. Hreapha began the meeting by explaining that they wanted to keep the upcoming birthday gift a secret from the *in-habit*, because in view of the fact that "Adam" had fallen in love with the Queen, and vice versa, it would make the *in-habit* very jealous to know that he was about to be replaced by a real live male. So the jam session was being held at a time and place when the Queen was in her bedroom making out with "Adam" and neither of them would know about the proceedings. Robert didn't buy this "in love" stuff, whatever it meant, but he was willing to go along with the idea of making sure that an invisible entity remained out of sight.

The meeting is called to order, Hrolf said. First order of business: volunteers for the expedition. I'll lead it, of course.

Count me out this time, Robert said. He didn't like speaking in dogtalk, but it was required.

The others all stared at him. Hrolf said, Do you mind telling us why?

I don't like human men, Robert said.

You're just jealous, his wife Hroberta put in. You just don't want any more competition for *her* affection and petting and favor.

No, hon, that isn't it, his mother-in-law said. Robert doesn't want to go on the expedition because he doesn't need to. He already knows where all the men are.

Is that true? Hrolf demanded of him.

He took his time replying. He didn't like the know-it-all attitude of his mother-in-law, but he was willing to grant that if there was any creature on this earth who did in fact know it all, it was she. Finally he grumbled, Yeah. If the purpose of your foray is just to *find* a man, I could save you the trouble and tell you where all of them are.

Holy cats, Hrolf said. So tell us.

Robert got to his feet. His joints were getting a bit creaky in his early middle-age, and he didn't relish a long hike anyway. But he had already been to the four little villages or almost-ghost towns that lay to the four points of the compass from this mountain, and he had inspected the few inhabitants of those villages, not one of whom was in the bud of youth, and he could present a catalog, as he now began to do, of all his findings. After he had finished describing to the best of his ability each and every man he had ever beheld, at least those who were not living with women, the members of the jam session discussed each in turn, and they came up with a short list, three of the best, or rather, considering that two of them were drunkards, three of the least undesirable. One was rather handy: the farmer who dwelt at the north foot of the mountain, from whom they had stolen Bess, the cow.

Bess spoke up, as best she could in dogtalk, not her natural tongue. That man is an asswipe, she said. I wouldn't give him to my worst enemy.

Another of the three lived alone in what had been called a

"hotel" in Stay More. Hreapha knew his name to be Larry but knew him to have a severe drinking problem and also to be possibly involved with a neighbor-woman named Sharon.

The third, the only reasonably sober one of the three, although Robert had observed him imbibing too, was a man named George who was in charge of the ham-processing operation in Stay More valley and lived alone at the west foot of Madewell Mountain.

The jam session was being held at Early Bright, to accommodate members who were nocturnal as well as the night sleepers, and as Early Bright changed to Later Bright, the meeting was adjourned so that all the nocturnals could grab a few z's. The meeting was resumed at Early Dark, and went on until Later Dark, when the night sleepers were beginning to nod off, but a vote was taken and a decision was finally reached: George was the man.

Second order of business, Hrolf declared. How for godsakes do we get George to come up here on the mountain?

Since Hrolf loved to organize and lead expeditions, he suggested a reconnaissance to George's domicile, and Robert grudgingly agreed to take them there. What became known as the Man-Snatching Crew consisted of Hrolf, Robert, Pogo, Dewey, Ralgrub and three of Ralgrub's grown sons, Rebbor, Tidnab, and Feiht. The brazen Ged wanted to go too, but her armor slowed her movements. They went not once but several times over the next several weeks, trying to gather as much intelligence as possible about the man, his appearance, his habits, and his movements. In time they knew almost everything about him that was worth knowing, and the more they learned about him the less Robert thought that George would make a desirable addition to the population of Madewell Mountain.

But the Queen's birthday was coming up in just another week or so and they had to fulfill their commitment. Woo, it wasn't going to be easy. Robert remembered all too well their acquisition of Bess; how they'd had to open her gate and threaten and cajole her away from the other cows and scare her into climbing the mountain and help her out of a ravine she fell into, where she lay bawling for hours, and, man, like try to get her to understand that she was not going to be harmed but given a chance to live in Paradise. How were they

439

going to persuade George? They couldn't just bark at him and nip at his heels and get him to climb the mountain.

George had a pick-up truck with a rifle mounted in the rear-view window, and he often drove that pick-up all over the back roads of the countryside. And it was one of those powerful machines that could climb the most rugged trail. Like Robert, George was in early middle-age, muscular but pot-bellied, a not unkindly face but not handsome either, never seen without a billed cap on his head, bearing an image of a redbird, a cap in which he even slept. He reminded Robert too strongly of Sugrue Alan. The Man-Snatching Crew, in their study of his movements, determined when they could expect that he might be driving along the road that passed the entrance to the winding trail on the north side of Madewell Mountain.

Ralgrub and her sons, true to their assbackward names, stole the contents of a case of whiskey from the Queen's storeroom, and under the cover of darkness positioned the contents at intervals away from the house, a bottle every so hither and yon left standing upright along a route from the house to the end of the North Way trail, a total of twelve bottles.

Then, on or around the Queen's birthday, Dewey, a magnificent buck with a rack of antlers having a dozen points, would be positioned strategically at the point where the North Way trail met the road at the foot of the mountain. It was going to be tricky, man. Dewey said he'd sacrifice his life if necessary for the Queen's birthday.

The idea was that George would come riding along, spot Dewey and take off after him. Dewey would head up the mountain trail as fast as his legs could carry him. George would not stop to load his gun but would keep driving in pursuit of Dewey, all the way to the top, where he would discover, just as Dewey disappeared into the woods, the first of the twelve bottles of good booze. George would take the edge off his disappointment at losing Dewey by sampling the fine whisky. At that point Ralgrub herself would sneak up behind him, snatch that prized cap off his head and run with it toward the second bottle of whiskey, where she would deposit it atop the bottle. George would find the second bottle, drink therefrom, replace the cap on his head, drink some more, and one of the other raccoons,

Rebbor, Tidnab, or Feiht, would grab the cap off his head and take it on to the third bottle. And so on, on up the path that led to the house. It was assumed, or hoped, that by the time he reached the house, George would be completely docile, if not totally sloshed, and would not object to becoming a birthday present for the Queen.

It is an ingenious strategy, but Robert, although he is proud of his contributions to the planning of it, is skeptical that it will work. And sure enough, as he takes his supervisory position at the foot of the trail on the afternoon of the appointed day, things begin to go haywire. For one thing, the whole motherfucking tense switches from past to present, a sure sign that expectations are either getting out of hand or else are so supercharged you can't tell your ass hair from your whiskers. He tests it: he turns this way and that, he shakes his head. No mistake, he's caught tight in the present. Hey Hrolf buddy, he calls to his companion, did you notice? Are we now in the *now?* You know, the *present* tense?

Yeah, Hrolf says, and don't look now but there comes our man George.

George drives his present-tense vehicle up the road, spots old Dewey, slams on his brakes, reaches for his gun, Dewey takes off lickety-split up the mountain trail, George turns into the trail, shifts into low-lock, spins his wheels, takes off after Dewey, but then slams on his brakes again.

George rolls down his window, sticks his head out, and yells at Dewey, "You're shore lucky it aint hunting season yet!"

Then George looks for and finds a place to back his truck and turn around and leave the mountain trail.

Ralgrub, Robert shouts, grab his cap *now!*

She leaps for the open window but misses and crashes into the door. George says to her, "It aint coon season yet neither!"

And then, in this crazy present tense, another vehicle appears. It is one of those big rugged automobiles, not a pick-up, which can go anywhere in the back country. The man driving rolls down his window. He and George exchange howdies.

"Have you been up there on the mountain?" the man asks.

"Naw," George says. "I was a-fixin to take off after a thirteen-point buck, and then I recollected the season don't start till November. If I had me a bow 'n air I reckon I could shoot him commencing October first, but that's still a ways off."

"Say, aren't you George Dinsmore?" the fellow asks. "Latha told me you were still around."

"Yeah, that's me. Don't I know you?"

"I reckon you ought to. We went to school together."

"Holy hoptoads, don't tell me you're old Ad Madewell! Why, I aint see you in a coon's age. And yonder runs the old coon."

Woo.

Chapter forty-six

Woo indeed. I have forgiven Bob for not believing in me. I had noticed, very early on, another difference between dogs and cats that he did not consider in the above soliloquy: dogs just drop their business in the yard; cats cover their business. They *conceal* it. As Robin had recently realized, apropos the wearing of clothing, all art is a form of a hiding and a seeking and a finding, and that which is hidden is more magically stimulating. Which is not to suggest, or even hint, that Bob, or any cat, considers his feces a work of art to be secreted and secreted. Rather, the point I'm clumsily trying to make is that Bob ought to have believed in me, as most who believe in God do, *because* I was hidden from ordinary perception.

Soon enough, in another tense, he will have plenty of reason to have faith in me, just as the clever reader has long since grinningly suspected that somewhere toward the conclusion of this marvelous tale I would materialize in the flesh so that we all could go have our breakfasts and get on with the workings of our lives.

I said to my darling Robin, early that day, *Darn if it aint your birthday again, and I reckon I caint give ye ary a thing.* I had spent considerable effort taxing my twelve-year-old brain to think of some way to give her, without the power to lift a gift, *something*.

And she said, "Dear sweet Adam honey, you don't have to give me anything. You know that. But there is something that the others are possibly going to give me, and I think I'd better ask you how you'd feel if…"

At that moment Adam Madewell, 46, was driving his expensive four-by-four SUV up the dirt road that winds out of Parthenon, and instead of bearing left toward the Madewell Mountain road he kept on going up the road that led to Stay More, which he had not taken on his previous visit eleven years before. As one's thoughts while driving have a habit of coming and going in rapid, random succession, he was recalling the way Linda used to challenge his occasional use of the Ozark language. "Do you 'reckon' on an abacus or a slide-rule?" she'd say. "And is it 'ary' or windy or gassy or what?" She couldn't even allow him to speak of "dusty dark" without asking, "Why can't you simply say 'dusk'? I don't see any dust."

There had been a time that Linda had taken an interest in his "roots," as she referred to them, wanting, as she said, to learn what made him tick. She had taken an interest in genealogy, long enough to thoroughly research his name, which she'd traced through its variations—Maydwell, Maydewell, Maydenwell, Maidwell, Maidenwell, Medwelle, Meidwell, Meadwell, etc.—back to Alanus de Maidwell of Northhamptonshire in the time of King Henry II in the 12th Century and his son Alan de Maydewell, Sheriff of Northhamptonshire (Adam was uncomfortable at the spelling of the given name, identical to the family name of his old nemesis Sog) but Linda had not been able to establish any connection between the titled Maydwells and those who settled in the Ozarks. "I guess you were white trash," she once said to him. One of the few magazines he subscribed to was *The Ozarks Mountaineer,* but Linda was not interested in glancing at it.

They had so few common interests, apart from barrels and wine. From the beginning, while still on their honeymoon in the Bahamas, they had disagreed on where they'd make their home. He liked his fine big house in St. Helena, but she wanted to live in Glen Ellen, near her father's winery (of which she was now manager), and talked him into it. The Mayacamas Mountains separated the two places, and there was a steep winding road between Glen Ellen and Oakville which he had to take to get to work, a daily nuisance. They were almost in different worlds, Napa and Sonoma counties. Red and white. Steak and lobster. Cabernet Sauvignon was the principal wine of the former, Chardonnay of the latter. Linda's father owned Chateau Duplessis, one of the best vintners of an award-winning Chardonnay, although at the time of their marriage the wine had not yet acquired its reputation; in fact, California wine in general was still little more than jug wine or at best the "fighting varietals" as the affordable but undistinguished table wines would come to be known. Linda's father was the first to admit that his Chardonnay did not acquire its excellence until he began to store it in barrels that were not merely from Madewell Cooperage but were the special "private reserve" barrels made well from Madewell oak staves from Madewell Mountain, Arkansas. Adam, wisely, was stingy in his distribution of these special barrels to certain select customers for their certain select wines, which, because he charged so much more for the barrel itself, became the first truly expensive California wines. Adam, while he still had a sense of humor, liked to joke with Linda that she had married him not for his money or his looks or his brains but for his barrels, which had made the Chateau Duplessis Chardonnay famous.

But it wasn't a joke that her father had never paid him for the barrels, and certainly Adam had never considered sending his father-in-law a bill. Adam's bookkeepers had complained; his sales manager had complained, but Adam had his accountants write it off as a loss for tax purposes, literally hundreds of thousands of dollars worth of barrels. Sometimes, particularly after one of his bitter quarrels with Linda, he wondered if indeed she and her father had simply plotted to have her marry him in order to get all those barrels. André Tchelistcheff had been furious when Adam had confided the situation to him. T remained Adam's principal confidant and, to the extent he had any friends at all, his only friend. For a number of years, they had lunch together at least once a week at Terra, St. Helena's best restaurant. It was T who had to listen to Adam's gripes about the wine industry in general, and to Adam's revelations of disharmony with Linda, and to

Adam's increasing dissatisfaction with the whole state of California, which he had come to feel had lost its soul, if ever it had one in the first place. T never disagreed. "Yes," T said, "Californians are all a bit runny around the edges." Adam could never forget those words.

When Adam was in his early forties and beginning to brood that his life had never yet reached any sort of fulfillment, Linda stopped speaking to him. But of course as with any marital rift, she claimed that he had stopped speaking to her. Eventually they visited a counselor, and Linda played back for the woman a recording she had made of Adam's silences, that is, her own observations and questions captured on the tape followed by complete silence from Adam. So all right, he no longer spoke to her, because, as he told T, "The more we talked, the more reasons we found for not talking." The counselor had also told him that his nightly dreams of flying were a wish to escape from his marriage.

Linda used that as the primary excuse for her affair. She announced, "I met someone who listens to me, who pays attention to me, who cares who I am." For a while, a few months only, Adam moved into an apartment in St. Helena, but then one day when he dressed for work in his suit he poured into his trousers pocket the handful of dirt from the floor of the cooper's shed he had kept since he was twelve. Then he simply called a meeting of the board of directors, resigned as chairman and CEO, appointed his able COO as the new CEO, sold all his stock in the company, and had a long final lunch with T, who was stricken to hear of Adam's intentions, but kissed him on both cheeks in parting and said, "Send me your address when you have one, and each holiday season for your birthday and Christmas I will send you a case of my '79 Pinot Noir."

But Adam wasn't sure he'd have any address to send to André Tchelistcheff. He had no idea what would become of himself. He only knew that, having felt homeless for over thirty years, he was going home. In the back of his SUV he had folded up a tent and a sleeping bag and an air mattress, as well as cooking equipment. He didn't know what to expect; his grandfather had built the house and barn and cooper's shed to last forever but they might have rotted away or been hit by lightning and burned...or maybe his failure to piss on the fire as his father had demanded might have caused the house to burn down. He also had with him all of his possessions worth keeping; three boxes of his favorite books, two boxes of his wine collection, and all the clothes he'd ever need, and he made a last stop at a supermarket in Harrison to pick up as many provisions and groceries as he still had room for.

He noticed that nearly all the houses between Parthenon and Stay More were abandoned. One of them, a ruin he recognized as the old Alan place, had a sign taped to the front door, and he drove up close enough to read it: "GONE TO CALIFORNIA." He breathed a sigh of relief because he hadn't relished the idea of having any contact with Sog Alan. As he approached the village itself, or what had once been the thriving little town of Stay More, tingles ran up his spine. *This here's my town,* he said aloud and laughed to hear himself speaking in his old Ozark accent.

There was just one building in town that still seemed to be occupied, the house and store that had once been Latha Bourne's and had once held the post office, shut down even before Adam had reached school age. On the long front porch, upon which he had sat himself many times in the company of other citizens of the town, there was now a man and a woman, neither of whom he recognized. He didn't know how to ask if Latha was dead. So he asked, "Latha Bourne don't live here no more?"

The woman said, "She lives up yonder a ways at the old Dill place."

"Thank ye kindly," he said, and drove on. He hadn't intended to visit Latha Bourne Dill, he hadn't given it a thought, but he was so delighted to know that she was still alive that he decided to stop at the old Dill dogtrot which he'd passed every day on his way to school.

He pulled into the yard, which was filled with cats and dogs. He remembered fondly how much she liked cats, but he hadn't known she liked dogs too. The dogs were yelling their heads off at him, and one of them, a big handsome golden retriever, was really yowling or yowering at him. Very soon Latha came out of her house and he got out of his SUV to meet her. She was white-haired and a bit stooped but just as gloriously glamorous as he'd always remembered her.

"Howdy, Miz Latha," he said bashfully.

She did not stare long at him. "Goodness gracious," she said. "Lord have mercy. Is that *you*, Ad?"

"Yes'm," he said. "You're sure looking pretty good."

She held out her arms to him, and they embraced. He had never been touched by her before, but now, as they held each other tightly for a long moment, he remembered one of his favorite movies, "Harold and Maude," and decided that he would just ask Latha to marry him, even if she was…he suddenly realized that she and T were exactly the same age.

"So how was California?" she asked.

"It was real sorry," he said. "It was the sorriest place on earth."

She invited him to lunch—dinner actually, which, he recalled, the noon meal was always called in this world. He furnished a 1973 Stag's Leap Cabernet. They talked well into the afternoon, and he reflected that she was easier to talk to than T had been. She brought him up to date on everything, that is to say, nothing, that had been happening in Stay More. He told her what he'd done in California. He mentioned having run into Roseleen Coe, and remarked, "I hope she doesn't bump into Sog Alan too."

"No danger of that," Latha said. "He passed on some ten or eleven years ago."

"Oh. I wish I could say that's too bad but I can't."

"Yes. It's a better world without him," she said. Then as he got up to leave she said, "So what are you fixing to do? Don't be a-rushing off. Stay more and spend the night with me."

"Thank ye kindly, but I reckon I'd better just get on up home."

"Home?" she said. "You don't mean the old Madewell place, do ye?

"Yes'm," he said. "That's where I'm a-heading. Why don't you just come go home with me?"

"Thank ye, I'd admire to, but I reckon I'd better not, this time." Before he got back into his suv, she gave him another hug, and said, "You must've really left a part of yourself up there at the old place."

"I sure did, ma'am," he said.

"You'uns be sure to come and visit me whenever you can," she said.

As he drove off up the Right Prong that skirted the east end of Ledbetter Mountain, he reflected that maybe he didn't remember Ozark speech as well as he'd thought. He'd always considered "you'uns," which is a contraction of "you ones," to be plural, referring to more than one person. In the Deep South, supposedly people said "You all" or "Y'all" when they were addressing only one person, but not in the Ozarks. Maybe he simply hadn't heard her correctly.

When he turns into the mountain trail at the north foot of Madewell Mountain, he notices another grammatical oddity, which gives him pause: time seems to have reallocated itself into the present tense, which doesn't bother him greatly. He understands that the present tense is more cozy and immediate, at least if you don't allow the urgency of it to make you nervous. And he isn't nervous at all. He's exultant. He's rapturous. He's going home.

Hardly has he turned up into the trail when he encounters a man in a pickup. He is quick to recognize good old George Dinsmore, who'd been just a year ahead of him in school. He is glad to have learned from Latha that George is one of the few remaining citizens of Stay More. But it takes George a little while to recognize him, and when he does he is flabbergasted.

They chat a while, and he asks George, "Have you been up yonder to the top lately? Do you know if my house is still there?"

George laughs. "I aint *never* been to the top of that mountain. I been practically everywheres else, but for some reason I never been up there. If you're a-fixing to go and see if you caint make it up to your old homeplace, why, good luck to ye."

Further up the steep trail, which is in such terrible condition it gives his mighty SUV the workout of its life, Adam encounters a bobcat, who scampers off into the woods. Before Adam reaches the gulley where he'd had to turn back before, where that fellow named Leo Spurlock had mired his pick-up, he encounters, or catches glimpses of, several other animals: a mongrel dog, a possum, three raccoons, and that thirteen-point buck that George had mentioned, a magnificent animal. Adam knows that this isn't typical of the animal population of these environs; he'd never in his boyhood seen such a diversity of animals together in one spot. As he is rounding a hairpin curve on the trail he glances into the rear view mirror and it appears that all those animals are following him! He stops, and waits, to see if they catch up with him, but the animals stop too, and keep their distance until he drives on.

Maybe it is the present tense, after all, which is making him feel funny. He is having distinct premonitions of disorder even before he reaches the spot where, he discovers unhappily, the trail comes to a complete end, far short of its original destination. He must stop and exit the vehicle, taking his rifle with him. He examines the terrain, trying to spot anything familiar, but apparently time and thunderstorms have transformed everything. The original course of the trail, over which his grandfather and father had driven so many mule-team loads of barrels and staves, has been totally obliterated. Not a trace remains of the ledges his grandfather had hacked into the bluffs. Now in every direction there are only deep gullies and ravines. In one of the ravines appears to be the remains of a burnt pick-up which had crashed, maybe years before.

Adam makes slow progress on foot. His bad leg hampers his descent into the ravines and his climbing out of them. Looking behind him, he catches an occasional glimpse of one or more of those animals who have been following him, even that big buck.

Finally he comes upon a very strange thing: in a clearing above one of the ravines, in a patch of grass, is standing a bottle of Jack Daniels Black Label whiskey! He opens it, sniffs it, and determines that it is a fresh bottle, untouched, undiluted, unpolluted, perhaps recently left behind by some hunter. But the hunting season, as George has reminded him, hasn't yet begun. His hiking has left Adam thirsty, so he takes a generous swig of the stuff, and it tastes just fine. He lights himself a cigarette. He carries the bottle with him as he continues his hike. But then he comes to another bottle, identical to the first. He does not open the second bottle but continues onward with the first, until he comes to the third, at which point he is distinctly beginning to feel funny, and needs more than a swig from the bottle to settle his nerves. From the lay of the land he has a distinct feeling that he is nearing his destination, and this drives him onward. By the time he arrives at the tenth bottle, he is stumbling not because of his bad leg but because he has consumed nearly a third of the one bottle he carries.

And then he hears the sound. At first he thinks it is just the wind in the trees, but as he listens, limping onward toward the source of the sound, he realizes that what he is hearing is too liquid to be the wind—it is an angel singing, or, no, not singing but vocalizing in wordless tones that rise and hide themselves and then reappear. He stops and listens, entranced. He is reminded of the soprano solo in Vaughan Williams' Symphony No. 3, the *Pastoral*, the soft off-stage *cantilena*, incredibly beautiful and incredibly haunting. Yes, that is the word: haunting. When he reaches the eleventh bottle he converts that adjective into a noun: *haunt*, and he looks down at the earth beside the eleventh bottle, seeing there an imaginary boundary line, and knows that something truly fantastic is happening to me.

This is not merely present tense, it is present tense first person singular, and I having reached my haunt have come at long last into full possession of myself.

But perhaps not completely full, just yet. Because as I reach the twelfth and last bottle, which stands at the very edge of my meadow, and I happily behold in the distance that my beloved house and its outbuildings are all still standing, I descry the source of that lovely singing. In the yard of my house stands a tall woman, nude, her blonde hair cascading to her knees but not concealing her nakedness. There is a serpent entwined around her neck and upper torso. My whisky-fuddled head is a vortex of thoughts; I am thrilled beyond measure to be home at last but I am uncertain if I am actually alive or just dreaming of some Eve in Paradise. I am Adam. And then practical reality takes hold of me, and I realize that probably my homestead has been expropriated by some hippies, and she is just some free-spirited flower child left over or lost from a previous time, as the Ozarkers themselves were left-over and lost from the mainstream. This thought fills me with chagrin.

And then she spots me. She seems to be having trouble focusing her eyes on me, but she has seen me. Although I have an impulse to turn and flee, I am visited by the last and most powerful of this day's haunting oddities; she may or may not be Eve, but I am certainly Adam, and I have not ever left this place, my haunt, nor shall I ever leave it again.

Chapter forty-seven

I t was the most challenging and wracking thing she'd ever had to do, and the doing of it had practically ruined this special day of days. She cared so much for his feelings and did not want to hurt him in any way. She really was deeply in love with him, but she had to make him understand that she simply could not face a future in which he not only remained ethereal and invisible but also remained twelve years old forever. What would it be like when she was thirty or forty or fifty years old, and he was still only twelve? She had hoped that his wisdom and mother wit, greater than she herself had possessed at twelve, would permit him to accept and even welcome the presence of the newest addition to the circus, but she could hear her own voice quavering when she said to him, "I think I'd better ask you how you'd feel if my eighteenth birthday present from the others was a man, I mean a real live one, I mean one who could truly lift things and eat what I cooked for him and even be able to go to sleep at night..."

In yore bed. His voice was matter-of-fact, and he added, *Tell ye the honest truth, I druther see a man a-sleeping there than a bar, but*

*you'uns would just have to be able to sleep with me a-watching over
you'uns.*

"And you'd be watching everything else we did, wouldn't you?"
she asked. "Would you be terribly jealous of him? Would you hate
me for it?"

As was so often the case that it didn't even bother her, he did
not answer. She waited, as usual, giving him plenty of time to come
up with the courtesy of a reply, and, as usual, he did not. She had
much to do today, to get ready, and as she put the layer cake into the
oven, she went on talking. "Don't you see? That's one of the main
things I want him for, that he'll answer me when I say something to
him, which you won't do." But he still did not speak. "Or at least, if
he won't answer, at least I can *see* his face and tell what he's thinking
or feeling. Don't you understand how frustrating it is for me that I
can't even see your face?"

There was not any response to that question, either. She poured
hot water into the tin tub and got a fresh bar of her special lavender-
scented beeswax lye soap. She climbed into the tub and said, "Would
you like to get in here with me? I'll scrub your back and behind your
ears and under your cods." But he did not make his presence known
or felt. She decided, for the first time, for this special occasion, to
shave her legs, which were just too downy and even hairy in places,
and she used Sugrue's razor to scrape it all off, although she nicked
the skin in a couple of places. "There," she said when she was finished.
"See how smooth they are. Put your hand on them and feel them."
But he did not.

She trimmed her fingernails and her toenails and cleaned under
them. She washed her hair and was tempted to cut it, and she asked
Adam if he'd mind if she cut her hair, but he wouldn't answer. She
decided not to cut it; she started braiding it but then determined it
would look better if she just let it hang loose to her knees. She studied
herself in the mirror, and carefully brushed some pokeberry juice onto
her lips to empurple them. She dabbed a generous amount of Tabu
around her chin, her neck and the top of her full breasts. "Before I
get dressed," she said to Adam, "could you see your way to making
love once again?" Surprise: he didn't answer. "Oh, Adam," she sighed.

"Don't you understand? When the man is here, I'll still always love you and I'll still make love to you whenever you want to. Whenever you get hard, all you'll have to do is let me know. We'll have to keep it a secret from him, but that shouldn't be too difficult, should it?"

She put on Latha's old-timey dress, which had already gone through several washings since Robin had acquired it, and was beginning to look faded and frayed. She studied herself in the mirror again with the dress on and was skeptical. She wondered, for the first time, how particular the man might be. Would he think she looked cheap? She had no idea what sort of man she'd be getting for her birthday. All she knew about him was that he'd have two arms, two legs, a head, and a dood...no, that would have to remain Adam's private word. And it was to be hoped that the man would be able to speak English. She believed without any doubt that Hreapha and the others *would* be presenting her with a man for her birthday. If she had asked them for an elephant, they would have got one for her. Or at least a horse, and now with her misgivings she began to wish that she'd asked for a horse instead.

She was starting to feel uneasy about the arrival of the gift, and she went into the storeroom to get a bottle of Jack Daniels. An entire case was empty, and she wondered if she had been consuming more of the stuff than she had realized. She opened a bottle, and drank straight from it, which she didn't usually like to do. "Care for a swig, honey?" she asked, but Adam was still sulking and silent and maybe even absent. Maybe he had gone out to the cooper's shed to escape from her entirely, and possibly he was curled up inside her barrel. He had told her that he was so proud of the barrel that she'd made with his advice and instructions that it had become his favorite place, not to sleep, since he never slept, but just to curl up and hide from the world. "Why would you want to hide from the world?" she had asked him. "Especially since you're invisible anyhow?" And for once he had tried to answer her.

Sometimes it's just too much with me, he'd said, and she had thought about that for a long time.

The man coming was of the world, and she feared that he might be too much *with* her. She didn't care if he was young or old, so long as he was older than Adam and ideally younger than Sugrue. She hoped he would be good-looking, and perhaps tall, and she hoped he would be intelligent enough to carry on a decent conversation with, and she certainly hoped, above all else, that he would be marvelous at sex. But what if he was too much *with* her? What if he couldn't accept her as she was? And *love*, or learn to love, her as she was?

And what am I? she asks herself. Do I know? The question haunts her almost as much as she is troubled by the sudden realization that her entire past, her whole story of eleven long years endured in this lonely aerie, is all now past, behind her, and she is living in and for the present, the very real but still fantastic present.

She removes the dress. She thinks aloud, "If he will have me, he will have me as I truly am, unadorned."

She takes another lusty swallow from her bottle, and steps outside the door. Many of her family are there, those who have not gone off on the quest for a man—Hreapha, Ged, Latha, Bess, Hroberta, Sigh and Sue, and Sheba, resting atop Sparkle—Robin lifts Sheba, gives her a kiss, and wraps her around her neck. Robin breaks spontaneously into song, or rather an inspired vocalization of abstract sounds born deep inside her lungs and transformed through all her vocal chords and tongue and the chamber of her mouth and even her nose. Such music delights most of her family, except Adam, who has complained that her melodious chants are *jist a lot of hootin and a-hollerin*. Another reason she wants a man, and with any luck a man who appreciates her singing.

She dances out to the cooper's shed and peers into her barrel. She is prouder of that barrel than anything else she's ever done. It is tight and solid and although she has not yet attempted to fill it, it will probably hold any liquid without leaking. Is Adam in there right now? She takes Sheba temporarily off her neck and puts her down. Then she whispers into the barrel, "Adam, dear sweet wonderful Adam, could you at least kiss me for one last time before he gets here?"

She begins to fear that Adam is permanently silent, perhaps even permanently gone. Maybe he has left his haunt and established another haunt somewhere else. But how could he do that? The afternoon is getting on, and perhaps those members of the family who have gone to find a man have not had any luck. She has not even tried to imagine how they might possibly have obtained a man. She has not wanted to risk trying to imagine. And possibly her birthday wish is not going to come true, after all. She decides to go inside and light the cake's eighteen candles that she has made out of beeswax.

Then she hears, far off, the faint sound of the motor of a vehicle laboring uphill. It is a sound she has not heard since Sugrue's truck made its final trip with her in it. She suspects that it is the man, coming up the mountain, and when she sings again, she truly sings with passion and joy. But the trills and tremolos in her soprano voice are not controlled and deliberate; they reflect her increasing anxiety. What if the man is simply not nice? What if he isn't interested in making love but only in raping her? What if he's cruel?

During her long wait, she practices her taekwondo. She discovers that she can sing and kick and chop at the same time. An hour passes, and her legs and arms grow tired. She has to save some of her energy for the actual employment of the taekwondo, if need be. As one more precaution, priding herself on the resourcefulness of the idea, she loads both barrels of the shotgun and all six chambers of Sugrue's service revolver.

She sets the weapons down on the porch, and resumes her singing, a distinct tone of elation now in her music, because she is ready. Ready for anything. Ready for the man, the world, for *life*. If the melody of her music consists of a hiding and a finding, then it is now mostly discovery, and the thrill therein.

Now she sees him, across the meadow. Her eyesight being so poor, she can only discern his fuzzy silhouette. Behind him stands the majestic silhouette of Dewey, his branchy antlers a calligraphy on the sky. She continues singing, interrupted only by her beloved dog, who says "Hreapha," that is, Happy Best of All Possible Birthdays.

Then Hreapha's son comes bounding across the meadow, barking HROLF! HROLF! HROLF! at the top of his voice. He arrives quickly and seems to be trying to tell his mother something. Behind him come Ralgrub and her thieving sons, Rebbor, Tidnab, and Feiht. And then Pogo and Robert, the latter running as if he's being pursued. But the man is not pursuing him. The man is walking slowly across

457

the meadow. In fact he is limping, and for a brief terrible moment Robin thinks that this is Sugrue's ghost, because the limp resembles that of Sugrue's final affliction, and even the man himself, what little she can see of him, seems to have Sugrue's shape. And worst of all, there is smoke rising from him, smoke coming out of his mouth, smoke from a cigarette in his fingers. And in his other hand he holds a half-empty bottle of Jack Daniels! Yes, it could be Sugrue, but her credulity, which can accept and even love an immaterial *in-habit*, cannot accept the idea of a daytime ghost.

Robin stops singing. As if to continue her music, Sigh and Sue on a nearby limb are cooing, or at least Sigh is, since Sue doesn't sing; and Bess is mooing, and Robert is wooing, and the dogs are barking, and there is even Ged on percussion, grunting.

She has not even given any thought to what she will say. Maybe the man, who has now almost reached her, will speak the first words, and all she'll have to do is think of something clever to say in response. Maybe he's just some guy who has lost his way and will ask her for directions…as if she'd know.

Will they do something as piddling as shake hands? Or will they rush into each other's arms? Or will they just keep their distance and make idle chitchat?

Suddenly her nakedness bothers her, and she wishes she had not chosen it. Her nervous hands try to arrange her long hair so that it covers her breasts and her poody. Then she can only stand and stare as he nears her.

He is only a few feet away when he stops. She can see him fairly well now. He is tall and extremely good-looking, but he is not young. He is perhaps as old as Sugrue was. She is relieved that he certainly is not Sugrue, nor his ghost. And he has thrown away his cigarette.

Finally it is he who speaks first. "Howdy," he says with a big smile.

"Howdy yourself," she says. She even imitates his accent, which is like Sugrue's, like Latha's, like Grandpa's. She realizes she hasn't thought of Grandpa Spurlock in a very long time, and she surprises herself that she is standing here wondering what Grandpa Spurlock would think if he could see her like this.

The man has an enormous smile on his face, as if she has said something funny. Or maybe he is just loopy from drinking. "You sure sing pretty," he says. "I'm sorry I interrupted ye."

Well, at least he doesn't share Adam's low opinion of her singing. "Thank you," she says. "I'm very glad you like it."

At her feet, her dog is asking, "Hreapha?" that is, Well, do you like him?

And she can only say, "Thank you, Hreapha. I guess he'll do." She won't tell Hreapha that the man is not exactly her ideal, and he certainly isn't perfect: in addition to his limp, he has an index finger missing from his right hand. Missing finger? She is beginning to have an uneasy thought. The thought is superceded or supplemented—she isn't sure which—by something she remembers Latha had said. Although she doesn't have any lemonade to offer the man, she can repeat Latha's words, "But here I'm being chatty and rude and haven't even told you my name. I'm Robin Kerr."

"Yes," he says, and holds out that missing-finger hand for a shake, and she takes it and accepts his handshake.

She waits, and then she says, "But you are being ruder if you don't tell me your name."

That enormous smile again, and there isn't a bit of humor in what she has just said. "I think you know who I am," he says. He waits for her to recognize him, but how can she? Then he says, "Why don't you take off that there snake and run in and put on your pretty dress?" And when her mouth drops open in awe or whatever, he adds, "Because, come to think on it, I reckon I'd want ye more in that there dress than I'd want ye as you generally are, a-running around all over creation a-wearing nothing but a smile." She cannot say a blessed thing. So he observes, "And you're not even wearing a smile, now."

Racking her brain, she comes up, at last, with a single word. "Adam?"

His smile is about to cleave his jaw. "Madewell," he says.

"I cannot believe this," she says. "I simply cannot even begin to believe this."

"If you're having trouble believing it," he says, "just imagine how I started out the day without any inkling of what I'd find up here at the old home place, and as soon as I step over the line into my haunt, here it all is! And here am I! And here are you! Boy, I'm plumb jiggered and struck all of a heap!"

"But where is Adam?" she wants to know. "I mean, if you're Adam, then where's the boy who *in-habits* this place?"

He touches his heart.

She thinks about that, and the thought disturbs her. "Do you mean I'll never see him again?"

"You never *saw* him to begin with."

"But I can't ever be *with* him again."

"You'll always be *with* him."

In time, she believes him, and believes in him, and her only disappointment is that she cannot show him the place because she doesn't need to. You'd expect, if a man came back to his boyhood home after thirty years, that he'd want to take a long, leisurely tour of the premises and see all the little changes, but Adam doesn't need to do that, since he's never left. She wants to show him the barrel she's made, and he dutifully inspects it, and honestly tells her that it wouldn't pass muster at Madewell Cooperage but it is certainly a remarkable piece of workmanship and he is proud of both of them, her and Adam, that is, himself, for having done it. She realizes that she doesn't need to explain the presence of a skeleton in the outhouse to him, because he knows all about it. "How do you feel about indoor toilets?" he asks, and she, remembering Latha's house, grants that they are a lot more convenient and comfortable than outhouses.

At least he can participate wholly in her birthday party, unlike the *in-habit*, who has never been able to sample the birthday cake except in make-believe. He can even light the candles for her, there in the midst of the whole menagerie, all her family and friends, and he can applaud, which the others cannot do, when she blows out all the candles. She will not tell him her wish, nor will she tell it to us, but only those of us with the most impoverished imaginations could fail to guess what it is. She wants to inform him that he is her birthday present, but she assumes he already knows that. He has retained, or has never quite lost, the *in-habit*'s ability to communicate with all the animals, and he tells her the fascinating story of how they had originally planned to acquire a man named George Dinsmore for her birthday, luring him with the bottles of Jack Daniels, but, owing to some of those quirks of fate which never cease to delight us, Adam himself came along and took George's place. So, in a sense, the animals have not presented him to Robin for her birthday. He has presented himself.

Nevertheless, he is still her present, and of course she is free to do with him whatever she has hoped. The adult Adam is experienced, far beyond the boy's wildest fancyings. As but one example, his adventures in France, where lovemaking is nearly as important as cooking, have left him with the ability to show her something called maraichinage, which is not just a kiss but an escapade, and the very first time she tries it with him she reaches so explosively that she can hardly stand it. Adam is so much better than Adam, and so much less inhibited or clumsy or inept or simply unknowledgeable.

They sleep late, and she is charmed that Adam can do something which Adam could never do—sleep. When he finally wakes, she shows him a present she has for him: hundreds of thousands of dollars in cash. He tells her that he is very touched to be offered such a large sum of money, but, if truth be told, he doesn't need it, and he would much prefer that she keep it and spend it on herself. "I'll give you many a chance to spend it," he promises. After breakfast she goes with him, holding hands, to the place where he has left his car, and she helps him in the slow, tedious carrying of all his worldly goods from the car to the house. For lunch he opens for her a bottle of what he says is the rarest, finest Cabernet Sauvignon of all time. She has never tasted wine before. She isn't sure, at first, that she likes it, but he tells her she will, as she will acquire a taste for all manner of things she has never known. He tells her that he would like to convert part of the meadow into a vineyard, if it's all right with her.

September is growing a bit chilly, and he does something else that Adam couldn't do: he chops up and splits a lot of wood for their stoves. She is so glad to be spared the chore; she can devote more time to preparing their meals. But there too he wants to use his hands and help her, and he knows things about cooking that the *Cyclopædia* couldn't have dreamt.

No, she decides, she hasn't lost her childhood playmate who became her phantom lover: he has just acquired all the talents and strength and wisdom of a *man*.

Chapter forty-eight

She does not like the present tense. So she bites it. She has tolerated it only for its ability to furnish a setting for the presenting of the birthday present: a man for Robin, but now that that present has been presented, the present tense is an annoyance and a hindrance, slowing everybody down, and she snaps "Hreapha!" at it and chomps her canines into its leg, and it will yelp and flee in panic, and in its running away it will be transformed into the future tense. Which will suit her just fine. Because the future tense will be everlasting, even eternal. She will realize that she is getting old and she will not be able to live forever (although she will have been happy to learn from Adam that Yowrfrowr will still have been going strong down in the valley), but as long as she will have this enduring future tense to live in, she will be able to hang around and watch all the wonderful things that will be happening.

Although the first time that she and some of the others will trot or creep or amble down the mountain to watch the strange men in their huge machines moving the earth and even building a bridge, one of the men will take his gun and fire at Robert. He will miss, but she will be indignant, even though she will continue to feel that her son-in-law is a rascal and a reprobate. She will run to Adam and will say to him, Master, those men are shooting at us.

Adam will go to the men, yell at them, talk to them, and he will collect all of their weapons, keeping them until such time as the men will have finished their job. He will pat her and say "Good dog," reminding her of the first words he will ever have spoken to her. She will be able to remember so many things about him when he was still invisible and unsmellable: how he had helped her find the scissors and the turkey caller, how he had told her how to find her way to Stay More, how he had assisted at the births of her children. She will have always felt that she was *his* dog as much as she will have been Robin's, and she will be especially thrilled that now she will have been able to actually feel his pats upon her head and his occasional hug. He will be purely and simply a nice man. A kind man. The nicest and kindest she will ever have known, so vastly different from her first master that it will be difficult to think of them as having belonged to the same species.

She will also appreciate the many ways that he will make Robin happy too. Not a day will go by that he will not tell Robin how beautiful she is, never in the same words twice, always with some convincing and well-spoken variation on the same essential theme: that she is, and always will be, the most attractive and desirable female on earth. And whenever Robin will raise her voice in song, the opaque tones that will drift out across the meadow will seem to express her joyful thankfulness for not just his kind words but his ability never to use the same words twice.

Hreapha will be sorry that sometimes their words to each other will not be entirely pleasant, and Hreapha will attempt to lower her ears and cover them on those occasions when the Master and Mistress will be having an argument. She will be especially sad when they will have discussed the coming of the strange men with their huge machines, even before one of them will have taken a shot at Robert. The building of the road and the bridge will have been the Master's idea; the Mistress will not have been certain that she wants it or appreciates it. When the men will have surrendered their weapons and gone on with their work, they will begin using what the Master will tell Hreapha is called "dynamite." The Master (he will have asked Hreapha not to call him that, but she will think it is at least preferable to "*in-habit*," which he will never be again) will organize on an October day what will be called a "picnic," far off in a glade on the western side of the mountain, where all of them, even Sparkle, will go to escape the horrible sounds, which they will only be able to hear in the far distance, the frightening sounds, worse than thunder, of great explosives blasting away the bluff where the bridge will be. The picnic will be so much fun, despite the distant explosions, that they will decide to have a picnic each week, which they will do regularly as long as the future tense will survive and weather will permit.

When the bridge will be finished, the road will be constructed onward to the dooryard, making it possible for Adam to park his vehicle at the house, and he will use his vehicle, for the first time after the road and the bridge are finished, to take Robin to Stay More, and Adam will explain to all the other animals that for this trip only Hreapha will be allowed to accompany them, because she is the first and oldest of all the menagerie, but that for future trips in this wonderful future tense he will give the others, even Sparkle, but not Bess or Dewey, a ride in his wonderful car. Hreapha will be thrilled, and although riding down the mountain sitting on the front seat with her head out the window will remind her of all the many long-ago times she will have ridden in the man's pickup truck down that mountain, she will come to understand what thrills the future, and the future tense, will have for her, riding in cars, and, that very first trip, riding down to Stay More to visit with Yowrfrowr and her daughter and grandchildren, and, my goodness gracious sakes, one *great*-grandchild. Adam and Robin will spend hours visiting with the nice old lady who lives in the dogtrot, so Hreapha will have plenty of time to visit with dear Yowrfrowr and the multitude of their offspring. If there is a heaven, this will be it. But Yowrfrowr will not be in good shape. He will say to Hreapha, Dear Girl, I am afflicted not merely with rheumatism but an host of other sufferings, and I fear I am not long for this world.

Hreapha will chide him for speaking in the present tense and she will tell him how she has bitten the present tense and chased it away. Sweetheart, she will say to him, in the future tense I will never let you leave us.

And he will give her a grateful lick. She will ask him if he understands that this man, Adam, is indeed *the in-habit*, the same one whom Yowrfrowr met in the orchard of the Madewell place that time that Yowrfrowr had helped them hunt for Paddington.

Yowrfrowr will say, Don't you recall, my dear, that it was I who taught you all about *in-habits* in the first place?

Adam will invite the nice old lady to ride with them back up to the Madewell place, and they will decide that they have room for Yowrfrowr too, although Adam will explain to all the others, to Hruschka and everyone and even the dozens of cats, that he'll give them all a ride too eventually, but for this trip he will take only Yowrfrowr, because he is the first and the oldest. Hreapha will be delighted, although they will have to sit together in the back end and will not be able to stick their heads out the windows.

Crossing the new bridge, which will be just wide enough for one vehicle but will seem to be suspended hundreds of feet above the ground below, both Yowrfrowr and his mistress will be amazed. "It's just a viaduct," Adam will say, "but it sure is extending our haunt."

Yes, their haunt will reach at least as far as Harrison, where Hreapha will ride with them one day to do some shopping at some of the same stores where the man had stocked up for his abduction of the little girl, and Robin will show Adam the house where the little girl lived, still there, almost unchanged, but inhabited by strangers. Adam will offer to knock and ask that Robin be allowed to visit the interior, but she will not want to. She will say to Adam, "I'm not ready. I don't want anyone to know who I am. Not anyone who doesn't already know."

One problem of Hreapha's new and greatly improved life will be the matter of returning after so many years to commercial dog food. She will have become so accustomed to a diet from the wild—of rabbits and squirrels and various birds—that she will not immediately relish the idea of Purina Dog Chow again. But Adam, with Robin's help, will pick out a lot of canned dog food of the very best grade, as well as cat food, and Hreapha will eventually decide that she appreciates the comfort and convenience, if not the taste, of not having to chase down, capture, kill and chew up her supper. It will be a comfort in her old age.

The viaduct and the new road will also make possible the crew of men who will come and dig big holes all along the mountain trail and plant in the holes tall poles, upon which will be strung wires. Just in time for their Christmas tree, a traditional red cedar, traditionally strung with Robin's garlands of popcorn and many of the stars she had cut from toilet paper tubes and hand-colored so many years before and had used every Christmas since. But in addition to those, there will now be many new glass ornaments and garlands and tinsel and bows and boughs and sprays, and, most marvelous of all, myriad wired bulbs, large and small, which, when Robin flicks a switch on the wall, in a ceremony in the presence of all of them, will burst with light and will sparkle throughout the holiday season.

But several days before that ceremony, Hreapha, knowing that it will be Adam's birthday, will say to him, Sir, as you know, I have always obtained, or directed the obtaining of, a pet for each of Robin's birthdays, including, for the most recent one, yourself, Sir, if you don't mind being called a pet, which you are, of course. Anyway, I should like to continue this tradition by getting *you* a pet for *your* birthday. You name it, I'll get it.

Adam will laugh and laugh. His eyes will water. When he will finally get control of himself, he will say, "Dear Hreapha, you are not merely a good dog. You are the world's best dog. But the 'pet' I reckon I'd like doesn't grow in these woods or anywhere hereabouts. And it isn't an elephant. It's something I've wanted all my life, which Robin almost wanted for her eighteenth birthday instead of me, or before she thought of me. You wouldn't have been able to get it for her either."

A horse? Hreapha will ask. And when he will smile and nod, she will say, Well, don't put it past me. I'll find you a horse, by golly.

"I have a better idea," he will say. And he will take her with him in his big car, just the two of them, and he will drive a long way, farther than Harrison, to a big farm surrounded by paddocks with many horses. He will hook to the rear of his big car another car, which he will say is called a horse trailer. "Now, pick one out for me," he will tell her, a tall order, but she will carefully examine all of the horses, and will choose the one which she considers most noble, most stately, and most handsome. They will take him home. When Robin will screech and whimper, he will tell her that for a Christmas present he will take her back to the horse farm and let her pick one out for herself.

So, that day, after they will light the Christmas tree, Robin and Adam will ride out together across the meadow and all over the mountain on two horses who Robin will have been named Wish and Desire, objects of envy and admiration for all the other animals. Much to Hrolf's dismay, neither Wish nor Desire will ever attempt to learn dogtalk, the official language of the menagerie. Rather, they will teach him a passable horsetalk, and he will spend the rest of his life, whenever he feels lordly, as he often will, speaking it.

Hrolf will remain always nominally in charge of the menagerie, even when, on those many occasions when Robin and Adam are gone away, sometimes for days on end, the care and keeping of the menagerie will be taken over by the very good man named George, the very same George who will have been intended as the original birthday present for Robin but through no fault of his own will have been relieved from that responsibility by the miraculous coming of Adam. Hreapha will like George very much and will often speculate about what life will have been like if he will not have been supplanted by Adam. George will not be nearly as handsome as Adam, nor as intelligent, and certainly not as wealthy, but he will have many admirable qualities which will always make Hreapha glad to see him, whenever he comes to feed them all during the occasional absences of Adam and Robin.

Adam will always tell Hreapha where they are going and how long they will be gone, and while Hreapha will wish she could go with them, she will know that she could not possibly ride in a vehicle which rises above the earth and flies over mountains and rivers and even oceans, which she will not even be able to imagine. She will be happy for them that they will be able to extend their haunt to the entire world, but she will miss them terribly while they will be gone.

While they will be gone, she will just take it easy and wait for them to come back. She will laze under her favorite tree, a white oak of course, and will watch the world either go by or fail to go by, as it will choose. Her favorite lounging hole, in the earthen floor of the cooper's shed, will have been covered with hard cement in the renovation of the shed. She will not have minded. That is, minded in the sense of being offended or bothered. The better sense of *minding*, which Yowrfrowr will have explained to her so many years before, namely, the faculty of knowing what is in one's master's mind, is a talent that she will continue to employ whenever in the presence of Robin or Adam, and which she will regret being unable to employ while they will be gone.

There under her oak tree, she will reflect that the nicest thing about an *in-habit's* becoming visible, as Adam's will spectacularly have done, is that one will be permitted to *mind* more readily by examining the lineaments and demeanor of the master. That is, one will be able to *read* and therefore to mind the visible face. You can't very well mind something you can't see.

While she will be having these thoughts, she will suddenly sit up, and she will perk her ears, and will sniff the air, and will look all around her, but she will perceive nothing, except, eventually, a small, timid voice, which will say to her, *Ma, things sure is a-changing hereabouts.*

Her memory will not be that good. It will be a voice she will not have heard for a number of years and it will be speaking in coarse, guttural accents. Because it will have no body nor scent attached to it, it will obviously be an *in-habit*, and she cannot *mind* it. Because it will have addressed her as "Ma," she will only be able to assume that it is a relative of hers, and she will correct it: Son, we will be in the future tense hereabouts. You will not be able to say 'is a-changing'. You'll have to say 'will be a-changing.'

Thanks for the grammar lesson, Ma, but don't ye know me? Or I reckon I should say 'will ye not be a-knowing me?'

She will be standing now, fully alert, and focusing all her senses on the source of the voice. In a voice as hesitant and awestruck as Robin will have first used to say to the rematerialized *in-habit*, "Adam?" Hreapha will say, Yipyip?

Ma, I'm sure sorry I took off with them fellers, he will say. *But I left my heart behind. I've actually been right here ever since but I just couldn't bear to let ye know it. Now I want to come home.*

Then come home, boy, she will say. This here will be the future tense and you will be able to do anything you will like in it.

She will gaze out across the meadow and will see him, in full trot. He will be an old dog, or at least a middle-aged dog, and he will have changed, but she will know him. It will be Yipyip, and very soon he will be surrounded not just by her but by his brother Hrolf and his sister Hroberta and all those of the menagerie who will have remembered him and all those who will never have met him but will be eager to sniff and ogle and listen to a wild dog of partial coyote parentage. He will be very hungry, but as soon as they will have fed him he will regale them all with stories of his many adventures in the pack of coyotes, who will have long since departed this countryside and roamed far away.

He will attempt to explain that he will have come home not only because of his desire to encounter his *in-habit* and return to his boyhood haunt but because he will have missed his mother, and he will never want to leave her again.

She will permit him to establish a loafing spot under her own private oak. She will attempt to bring him up to date on everything that will have happened around here, but he will hush her, saying, Ma, *in-habits* know all that stuff anyway.

She will not even need to show him all the improvements that will have been made around here, the renovations of the house and barn and cooper's shed and henhouse, as well as the construction of a garage and toolshed and greenhouse and something called a gazebo, because supposedly his *in-habit* will have already witnessed all of those.

But there will be one building that will not have been renovated, which will have been left exactly as it was, and Hreapha will direct her son's attention to it.

The outhouse, with its door open wide, will yet be occupied by a skeleton, the remains of a man who Yipyip will never have known. The skeleton will be wearing a big grin, and it will occur to Hreapha that he must be finding this future tense very funny.

Let me tell you all about him, she will begin to tell her son. Once upon a time, long ago, I decided to run away from him because

Chapter forty-nine

We will be charmed by darling Hreapha's conversion of this recital into the future tense, which, whether or not it is perpetual and boundless, is best-suited for *dénouement,* a graphic French word derived from the untying of knots.

The principal knot of this whole narrative will not of necessity have been our love story, but the more intricate knot of a girl's passage into womanhood in a condition of isolation and seclusion from the mundane milieux of society. The untying of *that* knot, consequently, will be a matter of that woman's decision either to remain in seclusion or to allow herself to accept and to receive certain satisfactions from the outside world. We will not wish to rush her into becoming sociable, because we ourselves will have led a rather private and circumscribed life, but at the same time we will feel obliged to steer her away from her determination to remain a hermit.

"I'm scared," she will confide to us one night in bed on the day that the finishing of the road has allowed us to park our suv in the dooryard. "What's to keep the whole world from driving up that road?"

"For one thing, a big iron gate at the bottom of the trail," we will assure her. "But I reckon nobody would have ary motive for coming up that road anyhow even if they could get in."

She will roll over into our arms. "Promise me you won't let anybody find out about us."

That will be easy for us to promise. But that iron gate will have to open to let us out, and there will be any number of places we will want to go, things we will want to buy, things we will want to do, pleasures we will have earned the right to enjoy. The first trip back to Harrison, for example, which Hreapha will have already mentioned, having been allowed to ride along with us. Robin will point out to us the modest little house in which she had spent all her early years, and we will drive past the Woodland Heights Elementary School, which she will have attended but not finished, and the Harrison High School, where she will never have been able to go. (A topic we will already have discussed: she will have been too old to go back to high school but will she want perhaps to prepare for some sort of high school equivalency certificate so that she will be able to go to college, if she desires? "I don't think so, but let me consider it," she will say.) Robin will even show us the roller skating rink from which she was abducted, and we will get out of the SUV and examine the low little balcony from which Sog Alan had snatched her. We will watch her carefully, we will *mind* her in Hreapha's sense, to see if any remnants of the trauma cling to her, but while she will obviously be lost in thought in the effort of remembering, she will not be disturbed. (Long, long ago we will have learned that one of the many things we love about her is her imperturbability in the face of hardship, shock, disappointment, and loss.)

Among the several and sundry stores where we will stop to load the SUV with all the food and goods and needs that we can haul, is the discount supermarket where once her mother will have worked. Robin will want to buy a few things there, including, for sentimental reasons, a quart jar of pickled pigs' feet, and she will call to our attention the fact that the manager of the store will still be the same Mr. Purvis who will have been her mother's boss. We will already have reflected and observed, not simply here in Harrison, that the world does not really change very much in eleven years, that except for the coming and going of new fads and fashions and the latest developments in technology, the world of this future tense will not essentially differ greatly from that world of the past tense in which Robin's story will have begun. Now she will tell us that she wants to speak to Mr. Purvis. She will not have spoken to anyone except us, our good friend George Dinsmore, and our excellent friend Latha Bourne Dill, and she will tell us that she will never have spoken to Mr. Purvis before. He will have seen her on several occasions at the ages of five, six, and seven, but he will not recognize her now, as she will have expected him not to do. The falls of her extraordinarily long hair (about which we'll soon be making suggestions) are concealed inside her winter coat.

"When did Karen Kerr quit?" she will ask him. She will have to repeat herself, because he will not immediately recognize the name.

"Oh, my, I don't believe she's worked here for a number of years," he will say. "You know, she married that FBI guy and moved to Little Rock, I suppose it must've been at least six or seven years ago. Are you a relative or friend?"

"Both," Robin will say, and will take our arm and lead us out through the check-out.

In time we will feel constrained to offer, "Robin, any time you feel like it, we'd be glad to take you to Little Rock to see your mother."

"Who's 'we'?" she will want to know.

"Well, I reckon it was just sort of an editorial 'we,' just meaning me myself."

"Let's not talk like that, okay?" she will request.

So we will—that is, *I* will—abandon the first person plural for the remainder of this untying of knots. But for a while there I will have liked to have thought, correctly I will hope, that I will have been including *you* in our story, as I will have been occasionally but consistently aware of you throughout. A good denouement will not merely untangle the knots of a story but will attempt to unscramble the reader's feelings, or, to use the overworked analogy of narrative climaxes and sexual climaxes, a good denouement will leave you sighing in dreamy contentment, exhausted but satisfied.

I will first, before taking her to see her mother, persuade her to go to Fayetteville, the Ozarks' most civilized city, for a variety of purposes: to obtain the latest things in the way of a whole new wardrobe, to have an ophthalmologist examine her eyes and fit her for contact lenses as well as an assortment of eyeglasses, to visit a dentist for some evaluation, x-rays, and cleaning (the man, Dr. Michael E. Carter, will express amazement to learn that she hasn't been to a dentist for a dozen years, and he will tell her that her teeth will be lovely once they are cleaned, and he will remark, "Looks like you haven't been to a hairdresser in a dozen years either.")

Although she will be smiling with clean teeth at her new ability to see the world in sharp detail, it will have been a major problem to have persuaded her to allow her hair to be cut.

"No," she will have said, holding her long tresses in her two hands, "this is something I *did.* I haven't done very much, but I *grew* this hair, and I plan to keep it."

"For how long?" I will have asked rhetorically and heuristically. "Until it reaches your ankles?"

We will have had several lover's quarrels centered around her locks, and I will have almost been swayed by her contention that the long hair will have been a symbol as well as a crest betokening her freedom, her originality, and her history. I will have admired her greatly on the one warm day that, totally nude like Lady Godiva, she rides Desire long enough for me to have photographed her long hair streaming down the mare's flanks. But I will slowly and methodically have brought her around to the realization that her hair will have stood in the way of her introduction to (I will almost have said "return to") civilization. And it will have been her desire to look her best when her mother will have first laid eyes on her that will, in the end, allow her to be taken to a Fayetteville establishment called Dimensions, where she will submit herself to the artistry of the town's best hairdresser, Patti Stinnett, who will cut Robin's impossibly long hair. The ends will be split, but Patti will know what to do, and the result will both startle and delight me. I will next want to stop at a good bookstore for a thesaurus, because I will have run out of fresh ways to tell Robin how beautiful she is. We (and I will be speaking only of she and I) will go to some fine restaurants and stay at the best hotel before heading down the Interstate toward Little Rock.

When Robin Kerr will meet Karen Kerr Knight on the latter's doorstep in the old Quapaw Quarter neighborhood of Little Rock, the former will be radiant in her beauty, neatness, stylishness and general marvelous attractiveness. The two women will only vaguely resemble each other, although I will suppose they might pass for sisters. I will note that Karen will seem to be several years younger than myself. She will of course not show any recognition at all of this old guy and this stunning blonde movie star standing on her porch.

"Hello, Mommy," Robin will say with a clean and lovely smile.

Karen will need a very long moment, not to recognize her long-lost daughter, but to accept the reality and the loveliness of the apparition. She will not be able to say anything. She will burst into tears. Blinded by her tears, she will reach fumblingly to embrace Robin; her hands will find her at the same instant Robin's find her mother, and I will admire the neighborhood while the two women have a long embrace.

Then Karen will examine me critically. "Is this him?" she will ask. "Is this the man who kidnapped you?" I will be afraid for a moment that she will be about to strike me, and I will reflect, as I will have done more than once before, that the difference between Robin's age and mine will be approximately the same as that between the kidnapped Robin and her abductor. "But you said he was dead," the woman will answer her own question.

"This is the man who kidnapped my heart," Robin will say.

"Well, don't just stand there," the woman will say nervously to both of us. "Come inside. Have some refreshments. Meet my husband. Meet your brother."

It will be an early Saturday afternoon, and we will be there for the rest of the day. Karen will require a long time to get her hysteria under control. She will be totally beside herself as she will introduce us to her husband, Hal Knight, and to their son, a boy of five or six named Richard, or Dicky, who will at least five or six times ask Robin, "Are you really my sister?"

Conversation in the beginning will be ridiculously trivial. Karen: "Where did you find that gorgeous dress?" Robin: "At Colony Shop in Fayetteville." Hal, to me: "What do you do?" Adam: "I'm retired. I ran a cooperage in California." Hal: "What's that?" Adam: "They make wooden barrels for the wineries."

Then Karen will have a flood of more serious questions, punctuated by practical questions from her husband, the professional questioner.

Karen: "Are you all right, honey? I mean, are you completely okay?" Without waiting for Robin's answer, she will ask me, "Is she *sound*? Is she having any bad problems, *here*—" she will touch her head "—or *here*." She will touch her heart. Flattered that my diagnosis will be sought, I will answer, "Your daughter is a survivor. She has endured indescribable adversity, but she has emerged from it with all her faculties intact, and a heart of platinum."

Karen and Hal will stare at me with thanks, and Karen will ask, "How did you two meet?"

Robin will answer that one. "The house where I have been living all these years was his boyhood home, and one day—in fact, it was my last birthday—he just showed up."

Hal will ask: "Of course I'm very eager to know who took you to that house in the first place."

"His name was Sugrue Alan," Robin will say.

Hal will smite himself on the brow. "I *knew* it," he will say. "He was my number one suspect, but because he was a police officer I couldn't seem to persuade the others that we should go after him."

"Where is this house?" Karen will ask.

Robin and I will have agreed, in advance of our coming here, that we will always respect our privacy by not divulging the whereabouts of our domicile to anyone who will not already have known it, namely George and Latha. We will also have agreed that we will never tell anyone who does not already know it, namely only Latha, not George, about *in-habits*.

"It's in the Ozarks," Robin will say. "I'm sorry but I really can't tell you where."

"You don't want me to come and visit?" Karen will say. And

before Robin can answer, Karen will have a barrage of additional, possibly related questions. "You've really drifted apart from me during all these years, haven't you? Don't you blame me for a lot of things about your childhood? Aren't you holding a lot of stuff against me?"

"No, Mommy," Robin will say. "I have the most happy memories of living with you and I have missed you terribly. But as I tried to tell you in that note I sent, I want with all my heart to stay there, so I can't tell you where it is. Not that you'd try to prevent me from staying there, but just that you'd *know* how to find me."

Hal will say, "You know of course that I could probably find out very easily where you live. I could simply find the locations of any places where Madewells have lived and check them all out. So you might as well tell us."

I will respond to that. "Your investigation, Hal, is over, and your case is closed. The victim has been found, and the perpetrator is dead."

"How did he die?" Hal will ask.

Karen will add, "You said in that note you'd tell us all about it. So tell us."

For the next hour or so, Robin will deliver a remarkably concise but comprehensive synopsis of her entire experience on Madewell Mountain, omitting, as we will have agreed, any mention of myself in the form of a twelve-year-old *in-habit*.

At one point, little Dicky will wander out of the room, and his mother will take advantage of his absence to ask Robin, "The monster repeatedly raped you, didn't he?"

"Not even once," Robin will say. "He was a sick man, physically as well as mentally, and fortunately for me he was impotent."

"Why didn't you try to escape, after you'd shot him?" Hal will ask.

"I was eight years old. I had tried to escape, but got lost. The trail that he had used to take me there was destroyed in a rainstorm. Winter was coming, and snow was on the ground." Robin will sigh, and will take a deep breath. "But even if rescuers had shown up in a helicopter, I would not have wanted to leave. I had several pets. I still do. I love them. And I love the mountain. Adam never wanted to leave, but they made him do it. And now he has come back. And he and I will live there happily ever after forevermore."

A long silence will seize the room after that, as if there is nothing more to be said, and in a sense there will not be. Or it will all be denouement. It will soon be time to leave.

"Let me show you the house," Karen will offer her daughter, wrapping an arm around her shoulders, and the two women will leave the room.

Hal and I will step out onto the porch to light our cigarettes. Robin will have nearly broken me of the nicotine habit, but it will be an addiction, after all, and I will need some time. I will need some time.

"You will need some time," Hal will say, surprising me, as if he will have been reading my mind. But he will not be referring to the breaking of my nicotine habit. "She's young enough to be your daughter, and she's probably just very grateful to you for coming along when you did, but now that you've helped her to find the rest of the world again, she might grow tired of you or she might discover someone else, you know?"

"I've considered that possibility," I will grant. "I'll take my chances."

"But thank you very much for returning her to us," he will say.

"It's just a temporary loan," I'll point out.

"You won't mind if I run a check on you?" he will ask. "Just routine. Just to see if you have any priors, or anything questionable in your past."

"My whole past was questionable, but you're welcome to check it all out."

"The name of the company you worked for?"

"Madewell Cooperage, Inc., St. Helena, California."

"Oh. You own it?"

"I did. I sold it."

He will notice my SUV parked at the curb. "Nice wheels," he'll say. "You going to be able to take good care of our Robin?"

"The best," I'll say.

And there will really not be much more to be said. All the knots will be free, straight, clear. We will live happily ever after forevermore. I will take the very best care of Robin. And she of me. We will want for nothing. The homestead on Madewell Mountain will have all the comforts and amenities that we will desire or will discover through our subscription to *Architectural Record*. I'll be an old man, and Robin in her elegant forties, before she will finally succeed in spending the last of the money from Sog's heritage. We will have taken trips to England, France, Germany and Italy, with pleasurable layovers in our favorite city, New York. But our happiest memories will be of the thousands of days and nights on Madewell Mountain, in the fragrance of oakwood, the sound of the nightingales, the taste of wild strawberries, and the sight of lightning bugs. With all of our pets, including those that Hreapha will surprise Robin with on her subsequent birthdays.

In time, the marvelous menagerie of Madewell Mountain will have two human additions, children born to us. Robin will name the first, Deborah, after the prophetess and singer of the Book of Judges, and I will name the second, Braxton, after my grandfather who built our homestead.

Each year on my birthday I will receive from California a carton of twelve bottles of the very finest private-stock Pinot Noir, with a card inscribed "Many happy returns, André," and each year for his birthday I will send to him the monetary equivalent in the form of a single barrel made from Madewell Mountain oak by the loving hands of Robin and the strong hands of myself. Our only hobby, hers and mine, will be the making of barrels—burgundy and bourbon barrels, as well as churns and piggins and firkins. And whenever we finish one of the latter, she'll say, "Did you say 'fuckin,' Adam?" and we will of course have to do that.

It will be so easy for us to live in the past, and to remember, to speak of, to reenact the scenes of our puberty together. Believing sincerely in *in-habits*, we will discover that Robin will have an *in-habit* of her own, who will be able to become any of the ages she has been, and to consort with my *in-habit* happily ever after. Our *in-habits* will cohabit.

There will remain only one chapter in this story, and Robin's *in-habit* will have it. There will remain only one more wonder in this wondrous journey: the moment when *your in-habit*, dear creative reader, will come into existence and will take possession of these pages.

Chapter fifty

Her mother will have said to her, when alone, "It just kills me that you grew up missing out on so many things. Don't you ever think about all the things you missed?" And although she will have nodded in acknowledgment that she will indeed have, her mother will have begun enumerating all the things she will have missed: education, friendships, fun, and knowledge of current events, of the world, of things like etiquette. "Every mother wants to teach her daughter some manners," she will have said. "But I was deprived of that chance. I was deprived of the chance also to help you with your social life, with boys, with going out on dates. My God, you never had a date! With nice boys your own age. And here you've taken up with that man and have nobody to compare him with! He's handsome and well-spoken and courteous, but he's the only guy you've ever known, except for that bastard who stole you away from me. It just kills me that you're planning to marry him and will have to live the rest of your life without knowing if there might be a far more desirable man."

"I'm not planning to marry him, Mother," she will have

said. "He has been married before, and doesn't think much of the institution."

"Really? So you're just planning to go on living in sin together up there in your hideaway?"

"Mother, I've read the Bible several times, cover to back. It was practically the only book I had to read. I have a pretty good idea of what sin is. Adam and I are without sin."

"Do you mean he's impotent too?"

Robin will have laughed. "Far from it."

"I guess the point I'm trying to make is that you have nobody to compare him with. How do you know if another man might not be…better in bed?"

"If any man were better in bed than Adam, he would be too much for me."

"Oh, let's not get to talking about such things, but I just want you to know how much I missed you, and how much I cried for you, and how much I will always regret all those lost years of your life."

"You never forgot me, did you?"

"Of course not! And your stepfather and I never stopped looking for you. Your Grandpa Spurlock is *still* looking for you, so you'd better let him know that you've been found."

Robin will be keeping lists of things to do, and she will add to that list a visit to Pindall to see her grandparents. She will not have mentioned to her mother the fact that Adam once met Grandpa Spurlock on the trail leading up to her Madewell Mountain aerie, and that if on that occasion either Grandpa or Adam had found her, she would have been deprived of some of the most wonderful adventures of her entire experience. But the Fate-thing will always have a way to prevent such happenstances.

Her mother will have told her about an organization called The Robin Kerr League, a nationwide group of the parents of hundreds, even thousands of abducted children. Her mother will have begged her to go on television or make a videotape to address the members of the League and tell them to have hope because she herself never gave up hope, etc., but Robin will have had to remind her mother that there will not be any publicity whatsoever about her existence.

It will have been a condition of their meeting and their resumption of their relationship as mother and daughter that there will not be the slightest public mention of the story.

Occasionally Robin will perforce give some further thought to some of the questions her mother will have raised, particularly one that will have already engaged her: despite her deep love for Adam, will she not be haunted by never having had a date to compare him with? Will she be completely happy with a man twenty-eight years her senior? Is it possible to fall in love only once and never again? To have that first love last forever?

Although she and Adam will watch innumerable movies because they both will love and crave that form of entertainment, their principal diversion will remain an overpowering thirst for reading, and they will consume enormous quantities of novels, the reading of which will provide Robin with a vast knowledge of human relationships that life will not have given her. Those many novels will also confirm her in her belief that her story will be unique, as well as settle whatever lingering doubts she might have about being madly in love with a man so much older. Eventually Robin will be strongly tempted to write a novel herself, but this future tense that Hreapha will have bestowed upon her will not extend that far into the future. And although she will come to understand the meaning of such novelistic concepts as self-referentiality, or self-reflective post-modernist fiction, she will have some difficulty accepting the idea of a novel wherein the main pursuit of the hero and heroine, apart from sex, is the reading of novels. Even if the setting for their reading, in that comfortably refurbished living room (the davenport alone will remain), with a nice fire going in their Vermont Castings woodstove, with glasses of Pinot Noir at hand or better yet the Sauvignon Blanc that Adam will make from his own grapes, will be sufficiently novelistic unto itself. Yes, she will allow, it might just be possible to write a novel about the reading of novels.

But she will have so many other things to do. The hobby of cooperage will keep both of them busy. And her garden: she will continue growing all their vegetables and flowers. Although she will have been slow and reluctant to accept all the advantages and material comforts that their unlimited financial resources can provide (she will never become materialistic, let alone acquisitive), and will have learned to lament PROG RESS, as it will have been spoken and lamented by earlier generations of Stay Morons, one benefit of PROG RESS which she will welcome heartily will be her Troy-Bilt® Rototiller, with which she will be able to make short work of churning the soil of her garden.

Of course she will be bothered by the noise that her Troy-Bilt® makes. And so will her pets, especially Hreapha, who will always escape deep into the woods whenever Robin starts up the tiller. Robin's readjustment to civilization will encounter several irritations, principally the *sounds* of civilization: the roaring of the tiller, the ringing of the telephone, the whirring of the fax machine, the screeching of the printer, the beeping of the microwave, even the midnight moans of the refrigerator. But somehow these noises will give her an appreciation of what she took for granted all those years of her growing up: the sheer loveliness of silence, when not even the wind is stirring the evening air. The soothing comfort and solitude of quiet. Likewise the distress of brightly lit rooms will give her a new appreciation of the darkness that was her element for so many years and will remain her favorite condition. And likewise the obtrusion of smells, of chemicals—cleaning products, repellents, her beauty products even—will make her love all the more the smell of dirt and the smell of *green*. She will learn to adore green as if she had never noticed it before.

Many of her garments will be green, a color that will go very nicely with her golden hair. She will frequently examine herself in the mirror, not with any trace of vanity nor self-criticism, but simply out of curiosity about her appearance as a modern woman, and her identity. Will she have remained and retained *herself* as she truly is despite fitting into society after a long absence? Will she really fit? What will show? Will anyone ever be able to tell just by looking at her that she will have been lost for all those years? Adam will continue to describe her to herself, each day without fail, in different words every time but with the same message convincingly reiterated: that she is a goddess incarnate, beauty personified, a living dream, a feast for the eyes. He will have said it so many times in so many different ways that she will almost begin to believe it, but there will always be the lingering doubt in her mind that any female who will have been subjected to such isolation and struggle, who will have been deprived of hygiene and balanced meals, let alone any knowledge of etiquette, algebra, civics and world history, who will never have had a chance to go out on a date, who will not have had a best girlfriend, who will have lived by choice in nakedness and wildness, who will without ever having learned the ugly term *masturbation* have practiced it so much throughout her later childhood and adolescence, whose only sexual experience apart from that will have been an eventual passionate affair with an invisible *in-habit*, could not possibly have expected to appear *real*, let alone normal, whatever that might mean.

"Adam, sweet honey," she will ask him one night during one of those postcoital moments of—what was the term he used? detumescent denouement—"do you think we ought to give up birth control?"

His silence will remind her of the way the *in-habit* Adam often would not answer her questions. Moments will drift by. She will hear him, in the dark, in the bed, quietly chuckling. Then he will say, "I reckon there's sure room for another of us."

There will be room for not just one but two of them, and the noise they make crying for her will be the one most tolerable noise in her life.

"This future tense is nice," she will sometimes comment to him. "Everything about you is nice. What's nicest about you is that you know me so well and yet you love me so much."

"Do you want to know when I first fell in love? Not the first time I watched ye reaching by yourself. That was pure frustrated craving, not love. The first time I knew I loved ye was when you weren't but ten or eleven and you told me that my initials which I burned into the first churn I made, 'AM,' could be taken to mean that I *am*, that I exist, that I have an identity. No one else could have given me that. You created me, Robin."

"I didn't create you. For the longest time I thought I might have just dreamed you up, and even when you appeared in the flesh

487

I continued to wonder if you were just a reverie, if maraichinage is just a mirage, but then you made me believe that I *am* too, that I am not merely some storyteller's wildest fancy, and that Madewell Mountain with all its inhabitants is really my domain, and, believing that I am, I know that you are."

"Future tense, remember? Always 'will be.'"

"Always will be *with*," she will say, leaving the sentence, like the future tense itself, unfinished, indeterminate, open to infinite possibility.

With a determination never to finish, they will go on expanding their haunt, to the world, but first to the world around them, until they will know every rock and flower of Madewell Mountain, and then beyond it to Ledbetter Mountain and all of Stay More. Robin will never feel truly sociable, and she will hate crowds to the point of being almost agoraphobic, but she will learn to feel comfortable with her neighbors. She will visit often with Latha. Adam will visit often with George Dinsmore. They will occasionally have Latha and George to dinner. In time Latha will introduce them to her grandson Vernon Ingledew and his lovely companion Jelena. Latha will introduce them also to her granddaughter Sharon and the man Larry she is living with in the old Stay More post office/store/house that had once been Latha's home. They will also meet another couple who will be living in the house that had been built by Daniel Lyam Montross, who was the grandfather or father of the woman Diana Stoving who will now be living in the house with her companion Day Whittacker. Montross had been the hermit who had kidnapped Diana as a child and been killed by Sugrue Alan. Robin and Adam will learn the stories of all these people, stories that Robin had already foretold to herself when she had created Stay More out of paper.

Denouements, Adam will have warned her, should not contain surprises, but there will be one little astonishment in the confession by Day Whittacker, a professional forester, that on one of his regular reconnoiterings of the timberlands of Stay More, a number of years before, he had stumbled upon the Madewell Mountain homestead, had taken a good look at a naked girl playing with a fawn in the yard, and had decided not to intrude upon her privacy.

Day's audience will have been curious: did he not wonder if she lived there alone? Was he not tempted to speak to her and find out? Had he ever wondered if she might be in need of rescue? "Something," Day will have said, "simply told me that she wasn't in need of me."

They will be in need of him now, will be in need of all of them, as friends. Eventually Vernon Ingledew, a very intelligent and wise person, will decide to run for governor of the state of Arkansas, and Adam and Robin will contribute gladly and generously to his campaign. Stay More will temporarily be invaded by others during the campaign, and there will be a few additional people that Robin and Adam will want to know. The old Stay More hotel, which had been the home of Vernon's ancestor, Jacob Ingledew, who had been governor of Arkansas during Reconstruction, and which Larry had temporarily inhabited when it was overrun with cockroaches, will become the home of a strange woman named Ekaterina, not from Russia itself but near enough to it to have piqued Adam's interest, since he will never forget André Tchelistcheff, who will continue until his death at ninety-three to keep in touch with Adam and send him a case of wine on his birthday. Two additional new residents who Robin and Adam will enjoy meeting will be an Oklahoma oil heiress, an Indian woman, and her manservant, also Indian. All of these people will also have their own stories, not ones that Robin will have foretold in her paper Stay More, but ones she will enjoy hearing and reading about.

Although there will come an occasion in the distant future when articles will be written about the coincidence, or design, that the impoverished backwater ghost town (one of which will propose a neologism, "*in-habit* town") of Stay More will have happened to have contained half a dozen millionaires, including Adam and Robin, no one, according to their proscription, will ever write about Adam and Robin, who will be allowed to enjoy their seclusion and privacy for as long as they will wish.

They will rarely leave except, before settling down to have and to raise Deborah and Braxton, their daughter and son, they will go to Europe. After her very first trip to England, which she will enormously enjoy, Robin will return home and will be surprised to discover that

Hreapha and the other animals have not missed her. She will be almost hurt, and will say accusingly to Hreapha, "You haven't seen me for several weeks, and you're acting as if I didn't even leave."

You didn't, a sweet female voice will say to her, and she will wonder if at last she has acquired the ability to hear Hreapha's speech.

She will stare at Hreapha, who in her nonchalance will seem to be smirking. She will think about what she will have thought that Hreapha will have just spoken. Can it be?

Welcome home anyhow, the voice will say. *I missed you. I wanted you back. I've always been the model of patience, but your absence was beginning to get to me. I'm* with *you now, though.*

"*Robin?*" Robin will say.

"Hreapha," her dog will say, that is, Well, it sure isn't *me.* And Robin will realize that she will be hearing Hreapha speak those words, that if her *in-habit* is now part of her, she will have acquired the ability of *in-habits* to know the language of animals, particularly dogtalk, that most noble of them all.

"Do you mean to tell me," she will ask Hreapha, "that my *in-habit* has been here *with* you all the time I've been gone?"

Yes, and she tells better stories than you do, Hreapha will reply.

Robin will give Hreapha a hug. Robin will give the *in-habit* Robin a hug, so happy to be *with* her again, and happier to have her and to be able to talk to Hreapha.

Robin's *in-habit* will look around in search of Adam's *in-habit,* and will find him, and the two of them will frolic and chat and cavort, and cohabit, conceiving Deborah, who, though created by sex between *in-habits,* will be born of woman and man.

Isn't this wonderful? the *in-habit* Robin will say.

Don't ye know it's future tense? Ye ort to say, "Won't this be wonderful?"

All right. But it sure will be wonderful.

She will be delighted in all the things that *in-habits* can do, in what they can say, and hear, and what they can see. She will be surrounded by all the eloquent animals of her menagerie, and she will recall those words from Isaiah, "The wolf also shall dwell with the lamb, and the leopard shall lie down with the kid; and the calf and the young lion and the fatling together; and a little child shall lead them." *I will have led them,* she will say.

In looking at the wonderful world through the eyes of her *in-habit,* she will not be surprised, because dear Adam will have already told her, that *in-habits* can see ghosts and she will be able to see Sugrue again. But Adam will have been mistaken about one thing. Sugrue's ghost will not be free to roam and prowl and trouble the premises. The poor thing will be imprisoned eternally inside the skeleton in the outhouse, like an inmate behind bars, sitting there forlorn and unhappy. She will stare at Sugrue's ghost with a return of the compassion she will have felt when she will have killed him. She will also know that none of this will have been possible without him.

Thank you, Sugrue, she will say.

About the Author

Donald Harington

Although he was born and raised in Little Rock, Donald Harington spent nearly all of his early summers in the Ozark mountain hamlet of Drakes Creek, his mother's hometown, where his grandparents operated the general store and post office. There, before he lost his hearing to meningitis at the age of twelve, he listened carefully to the vanishing Ozark folk language and the old tales told by storytellers.

His academic career is in art and art history and he has taught art history at a variety of colleges, including his alma mater, the University of Arkansas, Fayetteville, where he has been lecturing for fifteen years. He lives in Fayetteville with his wife Kim, although his *in-habit* resides forever at Stay More.

His first novel, *The Cherry Pit*, was published by Random House in 1965, and since then he has published ten other novels, most of them set in the Ozark hamlet of his own creation, Stay More, based loosely upon Drakes Creek. *With* is his twelfth novel. He has also written books about artists.

He won the Robert Penn Warren Award in 2003, the Porter

Prize in 1987, the Heasley Prize at Lyon College in 1998, was inducted into the Arkansas Writers' Hall of Fame in 1999 and that same year won the Arkansas Fiction Award of the Arkansas Library Association. He has been called "an undiscovered continent" (Fred Chappell) and "America's Greatest Unknown Novelist" (Entertainment Weekly).

The fonts used in this book are from the Garamond family

Other works by Donald Harington
published by *The* Toby Press

The Architecture of the Arkansas Ozarks

The Cockroaches of Stay More

Some Other Place. The Right Place.

The Toby Press publishes fine writing,
available at bookstores everywhere. For more information,
please contact *The* Toby Press at www.tobypress.com